PRIVATE VIEW

Also by Audrey Slaughter

Non-Fiction

Getting Through

Working Woman's Handbook

Your Brilliant Career

PRIVATE VIEW

Audrey Slaughter

All of the characters in this book are fictitious, and any resemblance to actual persons, living or dead, is purely coincidental.

PRIVATE VIEW
A BANTAM BOOK 0 553 40066 5

Originally published in Great Britain by Doubleday, a division of Transworld Publishers Ltd.

PRINTING HISTORY
Doubleday edition published 1989
Bantam edition published 1990

This book is set in 10/11½pt Plantin by County Typesetters, Margate, Kent.

Bantam Books are published by Transworld Publishers Ltd., 61–63 Uxbridge Road, Ealing, London W5 5SA, in Australia by Transworld Publishers (Australia) Pty. Ltd., 15–23 Helles Avenue, Moorebank, NSW 2170, and in New Zealand by Transworld Publishers (N.Z.) Ltd., Cnr. Moselle and Waipareira Avenues, Henderson, Auckland.

Made and printed in Great Britain by Cox & Wyman Ltd., Reading, Berks.

For
Cordelia
the extra bonus I gained
from marrying Charles

Chapter One

The light on the leaves hardened; the white and yellow and silvery greens stilled into a brassy gold. It was as though the image frame had jolted to a stop, as when the ill-treated school film projector went on strike. Even the air suddenly took on the smell of an airless, chalky classroom. Kate felt unable to breathe. She looked down at her shaking hands with dispassionate interest – they didn't belong to her. They were simply a part of the lengthening, surreal moment.

'Are you still there?' Geoffrey's voice had its familiar irritable edge but also something more – something suppressed.

'Yes. I'm still here.' Her words were all too accurate.

'I said, I won't be home tonight. The series has hit a major snag, and I can't see us getting away. I shall probably have to doss down on a couch in the studio and . . .'

'I heard you', she interrupted, 'the first time.' And all the other times since, she added silently.

But this time there was something about the tension in his voice, an excitement ineffectually damped down, a distraction that had never been there through all the other elaborate pantomimes he'd engaged in to mask yet another little affair.

His voice roughened with exasperation. 'Well for Christ's sake why can't you speak up? It was difficult enough to find a minute to ring you.' The slight, very slight softening of his consonants told her he'd been drinking.

'But you did manage to have lunch.' She was surprised at her own acid. She was always meekly acceptant of his excuses; it was easier that way, less painful.

She had always been ashamed of her lack of moral courage and would lie in bed at night, trying to generate sufficient indignation to enable her to talk to Geoffrey in an adult, reasonable way. 'It discredits you to treat me sometimes as a half-wit and at other times as a supernumerary secretary or maid of all work,' she was going to point out with sweet reasonableness. But in the bright light of day, her nerve for confrontation would always fail. Did it matter? Was it worth risking the violent eruption of Geoffrey's irritation, an annoyance always barely covered by a thin skin of bored indifference? She sometimes wished she could be an invisible presence in his office and studio, to see what he was like with other people, how they stood up to him.

'I can't stop to discuss my timetable,' he was growling now. 'You never understand the pressure under which I work.'

'Perhaps not.' She was crisp. 'Jeremy will be upset. He said you promised to help him with his maths tonight. He's panicking because his exams are next week.'

He was silent. Geoffrey was surprisingly patient at explaining things to Jeremy, and he was at home with mathematics.

He groaned. 'I forgot. But it wouldn't have made any difference. I simply can't get away. Tell him I'll make time at the weekend if I can.'

The line went dead.

Kate walked into the garden disturbing two badly dressed crows in shabby undertakers' suits pecking dispiritedly in a corner. Outdoors, she felt, she would feel normal again. She knew that Geoffrey's telephone call was a significant one. In a way, she had been holding herself in readiness for something bad to happen ever since her thirty-fifth birthday party a week ago.

Waves of shame and humiliation flooded back at the thought of that dreadful night. Geoffrey had been excited, his eyes hot, almost feverish. He had never made a fuss over her birthday before, but this time, when Charlotte had said, 'Mum, you'll have to give me a clue what you want this year, I'm absolutely stuck for ideas,' he had swept them all up in plans for a party.

'We'll go to Peppers, I'll book their upstairs room', he said gaily. 'We'll have the Milsoms. You're still fond of Michael and Penelope aren't you, Kate? And Felicity and Charlie Rutherford – haven't seen them for ages. Oh, and one or two more from the studio. I'll fix it. It will be fun. You like Peppers, don't you, kids?'

She and the children had been caught up in his exuberant planning, though Kate had felt a lurking heavy depression which she'd put down mainly to the thought of another birthday. She brooded about her lack of a natural lightness of spirit and *joie de vivre*. Her stomach knotted at the coming ordeal of being with Geoffrey's bright, chattering studio friends. Their vivacity always left her bereft of small talk, feeling a pale grey person.

On her birthday, at the last minute, Geoffrey called to tell them to go directly to the restaurant and he'd meet them there. He would come on with 'his lot' from the studio. As she drove with the children to Peppers, Kate was prepared to find Geoffrey absent, delayed by some 'crisis' that always sounded dramatic but, as she eventually learned, occurred less often at a conference table than round the office fridge.

To her surprise, he had arrived ahead of her, after all, with an entourage of eight other people from the television studios, including one beautiful young woman over whom he was bending, drinking from her champagne glass when Kate walked into the restaurant's private room. Only Derek Turner, who had worked with Geoffrey for years, was a familiar face. 'Ha,' Derek greeted her hastily, with an apprehensive glance at Geoffrey. 'Here's the birthday girl. Many happy returns, gorgeous.' He deposited a warm wet kiss to the side of her mouth.

Geoffrey looked over at her but didn't move from his limpet position next to the girl. 'Hail, Kate!' he called in a hearty golf club voice. 'Help yourself to a drink. You know everybody I think except Greta. This is Greta Lanson – she's to be our presenter for "Lifestyles" – she's terrific.'

Kate smiled and moved towards her. 'Congratulations. What is "Lifestyles" – a new panel game? Geoffrey hasn't told me about it.'

The huge, wide-set eyes gazed unsmilingly, assessingly, into Kate's. 'No, it is *not* a panel game,' she said evenly. 'It's an important new series about the way people live their lives. Contrasts. Rich and poor. Young and old. North and south . . . all kinds of contrasts. Geoffrey is a genius.'

'Don't tell him that,' Kate said, her eyes crinkling in a smile. 'He's conceited enough.' But there was no response. Neither of them was any longer looking at her.

Kate turned to greet some of the other new arrivals, whom she did know, and moved back into the shelter of the children's uncritical love. She felt dull, finished. All the old feelings of rejection, instilled by her mother's indifference, overwhelmed her.

By any reckoning, Greta Lanson was stunning. Wide cheekbones slanting to a piquant chin, a small, neat nose, sensuous mouth, and those extraordinary green feline eyes, alert and assured, under thick-lashed lids. Her hair, straight and heavy, fell to her shoulders in a dark shining curve. Such perfection had to be admired, but Kate saw no warmth there, and something subtly degenerate about the mouth. Not just sexuality, but a kind of complacent self-indulgence emanated from her, chilling Kate.

Kate had sipped her wine sombrely, trying to respond to the young television researcher on her left who was explaining the intricacies of his job. The studio crowd had obviously started drinking well before anyone else arrived and were now at that boisterous stage where any moderately sharp remark was greeted as a hilarious witticism. Greta sat like a sphinx on Geoffrey's right; Penelope Milsom was on his left, but Geoffrey hardly addressed a word to her. At the other end of the table, Kate was flanked by Derek Turner and Michael Milsom. Felicity and Charles Rutherford and Jeremy were somewhere in the middle.

Derek had pushed his red face into hers, his eyes rather unfocused. 'You're a dam' lucky woman if I may say so, *Lady* Katherine,' he slurred, emphasizing Kate's title offensively. 'I've worked with Geoff for years and the guy's a genius, I tell you, a genius.'

'So I've already been told this evening,' Kate smiled faintly.

'No, no, I mean it. That "Lifestyles" series will run and run and he's got Greta whoohooo.' Derek whistled to show his appreciation and gulped his wine. 'She's a star, that girl. Wunnerful on camera.'

'Geoffrey,' – Felicity, glancing quickly at Kate, had called loudly at that point – 'aren't you going to make a speech?' Geoffrey's hand withdrew quickly from under the table. Greta Lanson languidly moved her thigh as he got to his feet and smiled his lop-sided, charming little-boy smile. 'Of course,' he said, seizing his glass. 'This is a happy occasion. It could even be an historic one. Today, my friends, we saw the first pilot of "Lifestyles", and it was terrific. That is a plain statement of fact, no hype, no false modesty. Today, too, we saw the emergence of a new star – a real star.' He looked down at the woman beside him, mesmerized, clearly oblivious of everyone else.

'I want you all to toast one of the most beautiful women in the world, someone so talented that her name will very soon be in lights. Please raise your glasses to Miss Greta Lanson.'

For a minute there had been a shocked silence, even from the television crowd, who had looked embarrassed and uncomfortable, but then Kate had got tremblingly to her feet and somehow smiled.

'To Greta Lanson.' She raised her glass.

'But Dad,' Charlotte said fiercely, 'it's Mum's birthday, it's *Mum's* party, isn't it?' She glared at her father.

'Yes, that too, of course,' said Geoffrey, recollecting himself. He swayed slightly and smiled indulgently at his hot-faced daughter.

'Happy birthday, Kate.' He waved his glass casually in her direction and sat down, sliding his arm round Greta's shoulders and resuming his conversation.

Penelope Milsom pushed back her chair sharply. 'Jeremy, dear, do change places. I haven't seen your mother for ages, I must catch up.' She moved swiftly along the table towards the other end but Geoffrey was oblivious to the snub.

Years ago Geoffrey had been impressed that Kate knew Penelope and Michael Milsom so well. Despite his quick emergence from the yearly intake of anonymous trainees at the BBC, he was already restless, fretting in the knowledge that it would be a long time before he achieved a seat of power in the hierarchy. Within four or five years he was already casting about for other options. His careful, discreet soundings had gradually gathered together a promising mixture of youngish entrepreneurs: an absurdly rich young man star-struck by the glamour of television, a leather-faced pro who had started his career in advertising in Fleet Street and swiftly crossed to commercial television when he saw its potential, and a couple of programme-makers and producers like himself, impatient with the imposed slow climb and the tedious politics of the BBC. Geoffrey knew it wouldn't hurt to be on good terms with a few influential men like Michael Milsom.

Though Kate's father had buried himself in his archaeological studies for large parts of the year, he had kept a shrewd eye on ways to augment his all-too-inadequate income for someone addicted to expensive excavations, and had no compunction in accepting a number of non-executive directorships from companies who knew the solid value of an earl on their board and letterheads. He had been at Winchester with Michael Milsom, now the chairman of a big chemicals-to-soap-powder multinational, and a frequent diner at No. 10. The Old School Tie retained its pull.

Penelope Milsom was in her own way just as formidable as her husband. Active in the arts, she was a tireless fundraiser, taking under her wing children's charities, struggling orchestras and opera companies. Once Penelope's tiny, bird-like figure graced a committee, strong chairmen trembled, and opened company cheque books and became sponsors. She was tough, shrewd, intelligent and totally ruthless.

Geoffrey had persuaded Kate to introduce him, to ask the Milsoms to dinner, to buy tickets for the various charity performances. He hated opera, but he was prepared to sit with a suitably rapt expression through performances, to drop carefully rehearsed comments and reactions in a charming, quizzical way to the charity organizers afterwards, if it meant unlocking a source of finance. He had become thoroughly obsessed with the idea of putting together a new consortium to bid for a television franchise. If it came off, it was his chance to leapfrog into the top management league, have some real programme authority. He had studied the structure of the companies which had been awarded IBA contracts, and he knew the importance they attached to financial clout. He knew the Milsoms could be very useful, and not only as big investors; their powerful contacts could guarantee enviable prestige as well. As it turned out, he was right. Where Michael Milsom led, other powerful investors followed, and, indeed, the Milsoms had played an important part when the consortium had finally been set up.

Penelope's move up the table signalled the beginning of a general shift. Felicity and Michael changed places, and there was a bit more shuffling, so that in the end the television lot were one end of the table and Kate was flanked by friends at the other, their vivacious chat not hiding from her their sympathetic eyes, or their kindly attempt to show distaste for Geoffrey's behaviour by turning their backs firmly on the rest of the table.

Kate had played out the charade until the clock had crept agonizingly slowly round to an hour when she could decently break it up. Then at 10 she had had enough, and so had Felicity and Charlie Rutherford, Penelope and Michael Milsom; she had to release them from their ordeal of trying to pretend this was a perfectly pleasant, civilized party.

'Do you mind if we break up now? I have to get these two home to bed – they both have exams shortly. Do let's meet again soon.'

'Yes, we must go,' Penelope agreed hastily. 'We have an early plane to catch tomorrow.' As Felicity and Penelope scrambled to the cloakroom, she had gone over to Geoffrey and asked him to come home too, as the children were tired.

'This is your party, you stay,' Geoffrey had hissed fiercely. 'Why are you always such a wet blanket?'

Greta Lanson's predatory green eyes stared coolly at Kate. 'She terrifies me,' thought Kate, transfixed for a moment. She sucked in her breath. 'I'm sorry Geoffrey, but the children must get to bed – Jeremy has drunk too much wine. I have to get him home. And the Milsoms are leaving for New York early tomorrow.'

'Well you go ahead then. I can't leave our friends.' He'd turned away. 'Let's have another bottle,' he called aggressively to the waiter.

How Kate got back she didn't know. Jeremy was giggling and being very silly. Charlotte's face was tight with anger. 'It was your party and she spoiled it,' she muttered.

'It was a lovely party, dear, and I saw some old friends. Daddy *has* to entertain studio people – it's part of his job,' she said placatingly, but she was shaking with anger, an emotion she rarely felt – or allowed herself to feel. She usually assumed that everything was her fault. It was after 4 a.m. when Geoffrey crept into their bedroom. Kate lay stiff and wide-eyed, but he slid into bed and fell, almost immediately, into a deep sleep.

The next day, a Saturday, everyone was silent. Jeremy was cross and clearly hung over. Kate wondered how often the waiter had surreptitiously filled his glass. Charlotte did not speak to her father, and shook off his hand petulantly when he tried to draw her close to look at the book she was reading. He avoided Kate's eyes but talked in hearty tones about the latest political scandal, the neighbours' new car – anything but the studio. After lunch, he reappeared from his study with a cheque he thrust at Kate. 'I'm sorry I didn't have time to get anything for your birthday. Buy yourself something you'd like.' Kate took the cheque, said a chilly 'thank you' and went on reading.

The whole week had passed in oppressive politeness. In most of his previous affairs he had got home late, but he had always *made* it home. Kate believed that despite everything Geoffrey was genuinely fond of the children, and valued the solid family background they gave him. He wasn't the kind to throw too much away for the sake of a little sexual dalliance. She felt suddenly shocked at the way she had come to accept the fact of his affairs almost as if they were part of normal married routine.

Chapter Two

When Kate had first recognized, some years ago, the signs that he was in the middle of an affair, she had been deeply hurt, if hardly surprised. What *had* surprised her was that Geoffrey had taken any notice of her in the first place, let alone married her. How could someone, clearly one of the gods at Oxford, even consider her, a plain, half-educated, dull ignoramus?

It was her brother Tom, six years older, who had taken Kate to the summer ball. Tom, working towards his biochemistry PhD, didn't have a girl, despite being in a place teeming with attractive, lively young women. He'd introduced her to all his friends, but it was Geoffrey, a year younger than Tom, one of the cleverer post-graduate English students, Tom told her, who'd made a fuss over her, who'd danced with her virtually non-stop. 'C'mon, relax,' he'd said laughingly as she'd tried in her stiff way to emulate the bopping of the others. He'd pulled and pushed her slight body, his own intricate footwork and beautifully articulated body putting a gloss on her tentative efforts. Fed champagne, teased, hugged, tugged through the beautiful grounds as the evening softened into a warm, starry night, she had become a carefree, happy girl bearing no relationship to the pale, introverted, silent young woman she was as a rule.

And it hadn't stopped there. Flowers and phone calls, books with special passages underlined, with extravagant messages scrawled in the margins. Elaborate instructions to take a certain train, follow a bit of map, led her to a theatre seat with a confident Geoffrey lolling in the next one. Kate was bewitched, stunned at the suddenness of it all, unable to think beyond the wonder that anyone as insignificant and uninteresting as she felt herself to be, should have such a vivid, attractive creature as Geoffrey Cosgrove drawn to her.

Esme, once Kate's governess and now her companion as well as unofficial housekeeper to her vague, other-worldly mother, would listen to her lovesick outpourings, her ardent description of every little episode in the courtship with a non-committal silence. 'He knows, of course, that Tom is a viscount', she had once said mildly, and was taken aback by Kate's sudden and uncharacteristic fury. 'He's not like that. I don't believe he's even *aware* of Tom's title or who Daddy is – why can't you of all people believe that he might simply *like* me?' Her eyes had brimmed and Esme had rushed to restore her fragile confidence. If Geoffrey Cosgrove could make Kate aware of her own value, it would be worth her eventual suffering when the affair blew over. Kate was behaving like a normal teenager with a crush. It wouldn't last.

Esme had looked after Kate since her mother had hired her for the summer, during Esme's holidays from the dreary, East Coast boarding school where she was supposed to teach French and art. She had been happy and relieved when from the sultry warmth of a Greek dig, Lady Scott had asked her to stay on permanently as 'governess' to seven-year-old Kate.

In her ten years with the Scotts she had grown up herself, learned to be more worldly, to supply Kate with the love and companionship denied to her by her mother, and to stifle her own feelings of guilt about her lack of teaching qualifications.

Within six weeks Geoffrey had proposed, had been

tremulously and radiantly accepted by Kate, and had faced up to a sticky interview with Lord Scott of Trenthulme. 'He's not going to stand around watching the trees grow,' Esme thought, seriously disturbed, but this time kept silent about her misgivings. Lord Scott, despite his total absorption in the recondite book he was writing on prehistoric sun rites, was a good judge of character when he did surface. He had received Geoffrey with a cool, polite hostility. He couldn't understand Geoffrey's desire to go into television. 'Why?' he'd asked. 'What sort of life is that?'

Geoffrey was taken aback. Everyone else thought it glamorous. There were thousands applying for the handful of trainee openings with the BBC. *Why* didn't come into it. It was the smart thing to do, to be somebody in television. 'I – I want to create programmes, sir,' he blurted, feeling for the first time like a gauche undergraduate.

'Programmes? What for? What sort of programmes?' his lordship had asked in genuine bewilderment. What a strange ambition. 'I want to open a window on the world to people who have no other means of seeing beyond their own backyards,' Geoffrey quoted glibly from his application paper and ducked his head so that a lock of hair obediently fell over his right eyebrow. 'Poor devils,' Lord Scott had muttered, and stared at Geoffrey without speaking for so long that Geoffrey began to sweat.

'That chap Reith used to visit us sometimes – my father knew him. Terribly egotistical man. Never listened to anyone. You don't want to be like that do you? But Kate's always been a strange child. Never cared for history or archaeology. Always off with her governess sketching somewhere. I suppose this is all her doing.' Geoffrey smiled in bafflement. There was another lengthening silence. 'Right,' his lordship had suddenly said after minutes of looking straight at Geoffrey, standing up and holding out a hand. 'Goodbye.'

Geoffrey had found himself outside the study, not quite sure how he'd got there or what the upshot of the interview had been. It was Tom who had laughed uproariously and said, 'Just like Dad,' and told Geoffrey it would be all right. Kate, more fearful and despairing, had been sick with misery.

Tom was extremely fond of Kate, despite having been away at school through a lot of her childhood. The way she followed him around in the hols always touched him. She would hang on his every word, and would grip his hand convulsively whenever they were toured through the dark temples and eerie burial grounds and tombs which were their parents' idea of fun. He immediately gave his father a glowing report of Geoffrey's brilliant prowess at university, his work for the Oxford theatre which had already brought him to the notice of people in broadcasting and television, and dwelt craftily on his rowing blue. Lord Scott had rowed for Cambridge and was inordinately proud of the fact, though he affected to despise sportsmen. It all seemed to wash over his lordship, who did not even appear to listen. It was Kate herself who had made him capitulate. Trembling and pale, she had marched into her father's study and announced that she was pregnant.

Three months after Tom's summer ball Kate and Geoffrey were married in St George's, Westminster. Ancient relatives from all parts of the country were wheeled out and, as well, a large sprinkling of society were in attendance.

Geoffrey's side of the aisle was full of his Oxford friends, and a tiny, slight woman he introduced as 'Aunt Nellie – who brought me up.' Aunt Nellie was so painfully shy that she was barely able to speak, and darted frightened looks at Geoffrey whenever Kate or one of her aunts attempted to talk to her. She was so clearly out of her element that Kate felt a strong tug of sympathy; she knew how she felt. But Aunt Nellie resisted all overtures, looking so miserable that it seemed kinder to leave her alone with her shyness.

Lord Scott had played his part with a cool remoteness which only relaxed into charm when he spoke with the family or his business friends. During the short drive to the church he had stared out of the car window, and his face had been grim as he led Kate up the aisle. Her mother had drifted about indifferently, before the wedding, leaving Kate and Esme to make all the arrangements. 'It's your wedding,' she'd said once icily, when Kate had timidly asked her advice about the reception. 'You've always been an impossible child. And now you've managed to upset your father again with this charade. Personally I think Geoffrey is to be pitied. He doesn't know how difficult and self-willed you can be. I want no part in it.' Kate's heart had sunk and she realized that not even now could she get close to the mother she'd spent most of her life trying to please.

She was glad when the short reception had come to an end and she and Geoffrey could fly off to St Paul de Vence in the south of France for their honeymoon. She had felt relief and a great happiness as if now she could live, wipe the slate clean of all her past inabilities to be the beloved daughter of fond parents. Without Kate at home, they'd be able once again to devote themselves wholeheartedly to each other. And she, she had Geoffrey, who loved her, to love. It seemed a golden beginning.

Chapter Three

Now Kate wondered what she was to do. Could she go on playing the part of the devoted wife when she no longer felt any respect for Geoffrey and precious little love? As usual her thoughts circled round the children, and how they would react – Jeremy not quite fourteen, Charlotte a scant two years older. She had told her father a blatant lie in saying she was pregnant, but a bare two months after the wedding she had realized that, after all, she was, and Charlotte was born nearly ten months after the wedding.

When her father came to view his granddaughter he had said sombrely, 'I didn't realize you had your mother's single-minded determination to get her own way. I hope you won't regret this, Kate. I sincerely hope you won't regret it.'

She had felt, then, a stab of fear. Her anxiety to love and be loved, her desperate need to feel wanted after years of her parents', particularly her mother's, cold indifference and self-absorption, had not entirely protected her from a growing disappointment in Geoffrey, a gradual awareness that he wasn't quite the wonderful, godlike creature he had seemed. But she pushed such disloyal thoughts away, as usual blaming herself for unrealistic expectations; Geoffrey was simply human.

Now she felt in limbo; she had a sense of unreality. She drifted instinctively, for comfort, into the boxroom where she kept her paints. She felt real pain when she looked at the brushes, badly cleaned, stiff with old paint, jammed any old way into a chipped jug. The palette was as she'd left it years ago encrusted with daubs of dusty paint. There was nothing on the easel. She remembered painting in here, a good ten years ago, forgetful of time. She remembered, too, Geoffrey's contorted face as he'd burst in.

'What the hell are you doing in here when Ian Ferguson and his wife are coming to dinner, not to mention the Big Spender from Saatchi's? Are you mad? Do you want to ditch our chances of getting the IBA contract altogether?'

Kate had temporarily forgotten that Ian Ferguson, an IBA governor, together with a major prospective advertiser were coming, but it didn't matter for everything was ready. She jumped smilingly to her feet, but in his frenzy of anxiety Geoffrey was immune to smiles. He wanted, and had expected to find, Kate bustling in the kitchen, fussing over the flowers and table like any other helpmeet, not in a bare hole of a room frowning over a canvas and painting with a demonic concentration that surprised him.

He'd gripped her shoulder painfully and frogmarched her to the kitchen. 'This is where you belong,' he had snarled, his eyes three inches from hers. 'You're my wife and it's your job to help me.'

Kate had attempted to laugh it off, protesting that all was well, but Geoffrey would not be appeased. He kept up a cold wall of silence until their guests arrived, when he put away the icy disdain as if he were tidying up yesterday's newspapers and behaved as one half of a charming young couple, anxious to please. Indeed that dinner party had been a major success. Kate's sympathy and intelligent understanding quickly won over Ian Ferguson, the more forceful of the governors, and other women found an instinctive ally in her. But though Geoffrey had congratulated her afterwards, and made an apology, 'I'm sorry Kate, I was too wrought up – it was all too important to me', she was badly shaken by the incident. A couple of weeks later, when he seemed to have forgotten the episode and was in a sunny mood, she herself had broached the subject again.

'Geoffrey, I do like painting. I used to paint with Esme a lot – it was a kind of solace. You don't mind if I continue, do you? I thought I might take some lessons at Morley College now that Charlotte goes to kindergarten. I could easily manage it. I've never had any training and Morley welcomes adult students. They have a good reputation on the arts side I believe and it costs very little.'

His face had immediately hardened. 'There's too much for you to do here. I need to have people at home. It's important that we impress them, win them over. We absolutely must go out to all these functions, however dull or boring they may be. I have to be seen and known, and you have to reflect credit on me. You need to get your hair done more stylishly – I meant to ask you where you went – and choose smarter clothes. You're part of a double act, remember. I'm so close to getting all the pieces for the consortium together – so far in secrecy – but if the Beeb finds out what I've been up to these past few months I shall have to resign. Then I'm going to have to concentrate on the application and the funding every hour there is. You have to back me up. After all, I'm working for you and the children.' His voice had the ring of pious virtue. 'I want you to talk to your Uncle Harry, for instance, because we'll need more financial backing. You'll have to see what you can shake from the family coffers, my dear wife. There'll be no time for you to waste daubing.'

She had felt a chill of revulsion and a sense of shame, that he expected her to manipulate and exploit Uncle Harry and her father. Yet, she acknowledged grimly, she *had* played the role assigned her. Sick at heart as she was, she hadn't had sufficient spine to stand up to Geoffrey. She despised herself, but at least she knew it was wrong; she didn't think Geoffrey did.

* * *

One afternoon a few weeks later, as she'd been painting intently, engrossed in trying to make her brush do what her mind was directing, he'd come home early again, crept into the little boxroom and stood silently behind her, watching her struggle. When a slight movement made her turn, her eyes widening in delighted surprise, his face was impassive. 'Show me what else you've done,' he said. Happy that he was interested, she picked up a sheaf of paintings – some dating from the time she and Esme had painted together abroad, while her parents were stuck in some dig. Eagerly, she described the paintings as she showed them to him. 'This was meant to be an impression of the jungle, but there were so many greens, I couldn't get it right – it looks more like mud, doesn't it? Esme helped out on this one – you can see she has a much better graphic eye than I have. No wonder she's making so much money now . . .'

'For Christ's sake!' He had suddenly snatched the pile from her and thrown them on the floor. 'I've told you before – your job is to help me, not to waste time on schoolroom projects which as far as I can see merely demonstrate a unique lack of talent.' He had turned on his heel, scuffing the pictures contemptuously out of the way, and grabbed her wrist. Leading her roughly along the narrow tiled passage to the kitchen, he had pushed her in front of him so violently that she lost her balance and stumbled, her head cracking against the kitchen door.

For a minute she had not been able to see anything except exploding points of light, and then the pain started to throb. She had put her hand up to her temple, totally dazed. His expression had changed to one of guilt and contrition. 'I'm sorry, Kate. Are you hurt? Let me kiss it better.' He had pulled her to him and kissed her rapidly swelling temple and put his arms about her. 'You don't realize what a strain this time is for me,' he had murmured into her hair so that her knees weakened and she had looked up, eyes brimming, apologizing for any misunderstanding, assuming the blame for his having lost his temper.

She had ignored her throbbing head and run to pour him a drink. She made him sit down while she finished cooking dinner, conscientiously asking him about developments in his ambitious venture. Later, in bed, Geoffrey had pulled her to him, and silently, ferociously, made love to her. At the end, he'd said, 'Now do you realize why I want you, why I need you to help me?'

'Yes,' she'd murmured, happy at the word 'need'.

'And you won't waste any more time at that silly pastime?'

'No,' her reply had been low, uncertain, but he had given her bottom a pat. 'Good girl. Now I must get some well-earned rest,' and he had turned away and was soon breathing evenly in a sleep unmarred by a single restless toss. Kate had stared silently into the darkness until her aching head forced her to get up to take some more paracetamol. Geoffrey was right – she was completely talentless. She resolved to try harder to be more the kind of wife he needed.

Next day he'd behaved as though nothing at all had happened. He discussed their dinner plans, asked if Charlotte had had her typhoid, diptheria and tetanus shots, ignored her pale face and the bruise already showing on one temple and cheek, made a couple of light-hearted telephone calls and went off to his office.

A deep depression seized hold of Kate. She went to her boxroom, and stood looking at the strewn paintings, two of them marked by Geoffrey's footprints. She picked one up and looked at it intently. It *was* amateurish, even she could see that. Sudden tears poured down her cheeks, stinging as they touched her bruise. She dropped the canvas and went out, turning the handle quietly, as if not to disturb the dying.

It was clear by the cool way Esme treated Geoffrey, that she didn't like him and was impervious to his efforts to charm her. She had put up a stone wall whenever Kate had praised Geoffrey's good points and his efforts to establish a good career. 'Oh, I grant you that,' she'd said shortly. 'He'll do all right.'

By the time Geoffrey came home that evening she had decided that she, too, would ignore the incident. In an effort to be particularly sweet and loving, she took pains to disguise her bruise with make-up. She cooked some of his favourite foods, and asked careful, pertinent questions about his work. He only brushed her remarks aside. 'Kate, let me be – I've had enough of talking to people all day. I'm going to tackle some of the reading I have to do,' he announced with a heavy sigh. 'You have no idea of the detail involved. I have a lot on my plate now. Just do as I ask.' Silenced and mortified, she'd stood dropping warm slow tears into the washing-up water.

For some time, Geoffrey had been carefully cultivating a high profile with the press, as part of his carefully laid plans to leave the BBC. He was insistent that they go out to a great many charity functions and industry dinners, carefully appraising her appearance before they left. 'We have to come over as a team,' he told her, putting a firm finger under her chin and tilting her head to look into her eyes with his coldly intent ones. 'You mustn't let me down.'

When his new series 'Family Concerns' was launched, he was to be seen in every tabloid with Jeremy on his lap and an arm protectively encircling Charlotte, explaining to interviewers the awe and humility he had felt when his children were born, and how he hoped that as a result 'Family Concerns' would have a depth and understanding, a quality of reality that other parents would recognize and approve.

When indeed his series became a critical and popular success, he resigned from the BBC in a blaze of publicity, and announced his intention to help form a consortium to apply for one of the new television franchises.

It seemed to be the trigger for everything falling into place almost at once. Shortly afterwards, the last bit of venture capital was raised, and they managed to tempt Charles Wootton, a professional heavyweight, from a rival consortium to join them as Chief Executive designate in the application for the franchise. Uncle Harry had not only loaned Geoffrey a large sum for him to buy his own shares in the Company, thereby giving him a strong footing, but had persuaded his own financial advisers, Rothschilds, to become Crystal Television's merchant bankers. 'That husband of yours has family responsibilities,' General Walters had said to her. 'He's made the country aware again of the importance of the family, the solid traditional family, after all that sociological claptrap from those scruffy longhaired Leftwingers about extended families and communal living. Even a chap in my club mentioned he watched "Family Concerns".' That put the seal of Establishment respectability on the project as far as the general was concerned. Kate felt like a traitor, aware of how Uncle Harry had been calculatingly wooed by them both. Geoffrey, as always, had been touchingly grateful to Uncle Harry and asked him to be the adviser on his planned Second World War series.

When they went before the IBA a few weeks later, every brick had been carefully cemented in place. A solid line-up of businessmen, a sprinkling of titles, the highly regarded Charles Wootton as Chief Executive, four or five show-business celebrities and a leavening of creative talent. It was scarcely surprising that Crystal Television should be awarded a licence for one of the more well-heeled slices of the country! Now Geoffrey Cosgrove could leave Kate and the children to play Happy Families without him.

Kate rarely saw him as he and Charles raced about planning new studio buildings, enticing the more talented of Geoffrey's ex-BBC colleagues to join the new company, hammering out an identity for the station. Jeremy fell ill with a viral fever and she had her work cut out to cope with the demands of a fractious toddler who never seemed to sleep and wouldn't eat. It was a relief that Geoffrey now took to entertaining in restaurants and hotels, and that her family's social contacts and her own skills as a cook-hostess were no longer in such demand.

Geoffrey had asked Kate to come to the dinner after the Annual General Meeting, where Crystal Television's first year results had been received by the City with unusual enthusiasm. Michael Milsom, as one of the major shareholders, had been there, as had Kate's parents and Uncle Harry. A small group of influential City analysts visibly melted under the rays of Geoffrey's charm, and even talked guardedly of a Stock Exchange listing, an idea that was caught, and cleverly pinned down by Geoffrey as though such thought had never occurred to him. It ended with an invitation to the analysts, previously judiciously cool about the new station's profit forecasts, to a private view of their new autumn programmes. It was no accident that these same preview audiences were well-larded with television stars, a glittering breed the sober city types rarely met. Crystal Television received rave reports in the solemn City pages well out of proportion to their actual financial standing.

Afterwards, at home, Geoffrey was euphoric. 'It couldn't have gone better,' he crowed. 'Dressing the windows with all those City names is just what's needed to bring in the big advertisers. And they, in turn, were fascinated by the telly types. Just wait until the new autumn schedules come up – we'll have the media planners fighting for slots, and there'll be precious little talk of discounts either. You have an *extremely* useful family, my pet.'

He had led her to bed, where he'd made love to her, albeit with his usual emotionless despatch. Kate had nevertheless felt an upsurge of affection for him again. She'd been at fault, she told herself, in expecting a young man with talent and driving ambition to be totally attentive to her. He'd done wonders to achieve so much so soon. Hadn't everybody said so? He hadn't really neglected her lately, he had just been totally absorbed in a difficult project which he'd brought off brilliantly. Why did she have to be so crabby? Why did she let her old feelings of inferiority spoil things? She had responded to Geoffrey with an ardour fuelled by remorse, as much as longing, but he had simply come in his quick, efficient way, patted her patronizingly on the shoulder with a dismissive 'That was nice' and in seconds was breathing deeply in untroubled sleep.

Kate had long ago given up all expectations of lovemaking as a great galaxy of exploding stars, Hollywood style. Sex seemed a fairly overrated pastime to her, but when it had resulted in Charlotte and Jeremy, it had its points. She had assumed that her own ignorance and inexperience made it, as she thought, rather boring, but there didn't seem to be much she could do about it. She had heard about people being good in bed, and assumed that some people simply had a talent for sex, as they might for singing, or painting. Obviously she hadn't. Geoffrey's lovemaking was all over so quickly that she had trained her own responses to lie quiescent. What was the point of feeling aroused while Geoffrey slid into sleep beside her? She'd read a book about sex which recommended discussing difficulties and problems with one's loved one in a frank, open manner, but when once, bravely, she had tried to talk about it with Geoffrey, he'd roared with laughter.

'My poor sweet – you'll learn. Just take your time and leave it to me.' He had ruffled her hair affectionately, and Kate, anxious not to damage his sexual confidence, as the book had warned, didn't persist. But she wondered that her part should be such a passive one. Did women just have things *done* to them? It seemed most unfair. In time, she had given up yearning for the close relationship she'd believed marriage to be; she simply didn't allow herself to think about making love any more. Her mother had at least taught her how to absorb disappointment.

Chapter Four

When she explained to Jeremy that Geoffrey couldn't be home to help with his maths but that he'd go through it with him at the weekend, he was silent for a moment. Then he burst out, his face reddening, 'He promised! I *knew* he'd forget again!' And then, as if screwing up his courage he went on: 'There's no point in my taking maths. Mr Peters never explains anything so that I can understand it, and when I ask a question, he just makes me feel a fool.' He kicked the table leg. 'Will you ring school and ask them to let me drop maths, Mum? Even if Dad had been home, even if he'd really shown me, I know I wouldn't pass.' His eyes were too bright.

Kate saw how really upset he was. 'Blast Geoffrey,' she thought. But she was firm in refusal. 'Of course you can't drop maths – it's far too important. We'll find someone to give you some coaching. I'll bet one of Charlotte's teachers would be glad to earn a bit of extra money. Don't worry about it, darling – it's like rattling away maddeningly at a locked door, trying to turn a key, and it never seems to work and then someone comes up and says, "It's easy, look, a half turn like this, then a push and another half turn like this," and *voilà*, the door opens. Remember how I couldn't manage that can opener until you showed me how I just needed to tilt the tin slightly, and now I can do it every time.' She gave him an encouraging hug. Jeremy looked slightly comforted but not altogether convinced.

Charlotte merely shrugged when Kate told her later that Geoffrey wouldn't be home for supper. 'So what's new?'

She buried her nose in a book. Kate, with the new clarity induced by Geoffrey's phone call, suddenly realized that the façade she had tried to keep up that they were all living a perfectly happy, normal family life had fooled no-one. The children had already summed up their father. Her friends were well aware of his behaviour. Only Kate had cocooned herself from facing reality. She felt ashamed of her ostrich attitude. 'Even now, at thirty-five with two children, I haven't grown up,' she thought grimly.

She looked curiously at Charlotte, so seemingly self-controlled, already clear about what she wanted to do with her life. Although she had no problems with school work, she was not interested in it. She wanted to be an actress and was quite determined and single-minded about her aim, constantly reading books about voice production and biographies of actors. 'She's more mature than I am,' Kate realized. She had a sudden urge to talk to her daughter as to a grown-up woman. 'What do we do about your father? I don't think I can go on like this. What do you think?'

She sat gazing at Charlotte's head bent over her book, willing herself to broach the subject, searching for words that would sound light and natural, but at that point, to her combined relief and disappointment, the phone rang again. It was Penelope Milsom.

'How are you my dear?' she asked.

'Fine, thank you,' lied Kate. 'How was your American trip?'

'Short, I'm glad to say.' Penelope's voice was crisp. But she added, in a tone of elation, 'But while Michael was stuck in meetings I managed to meet both Placido Domingo and Grace Bumbry, and I *think* I got them to more or less promise to fit in a concert next year for my babies! Now I've to organize the rest.' Kate laughed, sharing her friend's pleasure. Penelope's babies were severely handicapped children who were taught, in a lovely home in Sussex, how they might eventually cope with life in the outside world.

'By "the rest" I suppose you mean dragooning a conductor and finding an orchestra and a suitable hall and agreeing on a programme – you're indefatigable.'

'Yes dear – and incorrigible. How about coming to lunch with me? I'd like to talk to you. We've known you for such a long time you know – Michael was very fond of your father, strange as he was sometimes. It seems ages since we've really had a chat.'

'I'm on the verge of becoming another of Penelope's projects,' Kate surmised, thinking back to the birthday party, but she made her voice light as she said, 'That would be lovely. When?' And they set a date.

Kate's introspective spell was broken, and pushing away the thoughts of Geoffrey, she had supper with the children and discussed how to go about finding someone to tutor Jeremy. 'Though I'm sure if you talked to your housemaster he'd help you get some extra coaching,' Kate said. 'Crested wants its pupils to do well.'

'No, Mum, no,' he protested. 'Peters hates me already. If he thought I'd complained my life wouldn't be worth living.' Jeremy was so fierce and seemed genuinely perturbed at the thought, that Kate felt totally inadequate. She really didn't know what school was like, since her own formal schooling had been virtually non-existent. Esme's teaching career had been short, her qualifications minimal – there were large blanks in her subject range. Her parents, who always seemed to believe they were on the verge of a big archaeological discovery, had as their only family concern that their unfortunate child should be kept out of their way. Her education was not of serious importance they thought, and anyway she ought to pick up a lot simply by travelling about with them. Esme was considered good enough to fill in the gaps. Kate relied for her idea of school life on dim memories of reading stories about other children, and she got the idea that it was mostly about winning matches and midnight feasts, and overcoming bullies and sneaks.

'I could ask Virginia – she's in the Upper Sixth and seems practically one of the staff,' Charlotte volunteered. 'Miss Bristow is the best, I think, but I daren't ask her myself – she always seems so polished.'

Kate laughed. 'What do you mean, *polished*?'

'Well she dresses so well – not a bit like a teacher. She wears terrific colours, and all her clothes seem so up to date. We swear that if we see that something's the latest trend in *Vogue*, Bristow's already been wearing it for a week. And her hair is always different – right now it's a sort of aubergine. She's got this snappy little black 'Golf' convertible, and Virginia said she has an amazing life. *Amazing!*' Charlotte rolled her eyes and made them laugh. 'I think she means she has lots of men.' Kate felt a stab of curiosity. What must it be like to have 'lots of men'? She had known only Geoffrey. But – had she ever 'known' Geoffrey, she wondered.

'Do you think she'd be able to keep her mind on Jeremy's maths while pondering her next outfit?' she asked.

'Oh, she's great in maths. She worked for IBM for *years* before she came to us.'

'Well, she sounds perfect,' Kate said dubiously, wondering how she would be able to face such a paragon. 'At least she'll know what goes on in the outside world. I could ring her direct. After all, she can only say 'No', and if she doesn't take you for maths now, it won't embarrass either of you.' Jeremy looked relieved and not a little intrigued. 'But it won't be any use,' he said with sad assurance. 'I'm thick.'

'No-one's thick,' Kate said firmly. 'I used to think *I* was but I just wasn't taught properly – and even when Esme came, we didn't bother with subjects she didn't like or, now that I come to think of it, she didn't know much about! I think she taught me a smattering of history, English by simply giving me one book after another to read, and arithmetic. I never knew what algebra and geometry *were* – still don't, which is why I can't help you.'

Jeremy beamed at her. 'Well, then, why do *I* have to learn them?'

'Because, my son, *I* never had to get a job or earn a living, and you will have to. I married Daddy when I was barely eighteen and until then I'd simply travelled around with my parents while they dug holes in places like Afghanistan or Egypt, and when I could escape from them, Esme and I used to amuse ourselves by painting and drawing. I can't *do* anything, but I don't believe I'm thick.' Apprehension gripped her as she said the words. Could she really be thinking seriously of leaving Geoffrey? She had little money of her own and no means of earning any. She felt a sudden desperation.

When her parents had died one shortly after the other there'd been no real family money. Her father's lucrative director's fees had ended with him. Most of their apparent wealth had been in land let to tenant farmers, since her father had not been interested in estate management. The house was a neglected, not particularly beautiful pile of stones – far too big to live in with any degree of comfort without staff; the estate had not produced a large enough income and had gradually been parcelled up and sold to the various tenant farmers for comparatively little, mostly to finance her parents' travels. There was not much left beyond a few stocks and shares, although her father had made an educational trust fund for Charlotte and Jeremy, and Tom had the rest.

'Mostly low-interest mortgage deeds on what seems to be a lot of loss-making farms,' Tom had said cheerfully. 'And I can't go into the stately home business with

Cheevers. It's not as if it was stuffed with priceless paintings. Who's going to pay to look at dark brown portraits of our ancestors by second- and third-league artists, I ask myself? There's no distinguished architecture, too many bits added on, too much of the early building knocked down and the so-called "home park" is now barely big enough to take half a dozen charabancs. It's just as well we have no sentimental feelings about it, eh, Kate? I don't feel fond enough of it to go into penury to save it. Do you?'

Kate had agreed. She had spent so little of her childhood there, only the last year or two before she'd married Geoffrey, when her parents had paused in their travelling for a bit. So, with little compunction, Tom had sold the house and what was left of the land to a hotel group. Kate's share from her parents' estate had caused Geoffrey to say peevishly, 'Well, they certainly managed to put on a big show for very little. The impression they gave was of having pots. Lived off his title, I guess your father did. It's a pity, my dear, that so little attention is paid to the value of an earl's daughter's title – I can't see many chairmen rushing to put Lady Kate Cosgrove on their letterheads.'

'Perhaps I could be a gossip writer,' Kate had snapped, uncharacteristically, needled by his vulgarity, and the distress of enduring another of Geoffrey's flings. 'There seem to be enough *liaisons* in television to provide fruitful copy.' Geoffrey had, for the moment, been silenced.

Chapter Five

The next morning Kate was still clearing up the aftermath of the children's rush for their respective bus and train when the phone rang. 'Kate? Will you come up and have lunch with me?' It was Geoffrey.

'Have lunch with you?' Kate was taken aback.

'Yes, it's not such a strange request, is it?' His voice was light, almost teasing.

'Well, I – I—' Kate stuttered, 'You mean, today?'

'Yes, dear. Lunch, today. The Savoy I thought, at one.' He enunciated carefully, as if he were speaking to a child.

'The Savoy?'

'Yes, Kate, the Savoy at one. Got that?' His voice had an edge.

I told Jeremy a lie, I *am* thick, thought Kate. I can't take in a simple sentence. 'I thought you were busy – too busy to come home last night.'

'Yes, well I think some of the problems have been ironed out. The Grill Room at one then, Kate.'

She hadn't had lunch with him since Crystal Television had come into being, when she had been asked to help entertain one group of businessmen after another. 'Your Geoffrey certainly knows the value of a title,' Esme had commented watching Kate enter in the kitchen diary more appointments passed on by Geoffrey's secretary. 'They have to get advertisers in now, before the programmes start, to help with their cash flow,' Kate had explained importantly, hoping Esme would be impressed by the business knowledge she'd picked up, 'But the advertising agencies always hold back on new projects. That's why they have to go direct to the client, the washing powder firms and the hair shampoo manufacturers and such. They're more interested in the glamour of the station than in asking awkward questions about numbers of viewers and costs. I just have to listen to their life stories and see that their glasses are constantly refilled. The advertising director and Geoffrey and whoever else they bring along do all the work. Sometimes the clients are quite sweet, really. It's not all boring, but I'd hate to do it every day. Imagine being a salesman!'

Esme had recognized Kate's ploy to divert implied criticism from Geoffrey. She had got into the habit of spending an occasional day with Kate, rarely staying on to supper. Her flat in Putney was just a bus ride away. Somehow she always had an appointment that meant leaving before Geoffrey came home. Kate accepted that the two people she liked best were not to be the best of friends themselves.

She rifled through her wardrobe for something to wear. Her wardrobe had reverted to the practical jeans and shirts or sweaters she mostly wore now. She couldn't remember exactly when she had been made redundant as Geoffrey's social helpmeet. Somehow, after the contract had been awarded, the opportunities for them going out together were few or far between. Something Savoyish she thought, wishing for an amused moment that Charlotte's Miss Bristow was at her elbow. She remembered a young cousin who had won a *Vogue* talent contest and who, as part of her prize, worked as one of the many fashion assistants at the magazine, saying with all the authority of two months' experience, that chic women never dress for a special occasion – their wardrobe was always well-chosen enough to cope with whatever their diaries might require. 'Good-bye chic,' thought Kate as she hunted. 'That is, if we've ever said hello,' but she found a Jean Muir red wool jersey dress she'd bought at a sale. It was so beautifully cut and the fabric so good that Kate felt that even the Savoy would approve. She pinned a large Eric Beauman brooch, a Christmas present from Tom, on the shoulder and dispensed with a coat. She would drive, and the underground car park was close enough to the Savoy for her to sprint if it rained.

She spent the short journey wondering what merited a lunch treat from Geoffrey. He obviously wanted something from her. She played with the idea of behaving like one of his business prospects, ordering whatever out-of-season delicacy was on the menu, and yes please, she'd like a pud. And a cigar if it is not too much trouble. Well yes, a brandy *was* a nice idea.

Geoffrey was waiting for her when she arrived, to her surprise, for once not forcing her to wait, sipping self-consciously at a drink. His face was serious, but he told her how attractive she looked.

'I haven't seen that dashing dress before, have I?'

'Well, I've worn it before – it's about three years old I think. I don't buy many new clothes these days.'

'You should, Kate, you should – cheer you up.' She ignored the implication, let him fuss over her chair, nodded acquiescence when he said 'Champagne cocktail?' and accepted the big embossed menu. 'Oysters, I think, Kate? The season's just started. A lightly grilled fillet with some field mushrooms – they must be a treat if they're genuine?' She felt even more like a business prospect.

'Anything you say – I'm not particularly hungry.'

'I thought it would be nice to talk, away from home and the children for once. And here where we're not likely to run into the studio crowd.'

'I should think there are plenty of people you know in a place like this,' Kate replied looking round. 'And some of

Daddy's friends come here – in fact I see Gerald Brooks in the far corner. He's a member of The Travellers too.'

'Well, they're not likely to bother us,' Geoffrey said, frowning slightly.

This amiable social chat until they'd finished their oysters made Geoffrey's next remark almost wind her. Putting his elbows on the table, he took her hand, and said 'Kate, I want you to give me a divorce.' It was so direct that she was unequal to response, but stared at him with a stiff face. His expression was gently blank, like a kind stranger's.

'I don't think we are very suited. You don't really like or understand my work. Things I believe to be important you disregard . . . no,' he held up his free hand. 'Don't speak or I won't be able to finish. I have been screwing up my courage to tell you all this because, believe me, I don't want to hurt you.'

Kate let out her breath and gave a faint smile. 'I think it's a long time since you have been able to hurt me, Geoffrey.'

He looked faintly surprised, but went on in the same even, reasonable tone. 'I think this is best for you. I think it's best for the children too – they don't see much of me in the evenings, but if we are in different homes I'll be able to make time for them at weekends. Believe me, I really minded about not helping Jeremy with his maths. Of course, we'll have to sell the house and get two smaller ones. I'll need space for the children to stay.'

It all sounded so cut-and-dried and unemotional. She felt her heart racing, but her mouth was too dry to allow her to speak. Was this how things ended? A sentence or two, spoken in a reasonable tone, just as if you were exchanging damaged goods in a shop?

'You see, I want to marry again.' He couldn't keep a shining look of happiness from spreading over his face.

'It's Greta Lanson. I'm in love with her and want to marry her.'

Kate felt a deep stab of envy, and pity for herself. She had never inspired this kind of reverence even at the beginning. He had been gay and teasing, but, now she realized miserably, had never shown any depth of feeling for her. At first, when her faint disappointment with him had made her feel disloyal, she thought that his character was simply an unemotional one. He was outgoing and exuberant when he wanted to be, but he never seemed deeply moved by the arts or nature, or even particularly excited at becoming a father.

She could hear again her mother's voice. 'Go away, go and play somewhere else. You're such a hindrance.' 'Kate, stop following me about. Why are you such a nuisance? Go and ask cook for a drink. Don't bother me.' She remembered watching her mother scrape away at the hard, dry clay, whooping with excitement when she uncovered bits of broken pots, which she'd laid out reverently on a piece of carpet with more gentleness than she'd ever shown Kate. She had so much wanted her mother to show the same pleasure and animation when she looked at her that Kate had carefully dug away at the loosened soil near the top of the hole with her spoon and buried the pieces again. She would dig them up again after her mother had finished her lunch, and give them to her. She'd be so pleased with her, reasoned the six-year-old.

She had been bewildered when her parents and their assistants had emerged from their tent and started to bellow and shout at the sight of the bare carpet. Accusations were flung, her mother had stormed at one of their fieldworkers, and Kate had looked on, terrified at the commotion. She'd dug out her hoard, put them in her little cotton skirt, and offered them with shy anticipation to her mother. Kate could still feel the stinging slap she'd received, the words her mother screamed at her: 'You meddling little beast – you've undone a whole morning's work. I wish you'd never been born!'

Kate had run off crying bitterly, uncertain what she'd done that was so terrible, aware only that she was a nuisance and her mother didn't want her. It had been hours before a couple of students, amateur fieldworkers, had come to find her. The tears had dried on her dusty cheeks, she'd been frightened of the enveloping dark as the sun dropped swiftly behind the hills, but she'd been too terrified to try to find her way back to the camp and face her mother's anger. When they brought her back, her mother was sitting in the centre of a little group, laughing and talking as she sipped her drink. Her face had darkened at the sight of the small huddled figure clutching the neck of the young student who was carrying her.

'Get Hereena to put her to bed,' she'd said in a cold voice, and turned back to the others. Even at six Kate had realized that her mother hadn't worried about her absence, or thought of interrupting her other concerns to look for her.

From then on she'd kept out of her way, unhappy in her rejection, bored and lonely until Esme had arrived. She realized now that her mother must have been very odd, but her deep feelings of inferiority persisted.

The familiar tight misery uncurled itself as she rolled the wine around in her glass, staring at the liquid as if deeply fascinated by some extraordinary phenomenon. She gulped the last of it and took a breath. 'I see. She's very beautiful.'

'And we have so much in common,' Geoffrey went on eagerly. '"Lifestyles" has proved how well we work together; we're on the same wavelength. I'm sorry,' he broke off, suddenly embarrassed. 'This must be very painful for you.'

'Yes. It is.'

They were silent for a long moment but then he burst out impatiently. 'Then you do see why we have to sell the house? I'm doing very well with Crystal, but I haven't any capital, as you know. I can't cope with a hefty mortgage, even on my salary – or furnish and decorate it as Greta would wish. She has marvellous taste, but good taste costs a bomb.' He gave a fond, indulgent laugh.

'Yes, I do see that she'll be expensive,' Kate said levelly. He looked up sharply but decided not to challenge the remark.

'I will pay for the children's education, of course.'

Kate looked at him directly and he dropped his eyes. 'Well, top it up. I know the trust pays for most of it but it was made before school fees went up so much. And Kate,' he took her hand again and dropped back into his silky voice, 'let's do it quietly, by agreement. We don't want a great publicity fuss do we – you especially? I have to face the fact that, well, thanks to Crystal and my job, I'm news, and so, of course, is Greta – the poor child is absolutely hounded by magazines and newspapers wanting to write about her. She has really taken off in "Lifestyles". It would be damaging to her image to be mixed up in a divorce case.'

'I quite see that,' Kate agreed again in the same flat tone. 'I don't suppose I have an image, whatever that is.'

He squeezed her hand. 'Good girl. I knew you'd be reasonable. Look, I'll move my things – why don't you and Esme and the kids go away for the weekend and I'll get them out then. I'll stand you all the treat.'

'Esme's in America. Besides, I don't think I want you to "stand us a treat" as you call it, right now. I'll let you know a good time – when the children are at school. I'd like to go now. I don't think I can finish my lunch.' She stood up.

Geoffrey, unusually for him, looked awkward and

embarrassed. A swoop of waiters bustled about their table, ready to serve the main course. Guilt – could it be? – stained his face for the first time. He waved the waiters away with a faint gesture. 'I'm sorry it's worked out like this, Kate. You'll find someone else, I'm sure. You're quite young and attractive – and a splendid cook.' It sounded such a humblingly trivial set of accomplishments that Kate wanted to hit him. 'I'll get you to write my cv,' she said as she picked up her bag. 'Goodbye Geoffrey.'

She was proud of her slow, poised exit from the restaurant. It took some doing. Perhaps Charlotte gets her acting ability from me, she thought, regarding herself with detachment in a mirror as she negotiated the stairs and corridors to the river exit nearest to the car park. The Jean Muir did a lot for her figure, she noted. Geoffrey hadn't put *that* attraction on his list!

Chapter Six

Outside the Savoy her air of self-assurance crumpled. The early September sun poured through the thinning branches of the Embankment plane trees. Drivers leaned on their car bonnets, exchanging gossip and racing tips, waiting for their employers to finish their expense account lunches. As she felt the cold whip of an easterly wind, Kate wished she'd worn a coat.

After the cold brilliance of the sun she stumbled almost blindly through the car park's underground gloom, trying to remember where she'd left the car. She felt terribly lost. She walked up one lane of cars, staring but not seeing them, and then tackled another farther on. The cars all looked alike, in this forest of silent, menacing vehicles that seemed to leer at her with shiny chrome teeth. She desperately strove to remember the number or the colour or make of her car, and wondered if she could get lost in the shrubbery of metal and plastic, if people could actually die of frustration searching frantically for their cars. Her heart thumping in panic, she leaned against an oily cement pillar to calm herself and shut her eyes.

'Are you all right?' Kate opened her eyes on a little man in an absurd wrinkled pinstripe suit and stiff white collar who was peering at her anxiously.

'I'm sorry.' She squeezed her eyes shut again as the pain hit her. 'I'm sorry. You see, I've just lost someone.'

The little man's face rearranged itself from anxiety to sympathy. 'How awful. Has it just happened?'

'Yes,' said Kate, and to her astonishment felt tears

coursing down her cheeks. 'Look – please don't trouble. I'll be all right in a minute.'

'Come into my office. It's just along here. Were you looking for your car?'

'Yes, but I can't remember where I left it or what its number is.' Kate started to sob. She felt desperately ashamed of herself.

'Don't worry madam, we'll find it. Now sit there, and have a cup of tea – I keep the kettle always on the boil in here.' He gestured round his little cubby-hole of an office, black with car grease, with odd car keys and numbers hung on a panel of hooks, and an assortment of improbably pumped-up nude young women staring boldly from posters and calendars donated by oil companies.

The kettle was sitting on an old-fashioned gas ring in the corner and Kate's hands were wrapped round a tannin-stained mug of strong stewed tea. The dear old chap seemed afraid she might drop it.

She brushed her eyes with the back of her hand and searched for a tissue. He tore off a piece of absorbent paper on a huge roll above his desk and gave it to Kate. 'Don't worry, my dear. We all have to face up to loss sometime. I lost my Annie nearly five years ago. Cancer it was. But you make your life again. You have to, don't you? Was it your husband?'

'Yes.'

'I hope he didn't suffer too much. My Annie didn't, thank the Lord. It was all too quick.'

'No, no, I don't think he suffered at all,' Kate said slowly.

'Well that's a blessing isn't it? Was it an accident?' He seemed avid for details, but his face still looked rumpled with concern.

'I think so,' Kate said. 'He was always incautious. There was nothing I could do.' He patted her arm in a clumsy gesture that slopped the tea on to some invoices on his cluttered desk. 'I'm sure you did all you could. What hospital was he in?'

Kate stood up quickly in agitation, slopping more tea. 'Look I've remembered I have my car registration number written in my diary. Here it is. It's a red Mini. Do you think you could find it for me? I must get home to my children.' She felt a hysterical compulsion to go on embroidering the details of Geoffrey's sudden demise, and visualized herself and this crumpled little man swapping tales of their loved ones' last hours for the rest of the afternoon in the stifling little room.

At the word 'children' his face found yet another sympathetic rearrangement, but he shot obediently out of the office.

''Ere Fred, on the double, red Mini, BKF 589G.'

Kate gave the man a grateful kiss on his grey-stubbled cheek when her car was driven up to the office door. 'Thank you so much,' she whispered, as Fred looked on in astonishment. 'You've helped me so much. I'll never forget your kindness – or the tea.'

Suddenly, as she drove out of the garage, she felt inexplicably light-hearted. That poor man, believing her recently bereaved. Giving her tea and sympathy when she was merely one of an army of wives cast off when someone younger and more attractive came along. It was touching, but it was really very funny. Very, very funny.

She started to laugh helplessly as the traffic jerked into movement. Accelerating heedlessly, she changed up a gear, turning the old Mini's blunt nose to go under Admiralty Arch, replaying the scene in her head. What was that song? 'Breaking up is hard to do'. It had been, in fact, incredibly easy.

'Unless you have anything better to do I suggest we go to

the cinema tonight and eat at the Pizza Parlour,' Kate kept her voice casual. 'I somehow can't face cooking again.'

'Dad out?' Charlotte asked indifferently.

'Yes.' She wasn't ready to tell them the news just yet. She needed to get used to it herself. She would have to ring Geoffrey to see what he felt about breaking it to the children. They'd left too many details in the air. Or *she* had, going off like that. It would be better tomorrow when she had taken it all in. She'd make notes tonight, when the children were in bed, of all the things they needed to discuss. You couldn't break up a marriage of so many years with just a few sentences and half a lunch at the Savoy, could you?

Fortunately the film was the latest Bond. Jeremy loved it, and she and Charlotte shrieked with laughter as one improbable piece of derring-do and absurd coincidence followed another. It was good therapy, and the Pizza Parlour was cheerfully noisy, full of young people sprawling and gossiping and drinking coke. Charlotte suddenly became self-conscious, tossing her hair and posing in the mirrored wall. Kate was aware that several boys were looking at her with interest and behaving just as self-consciously with *their* friends. 'The mating game,' thought Kate, hoping that dear, single-minded Charlotte would not fall for the first charmer who made a fuss over her. 'I'm responsible for her entirely now, and I just don't know enough about men to help.'

Despite being wearily aware of problems ahead, Kate slept soundly and felt not only refreshed but amazingly cheerful the next day. A feverish energy gripped her. All right, her marriage was finally over, but her life wasn't. There suddenly seemed so much to do, so much to tackle that was unfamiliar, that she felt an unexpected surge of excitement and adventurousness, spiked by fear. She would have to talk to the family solicitors. And she'd also have to face up to earning a living somehow. She knew she had an income from her father's estate, but Geoffrey had made it clear at the time of his death that it was disappointingly small. She had enough pride not to want to be dependent on Geoffrey. She could imagine him grumbling over their various bills while he forked out happily for Greta's latest piece of designer 'good taste'. She had a sudden pang as it occurred to her that Greta might have Geoffrey's children. No, he wouldn't want another family, surely? It would be like disenfranchising Charlotte and Jeremy. But Greta was young, she would want children of her own, wouldn't she?

Tomorrow she would start to think about a job. Her mind was uncomfortably blank on that score. She couldn't think of anything she could do that would command a salary. She didn't even know how to set about looking for a job. She couldn't type and hadn't the merest O-level to her name.

But first she would have to talk to Geoffrey. Yesterday was too unfinished. 'Geoffrey,' she said when she got through his stonewalling secretary eventually, 'We didn't discuss how we were to tell the children. I think that has to be done as soon as possible. They're going to be upset in any case, but I think we'll have to talk to them together, don't you? I couldn't bring myself to say anything when I got home last night. I was still getting used to the idea myself.'

'You sound remarkably crisp,' said Geoffrey.

'And you sound rather cross that I am,' Kate said evenly. 'Let's not pretend that a happy marriage is being broken up. You were sensible to take action. I would have gone on procrastinating forever, I suppose. But we have to face up to making it as easy as possible for the children to take in the news. And then, I suppose, our lawyers will take over.'

There was a nonplussed silence. 'I thought you were

fond of me, Kate,' he said with a note of petulance in his voice.

'I was.' She paused to steady her voice, which threatened to break with self-pity as she recalled the besotted girl of eighteen.

'No inquests, Geoffrey – such a waste of time. Do you think you could come home this evening, so that we can explain it all to the children? If you got here before they arrived from school I could have some of your things packed to stow away before they come home. I don't think they'd like to see you marching out with suitcases. You can pick up the rest later.'

'All right. I didn't realize you were so businesslike Kate. I'll arrive about four – is that all right?'

Kate was pleased at her calmness when she put the phone down, but she was starting to tremble again. It all seemed so unreal. She called the hairdresser. 'Can you fit me in *now*?' she said urgently. She wanted to get out of the house, to be pampered. Yes, Mr Eric could fit her in, it being a Tuesday, and if she could be there within half an hour? Kate parked the Mini on a double yellow line outside the hairdressers, marvelling at her irresponsibility. 'Mr Eric,' she said tentatively, looking at him in the mirror as she sat swathed in a pink overall a few minutes later, 'Do you think I could go aubergine?'

Chapter Seven

Charlotte and Jeremy, stony-faced, sat side by side on the sofa as Geoffrey adopted a hearty cheerfulness, launching into what seemed a carefully rehearsed script.

'Your mother and I feel we've grown too far apart to enjoy living together any more. But that doesn't mean we don't love you. We're still your parents and you'll see me perhaps more often than in the past.

'Mummy and I are going to buy another house each, and you'll come and stay with me some of the time. It's really for the best . . .' He trailed off in the face of the two impassive expressions, and looked helplessly at Kate. She felt again the hysterical impulse to laugh, particularly as, moving to squeeze beside Jeremy on the sofa, she caught sight in the nearest mirror of her newly shorn aubergine head, which Geoffrey had regarded with amazement when he arrived. She put her arm around Jeremey's slight shoulders and gave him a gentle squeeze.

'It will be all right,' she said quietly. 'It's just the end of a chapter, not the end of the book.'

'Why have you changed your hair?' demanded Jeremy with sudden hostility, and Kate could see his chin trembling and dimpling as it did in his infancy when he was about to cry.

'I wanted to be polished like Miss Bristow,' she answered with a smile. 'Don't you like it?'

'You're different.' He said it like an accusation.

'I like it,' said Charlotte with conviction. 'You look chic.'

Geoffrey snorted. 'Well, if we've nothing better to do than discuss hairstyles perhaps I should be on my way.' He was both relieved and irritated. There was a silence. Then Charlotte looked directly into his eyes.

'Goodbye, *father*,' she said with heavy emphasis. 'I have to get on with my prep. We're in the middle of exams at school.' It was said formally, politely, as if to a stranger. Geoffrey flushed.

'Your mother and I will make arrangements over the phone,' he said hastily. Jeremy looked at him silently, unblinkingly.

'Bye, old chap. We'll have a go at those maths soon.'

'You said that before.' His voice, like Charlotte's, was empty of emotion. 'Mum's going to ask one of Charlotte's teachers to help me. She worked for IBM, and she probably knows everything about computers.'

Awkwardly Geoffrey made to kiss the children but, without making overt rejecting moves, they managed to dodge the embrace. Their bodies were stiff with stoppered animosity. Geoffrey looked at Kate uneasily. He didn't know how to deal with criticism – he wasn't often in line for anything but praise.

'I'd better go then,' he said feebly. 'I'll give you a ring soon.'

They sat in silence as they listened to his feet on the short terrazzo path to the gate, and the car engine making a few false starts before it purred away. 'Have a drink, Mum,' said Charlotte, then. And added, 'Let's have some champagne.'

'Charlotte!' Kate exclaimed, scandalized.

'We both had wine at your so-called birthday party,' said Charlotte calmly. 'I don't see why we shouldn't have some now.'

'You really are growing up,' Kate said wonderingly.

'Kids do.' Charlotte dropped a kiss on her mother's forehead.

Kate now wanted to cry, but managed to smile instead as Jeremy with an air of importance got a bottle of champagne from the larder and started to wrestle with the cork. Watching her two children she felt the youngest by far.

'What are you going to do, Mum?' asked Charlotte. 'Do you want to move?'

'Do you?'

'I don't really mind. It's sometimes so noisy here – every plane between here and Heathrow seems to fly over us, but it's quite easy for school. The tube is so handy.' Jeremy looked anxiously from one to the other.

'There's no rush,' Kate said gently, and watched him relax. He was, despite his bravado, very young. He couldn't take too many changes too soon. 'You'll have to help me decide what I can do. It will be strange going out to work, assuming I can *find* any! Who will have me?'

The rest of the evening passed with outrageous suggestions for Kate's future employment, each more hilarious than the last.

'Really, that champagne has gone to our heads,' Kate gasped, wiping a tear, as they collapsed laughing at the suggestion that she could try to be a taxi driver. Her total blankness about geography was a standing family joke. 'I think it's bed for us all now – we'll be more sensible in the morning.'

She was touched by the extra-close hugs they gave her as they said good night. Really, children understood more than they were given credit for. She felt grateful for their support.

Next day, however, Kate felt very low. The children had been pale and heavy-eyed at breakfast, as if they had not slept much, and they'd all been rather silent. Her reactive euphoria had dissipated and her sense of failure and inadequacy returned. She made an appointment with her solicitor, wrote a brief letter to her brother, now working in Scotland – after all he'd introduced her and Geoffrey, and he should be the first to know about the breakup – and studied the job advertisements in *The Times*. '£20,000 for telephone sales professionals under 30,' ran one advertisement. 'We urgently require several highly motivated, articulate and successful sales people who can negotiate at senior management level.' 'Girl Friday for busy advertising agency chief. Able to use word processor, charm clients and temperamental creative people, read minds, and organize timetable of frantic media planners. Age 20–25.'

She couldn't offer either the age range or any of the required skills. She wasn't even sure how much she needed to earn. And as for buying another house – surely the proceeds from this one wouldn't stretch to two? Besides, she was fond of this one. Her father had bought it for Geoffrey and her. They had converted the small rooms, and she felt a sense of belonging here. She felt quite pleased at the way she'd overcome the difficulty of the narrow frontage, thrown two small rooms into one long sitting room, and created a large kitchen out of a scullery, outside lavatory and laundry room, winkling the little boxroom for herself from the abrupt turn made by the corridor and a redundant cupboard. It had all worked comfortably, attractively. They had been able to furnish cheaply, with a few nice pieces from her old home, and some good finds at the grubbier auction houses.

Musing, she drifted to the boxroom, and began cleaning up her paints. The place was filthy. She had not let Mrs Shepherd in here to clean, and she hadn't had the heart in some time even to go in herself. Now she dusted and vacuumed, threw out the brushes and tubes of paint hardened past redemption, and did her best to resurrect those that were left. With surprising determination she drove to the high street, making straight for the art shop she mooned over every time she went shopping. There was no-one now to make a scene or put her down and she yearned to lose herself in painting once again, enjoying the concentration of wrestling with colour and shape. It was, she acknowledged, a kind of drug, and ever since that dreadful time when Geoffrey had so denigrated her paintings, she had felt bereft, experiencing strong withdrawal symptoms each time she went past the boxroom door, or even thought of her little work haven.

Back with fat tubes of paint, some shamingly expensive brushes and some canvas paper, she put aside all thought of the jobs she ought to be doing in the house, and set about painting. It was painful, frustrating, but for the first time in months, if not years, she felt contented.

Wrestling with cadmium yellow which threatened to engulf the canvas, bemoaning her lack of skill, she painted until she heard Jeremy calling out in panic 'MUM . . . Mum, where *are* you?' It was nearly five o'clock!

'Darling, I'm here.' She opened the long-unused door in front of his worried little face, making him jump. Had he thought *she'd* abandoned him too?

He rushed to her, a mixture of anger and fear fighting in his expression, and burst into tears. 'The house sounded so quiet, so empty. I thought something had happened!' She hugged him, and her own throat suddenly closed with tears. She had the children, she was very lucky. Soothing him with comforting inconsequential chat, she steered him, her arm about his shoulders, through the narrow house to the kitchen, and made toast and tea, pondering the comfort there was in sipping hot tea. She suddenly remembered that Charlotte's Miss Bristow was coming to see them that evening; she had totally forgotten the appointment.

'I can't wait to see her.' She smiled conspiratorily at Jeremy. 'I wonder if we'll have matching aubergine hair?'

'I do like yours really,' he said shyly. 'You look different, but it's nice – modern.' 'Modern' was the favourite word that week at Crested. Kate felt grateful, pleased at the compliment, all too rare in her life.

Chapter Eight

Miss Bristow turned up on the dot of seven, wearing a short black leather skirt, a colourful, intricately knitted sweater that Kate recognized as a Missoni, and blue tights to match her hair. She smiled cheerfully at Kate. '*I* was that colour last week,' she said. 'Did Daniel do it?'

'Er no,' said Kate nervously. 'Eric – in the high street.'

'Fulham?' Her eyebrows disappeared under the blue fringe. 'How brave! I must let you have the eyeshadow I used with that colour – it's fantastic. But I won't use it again. I never go back to the same shade twice. Too boring.'

She walked into the house, looking about in frank appraisal. Jeremy was standing open-mouthed at the table.

'Hi, kid,' Miss Bristow tossed at him casually. 'You in a mess with maths? Let's look at your books.' Jeremy promptly passed them over.

Miss Bristow turned to Kate. 'I can do an hour after school, two – perhaps three times a week. OK? Fifteen quid an hour. OK? Do you want me to start right now?'

'Well, er, I just thought we'd have a talk first, you know, find out what you've done, your qualifications, er . . .' Kate said bravely.

'First at Cambridge in Applied Mathematics, post-graduate fellowship in pure mathematics and computer studies, three years in the US with IBM, chiefly on programme research and data bases, one year IBM Europe based in Germany, teaching diploma from Bedford, one year maths teaching at Sherborne, head of Maths Department here at St Anselm's since 1986. Anything else?'

'No,' said Kate faintly. 'Except it seems odd that you should need to teach, I mean . . .' she floundered, embarrassed.

'You mean how come with my qualifications I'm not Chancellor of the Exchequer or a Treasury mandarin?'

Kate nodded, faintly relieved at her quick grasp of the import of her hesitant question. 'Something of the sort. I mean, why do you want to teach in the evenings as well?'

'If you'd gone from an IBM salary to a teacher's without modifying your expensive tastes, you wouldn't ask such a question.' Miss Bristow looked impatient, as if the catechism had gone on long enough.

'Well, I'm sure you will be a great help to Jeremy. Er . . .' Kate said awkwardly. This woman took her breath away. Miss Bristow stood up abruptly. 'Good, we'll get on with it now then, shall we? Fee all right?'

'Yes, oh yes,' Kate said hastily, wondering if she could, indeed, afford it. Perhaps this could count as 'topping up the school fees' she thought mischievously.

'Well, perhaps you'd leave us together so that Jeremy can show me what's he done so far, right, kid?' Jeremy nodded speechlessly, throwing a scared look at Kate, as she stumbled over her feet out of the room. She had been dismissed. What a terrifying woman!

She was watching the end of Channel 4 news and jumped when Miss Bristow knocked and came in.

'The kid's all right. Just in a muddle. Some cretin has taught him badly. I'm going back to basics to try and undo some of the tangle but there's nothing wrong with his brain. Who told him he was thick?' she demanded aggressively.

'I don't know,' the steely stare was like an accusing jab to Kate's chest. She stuttered guiltily. 'He got it into his head that he'd never understand maths and the harder he tried the more baffling it seemed. He's been frightfully worried.' She gazed back at Miss Bristow. Her eyes, astonishingly, matched the vibrant blue of her hair and tights. 'Coloured contacts,' said Miss Bristow briefly.

'I'm sorry,' Kate almost jumped again. 'I didn't mean to stare. I've never seen such blue eyes.'

'Sometimes they're green,' Miss Bristow said easily. 'Sometimes violet. Occasionally brown, but I only have brown eyes when my hair is blonde and that's not often. Blonde's so boring, don't you think? Do you have any drink in the house? I'm gasping.'

Kate was a little startled. 'Yes, yes of course – how rude of me. What would you like?'

'A whisky would be just what the doctor ordered. I'm bushed. Late night last night. A hundred kids today – at least it felt like it.'

'And now Jeremy,' said Kate sympathetically. She poured a large whisky.

'Hey, you're my sort,' said Miss Bristow holding up the glass admiringly. 'Is that yellow streak on your cheek deliberate or just a happy accident?' Kate rubbed her cheek self-consciously.

'I'm sorry, I've been painting – I forgot the time and I haven't washed. Jeremy came home before I realized it.'

'Looks great,' Miss Bristow said sipping her drink. 'I might try that.'

Charlotte came tentatively into the room. 'Hi, Charlie. How did the rehearsal go?' Miss Bristow greeted her from where she was slumped back in the chair, her long blue legs stretched out across the hearthrug.

Charlotte blushed and threw a self-conscious look at her mother.

'I wasn't very good. I forgot my lines twice.'

'Bloody difficult part – the play's too ambitious for the school, I think. Do you realize they're doing *Antigone*?'

she demanded of Kate, who immediately felt somehow to blame.

'Miss Cundell thought we could manage it,' Charlotte said shyly. She seemed absurdly young tonight, not a bit like the cool, matter-of-fact know-all she was most of the time.

'She's probably right. It doesn't hurt to be ambitious. I knew her at Cambridge. She was a leading light in the ADC. When she produced *Rosencrantz and Guildenstern Are Dead*, Tom Stoppard was in the audience at one performance and came round afterwards and congratulated her. You're lucky to have her for English, but I'm not sure she isn't wasted as a teacher. She should be directing.' She took another swig at her drink.

'Wednesday be all right?' she turned abruptly to Kate. 'I think he should have me three times a week for the moment – lucky young devil.' She laughed mock-lewdly. 'But I don't think it will be for long. Three or four weeks perhaps and then I need come only if that fool who purports to teach him now gets him screwed up again. I'll just go and see if he's finished the exercise I gave him and then I'll be off. See you Wednesday then.' She uncoiled from the armchair with a natural grace, downed the last of her drink and strode out of the room with a half-wave of the hand.

Kate looked at Charlotte in amazement. 'Is she always like that?'

'Always,' said Charlotte. 'I did say she was trendy.'

'"Polished" was the word you used I think. Hardly an apt one I would say. She seemed familiar enough with all your activities,' Kate said jealously. 'I thought you were a bit afraid of her.'

'I think she's *wonderful*,' said Charlotte passionately. 'She takes an interest in everything, only she makes me feel so dull and boring. I could never be like her.'

'Dull and boring *she's* not, I agree,' said Kate lightly.

'And neither, my pet, are you. What about the play? Is it difficult?'

Chatting companionably, they got the supper ready. Kate was secretly perturbed at Charlotte's fervent interest in acting. Wasn't it too difficult and competitive a profession? She had a good brain, as her results showed – shouldn't she be encouraged to think about a more secure and prosaic occupation? Kate felt herself sink into the familiar swamp of inadequacy. She *must* learn to cope, to find out how best to help Charlotte – no-one had ever called her Charlie before – but a larger dose of Miss Bristow was unthinkable. She wasn't sure she could cope with too many rides on a roller coaster herself.

Chapter Nine

It was unbelievable how the days settled into a serene routine almost immediately. Could it be that they had all felt Geoffrey's presence as disruptive? Kate could hardly wait for the children to go off to school before she raced to the little room and started painting. It was no more than therapy, she told herself, an escape route from the difficulties she knew she would have to face soon enough, but nevertheless she painted obsessively, perhaps trying to make up for the lost time. Almost unconsciously, she set a date for coming to terms with reality after she had talked to her solicitor and found out her exact position. In the meantime the future was hazy.

She took a bus to her lunch with Penelope Milsom, trying to think how she could break the news without making herself seem a pathetic, abandoned wife. In the end it came out as a joke.

'You've got to get rid of that husband of yours,' Penelope Milsom said almost as soon as she had pressed her monkey cheek in greeting against Kate's.

'I have,' said Kate simply. They gazed at each other in astounded silence for a second or two and burst into laughter.

'A strong drink is indicated.' Penelope drew Kate into the large square sunny drawing room. 'Tell me, what are you going to do?'

Reaction set in quickly after the worldly exchange and Kate sniffled a bit. 'I feel such a failure.'

'Nonsense.' Penelope was crisp, shoving a tissue into Kate's hand. 'Lots of people's marriages come unstuck. It's not the end of the world. In fact, for you, I think it could be a beginning. How old were you when you married? Twenty?'

'Eighteen.'

'Ridiculous. What were your parents thinking of? I always thought it was appalling that you were dragged around the world with them, and said so, but your mother would never listen. I think her charming vagueness was a protective covering, a way of not facing up to anything unpleasant.' She considered Kate through the pall of her cigarette smoke. 'You can't live your life in someone else's shadow – you *mustn't*. You've never really found an identity of your own, you know. Don't be silly about the divorce settlement.' Kate jumped at the change of direction. 'Your father gave you the house, your father helped G. Cosgrove get his act together, you have two children to worry about and you mustn't let Geoffrey get away with everything. He should support you properly. It's his *duty*,' she said decisively.

'I don't know what to do,' confessed Kate. 'I've never had to get divorced before.' She tried a smile to banish the wave of self-pity that engulfed her. 'The one thing I'm sure about is that I'd rather starve than take any money from Geoffrey for myself. He wants to sell the house so that we can buy two smaller ones. He hasn't any capital.'

'You can hardly buy anything smaller than the one you've got.' Penelope dismissed the little terraced house that Kate loved so much as if it were a rabbit hutch. 'Don't worry about Geoffrey's lack of capital. That's his problem. Sit tight and let your solicitor battle it out.' Penelope was firm. 'Do as he says – you're still with your family's firm?'

Kate nodded. 'I don't really know how much money I need to live on, or even how much I have. There's a tiny income, I know, and Father set up a trust fund for the children's education, but I don't know how I'm to earn a living. I can't *do* anything.' She felt ashamed.

'Nonsense,' Penelope leapt up briskly. 'Everyone can do something. You just don't know your own value. You could help me in my fund-raising, for a start.'

'I can't type,' said Kate helplessly. 'I've never worked. I don't know what it's like to be in an office – I'd be terrified.'

Penelope stopped her pacing to stand in front of her. 'Think of what you *can* do. Didn't you help Geoffrey when he was setting up the station?'

'Yes, but only as a hostess. I just saw that people were fed and watered and chatted to those who seemed left out of the conversation . . .'

'Well that's virtually what a PR does,' Penelope commented drily. 'They wrap it up a bit but as far as I can see that seems to be the crux of the job.' Kate smiled in gratitude. 'You're lying, but you're a comfort. I suppose I could learn to type – it can't be that difficult. Or sell – some of the shops seem stuffed with languid girls who don't seem to have much more idea than I do.'

'I'm on so many committees I know I can find you a job. You could be my social secretary, for instance. I've been thinking I needed someone more than a typist and my poor girl is intimidated by me. I can't think why, she towers above me. But she doesn't *think*. She doesn't know how to arrange luncheons and dinners – sits all the wrong people next to one another. And she has no charm. That's an essential ingredient in fund-raising.'

'And being a bit of a bully,' Kate said with a sly smile.

'Yes, well that too.' Penelope grinned back. 'But someone has to help the arts if we're not to live in a cultural wasteland, and it's clear the government is not going to do more than the absolute minimum that they can get away with. Sometimes I get so furious I could personally wring the prime minister's neck. Isn't culture supposed to have a civilizing influence? When I read my morning papers it's clear that *culture* is not getting the upper hand! How could you mug two elderly ladies for their pathetic ha'pence if your spirit had been uplifted by good music or you'd stared for five minutes at a Cézanne?' She broke off in embarrassment at her own vehemence, and her little brown wrinkled face screwed up even tighter. 'You could do it all so beautifully . . .'

Kate kissed her spontaneously. 'You're much too kind. But,' – and she was surprised at her own firm voice, 'I've got to stand on my own feet. You've just said yourself I mustn't live in someone else's shadow. You cast a pretty big one yourself, despite your small size. I can't lean on you. I used to lean on Esme, and Tom, and then I let Geoffrey take over. This is a big break, not of my seeking, but if it hadn't happened I would have gone on drifting, more and more hurt by Geoffrey, more and more miserable. I know I'm untrained, unskilled, but other women manage, and I at least do have some money. For the first time – just that minute as you were talking, I could see myself like a post-office parcel, constantly re-addressed, and suddenly I wanted to find my own destination. It was almost like getting the proverbial flash – everything suddenly seems exciting.' Kate stopped, embarrassed in her turn by her passion.

Penelope looked thoughtful. 'You'll make it – if you don't put yourself down too much. Let's have lunch – and one of Michael's best bottles of wine. I think this is a celebration, my dear.'

Although nothing had changed, Kate came away from Penelope's feeling cheerful and confident. It had been a comfort just to talk to the older woman, and she had reiterated her offer of some vague kind of job. Even if she weren't to take up the proposal, it gave her a slight sense of security.

She went back to Fulham by bus again, soothed by its

slow trundle through the crowded Chelsea streets, the amusing wild-looking girls in King's Road – almost as colourful as Miss Bristow – the comfortable pensioners tucked into their seats around her, enjoying their free ride as they gossiped. 'I'll go to the library tomorrow and look at career guides,' she thought. 'There must be some niche for me. I can't just die off like a hardy annual just because a husband doesn't want me.'

The children looked at her curiously as she buzzed about getting supper, humming as she did so. She asked Jeremy to show her his books, to see if she could understand anything, and wanted Charlotte to tell her about the girls in her class. What were they going to do? How did they know what they were going to do? How did they set about doing it?

Charlotte grinned. 'I'm not going to ask our careers mistress to come home and coach you too,' she said, aware of what was behind Kate's sudden interest. 'Anyway, most of them don't know what they're going to do. They're just programmed by their parents to swot for their O-levels and A-levels and haven't a clue beyond that. They're pretty wet.'

'What makes *you* so sure you want to be an actress?' Kate asked curiously. Once more Charlotte's grown-up decisiveness and assurance was making her feel the child. 'I just feel it in my bones. I'm simply not interested in anything else. I don't want to go to university.'

'But plenty of actresses do, and a lot of them are discovered there, because there are drama societies which attract talent-spotters. Daddy, you know, used to be a leading light as a producer and that's what helped him get his first BBC job.'

'I know but I don't want to waste time. I want to go to RADA and if I can't get there I shall try for a repertory company. What would I do at university?'

'Well, read English for a start – it will help your understanding.'

'I read endlessly now, I don't need some dusty don to make me write useless essays when I could be learning to move, to control my voice, to interpret, oh, *all* that stagecraft that people like Maggie Smith and Vanessa Redgrave seem to've been born knowing.' She spoke so passionately that Kate was awed and envious.

She found herself, the next day, looking forward to Miss Bristow's second visit. What would she look like this time?

Disappointingly her hair was still the same electric blue and the short black leather skirt was the same, but this time it was partnered by a comparatively sedate waist-length fitted jacket like a bell-hop's, over a blue-and-black spotted shirt. Her long legs were displayed in black tights, ending in pert little ankle boots. She looked almost conventional. 'Hi,' she drawled at Kate. 'Kid in?'

'Yes, he's in the dining-room as before.'

'OK, I'll see how he has got on.'

Kate was reading when she came in later. She looked up and smiled. 'There's a drink all ready. Whisky, as before?' Miss Bristow nodded. 'Thanks. Aren't you drinking?'

'I hadn't thought about it. I don't drink much when I'm on my own.'

'Well you're not on your own now,' Miss Bristow pointed out. 'I've left the kid struggling with another exercise. He'll be better able to think things out on his own. Maths is just common sense really. It's only when some self-important idiot tries to make it seem over-complicated that the rot sets in.'

'I always thought maths was creative,' said Kate, pouring herself a drink every bit as stiff as Miss Bristow's. 'Surely it is the mathematicians who made space travel a reality?'

Miss Bristow's face lit up. 'You're dead right. If they got a tiny millimetre wrong, kaput.'

Kate felt rather pleased with herself for making an acceptable speculation, but was afraid she would lose points if she got out of her depth any further, so she hastily offered that she herself had not had any formal schooling and was just as much at sea as Jeremy.

'You're not asking me to take you on too, are you?' Miss Bristow snorted with laughter, and Kate joined her.

'No, it's too late for me. But as a matter of fact, I have been wondering what I could do. I have to earn a living and I've never done it before. I've no idea where to start.'

'How come?'

Kate, relaxed by the drink, began to tell the brilliant creature a bit about herself.

'Do you mean you married the first man you met at *eighteen*?' Miss Bristow was scandalized. It was a replay of Penelope's reaction, but much more direct. 'You've never been to school or college? Ye gods. I can't believe it.' She downed the rest of her drink in her amazement and held out her glass. Kate was amused. Somehow her gestures weren't rude, just totally relaxed and unselfconscious. She refilled both glasses. It was quite heady to have an audience, to talk about herself, and not tiptoe round someone else's ego.

'It does sound strange now, even to me, but I didn't realize what I was missing at the time.'

'Well you'll have to make up for lost time.' Miss Bristow grinned, 'Do you want to come with me? I'm going on to a party after I've dealt with the kid. It's not far from here – World's End and very casual. You can't sit here alone for the rest of your life. How old are you, anyway?'

'Thirty-five,' Kate said faintly.

'Three years younger than me! It's incredible.'

'I don't think I *can* come, thank you all the same,' Kate was suddenly shy. 'I can't leave the children.'

'But Charlie's here isn't she? She's nearly sixteen going on thirty for God's sake. And Jeremy's not a baby. They know how to use the telephone, don't they?'

'Perhaps another time,' Kate smiled, but her tone was firm. She'd pictured herself in her careful classic ladylike clothes among the bird-of-paradise guests she imagined would be at Miss Bristow's party, like the young women she'd seen from the bus window in Chelsea. 'I mean it – I would love to be invited again but I don't think I'm mentally quite up to it just now.'

'Suit yourself, but it'll be fun.' She uncoiled from her chair in one smooth movement. 'She's like a wild animal,' Kate thought; she couldnt imagine her caged in matrimony.

'I'll go and see what the little horror's up to.' She nodded briefly at Kate. 'And take myself off. Friday, I thought?'

Kate nodded, disappointed at the imminent loss of such colourful company.

'My name's Phillipa,' Miss Bristow added, draining her glass again. 'Commonly known as Flip.'

'Mine's Kate.'

'Yes, I thought it would be. Or Emma. Cheers.' And she strode out of the room as informally as she had arrived.

Painting feverishly again next day Kate found herself thinking about Miss Bristow – Flip, she corrected herself, amused. Did she have many lovers or just one at a time? She must spend a fortune on her clothes, and her car was newish. What could it be like to be independent, to be able to earn a living, to be unshackled by emotional involvements, to be free? It seemed so enviable.

She had studied the morning paper again for possible jobs and even telephoned the Job Centre. When she explained that she had never worked, hadn't any educational qualifications or experience, the interviewer's voice had sharpened in disbelief. 'You might find something in catering – but you must come in for an interview.'

Depressed, Kate had said she would but she had gone into the boxroom and started to paint again. If only Esme were back from America. *She'd* think of something Kate could do. For herself she had no ideas except perhaps to cook. She knew that some young women trained as Cordon Bleu cooks, cooked for company dining rooms, and half the time ended up marrying one of the bright young executives. It seemed a good marriage market. But she wasn't sure her self-taught cookery was good enough, and neither youth nor looks were on her side.

Startled from her musings by the doorbell, she was confronted by a stocky, dark-haired man with a wide-mouthed ugly face redeemed by a humourous smile. 'Kate Cosgrove?'

'Yes.' She looked puzzled.

'Then you don't remember me. I was at school with Tom. I once spent a summer with you at Cheevers. I've just left Tom in Edinburgh. I'm *en route* to Spain, and he asked me to call to see you. He was worried by a letter he'd had from you.' Kate struggled with memory, opening the door more widely but with a certain ungraciousness. She didn't want to be interrupted, certainly not by a near-stranger, possibly an over-curious one. She flushed at the thought of Tom revealing the contents of her letter.

'I think I do remember you,' she said shortly. 'I seem to recall a thin, dark boy Tom brought home one summer. Your parents were in the Far East then. Nick, isn't it? Nick Menton.' His smile grew.

'Correct, but, as you see, no longer thin.' He patted his stomach. 'And—' he swept his hand over his greying hair deprecatingly, 'my parents are still out East – they both died there.'

'I'm sorry,' Kate regretted her ungracious manner.

'Oh, some years back now.' He followed her into the sitting-room. Damn Tom. She struggled with her irritation. She didn't want people popping in being kind to the abandoned little woman treating her like some terminal case, lowering their voices, tiptoeing round her misery, laundering their chat for fear of upsetting her. She could imagine Tom telling this Nick Menton to go and cheer up his poor sister. After yesterday's bracing chat with Penelope she was looking forward to the future, not sunk in gloom. She frowned. 'Would you like some tea?' she asked grudgingly.

'That would be nice.' He seemed unaware of her irritation. 'I came down on the shuttle and I'm parched. I didn't stop for anything because I want to get to Madrid tonight.' He smiled at her again with such infectious goodwill that Kate felt slightly ashamed of herself. 'Well have a look at the paper – I'll make some. Would you like some toast?'

'If it's not too much trouble, yes, please.'

She disappeared to the kitchen, trying to damp down her exasperation. It was amazing how these hours alone in the house, with just her paints to keep her company, had soothed her spirit. She realized how jealous she was of the time spent away from her easel and how much she had missed the physical therapy of working brushloads of paint into a canvas, moving the shapes around, battling with the distance between what was in her head and what her hand produced. She banged each cup into its saucer to relieve her feelings. Really, she was being unreasonable. He'd broken his journey at Tom's request, just to be able to reassure her brother that she was all right. It was unfair to be so rude. As she was buttering the toast and cutting off the crusts he walked into the kitchen and picked up the tray.

'Let me take that. I'm sorry if I interrupted you. I would have rung from the airport but there was such a queue for the telephone boxes. Is that painting yours?' he added conversationally. She stared at him speechlessly, rage pricking her scalp. 'What do you mean?' she demanded outraged. Had he actually gone into her room!

'I'm sorry.' He spread his hands and shrugged his shoulders in a faintly European manner. 'I just followed my nose. Turps. I used to believe I could be a painter and the smell of oil and turps is still evocative of some very happy times. That was before I found out the truth about myself. I couldn't help taking another nostalgic whiff of what might have been.' He smiled disarmingly.

He helped himself to a piece of toast and bit into it as he remarked, 'Tom didn't tell me you painted.'

'I don't.' Kate was still trying to regain her calm. That little room was hers – she didn't want it violated.

'I thought what was on your easel was very exciting.'

'Exciting?'

'Yes – and fresh. Could I see some more of your work?'

Kate could only stare. 'Tom didn't tell you, I suppose, that I followed the path of other failed artists: I became a dealer.'

Kate shook her head, still speechless.

'That picture has something, but I'd need to see more.'

'I don't have any more,' Kate said slowly. 'My husband didn't like me painting,' she offered at his look of incredulity.

He sipped his tea in silence. 'Do you have a job? Tom said you had two children.'

'No. But I gather Tom has told you my marriage has broken up.' She didn't look at his face as she said this; the words were still painfully new. 'I shall have to get a job now. I've just been trying to think of what I can do.'

He bit neatly into the toast. 'I'm a picture dealer, but I do have lots of contacts in the commercial world. Have you thought about the art department of, say, an advertising agency or a design studio?'

Kate gasped. 'But I haven't any *training*! I've never been to art college – I've only painted with my old governess.' As she mentioned Esme, Kate felt a sudden stab of excitement. Esme was earning a very good living painting greeting cards. She was self-deprecating about it but all the same her skill, untrained like Kate's, was in constant demand. Esme had put crayons and then paints in Kate's willing hands ever since she's first come to the Scotts' unconventional household, and they'd spent hours contentedly painting and drawing together. Esme was passionate about art and whenever there was an opportunity they had escaped to an art gallery or exhibition. Perhaps she wasn't as untrained as she thought, with a flash of elation.

'Training . . . pshaw. It doesn't give you an eye, or a heart, or an imagination. It merely develops technique and that can be acquired by practice and observation. And self-criticism,' he added with a smile. 'But perhaps you have too much of that already.'

Kate stared at him, her cheeks flushed. He was a bit too penetrating for comfort but he was offering the first idea that seemed remotely feasible.

'Do you think I could get a job in a . . . in an advertising studio or something? I wouldn't mind doing menial jobs if I could see how it all worked and perhaps learn at the same time.'

'I don't know.' He made a brief note on a gilt-edged leather notepad. 'Ad agencies have to be so competitive, that they haven't the time or personnel to teach people, but you could hang around a good creative team and learn a lot if you made yourself useful in some way. I'll ring a few contacts and see what I can do. It's a pity I'm off to Spain tonight but it's only for a few days, and,' he smiled a puckish smile of great charm, 'I believe the Spanish have telephones.'

Kate smiled back. 'Thank you so much. I'm sorry I was so ungracious when you arrived, but I couldn't bear to be interrupted and I thought Tom was being unnecessarily big brotherish.'

'Tom's very fond of you – we happened to be having dinner together the day your letter arrived, and he was deeply concerned. It was all I could do to stop him hurtling down himself, but he's in the middle of some amazing work that looks as if it's close to a great climax. To break off at that critical point would be . . . he was going to telephone but as I was passing through . . .' He spread his hands and gave a shrug, his smile a little self-deprecating. 'But I think you should telephone him; you *are* his only family.'

Kate looked down to hide the sudden rise of tears. She was remembering how Tom had jollied her father into accepting her marriage to Geoffrey. It was sad that they were so far apart geographically.

Nick was getting up. 'Thanks for the tea – and the toast. Perhaps when I get back you would have lunch or dinner with me and I'll give you a progress report.'

She looked at him shyly but held out her hand and shook his firmly. 'I'd like that very much.'

'Goodbye then.' From a window she watched him hurry down the road at a pace almost approaching a trot toward the tube station. Poor man might miss his plane. She was a thoughtless bitch. She would have to learn to be less defensive.

Chapter Ten

After Nick had gone Kate whirled round the room, unable to suppress a mounting excitement. Confronting herself unexpectedly in a mirror, she gazed at her shining face, looked herself in the eye and said resolutely, '*You can do it.*' It was odd – she felt scared but suddenly immensely, astonishingly confident. Nick's words had caused a thrilling flash of self-revelation. She remembered saying to Jeremy, 'It's all a matter of someone's showing you how to turn a key in a lock, when you've been rattling away at it without results . . .' She hadn't the faintest idea what sort of work advertising art departments did but whatever it was didn't, now, seem impossible or beyond her. Nick had offered her a key. It was up to her to find a lock it fitted and discover how to turn it.

She tugged at a pile of old magazines on a bottom shelf and looked at the advertisement pages. She'd never really paid attention to them before. She sobered down as she flicked through and saw that most of them were photographs. Here and there were small line drawings of very pedestrian merchandise, but she couldn't see any outlet for someone who painted. Her spirits plunged. Probably Nick Menton was out of touch. An art dealer would not have much contact with the advertising world, and though he might have a few successful friends in it he probably had little idea of what they actually did.

That was a short-lived freedom dash, she thought, feeling a bit sick with disappointment as she turned away from the magazines to prepare supper. She didn't feel able to go back to her paints now.

Charlotte was home before Jeremy today. He'd been chosen for the soccer team and they were having some after-school coaching. 'What's up, Mum?' she asked, gauging her mother's mood from her expression. There was a look of strain about her own little face, as she visibly made an effort to understand. Kate shrugged and attempted a laugh. She knew she must reassure Charlotte that nothing else awful had happened. The children had been fairly quiet and noncommittal, trying hard to cheer her, making touching attempts to show that they loved her, that they were on 'her side'. But she mustn't forget that they too had lost their trust in their father and were probably feeling confused and depressed.

'Oh nothing, really. A friend of my brother's called today and at first I thought he had a good idea for a job for me – he suggested that I might find work in the art department of an advertising agency.'

Charlotte looked mystified. 'He saw my painting,' Kate added apologetically. The children had never seen her work on a canvas and had rarely bothered to enter the boxroom, merely wrinkling their noses at the turps-and-oil smell that hung about so obstinately. 'It sounded like something I could do, but when I looked at the advertising pages in those old magazines they seem to use mostly photographs. I don't suppose he knew anything about it really. Just trying to be kind. He raised my hopes for a bit – that's all. There seems so little I can do.'

'You used to draw for us when we were little,' Charlotte said, remembering. 'I didn't realize it then but the pictures were *good* – I've still got some of the birthday cards you made me.'

'Oh, Esme's the greetings card whizz,' Kate said. 'I

don't think I could do those on a commercial scale – she has a sense of what will sell.'

'How do you know?' Charlotte demanded reasonably. 'Perhaps you could go into partnership with her.' Kate pulled herself together and started slicing the carrots. 'No – although I studied with her – it's about the only subject we did study, now that I come to think of it – we always saw things differently. We could be painting or drawing the same thing, but looking at the finished product, you'd never know it. She has an amusing, sardonic eye. She used to almost caricature the subject, whereas I was a bit more poetic, sometimes rather abstract. No, I don't think I could do a greetings card,' she said decisively. 'How did you get on today? Did you get your chemistry test results? I hope you'll now appreciate the need to be trained in *something*, get a degree or a recognized skill.' She wanted to change the subject; thinking about herself was too dispiriting.

Charlotte rubbed her cheek comfortingly against Kate's shoulder. 'I got 73%. Miss Martin keeps going on about taking it for A-level. She's so dreary. I'm fed up with her nagging me to make a decision. She's arranging a party of the sixth formers to go to ICI's dyestuff division and she wants about four of our class to go with them, to stimulate our interest I suppose – turn us all into little chemists.'

'That sounds very nice of her, I think you should go – after all, you might have to *play* the part of a chemist one day,' Kate said suggestively. Charlotte gave her a sardonic look. She was far too sharp. Kate wondered how she'd grown up so quickly – hardly by using *her* as an example. Charlotte seemed to have overtaken her effortlessly.

The telephone interrupted them. It was Flip. 'How are you fixed for Friday?' she asked without preamble. 'I'm going to a new club with some friends. They're supposed to have good food, which I doubt, and good live music from some new groups. They let them try out there for peanuts I suppose. Why don't you come with me after I've given Kidlet another dose of maths?'

Kate smiled. 'I don't suppose I've been to a club more than twice in my life, and I doubt whether I'd know one group from another.'

'Well then, there's no time to lose.'

'But I – well to be frank, I don't think I have anything suitable to wear. Marks and Spencer cut-price cashmere jerseys and a three-year-old Jean Muir bought at a sale would scarcely count among your friends.' She laughed.

'Forget trivia. Are you coming?'

'Honestly, I don't like leaving the children. Supposing there was a burglar . . .'

'Or the house caught fire. Or Kidlet got appendicitis. Sure, all those things can happen. But are you going to live your life on the off-chance of missing an emergency? Get your ex-old man to babysit if you're that worried.'

Kate laughed aloud at the idea of summoning Geoffrey to look after his offspring while she went out to enjoy herself.

'All right,' she said on impulse. 'I'll come. I'll arrange for someone to come in. But . . .'

'But me no buts. That's settled then.' And the telephone clicked off before Kate could think of any more objections.

It's only an evening out for God's sake, she thought to herself as, trembling slightly, she went back to the half-prepared supper. 'That was your Miss Bristow,' she told Charlotte. 'She wants me to go out on the town with her on Friday.'

Charlotte's jaw dropped. 'Crikey! What will you wear?'

'My sentiments exactly,' said Kate.

'Buy something new. You've *got* to!'

'Darling, I can't rise to the heights of Miss Bristow – Flip, by the way, as she told me to call her. I can't rush off and buy something extravagantly trendy for one night at a club!'

'A *club*!' Charlotte sat up with avid interest. 'Which one?'

Kate was astonished. 'What do you know about clubs?'

'I read. I can't wait to go to one. Some of them have marvellous *live* groups like Simply Red.'

'Flip said it was a new one. She said they have little-known groups trying out, and supposedly good food, but she didn't believe it.'

'It must be Mickey-Michaels. I read about it in *The Face*. It's supposed to be wonderful, all done out in gold with gold lamé tablecloths and a red glass dance floor that rises and flashes lights. You eat on a balcony overlooking the dance floor and the food is Creole. It was all in *The Face* last month. It looked amazing,' she rolled her eyes for emphasis. 'The owner is a transvestite,' she added casually.

'*What!*' Kate was rattled.

'They're quite harmless, you know,' she said calmly. 'Very funny, usually. You won't have to join in.'

'I should hope not. I shall be a fish out of water. I won't have to dance, will I?'

'Moth-*er*, you don't have to do anything you don't want to. But what have you got against dancing? You look young enough not to look soppy.'

'But I don't know how . . .' Kate almost wailed. The whole thing was a mad idea and she'd simply tell Miss Bristow – Flip – when she came on Friday, that she couldn't make it.

'Oh Mum, you're so silly – it's just a dance. You just rock about. You've seen how it's done on television. And you must have gone dancing with Dad, didn't you?'

'But they're all so young on television – *your* age. And I haven't really danced with your father since he was at Cambridge, and that's more than seventeen years ago.'

'Well then, there's no time to lose.' She sounded so like

Flip that Kate looked sharply at her. Surely they had not colluded?

'Anyway *you're* young. The girls at Open Day thought you looked smashing. Do you realize,' she said, 'people are living a lot longer today. You'll probably live at least another sixty years.' She was pink with an air of self-assurance, just like a television presenter on a science programme. 'That means you have nearly two-thirds of your life still to live. You can't waste it!'

'If you go on like that I shall start calling *you* "Mum".' Kate chucked her under her determined little chin. 'Well since you're so knowledgeable, what *shall* I wear?'

'Ring Beatrice. Didn't she work on *Vogue*? Where is she now?'

'That's a great idea! She's a fashion PR now. She sent me a card. Wait – I've got her new number somewhere,' Kate said excitedly.

She rang Beatrice at once. Unsurprised, her young cousin was casual. 'Come and have lunch with me tomorrow. I've got a brand new account – he's the up-and-coming designer now. A bit pricey, but I can get you a good discount. Where are you going?'

'To a club as a matter of fact.'

'A *club*? I didn't think that was your scene,' Beatrice said tactlessly. 'I suppose Geoffrey wants to be trendy?'

'Geoffrey and I have separated,' Kate said awkwardly. She still couldn't get used to the words. 'We're going to divorce. I'm going out with some friends.'

'I'm sorry,' Beatrice said after a beat. 'I shouldn't have blundered on like that.'

'That's all right. It doesn't matter – it's the sensible thing to do. But are you sure you're free for lunch tomorrow? I could just pop into a showroom or something.'

'I'd love to see you,' said Beatrice sincerely. 'You were so sweet when I won the talent competition – you sent me flowers. Everybody else saw it as a huge joke.'

'Well I'll come to your office about 12.45, shall I?' She had the feeling there was no turning back now.

'Lovely. I've just remembered something from his new collection that's absolutely devastating. It will be good for his image for you to wear it in a smart club. If money's a problem he'll probably lend it to you.'

'No no,' Kate said hastily. 'That would be too much of a worry all night.'

She rang off after Beatrice had given her directions for reaching an obscure little street. 'It looks scruffy outside,' she'd said, 'but the woman who runs this agency has just started on her own – that's how she got me. I'm cheap,' she explained, adding firmly, 'for the moment.'

Jeremy looked bemused by the intense chat between Kate and Charlotte over supper and felt aggrieved that they cut short his description of how at football practice he'd had to keep heeling and toeing the ball until his thigh muscles trembled with tension. Charlotte insisted on tuning to Capital radio so that Kate could listen to some of the new discs throughout the meal. They all sounded roughly the same to Kate and the words when she could hear them were so banal and repetitive that she wondered why they bothered with lyrics at all, but she thought she'd keep quiet since Charlotte was so bent on educating her.

Beatrice took her to Le Caprice. 'Everybody comes here,' she said. 'I have to be seen in the places where the press goes.' She looked so young and self-important that Kate smiled. A slightly older Charlotte with the same sense of direction. 'Have you got someone else?' she asked abruptly. 'Because if so I'll go after Geoffrey. I always fancied him. He was so glamorous.'

'Still is,' said Kate with a slight pang of regret. 'I'm afraid he's found someone else. Greta Lanson.'

'The television woman?' Beatrice gasped. 'She's *beautiful.*'

'So Geoffrey thinks,' Kate agreed.

'I'm sorry,' Beatrice looked abashed and suddenly gauche.

Kate smiled. 'I expect it's all for the best. I'm going to have to be a career girl now – a belated breadwinner. *If* I can find something I can do.'

'Right – well, you have to package yourself. I can help with clothes – Miffe says if you look expensive no-one *dares* offer you peanuts.'

'Steady on – I can't spend a lot. I haven't dared sort out finances yet – I'm too cowardly.'

'It's not what you spend, it's how you spend it.' Beatrice was back on her own ground, authoritative and confident. She tilted her head critically. 'I like your new hair colour, but you need to change your make-up. Very pale skin I think, and an ox-liver lipstick.' Kate shuddered. 'Not now while I'm eating, please. I'm not enamoured of offal.'

Beatrice giggled, and plunged into gossip about some of the fashion editors she had to deal with; how some of them would wear the clothes she sent over for photography and return them creased and spotted with food or drink, sometimes covered in make-up. 'They think we don't know but one of them was caught out wearing a Zandra Rhodes she'd borrowed, ostensibly to photograph for their Christmas issue, and she bumped into Zandra at the same party. I must say Zandra was very understanding about it, which is more than my boss would be. She's a terror, but knows her business and commands respect. Frankly I'd much rather do the styling for ads,' she went on. 'For one thing they have to pay for the loan of the garments, and they come to the showrooms and look at the collections. I don't have to send a taxi-load of garments as I do for the fashion editors, some of whom never take proper notes at collections and are too lazy to turn up and pick things out for their fashion stories themselves.'

Kate's ears pricked. 'Advertisers? Of course I suppose they have to choose clothes for their photographs.'

'Or the television commercials. Of if they're doing a big presentation, one of the artists sketches the newest shapes.'

'But I hardly see drawings in ads,' Kate was rapt.

'Not so much in magazines, but they have big art departments preparing what they call visuals to show clients. And of course a lot of posters are all art work – especially on the Underground, but they still need a fashion stylist to get the details right. And the pay's *terrific*. One of the *Vogue* fashion girls used to moonlight and she'd be paid £500 for an evening's work.'

'What a lot you know.' Kate was sincerely admiring.

Beatrice looked pleased and gratified. 'Let's go and look at the clothes.' She called for the bill with a touching show of authority. 'Now I've seen you again I've changed my mind. I didn't know you'd transformed your hair so dramatically.' And that's not all, thought Kate, projecting a picture of herself in a gold lamé club tomorrow in company with the outrageous Flip Bristow.

Chapter Eleven

While Jeremy was having his maths coaching, Kate got ready, critically supervised by Charlotte. Beatrice had produced a slim, bronze silk dress with a plain high neckline and a wide, v-shaped bare back, plunging to the waist.

Kate had shaken her head. 'I couldn't wear a bra with that.'

'No,' Beatrice had agreed, 'you're not supposed to.'

Kate had protested, twisting and turning to look in the mirror, that it was too daring for her.

'Well I agree, if you wore it back to front.' Beatrice handed her some long, tasselled earrings. 'Wear these. Vernon would be furious if you didn't put his whole look together.'

Now she obediently shaded her lids with the bronze eyeshadow Beatrice had suggested, dutifully adding more as Charlotte said, 'No, stronger, it needs to be stronger,' and applied the strangely deep-toned lipstick she'd bought from the girl in Selfridges who seemed totally indifferent to the fact it was a far cry from the soft pinks Kate usually wore. She had bought some metallic bronze Maud Frizon shoes from Brown's in South Molton Street, as directed by the imperious Beatrice, so expensive that she suddenly wondered where the money would be coming from. While they were so vague and hazy, her financial problems didn't seem threatening. After she'd seen her solicitor there would be time enough to face the cold facts of her financial future.

'Mum, you look *wonderful*!' Charlotte gazed raptly at her mother. 'Good old Beatrice. She's a genius.'

Kate felt a strange mixture of shyness and excitement. She blushed as she saw her nipples under the thin fabric and she instinctively crossed her arms in front of herself. What was all this gilding and dressing up *for*? She felt vaguely that being scented and packaged was like being offered for sale. Yet it was pleasant to feel attractive and the centre of attention, if only Charlotte's.

'Oh well, I expect I shall be a fish out of water anyway,' she grumbled, trying to regain some poise as she went down to tell Mrs Shepherd that there was supper in a low oven, and not to hesitate to ring her if there were any problems.

'Heavens, Mrs Cosgrove, there's nothing to worry about. The children don't have to be put to bed. They're too old for me to look after, really, but I suppose you wouldn't enjoy yourself if you were to leave them alone. I'll just watch telly and take myself off to the spare room when my programme's over. "Lifestyles" is my favourite programme – tell Mr Cosgrove. Ever so interesting, and that Greta Lanson is *so* beautiful. My husband can't take his eyes off her.'

'Nor can mine,' thought Kate, but she didn't bother to enlighten Mrs Shepherd, her twice-weekly help. The news would trickle out in time.

Flip's eyes flicked judicially over Kate as she came out of the dining-room with a smiling Jeremy, but she didn't comment, merely put her arm round his shoulders as she said to Kate, 'I think he's cottoned on. He's doing brilliantly. Tonight he sailed through the exercise I gave him. I think that guy who pretends to be a maths teacher ought to jump in the lake.' She gave Jeremy a friendly push. 'Don't get too cocky, kid; I've got more up my sleeve.' They grinned at each other in understanding. 'Well, let's be off.' She turned to Charlotte, hovering on the bottom stair. 'No boys, mind. We might come back unexpectedly early.' Charlotte blushed self-consciously.

Kate asked her for the name of the club they were going to so that she could give Mrs Shepherd the number. Flip looked amused. 'My, it *has* been a long time since you went out. We're only starting off at Mickey-Michaels.' Kate heard Charlotte's rapturous gasp behind her. 'We usually move on. But here.' She fished out a card. 'If it makes you relax.' She gave Mrs Shepherd the card and the three of them watched as Flip went with her long, loping stride to the car, with Kate trying to walk unselfconsciously but feeling a stranger to herself. Her heart was thumping. 'Anyone would think you were a gauche teenager,' she chided herself, 'instead of a gay divorcée.' She felt a touch overdressed besides Flip, who was wearing a short, narrow cream skirt with a matching soft blouson jacket buttoned almost to the neck. Her hair, tonight, was silvery white, razored all over so that her head, a beautiful shape poised on a long neck, looked delicate and vulnerable.

'How long will it take to grow out?' asked Kate as she settled into the black Golf.

'Two or three weeks, but I might keep this cut – it's so easy. But I get bored so easily. It's probably the major one of my many failings, and since it's too disruptive to keep changing my life, I change my looks instead.' She pressed firmly on the accelerator as they moved out into New King's Road.

'Is that why you've never married?' asked Kate curiously.

'Who said I'd never married?' She turned her head to look at Kate as she cut by a furiously hooting taxi. 'At the last count there were two husbands. Ex-husbands,' she added succinctly.

'I'm sorry – I didn't know.' Kate was astounded.

'One lasted three weeks.' She hooted with laughter.

'And the other all of three months. I'm not cut out for marriage.'

'Don't you want children?' Kate's curiosity got the better of good manners.

'Nope. If I did want them I could have them without being married. But I'd be a hopeless mother. Far too self-centred. I like kids, which is why I teach now, but only when they are at a civilized age. All that feeding, and the sick and the nappies. Yuk. Not for me. And I'm not big on the self-sacrifice. I like spending money on *me*, not screwing and scraping to send the little blighters to good schools.'

She smiled at Kate's blank face. 'Not an admirable character. By the way, peel off if you hate tonight. You don't want to be forced to enjoy yourself. I like the odd rave-up after a day in school, and I'm mad about R & B – that's how I married my first husband. I was besotted by his playing – might just as well have gone to bed with a guitar.' She gave a snorting laugh. 'But don't rely on me for a lift home. If there's no-one I want to split with, I don't mind dropping you off – but otherwise you'll have to make your own way. And if you see some talent, don't worry about me.' Kate was aware of Flip's amused eyes on her face; she was hoping to catch the giveaway shock, but Kate looked calmly ahead, hoping the bus in front would reach Sloane Square before Flip swung out to overtake it, slipping between it and an oncoming coach, as she had done outside Chelsea Town Hall.

The club, on a small street in Soho, was not full when they arrived, but it was thumping to the sounds made by five young men in shorts and morning coats, with waistcoats and top hats made of the Stars and Stripes.

Flip's lip curled. 'The quality of the music is in direct ratio to their gear,' she said briefly. 'Let's go to the cloakroom.' There Kate was stunned to see the cream jersey jacket peeled off to reveal a darkish pink double chiffon top ribbed in knit at the neck and sleeveless armholes. Under the gauzy fabric, Flip's small pointed breasts, tipped with dark brown nipples, were clearly visible. She suddenly felt her long-sleeved dress to be, if anything, too decorous, back dip or no.

'Watch out for Brian,' Flip hissed as they went upstairs to the balcony. 'He's not called Octopussy for nothing.' Enthusiastic waves of greeting rose from a far table in a corner. 'There's the gang,' Flip said. 'With, I'm happy to say, one or two promising recruits.'

There were seven people round the small dark corner table. A tall thin man with close-cut curly fair hair, fair eyebrows and eyelashes, and a lazy, good-natured smile stood up and hugged Flip in a casual, friendly fashion. 'At last. My favourite raver. What colour do you call that?' He indicated Flip's transparent top. 'Dark mouth,' Flip said easily and gazed with frank interest at a thin, dark man still seated. 'This is Freddy.' The fair man introduced him, and taking hold of Kate's hand, said, 'And whoever you are you'll sit by me.'

'That's Kate.' Flip reached for the bottle in the middle of the table. 'Kate, Jon without an H is the fast-worker holding your hand, Brian, still, I see, wearing that awful shirt, and Natalie, our resident glamourpuss.' Natalie shook back a sleek Louise Brook bob and gave Kate a sideways glance from under incredibly long lashes. 'Hi.' She was wearing a black strapless dress, and with her elbows on the table, looked half-naked. There was an older man, forty-five, Kate judged, looking very much a City gent in a navy pinstriped suit, with a waistcoat and beautifully crafted shirt, who was introduced baldly as 'Dave', and a young sulky-looking man called Jim who must still be at university, Kate thought, watching him watch Natalie. Kate sipped the glass of raw red wine poured for her by Jon when he'd snatched the bottle back from Flip. The kind of polite small-talk she was used to making at cocktail parties would not go down very well here. 'And Jon, do you teach too?' She smiled at him.

'No. I'm a grocer.'

Kate gaped. 'A *grocer?*'

'Yes madam, at your service,' he said, and pulled a forelock obsequiously. 'May I take your order? Everything delivered within a five-mile radius.' He broke off and picked up his glass, lifting it to her, looking deeply into her eyes, so that she felt a flush creeping up her neck. 'Do you really want to talk about *jobs*? What do *you* do?'

'Nothing.' She was going to say tritely, 'I'm just a housewife,' when she caught Flip's admonishing look. 'I – I'm looking for work at the moment.' Flip smiled her relief and sank her nose into her glass. 'Tell me,' Kate plunged bravely. 'Have you heard this group before? They look extraordinary.' She half-turned her back to look at the stage below where the musicians were playing gamely despite almost total lack of interest from the audience. She felt his finger stroke softly down her spine. She had quite forgotten that her dress was backless.

'Does that do something to you?' He had brought his mouth so close to her ear that his soft whispered breath sent a little shiver down her spine. She hastily turned back and smiled too brightly. 'Yes, of course. It felt like a zip closing.'

Jon's sultry, sexy expression vanished and he laughed appreciatively, pouring himself another drink and calling the waiter for more. 'Bring a couple more bottles but not of that vinegar, there's a good chap. I'm sure you've something drinkable tucked away – if not I'll sell you some myself. And don't forget – I know the wholesale prices.'

The waiter grinned. 'Mr Daniel, you don't come to clubs like this for good wine, you know. No-one here appreciates it.'

'Well *I'm* here and *I* know the difference, and so I'm

sure do my friends. Find something Mickey-Michael drinks himself.' He had tipped his chair back and stretched his arms along the backs of Kate's and Natalie's chairs and was stroking Kate's back again with his finger. Kate wondered if Natalie was getting the same treatment, but if so her expression betrayed nothing.

Flip stood up. 'Let's see if you can dance too,' she said, clutching Freddy's hands and pulling him to his feet. 'Too?' He bent his head and gazed at her mouth. Flip looked boldly back and ran her tongue slowly over her lip. 'Too.' She turned and led the way downstairs to the floor. Jon laughed again. 'She's hopeless.' He turned to Kate. 'Would you like to dance or,' as the rest of the table paired off and followed Flip and Freddy to the floor, 'stay and talk to me?'

The floor was so thinly peopled that Kate was unwilling to reveal her so-called dancing. She watched fascinated as Flip's slim body writhed freely to the music, her head thrown back, revealing the long line of her throat and her open, inviting mouth. Freddy was cool, in charge, challenging Flip with his own body movements and intricate footwork, yet they moved in perfect harmony.

'I'd like to stay and watch them,' she said warmly. 'They look so lovely. And I'm afraid I don't dance very well. I haven't been to a place like this before.' She thought she might as well confess, rather than make a fool of herself on the floor. 'I rarely go dancing and then it's usually been a rather sedate, formal dinner dance.'

The waiter arrived with the new bottles and Jon made an elaborate show of tasting the wine before nodding and saying to Kate, 'Young but it has potential – like me.' They drank companionably, and Kate felt relaxed and amused. It was so good to have someone bother to flirt with her.

In fact she drank too much of the wine, remembering too late that she had not had anything much to eat during the day, having been far too keyed up about the evening. Jon refilled her glass whenever it was only half-empty, so that she lost track of how much she was drinking, but it was a pleasant sensation. When Jon took her hand and led her in an offhand way to the dance floor it no longer seemed an ordeal but a rather daring experiment. She wished Charlotte could be watching. Jon, as Geoffrey had done years before at the Oxford ball, pushed and pulled her to the rhythm until she was laughing and moving uninhibitedly to the music. It didn't seem at all difficult, but she watched the other women out of the corner of her eye, trying to copy them. When they went back to the table, Kate was hot and breathless, but inordinately pleased when Jon put an arm round her shoulder and said, 'I thought you said you couldn't dance.'

There seemed no sign of food and though she was hungry, Kate was too busy storing up things to describe to Charlotte. A third group came on, dressed in white shirts and black trousers, their faces serious, intent on their music. Their strong, sensuous rhythm played on Kate's relaxed and heightened senses, releasing in her a sad yearning. She was dancing with Jim then, and she gripped his arm as he moved in front of her, intent on his footwook. 'Hold me,' she implored anguished. Jim's bland young face split into a faintly embarrassed schoolboy grin. 'You bet,' he said, and hugged her tight to his chest with both arms while continuing his complicated steps. Kate laughed. His body was as thin and hard as a plank, so that her yearning for something undefined, romantic, vanished. 'Stand on my feet,' he commanded, 'and I'll show you what we do in rehearsal.'

'Rehearsal?' Kate repeated.

'Yep. I'm a dancer. Have you seen *Cats*?' She shook her head.

'I thought everybody had. Well anyway, I'm in that.'

Kate was planted on his insteps and found herself jerked

like a puppet to his steps. She collapsed laughing. 'How old are you?'

'Twenty-two.'

'That accounts for it. Let's go back to the table. Not only am I a lot older than you, I'm out of condition.' Jim gave her a companionable smile. 'I used to try that with my little sister. You know, you move well when you stop being selfconscious.' Kate was pleased. Really everyone was so nice. Back at the table the food was being served, but Flip was missing, and so, Kate noticed with a touch of panic, was Freddy. Had Flip left without her? She had warned she might but Kate hadn't really believed her.

'Don't worry about Flip,' Jon said, noticing her wild glance round. 'She has found a new man to conquer. She can look after herself.'

'Quite. But I vaguely imagined she was going to give me a lift home – I didn't bring my car.'

Jon laughed. 'Giving female friends a lift home is not Flip's aim in life. I see you haven't known her long.'

'Not very,' Kate sipped more wine. 'I'll get a taxi.'

'I'll drive you home,' Jon said lightly, and piled her plate from the assortment in the middle of the table. 'But not yet. Eat up.'

Kate's recollection of how the rest of the evening went was hazy. There was another group, very loud, very discordant, and she noticed vaguely that Jim returned from a prowl about the club bringing with him another young, slim look-alike man with incredibly light sky-blue eyes who seemed to galvanize Dave into frenzied animation. He spent the rest of the evening joining in their fervent conversation; apparently Jim and the newcomer had been in another musical together and had to catch up on the gossip. Kate caught the pathetic wistfulness beneath Dave's assumed animation as he tried to divert a little of their attention to himself. She felt sorry for him and sent him a sympathetic smile across the table. He frowned back at her, humping his shoulders, setting up a pinstriped barrier against her.

Natalie was bored. Clearly Dave was a dead loss, she had known Jon too long and too well for him to have any novelty value, and Brian was making himself very unpleasant. Suddenly Natalie sent her chair sprawling as she pushed it back yelling, 'Fuck off!' Brian had attempted to slip his pudgy, putty-coloured fingers into her dress, saying 'Let's see this, let's see this little titty.' Jon looked at Kate and stood up. 'Time to go, I think.'

'You're dead right,' Natalie stared at Brian with venom. 'Let's go to Victor's. Perhaps we'll find fewer cretins there.' She spat the words at the helplessly giggling Brian.

'Naughty, naughty.' Brian shook his finger, a foolish, drunken smile slipping loosely over his soft, pale face, damp with sweat. Jon propelled both women to the exit. 'Get your things while I settle the bill.'

'Some evening this is.' Natalie frowned crossly into the cloakroom mirror. 'I hope Victor will make up for it.'

Kate smiled fuzzily. 'I've had a lovely time.'

Natalie marched out, heaving a theatrically impatient sigh. She stared furiously at Jon as he made it clear he was not going on to Victor's. 'Sweetie, you know everyone there, you're a big girl now, you can go in alone. I'm taking Kate home and then I'm going to bed.' 'In that order?' asked Natalie maliciously. Jon smiled. 'If you're good I'll drop you off at Victor's on the way.'

Kate leaned back languidly against the luxurious black upholstery of the long black Porsche after they'd dropped Natalie, who was white with anger, at the nightclub. She had slammed the door so viciously that Jon had winced. 'It hasn't been a good evening for our beauty queen.' It was warm and comfortable, and Jon turned on the radio as they moved swiftly through the empty streets. 'This is an opulent car for a grocer,' she said sleepily. 'I'm an opulent grocer,' Jon said lightly. 'Where, exactly do you live?'

'Fulham.'

'Fulham? Not the right image, I think.'

'I don't have an image,' Kate said pathetically. 'No image. Just plain little Kate.' She sat up suddenly. 'I've had too much to drink,' she said accusingly.

'Good for you now and then,' Jon said, his hand resting lightly on her thigh. Kate peered at it with interest in the gloom of the car. 'Lets out your inhibitions.' He kept his eyes on the road as he moved his hand slowly up and down her lap, kneading slightly as he moved it between her legs.

Kate stared ahead too. It was a nice feeling. He was a nice man. She'd had a nice evening. She put back her head and gently snored.

When they reached her home she was wakened by a smiling Jon bending over her and saying, 'Well, it's a long time since I had that effect upon anyone. You're not very good for my male ego.' Kate blinked and gasped into consciousness. 'Heavens – we're home. I'm so sorry. Thank you for driving me. I – I don't usually drink much.' Her head was whirling and she fumbled to open the door. She couldn't find the handle. What a performance. Taking a deep breath to try and collect herself she turned to him and said with elaborate dignity, 'Thank you so much again. You've been very kind,' and held out her hand.

'No I won't come in, thank you,' Jon laughed in her startled face. 'You have been out of circulation for a long time.' He put his hand behind her head and pulled her to him, kissing her deeply on a mouth opening again in apology. 'I'll call you.' He released the lock on the car door and opened it widely for Kate. 'Good night Cinderella. Don't lose your slipper.'

Kate stood looking dazedly after the car as it slid away down the road and then let herself in. She had a raging thirst and went into the kitchen for water. The warm familiarity of the room recalled her to her senses. What on earth was she about? But despite her sleepiness and the drink, she could still feel the pleasing throb stirred into life by Jon's hand.

Chapter Twelve

Kate attempted to satisfy Charlotte's eager questioning next morning as Mrs Shepherd got breakfast, but she eyed the fried eggs with queasy distaste and passed hers on to Jeremy. 'Yes, there were lots of glamorous women there. Yes, I did dance. No, I don't remember what the groups were called – one wore morning coats and silly boxer shorts, and one, which I liked, had simple white shirts and black trousers. Your Miss Bristow, Flip, says the best ones have the fewest gimmicks. There was a male dancer there who's in *Cats* – Jim somebody – I danced with him.' Charlotte squealed. 'You danced with someone from *Cats*? I can't believe it! What did he *say*?' 'He made me stand on his feet, as if I were a puppet being worked.' Kate smiled at the memory. 'And he showed me some of their steps. It was exhausting. Oh, and he said I move well. Now be off or you'll be late.'

'Moth-er,' Charlotte wailed.

'I'll tell you the rest tonight if I remember. Now shoo.'

When a curious Mrs Shepherd had been paid and sent on her way too, Kate lingered over her coffee. She recalled Jon's kiss and his hand between her legs and felt hot with embarrassment. She had behaved like a gauche schoolgirl, drinking too much, being easily bowled over.

The doorbell rang. She was still in her towelling wrap. Squinting at the dark figure standing in the doorway against the brilliant morning sun she was stunned to realize it was Jon, behind an enormous bouquet of flowers, looking fresh and groomed. 'Hullo,' he said cheerfully. 'I thought I'd catch you before you went out.' Kate gaped foolishly. 'Well, you are going to ask me in this morning, I hope. I'll forgive last night – but twice,' he shook his head.

'I'm sorry. I was too surprised. Would you like some coffee?'

'Not particularly, but if it pleases your conventional little soul, I will. I came to go to bed with you.'

'Bed?'

'Yes, you cheated me last night by being too tight and too sleepy – not the best condition in which to make love, I find. So I came this morning.' He dumped the bouquet on the hall chair, put his arms round Kate and kissed her. Then he bent his head and kissed the nape of her neck, and then her ear, and started to slide off her wrap. He kissed her shoulder and brushed his lips over the curve of her breast. Kate recovered herself. 'Stop, what do you think you're doing?'

His eyes looked up from her chin as he was still nuzzling gently at her breast. 'I think I am about to make love to you. Don't you like it?'

Kate twitched away. 'That's beside the point. I hardly know you.' She could imagine Flip's lip curling as she said the faintly Victorian words. She was flustered. 'Besides, how do you know I want to?'

'It's normal to want to.' He sighed. 'I suppose you want to hold hands over candlelit dinner tables and be wooed and pretend you're in love with me. Such a waste of time. Don't you like sex for its own sake?' He stood tall again and looked down at her, catching her hands loosely.

'It's not something to which I've given much thought. I'm married,' she blurted, feeling again like a schoolgirl.

He looked surprised. 'What's that got to do with it? I can see we'll have to have that coffee.' He spoke with amused resignation.

She pulled her wrap round her again and belted it

firmly. 'I think *I* need some even if you don't.' She led the way to the kitchen, picking up the flowers to put in water. To her surprise Jon opened cupboards, found the coffee beans, located the grinder, tipped away the cold coffee she had been drinking, all with spare, efficient movements; he made some more, poured orange juice from the fridge and sat across the kitchen table from her, gazing at her over the rim of his cup. 'Now, does that make you feel better?' he mocked. 'Cosy and domestic and *safe*. What happened to your husband?'

'He went off with someone else.' Kate felt the familiar stab of pain and failure.

'Did you love him?'

'At first, of course, yes. But I wasn't the right woman for him.'

'Or possibly he the man for you. Unrequited love is rarer than you think. People quite often love those that love them – something to do with believing themselves unlovable I suppose. It reassures them. I guess most people rub along for a time, turning a blind eye to each other's inadequacies, investing the other one with qualities they don't possess and never did. And then when they wake up, they find out there isn't anything for them there. They try to hide their disappointment because not only does it reflect badly on their own judgement, but if they admitted it they would have to take some kind of action.

'Disappointment corrodes – that's why you find married people picking on each other – they're driven mad by ridiculously small irritations. They try to smother their exasperation but they're seething underneath. At best they have frequent, blazing rows. At worst, total indifference.

'Yet people are afraid of being alone. It's the Noah's Ark syndrome. They would rather be with someone, *anyone*, than face life on their own.'

Kate had a sense of unreality. What was she doing at this time of the morning, unfamiliarly hung-over, not yet dressed, listening to a virtual stranger pontificate about marriage? It was bizarre.

'You sound more like a sociologist than a grocer,' Kate sipped her coffee, staring at him.

'You have the most lovely, frank, tranquil gaze,' he said, leaning across the table to kiss her nose. 'Do you feel more settled now, after all that serious chat? How long are you going to go on drinking coffee? Let's go to bed. I suspect you haven't been to bed with anyone other than your husband, have you? How quaint.' He took Kate's silence as agreement. 'Think of it as an adventure. Don't you like adventures? Of course you do.' He indulged in this amiable coaxing as he drew her to her feet, put his arm round her waist, and ushered her to the stairs. 'I want you,' he breathed into her hair. Behind her on a lower stair his eyes were level with hers, and they were quiet, serious, determined.

Kate felt a leap of apprehension and pure excitement. Why bloody not? She had spent her whole life being timid and conventional. She was grown up, her husband didn't want her, and this kind attractive man apparently did. She looked at him calmly.

'Good.'

In her bedroom the bed was still unmade, her bronze dress thrown over the chair, the shoes kicked off as she'd stumbled in last night, but Jon simply slipped off his clothes in a smooth, practised way, pulled her on to the rumpled bed saying: 'It will look much worse when we've finished,' and began kissing her, hundreds of light, tantalizing kisses smothering her face and eyelids, her ears and neck, sliding his hands over her body as he eased off her robe. Kate felt as if she couldn't breathe. She was overwhelmed by the suddenness, by the strangeness of it, by the sight of his unknown body writhing on her very familiar bed. She blushed as she felt his lips move down her body, flicking his tongue over her belly, on down to her pubes. Geoffrey had never done that. She stiffened in embarrassment. 'You're lovely,' he breathed, sliding up over her body again until he could bring his mouth down on hers, probing with his tongue. Hands and lips never still, he rubbed his body against hers. Kate could feel him hard against her but he made no attempt to penetrate. She kept her arms round him, stroking him tentatively. She wished she knew what the secrets of 'being good in bed' were. It was so pleasurable to touch him, his skin was warm and dry and just faintly scented. She tightened her arms involuntarily and slid her hands over him more urgently.

She cried out as his fingers went inside her, probing, moving, insistent. All the feelings she'd had to damp down and keep under control with Geoffrey burst through and she began to respond naturally, copying his movements as she had on the dance floor, arching her body against his, kissing him back, letting her tongue dart too. 'There,' he lifted his head to smile at her. 'Was a second cup of coffee worth missing this?' and laughing, he plunged into her, thrusting and moving, smiling into her eyes. Laughter had never been associated with sex in Kate's experience; it seemed almost sacrilegious.

He took her hand and moved it to her vagina. 'Feel there. Isn't that nice and warm and slippery?' He took her damp hand back to her nose. 'Smell it. Taste it.' She was bewildered by the excitement she felt, and yet she was embarrassed. Women didn't behave like this, surely? He rolled on to his back and brought her on top of him. 'Come along. Don't be shy. Enjoy it.' Desperately anxious to please, she moved on top of him, his eyes were half-closed in lazy, sensual enjoyment, his mouth open as he gave little gasps of pleasure. Looking at him, she felt a sense of triumph, and moved more daringly, closing her eyes and throwing back her head as her own sensations mounted, and his hands cupped her breasts. She couldn't believe the intensity of her feelings; she was outside herself, shaken, fearful, trembling. She had never experienced such fervour before. She sat panting, almost unconscious of him as he came too, and she collapsed on him, his mouth wet against her breast. She lay with her cheek pressed into the pillow, feeling a drowsy sense of peace. 'I must change the sheets,' she thought irrationally, and laughed in self-ridicule. She waited to feel guilty and ashamed but her only feelings were ones of pleasure and enjoyment. Jon lifted his head.

'What are you smiling about?'

'You. I haven't met anyone like you before.'

He kissed the corner of her mouth. 'I have to get to the shop,' he sounded remote and businesslike. 'This is just unfinished business from last night. We'll do it properly next time.'

Kate was absurdly disappointed 'Wasn't that "properly"? I enjoyed it,' she said shyly.

He smiled and touched the tip of her nose. 'So did I, sweet. There just isn't more time right now.' He went into her bathroom and she felt a sense of loss as she heard the water running. Coming back he dressed just as swiftly and efficiently as he'd disrobed. Kate stood up and belted her robe again and trailed disconsolately after him down the stairs. 'I suppose you are very, very experienced with lots of women,' she said.

The very slightest frown dented his forehead. 'Yes,' he agreed. 'Lots. 'Bye now – I'll call you. Oh—' He turned at the front door. 'What's your name?' Kate burst out laughing. 'Cosgrove, Kate Cosgrove.'

He waved from the gate. 'Flip introduced you only as Kate. 'Bye.'

He slid into the car and it moved smoothly and quietly away. Kate shut the front door and leaned against it. 'I'm an adulteress,' she told herself. And then wondered if it counted when her husband had already left her. She hoped it did. It gave her a delicious feeling of being wanton and desirable, and even she ruefully admitted, being one-up on Geoffrey.

She ran back up the stairs and ran her bath. Everything had happened too quickly. She needed to get a grip on herself again.

Chapter Thirteen

Before she could examine her feelings in the quiet of the empty house, the telephone rang. 'James Bennett, of Marrer, Lyon & Co,' said the measured tones of her solicitor. 'I'm just confirming our appointment this afternoon at three.'

'Yes, yes, of course,' she said flustered. Damn. She had forgotten. She wanted to think about Jon. 'I'll be there. Do I need to bring any papers with me?'

'No, Lady Kate. We have your father's will and the trust document and everything we need for the moment I think. Perhaps you would find out the name of your husband's solicitors.'

Kate's heart sank. It was all so sordid. She didn't want to pick over the bones of her marriage with a solicitor she barely knew. But she remembered Penelope's advice. 'Be guided by your solicitor.'

She rang Geoffrey. His voice was non-committal. 'Hullo, Kate,' he said formally. 'How are you?'

'Fine, fine,' she almost sang the words.

'You sound very cheerful,' he said accusingly.

'Marrer's want the name of your solicitor,' she said crisply, ignoring his comment. 'I am going to see them this afternoon, and I suppose they'll want to communicate with yours.' He gave her the name and then said: 'When am I to have the children?'

'Oh. I hadn't thought about it. Have you somewhere they can stay?'

'Greta has rented a furnished flat off Regent's Park; there's room for the children.'

'Regent's Park!' Kate's voice rose incredulously. 'Flats there must cost a small fortune. I thought you were supposed to be short of money.'

'I didn't think you were so calculating Kate.' He had put on an injured voice. 'It is only temporary, until you've sold the house and I have some capital.'

'The house and other matters will be decided by the solicitors,' she said curtly. 'I'll talk to the children tonight about the weekend. They may have football matches or rehearsals or something fixed up. I'll ask Charlotte to call you later, if you give me your home number.' Her voice trembled over the last words. This was his home. She was his wife. They were their children. She didn't want to share him – or them – with Greta Lanson. It suddenly seemed as if everything was moving too fast, outpacing her efforts to adjust; it was all too different and alien. For one wild moment she wanted to plead with Geoffrey to start again, to come back and not to put them through this torment.

When she put the phone down she realized soberly that this was an inevitable step, an overdue part of growing up, something she should have done years ago. She had faced the fact that Geoffrey had never loved her in the way she had schoolgirlishly imagined her husband would. But it was obvious that he was infatuated, perhaps genuinely in love with Greta Lanson, and sadly she acknowledged that for her, too, the relationship was over. She couldn't go back; she'd become a different woman from the idolatrous girl Geoffrey had married.

Her visit to the solicitors was unnerving. James Bennett was abnormally tall. He towered over Kate, bending his head to avoid hitting the ceiling of the small room tucked away inside an old Dickensian Court in Lincoln's Inn.

Kate was fascinated to see a real coal fire burning in a small grate in the corner of the room. The room, painted a flat green with dark green velvet curtains screening much of the grey outdoors light, looked cosy and friendly in the ruddy glow of the dark red damask lampshades. Through an alcove were visible ceiling-high shelves housing volumes of law, but in his room the impression was merely one of a pleasant study. He'd offered her tea, so his subsequent relentless questioning and probing were all the more nerve-racking.

Had Geoffrey moved out? Had he actually asked for a divorce? Was that what she wanted? Had she any, ah, special male friend? Had he offered financial support? Who was to have custody of the children?

'My husband doesn't want any adverse publicity. You see, he's a television executive and the tabloid newspapers would splash this kind of gossip . . .'

'Except that it isn't gossip, is it, Lady Kate? It's fact, isn't it?' he cut in. 'Divorce is an unpleasant mess at the best of times.' Distaste was in his steely tone.

It made Kate feel faintly grubby. 'It happens a lot, I hear,' she had said with spirit.

'Indeed. Our firm's fortunes were made out of some spectacular divorce cases in the past which is the more remarkable since our senior partner was such a staunch Roman Catholic.'

He had then explained her father's trust fund for the children and informed her that her income was somewhat under £4000 a year. 'Since that is unearned it is tacked on to your husband's income at present. We must get that separated immediately. The school fees are paid for, and have remained reasonably steady. I think there was a shortfall last year of a mere £272,' he had told her. 'But you say your husband has offered to pay any difference.' Kate had assumed from what Geoffrey had said that the trust income fell woefully short of the school bills.

When she left him she was seething with rage at her own pitiful ignorance. She had been humiliated at his pointing out that she would need money from Geoffrey to manage. His expectation of her finding a worthwhile job seemed even lower than her own.

'There is no question of your selling the house and giving half the proceeds to your husband,' he had said categorically. 'The house may have been a wedding gift to you both but the deeds are in your name. Your father insisted. If the house is a big one, perhaps there is a case for selling it and trading down, so to speak, but you'd need any profit realized just to manage.' He'd made a list of her outgoings – rates, fuel, insurance payments, clothes for the three of them, travel, food, cleaning and laundry – it seemed endless and frightening. Her blithe indifference to money vanished. She wished she hadn't spent so much with Beatrice. It had been madness. Panic gripped her. She needed urgently to get a job even if she had to go back on her brave words to Penelope and ask her to find her something.

Mr Bennett had said he would write to Geoffrey's solicitors to ask him to suggest an allowance. 'Legally, he must maintain you and the children. But it is better for the husband to make a suggestion. If it isn't adequate—' his expression hardened – 'then we have to propose a figure.'

'I don't want his help,' Kate had been mulish.

'Then how do you propose to live?' James Bennett asked. 'I've three children at schools like yours; there are always educational trips of some kind or another, not to mention the cost of teenage clothes and pocket money. You won't be able to manage without a struggle, even if you get a job.'

She could imagine Greta Lanson's scorn as Geoffrey reluctantly made her an allowance. Greta had talent and looks, she was earning a large salary, she had effortlessly taken Kate's husband; she would find Kate pathetic.

'If I can manage without help from Geoffrey I will,' she had insisted, like an obstinate child.

'You can't,' Mr Bennett said flatly. 'You must let me handle this.'

Kate had sunk into the armchair, shivering despite the fire, feeling diminished and defeated; it was all so squalid. An image of her father's disappointed face rose in her mind as he'd said, 'I hope you don't regret this, Kate. I sincerely hope you don't regret it.'

Chapter Fourteen

Both children flatly refused to go to Geoffrey for the weekend.

'Not if *she*'s there,' said Jeremy glumly, and Charlotte shook her head firmly. 'No fear.'

'I think Daddy has a right to see you,' Kate said carefully. 'He's still your father and he loves you both very much. This is probably quite difficult for him too.'

'I'm not ready to talk to him,' Charlotte's mouth compressed stubbornly. 'Then you must telephone him and explain that you have too much to do, but arrange another time.' Kate was equally firm. Charlotte fussed around a bit but eventually rang Geoffrey and Kate heard her voice get high-pitched with argument. She flounced back into the room, her eyes bright with tears and two red spots burning her cheeks.

'He wants to talk to you, Mum.' She threw herself into an armchair and folded her arms.

'Kate, what is this? Have you been turning the children against me? I have tickets for *Cats* on Saturday, Greta wants to take Charlotte clothes shopping and now she says she can't come. She's "too busy". Did you put her up to this?'

'Geoffrey, calm down, of course not. I think they are having a job to adjust to all this. It's natural apprehension. But Charlotte *is* busy with rehearsals for the school play and neither of them knows how to treat Greta. We have to be understanding – it's been a great shock for them.'

'Of course. I'm sorry,' his voice dropped in contrition.

'Well, please do talk to Charlotte again and get her to change her mind? Jeremy simply follows her lead. They'll have to face up to it sooner or later. Let me talk to Jeremy.'

Jeremy looked nervous. Yet of the two chldren, he probably missed Geoffrey the most. Kate heard his voice low and monosyllabic. He came back looking pale and shaky and glanced at Charlotte.

'Dad wants us to go on Saturday,' he told her miserably. 'He's got tickets for *Cats* and he promised to take me to the Planetarium.'

Charlotte's lip curled. 'So he told me. Bribery.'

Jeremy looked down at his feet. 'I'd like to see him. He told me he missed me,' he said, and bolted out of the room. Kate and Charlotte looked at each other.

'I think he really wants to go,' said Kate quietly. 'Don't you think *you* ought to?' Charlotte was obstinately silent.

Kate left the room worriedly. Jeremy was more deeply upset than she'd realized. Going towards the kitchen she paused outside the cloakroom. She heard the noise of vomiting. She went in to find Jeremy on the floor of the tiny room, clutching the lavatory bowl, retching miserably, his eyes streaming with tears.

'Oh darling.' Kate gathered him in her arms, wiping his mouth and smoothing his hair. 'It's not that bad. You mustn't distress yourself. Everything will work out soon, don't worry.'

'I didn't really mean it when I said I wouldn't go. It's *her* I don't want to see, not Dad. Now Charlotte won't budge, and I'll never see Dad again,' Jeremy blubbered like a small boy against her shoulder.

'Of course she will. You know Charlotte – she gets angry but she gets over it. She's just feeling cross with Daddy right now – I bet she'll ring him up later and say she'll go. You know how crazy she is to see *Cats* anyway. It's been on a long time, and she's about the only one in her form who hasn't seen it.' She laughed gently. 'And there's a shopping trip – I bet she's kicking herself right now for saying no. Come on, let's go and see.'

Charlotte, looking slightly frightened, had lost her obstinate expression and looked definitely out of her depth at the sight of Jeremy's distress. Kate deliberately kept her voice light and asked them about their school day. They had supper, and watched a wildlife programme on television. At the end Charlotte stretched and said nonchalantly, 'I must go and do my prep. If you like I'll ring Daddy and say we'll go.' She scuffed her shoe into the carpet as Jeremy looked up sharply. 'I suppose we might as well get it over with, but don't expect me to be nice to *her*.'

Kate smiled approvingly. 'I think that's a very grown-up thing to do – even more so if you behave properly to Miss Lanson.'

She wanted to scream, '*Don't* go – she shan't have my children as well as my husband!' and for a minute thought she'd have to rush to the cloakroom too, but she cleared the table instead, merely slamming the dishwasher door so fiercely that the motor gave an ominous clatter as it started.

Geoffrey arranged to pick up the children early on Friday evening and Kate saw the weekend stretching ahead, bleak and empty. She wondered what to do with herself. She felt in an alien no-man's-land. It was strange that until now she hadn't realized that she hadn't any close friends. Esme had been all in all to her before Geoffrey came on the scene, and since her marriage, she'd been too busy to make new friends, first with the entertaining Geoffrey had wanted her to do before the station was set up, and then with the two babies.

She wandered about the house on the Friday afternoon before the children came home from school checking and re-checking their weekend bags. She didn't want Greta Lanson's cool, assessing eyes noting that she'd sent the children without enough socks and knickers. She recalled Jon's saying, 'We've all been brainwashed into thinking that being alone is something to be feared . . . before we've tasted true independence, and learned that it isn't frightening after all.' Perhaps Jon would call, or Flip, she thought hopefully. Then she felt ashamed of herself for being unable to face forty-eight hours of her own company. She remembered that she'd forgotten to cancel Jeremy's coaching and that in all probability she wouldn't catch Flip at school now. But when she got through to the staffroom number, Flip's low, languid voice came on the line.

'I'm sorry,' Kate said in a breathless voice, 'but Jeremy is going to his father this weekend and I'll have to ask you to postpone the coaching. I hope it isn't inconvenient – I'll pay for the wasted lesson, of course,' she added awkwardly.

Flip gave her rasping laugh. 'Instead of that you can give me some supper,' she suggested. 'I want to hear how you enjoyed Mickey-Mike's.'

Kate felt hot with embarrassment as she thought of Jon's lovemaking. She certainly wouldn't include an account of that. 'It was a lovely evening,' she said, 'and it would be very sweet of you to come to supper. To be honest, I was feeling a bit at a loss, with the children going away.'

'You must be mad,' Flip said. 'Most mothers would love it. I'll come round at about 7.30 – is that all right? Don't make a fuss – a frozen tv dinner would be fine.'

The children went off in a rather subdued fashion. Kate was relieved that Geoffrey hadn't brought Greta Lanson with him to pick them up, and was amused at the way he put on his fervent geniality like a children's party entertainer. He didn't quite meet her eye. She saw him look speculatively at Jon's flowers, arranged rather showily on the coffee table. She had carefully laid the dinner table for two in advance and he glanced at that, saying, 'Esme coming?'

'No, she's still in the States, I believe. The card company was planning a hectic coast-to-coast-in-store promotion of her work, she told me when I last heard from her. She was having a lovely time then, but is too exhausted to write I expect and I can't ring her because I don't know her schedule.' Kate was being deliberately oblique; she had no intention of satisfying his curiosity about her guest.

Chapter Fifteen

Flip came wearing jeans and a white ribbed sweater, and very little makeup; she looked rather washed-out. 'Have you ever acknowledged how tiring children are?' she demanded, following Kate through the narrow passage to the kitchen. Kate handed her a glass of chilled white wine.

'I don't know how mothers manage. Those kids at St Anselm's never seem to stop. I've got three sixth-formers whose parents will kill me if I don't get them at least an Exhibition to Oxbridge. And I've let Cundy talk me into helping with the play.'

'And you have Jeremy's coaching,' Kate paused wickedly '—as well as an *amazing* social life.' She rolled her eyes as Charlotte had done and laughed. Stirring a saucepan, she sipped her own drink. 'I'm feeling a bit frazzled too. I had to see my solicitor this week and it wasn't very pleasant. He made me feel like a useless piece of furniture stashed in an attic.'

'You have to admit that you're rather odd.' Flip didn't bother with superficial politeness. 'Never been to school, never had a job, married, unsuitably it seems, at eighteen. What have you done with your life so far?'

'Well, I've produced two children,' Kate was rather nettled. 'And my husband needed me to do lots of entertaining when he was helping to set up Crystal Television. There seemed to be a function to go to or people to dinner every other night.'

'How did you learn to cook?' Flip was casual. She

sniffed appreciatively at the stove, 'That's not a tv dinner I recognize.'

'I read cookery books and fell on *Good Housekeeping* every month.'

'So you could teach yourself cookery when it came to the point, but not anything else? Cooking for a family is hardly a full-time career, I wouldn't have thought. Didn't you have a hunger to learn other things too? What else did you read? Weren't you affected by the women's movement – did the 70s entirely pass you by?'

'It washed over me.' Kate was candid. 'All that unrest somehow didn't seem to include me. I remember the fuss over the graduate housewives supposedly isolated on housing estates letting their brains atrophy, but for one thing I didn't have a brain, or at least a trained one, and for another I was quite grateful to be living in a nice house caring for two delightful little children. I was tired of being dragged all over Egpyt and India and Afghanistan looking at temples and relics and watching my parents get excited about broken bits of pots and ancient implements. I got so I didn't care if I never saw another museum in my life! It seemed such bliss to stay put, somewhere modern and clean and convenient. I enjoyed learning to cook, and I adore gardening. I seemed to be pretty busy.' Her voice was defiant.

'Until,' Flip sipped her drink again and looked coolly at Kate, 'you're abandoned by some man and are flailing about like an upended turtle.'

Kate was hurt. She turned her back on Flip and went on slowly stirring in the saucepan. 'I can't really blame Geoffrey for being bored with me,' she said at last in a small, muffled voice. 'He's talented and attractive and has a job which interests him. Once I'd got over my first infatuation, and realized that after marriage one doesn't necessarily live happily ever after, I settled down fairly contentedly.' She stared unseeingly into the sauce as she tried to picture herself then. 'I didn't look very far into the future.'

Flip banged her glass down on the table, got to her feet and strode about the kitchen.

'You make me so furious. My God, you have some growing up to do! Why, any of my little Anselm's kids would put you to shame. Why are you so – so *accepting*? So ready to acquiesce to your husband's verdict of you, never questioning that your parents' attitude was repellent and irresponsible? What were they doing dragging you around like that with a half-baked tutor?'

'You make me think my whole life is a failure,' Kate hunched her shoulders.

'It will be if you don't do a bit of serious thinking for yourself. If you've made a mess of it so far, start again.'

'I'm not sure I know how.'

'Become a brain surgeon, a Prime Minister, a nuclear physicist – anything's possible. You're talking like an old woman! Masses of people start new lives, learn new things, discover latent talents halfway through their life. I switched from a business career to teaching when I was over thirty, though I sometimes wonder why. You're Geoffrey Cosgrove's wife, you're Charlotte and Jeremy's mother, but have you asked yourself who the hell is Kate Cosgrove? For God's sake what do you *want to do*?'

'Paint.'

Flip paused and stared. She hadn't expected so prompt and unequivocal an answer.

'Paint then.' She drained her glass and helped herself to a refill. '*Can* you paint?'

'I don't know whether I do well enough to earn a living, but it is the only thing I've ever *wanted* to do,' Kate felt again the deep pang of loss experienced over the years she had had to stop.

'But surely you could have painted at home as well as being a housewife?' Flip was genuinely puzzled.

Kate's voice dropped in shame: 'Geoffrey didn't like it. I thought when I was first married that at last I would have the time to take a proper course – there's a woman who lives in this road who is now um, fifty-three. She was forty-one and learning the cello when I met her – I'd helped her stow the great thing into her tiny Fiat one morning – and she told me that she went to Morley College where they have a very good arts faculty and encouraged mature students. It seemed ideal, but when I broached the idea to Geoffrey, he was furious. He said he needed me to help him.' Her mouth unconsciously tightened and her voice trembled as she remembered the awful day when Geoffrey had been beside himself with rage at catching her 'wasting time' painting, and marched her so roughly into the kitchen that she'd cracked her head on the door.

'He wasn't a husband, he was a bloody employer!' Flip controlled herself and touched Kate's shoulder contritely. 'You're too nice. I'd have kicked him in the balls and registered for a full-time course the next day.'

Her sympathy on top of the anger made tears snatch at Kate's throat. In a minute I shall cry with self-pity, she thought. What a gulf there was between their characters!

'Let's eat,' she said abruptly, leading the way to the small dining room next to the kitchen. 'Bring the rest of the white wine, if you haven't polished it off by now.' She cheered slightly at her little retort. For a minute or two they ate in silence, and then Kate looked up. 'Don't you think a family is worthwhile? Are you really saying that *all* women should have careers? Isn't creating a family and looking after them just as vital?'

'I don't know.' Flip shrugged. 'Half the tensions and cramped egos and damaged characters, not to mention straightforward physical abuse, if you read your newspapers, seem to start with the family. We seem to have two opposite images: the glutinous telly mother or the automaton self-seeking career women. I can't decide which I find more repulsive.'

'How else would you bring children up if not within a family?'

'That's the problem. I don't know. Kibbutz kids don't seem any more self-reliant or well-adjusted or – more important – kinder to other human beings. I don't really have an answer. Perhaps the much vaunted new technology will produce a society such as existed before the Industrial Revolution, when there were small communities. We'll all be sitting at home with our VDUs and fax machines, our meetings and far-flung conferences on closed circuit television, press-button shopping and banking, and what is it called? Distance learning, on the lines of the Open University. Then everyone can take a hand in bringing up the children, and cope with the handicapped and the elderly. But I expect there'd be snags. We'd all have square eyes, constipation and robotic voices. I get very gloomy about mankind, don't you? It's all so unfair and yet changing attitudes is such an impossible task that I for one don't do much more than use my vote, and a fat lot of good *that* does – it's choosing between the bad and the indifferent. Inertia's our besetting sin, really. I sometimes think I'm leading a solitary, non-productive life as my subconscious contribution towards wiping out the human race.

'Russia made a stab at sharing out the wealth, and what was the result? Immovable bureaucracy and the status of a third-rate banana republic.'

The telephone interrupted the soapbox oration, and Kate bounded up, convinced it was the children demanding to come home, but it was Nick Menton.

'How are you? Are you free sometime tomorrow? I've talked to a few friends and one of them would like to see you next week if you can manage it. He's with one of the bigger agencies, so he knows what he's about. I don't know whether he can offer you anything, but it's a start. I thought we ought to talk.'

'Yes. How kind. Thanks. Yes,' Kate said, disconcerted.

'Could you have dinner with me? There wasn't much time to talk when we last met, and I've found out a few things about the sort of work you could do, if that would help.'

'It seems unfair that you should take me to dinner on top of all that effort,' Kate said. 'But I'd like it very much.' They set a time and hung up. So much for the empty weekend, she thought elated. She determined not to get unduly excited again. Nick's art director friend was only seeing her because Nick had asked him to; how could her amateurish 'daubing', as Geoffrey had described it, land her a job in a small agency? But she couldn't help feeling cheered.

'A friend of my brother's,' she explained to an openly curious Flip. 'It was he who suggested I might get work in the art department of an advertising agency, and he's asked a friend of his to see me.' Kate brought in the next course, breast of duck sauced with the morellos she'd frozen in the summer from the little espalier she'd planted against the back of the house ten years ago, and poured the red wine.

'Has he seen any of your work?'

'Just one picture – I don't have any others. In any case the sort of thing I have painted so far was only for my own interest, it is not commercial. Esme – the one you unfairly called my half-baked tutor – has a strong, very special talent. She's become the queen of the greeting card industry here and now in the States. I know I couldn't do that kind of thing, but there might be *something*.'

'Everyone can do *something*. And plenty of people bluff their way through jobs. You might be strangely naive but I don't think you're unintelligent.' Flip grinned at Kate, conscious of her earlier toughness, challenging her to rise. 'You shouldn't put yourself down. Say "yes" if you're asked if you can do the job.' She narrowed her eyes to look consideringly at Kate. 'Underneath that amazing ignorance there could be a strong character clamouring to get out.' She uncannily echoed Penelope. 'Tell me about what happened after I left Mickey-Mike's,' she said with a sudden change of direction. 'Did you take a cab home?'

Kate blushed. 'Jon drove me. I'm afraid I had too much to drink and I fell asleep in his car on the way back.'

'That must have been a new experience for him!' Flip guffawed. 'Before all that money and those looks most women seem to go down on their knees.'

'Money? He told me he was a grocer.'

'He's right. He has about ten hypermarkets outside big towns all over Britain and a snob flagship in Belgravia. His mother started it all. An amazing little Frenchwoman who was widowed early. She started simply importing interesting foods because she was appalled at our shops. Then she realized how many professional women didn't have time to drift about shopping every day, and she opened one of the first specialist supermarkets. It took off from there. Jon runs it now but she's still in the background. Did he make a pass?' Her eyes narrowed in amusement as Kate hastened to the kitchen on the pretext of fetching the pepper grinder.

'What about Freddy?' Kate made her own attack on her return.

'Oh he's a sexy bastard. I like men like that who are obvious creeps. You know exactly where you stand, no emotional involvement, a few good times perhaps, and then kaput. No hard feelings.'

'Don't you ever fall in love?' Kate felt as if this evening was becoming a crammer in independence.

'If I feel a bit too keen I cut out. I don't want heavy love – all I require of men is sex and a little amusement. It's a big relief for them, really.' She chewed appreciatively. 'This is delicious. Most of the time men are only looking for a good lay anyway – and they're right! Just because there's a bit of sexual chemistry between you doesn't mean you have to link up for life. You should try it for a bit. Good for you.'

Kate watched her eat with gusto and enjoyment. No fussy picking over her plate sorting out the fattening bits. There was altogether something animal-like about her.

'My way,' she went on, 'I can say to the man, on equal terms, "I fancy you" and if he returns the compliment, there's a lot of good sex which always makes me feel as satisfied as a fat cat. Some transient companionship is what I want – and that's all. Freedom.' She yawned, mopping up the sauce on her plate. 'I must get some sleep. I'm going to a party tomorrow – want to come?' Kate was disappointed. She wanted to hear more, to argue more. 'No coffee, cheese, fruit?' Flip shook her head. 'I've eaten far too much and I'm absolutely whacked. Come to the party – there'll be some interesting people there unlike the ones at Mickey-Mike's.' She was clearly drooping.

'Thanks, but I'm going to have dinner with Nick so that he can tell me about this job prospect. I don't suppose anything will come of it, but I have to start somewhere – my solicitor made that quite clear.'

'Just say "yes" and "I can" and don't worry. Shall I come for Jeremy next week? OK, then. It was a super meal – you can always cook for a living! Just think of all the things you can do. Get a little angry with your lot. And you can tell me to shut up and mind my own business a bit more.'

She sounded like Penelope again and Kate was surprised and touched when she gave her a good night kiss on the cheek. She was an extraordinary woman.

Chapter Sixteen

Saturday was chilly, with a sharp frost that gave way to a piercing little wind. Kate pottered restlessly in the garden but it was too cold to stay out for long. She tidied up the plants winding down for their hibernation, mourning the onset of the winter. She wondered if she would still be living here next spring. No-one else was about in the row of small crumbling walled gardens patched with ancient fencing, and she felt saddened by the thought that they hadn't made friends here.

It was one of those streets that had been gentrified when young marrieds overflowed from the too-expensive Chelsea. But the inexorable price rise had gone on, and Fulham had rapidly become smart as well. New restaurants had opened, vying with each other in decor and ambience if not in cuisine, the existing shabby junk shops had turned into antique shops. There were boutiques for designer clothes and expensive interior design studios.

There had been a feverish turnover of house ownership as people expected the bubble to burst. The first settlers, young couples about to start families, took their profit, bought bigger houses farther out in areas like Woking and Reigate, from which rail commuting was easy and schools were full of pony-clubbing middle-class children unlikely to infect theirs with Cockney accents.

Once working class, Fulham was now full of thrusting young executives who left the little streets early in the morning, returned late at night, and gathered for Sunday lunch in some of the big smartened-up old-fashioned pubs. Kate had seen them spilling out on to the pavement in the summer round the two little greens, reading newspapers and flirting amiably.

Kate and Geoffrey had lived in their road longer than most, except for an Irish policeman and his wife and their five children three doors along, and the middle-aged amateur cellist.

'Perhaps I haven't enough curiosity?' Kate thought, as she cut down some blackened, withered stems. As she came back into the empty house, depression settled on her. There seemed so little to do with Charlotte and Jeremy away. It was true, as Flip had said, she had built her life round Geoffrey and the children. A bleak fear clutched her as she pictured a life without a husband and sooner or later, of course, without the presence of the children. Perhaps her mother had been right to put her own interests first, but then she had shared her husband's, they hadn't been on different tracks. The two of them had been friends, with a deep companionship that, looking back now with a new insight, Kate could see came from a mutual respect. Had they ever been bored with each other? She didn't think so. Her mother, under that otherworldly air, had been pure steel, with trenchant views of her own, even at times challenging her husband's assumptions about their discoveries, although he'd been the greater authority. She, Kate, and possibly even Tom, had been incidental, probably in both cases an accident – certainly in her case. They hadn't needed anyone else, not even their children.

She wondered whether, if she had really tried to understand Geoffrey's work, taken an enthusiastic interest, they would have become closer. Why hadn't she talked to him more, asked questions, made him more aware of her as a person? In the beginning he had seemed so wonderful, teasing her, buying her funny little presents, deciding on impulse that they could afford to go to France for a long, unexpected weekend, choosing things for her to eat, buying a bowl she admired or a cushion for the house. Had he changed or, more to the point, had she *not*? Could she have developed, lived up to him, met him on equal terms?

Instead, she had metaphorically clutched his coat-tails as he'd raced around, had acted as a dutiful housekeeper accepting the orders for the day. But he never treated me as anything else, a small rebellious inner voice said. Right from the beginning I was a stepping stone, a useful business connection, though I didn't see it at the time. She wondered what would have happened if she had turned on him over the painting, demanded an apology when he'd damaged her work, insisted on going to art classes despite his objections. Wouldn't he have had more respect for her? Wasn't it true that bullies fed on weakness? For she'd *been* weak, a non-person, always too blindly adoring.

Admitting the truth hurt. She forced herself to look at the relationship shorn of the haze of romance and infatuation that protectively clouded her memories. She realized that it wasn't just Greta's beauty that had captivated Geoffrey – she knew where she was going, what she wanted out of life. She was as single-minded as Geoffrey, and that shared enthusiasm for their work was a bond for them. She tried to remember a time when Geoffrey had sought her views on anything. Flip was right, she had been, in effect, hired simply to do his bidding, to help him achieve his ambition. Bleakly, she realized that she had been a willing accomplice in fashioning her own colourless role.

She tried to distract herself by reading the day's newspapers, but nothing seemed as important as pursuing her own self-critical thoughts. Flip was right in saying that she hadn't questioned her life enough. She'd lived within herself, an introspective child full of dreams and vague yearnings, clinging to Esme, always desperately anxious not to get in her mother's way or provoke her exasperation.

She went into her boxroom and picked up her brushes. Absorption in her work gradually blotted out all these unpleasant thoughts. She painted fiercely, in great hurried strokes, without conscious thought. After a while she felt her depression lift and give way to a sense of excitement; she felt the canvas yielding to her, the shapes and colours moving in an obedient, highly satisfactory way. All her pent-up unhappiness, her frustration with her own incompetence seemed to direct the strange images emerging on her canvas. She felt that if she could express graphically her mental confusion and her hazy, fearful view of what might, or was going to happen next, it would somehow clarify her situ-ation, her feelings. The canvas was releasing something demonic inside her. She couldn't stop, but struggled, repainted and tried to carry on even when the light went. It was a shock when she realized that it was nearly six o'clock and she still had all her brushes to clean. She stood back and looked at her picture. She was sure that it was better than any she had done before. Full of abstract shapes that were quite meaningful to her, it had an urgency, a coherence that was profoundly satisfying. It was melancholy, enigmatic perhaps, but she recognized, with a *frisson* of excitement, a new kind of authority in her work.

She cleaned her brushes lovingly, with meticulous care, in a happy trance. They were the fat new ones she had bought since Geoffrey left. They were exquisite, she thought, sensuous, capable of giving pleasure and not a little torment – she loved them.

When Nick called very promptly at seven she was just ready, wearing her red Jean Muir again. She was suddenly conscious of the limitations of her wardrobe. She had bought very few 'social' clothes once Geoffrey had ceased to need her to help him entertain. But she knew that she dare not go to the extravagant heights she had when she'd called on Beatrice to help her find something for her night out with Flip. That reminder of Jon made her go hot; sex with him had been a revelation.

She greeted Nick much more warmly than when he had called before. He caught her hand and at once noted a faint brown smudge on the side. 'That looks surprisingly like paint. Have you been working?'

'I can't help resorting to that room, now,' she said, handing him a drink. 'But I haven't done anything, I think, that might impress your friend. I haven't the faintest idea of what he is likely to look for.'

'We'll talk about that later. Are you going to be cross with me again if I ask to look at this new work?' He had a humorous, curly smile that lightened his heavy dark face when he smiled.

'I was a pig that day,' Kate said, smiling sheepishly. 'I hated being interrupted. And I thought you were going to be pitying. I was furious that Tom had told you about my letter – I thought that was too personal to be shared with a . . .'

'Complete stranger,' he interjected. 'I understood. But it's different if you *invite* me to see your work, isn't it? I'd like very much to see what you've been up to.' He sniffed the air with pleasure as Kate led the way to the boxroom, saying, 'It sounds like a busman's holiday to me. I would have thought you wanted time off from looking at pictures. You're not just being polite? I always feel sorry for doctors who are buttonholed at parties for medical advice. Isn't this much the same thing?'

'Not to me. I never get tired of looking at paintings,' he said with genuine enthusiasm. He stood looking at her unfinished picture, his drink disregarded in his hand.

'You are very unsure and unhappy now,' he said after a long moment. 'This shows a painful vulnerability, if not actual terror. Where did you learn how to use colour like that?'

'My governess and I used to paint together non-stop – it was one of her passions. And we went to lots of galleries. She's very knowledgeable about painting. I suppose that something has rubbed off from all that. I was feeling rather pleased with this – it's not finished, of course, but today, for the first time, I felt I was making the paint do what *I* wanted, instead of floundering. Is it too gloomy, do you think?'

'Gloom doesn't matter, but it does show a struggle. What made you, for instance, put that tiny patch of bluish white in that corner?' Kate peered at the spot with interest. 'I didn't know I had. I don't know.'

'I think,' he said sipping his drink and turning to look at her. 'I think that's your little bit of hope. You do see some happiness – why else in the midst of all that dark, low-keyed colour have that small bright shape so carefully apart, a long way off but reachable?'

'Perhaps you're reading too much into it,' Kate said hastily. 'I didn't set out with a deliberate idea – since I've started again I'm really still just battling with technique – I'm so out of practice. But this picture seemed to evolve almost by itself – it seemed to have a pattern, a volition of its own.'

He didn't say any more but walked to the door. 'I've booked a table at a little restaurant not far from here, cheek by jowl with the gasworks. I have an idea they've hooked themselves up to it somehow and do all their cooking free. But I don't know how good it is – I apologize in advance.'

Over the meal he explained that Joe Grimshaw was looking for an art assistant. 'Someone who can take work to paste-up stage,' he grimaced at her baffled look. 'I know, I hadn't heard the term before either but it means being able to rough out the visual thoughts of the creative team, well enough to give clients the ideas, so that once they get the go-ahead, they can hand it over for finishing to an artist. Sometimes it will be a series of strips, a bit like a comic, I suspect, for film and television commercials – or it might be a full-sized image.'

'I suppose that means mostly line drawing? I haven't done much of that.'

'Probably – I'm not sure. But very quick, very rough. You'll have to ask Joe. A bit dogsbodyish, I'm afraid, but the salary isn't bad in my opinion – £9,000 or £10,000 – more than most of my fine artists earn, I regret to say.'

Kate gasped. 'But that's a fortune! I wouldn't be worth that!'

He was amused. 'You're not much of a businesswoman, are you? Let *them* find out if you're worth it. On very small evidence, I admit, I think you have talent. Too much for a job like this, in all probability, but the important thing is to get in there and then flannel around until you find out how it all works.

'Ask to see the studio when you meet Joe – he's very civilized. In fact he is a very good illustrator himself – he does some fine work in his spare time for one of the better publishers.'

He looked down at his plate, as if trying to identify something edible in a sea of gravy, and Kate studied his face. He must be older than Tom, she thought, noting the lines around his eyes and his thinning hair. He had very black brows over rather sad brown eyes, above a blunt nose. His face was fleshy, rumpled like a dough that hadn't been properly kneaded before baking. He wasn't at all handsome, but when he smiled his face looked good-natured, benign.

'This looks terrible, but it tastes surprisingly good,' he said chewing experimentally. 'Try it. You're not eating.'

'I *ought* to be hungry. I didn't stop for lunch but I'm too nervous about seeing this man.' She speared a piece of meat. 'A friend tells me I have to bluff, but I haven't had a lot of practice at that. Will he be very fierce if I've wasted his time?'

'I should think so. Probably throw you out and your portfolio after you and never speak to me again.'

Kate smiled. 'I can't help being apprehensive. I've never even had an interview before! And I certainly don't have a portfolio!' Anxiety again shuttered over her face.

'You can scribble a few roughs between now and Thursday, I'm sure. Draw some everyday things, put some wash on them, do a few figures – anything. This won't be a senior job, you know – you'll have to do all sorts of odd junior work – probably even clear up after the others.'

Kate set her jaw. 'Well, I have nothing to lose. I shall just have a go. It's good of you to fix it up.' She tucked into the food. It *was* good and she *was* hungry. 'Tell me about Madrid – what were you doing there?'

'I was on the trail of a certain picture for a client. Art dealing is something like detective work half the time. Sometimes I feel that I'm a sort of glorified filing clerk, keeping tabs on where pictures are, and who might be wanting to sell them. I sell more pictures outside the gallery than in. I opened it originally in the naive hope that I'd be able to show new artists, but if I'd kept to that line I'd have starved. All but a handful of genuine, discerning collectors want art that's already established. And sometimes I despair of finding really original, unknown artists.'

They talked for a while about contemporary painters, agreeing and disagreeing – about Hockney, Bacon, and others. Kate felt elated. She hadn't talked with anyone about art since Esme had left for America. It was pleasant to feel confident, to be sure of her ground after the recent days of misery. Kate sipped her wine and talked about Penelope's efforts to raise funds for music and artists.

'Penelope Milsom? She ought to be given a medal for what she does. She's tireless – I'm very fond of her.'

'So am I,' Kate said. 'Her husband Michael was at school with my father, and they've always been very sweet to me. They were very good to Geoffrey too when he was working at setting up Crystal Television, but when I lunched with her the other day, she advised me quite bluntly to leave him. She was overjoyed when I told her we'd separated.' Kate was hardly aware that she was treating Nick with the easy familiarity of a family friend.

'I think Tom felt rather the same way,' said Nick carefully. 'He thought you'd be cut up, but I gather he didn't rate your husband very high.'

'Something happened between them – I don't know what. But at Oxford they were friends – in fact it was Tom who introduced us.' Her eyes misted as she thought of herself at that time, besotted as she'd been.

Nick looked at her. He couldn't tell her that Tom had found Geoffrey with one of his more attractive students just after he'd married Kate. 'Everyone ought to have one great love affair when they're very young. It shouldn't be a tragedy if it doesn't work out. If you hadn't married so hastily, by now it would probably be a beautiful, romantic memory of your youth. One day you'll forget the present pain and only remember the good part.'

Kate smiled gratefully. 'You sound a philosopher.'

'It comes with age,' he said, his smile a little lop-sided. 'Shall I get the bill?'

Kate nodded guiltily as she stared round and saw that the restaurant was nearly empty and their waiter was leaning against a nearby wall looking at them a little resentfully.

'Heavens, I didn't notice the time. Today seems to have

flown and yet I was dreading the weekend. The children are visiting their father.'

At her door she was disappointed when he wouldn't come in for a coffee. Their conversation had left her feeling stimulated, alive, and she wanted to go on talking.

'I'll telephone you after you have seen Joe.' He took her hand as if to shake it, but merely gave it a slight, impersonal squeeze. 'I'll be interested to know how you get on.'

Kate watched him drive away, reluctant to go into the dark, empty house alone, disappointed that she didn't seem to have charm enough to keep him talking the small hours away.

Chapter Seventeen

Getting up very early next morning, Kate went purposefully to the kitchen and pulled various branded packets and tins out of the cupboard. As she stood leaning against the sink eating a piece of toast and sipping coffee, she considered what in particular would induce *her* to buy such items.

It was an amusing exercise. She tried to remember some specific television commercials. Supposing she had been working in the studio before they shot them, how would she have put them over to the photographer or 'finished' artist? She sat down at the kitchen table and practised drawing the boxes and cans. That wasn't difficult; what was unfamiliar was trying to imagine the items as the stars of an advertisement or commercial. She looked through the Sunday papers – they always took the lot in case Geoffrey's programmes were mentioned – and studied the advertisements with a new, intense interest. She'd barely noticed them before. They were very clear, she now realized. They appealed, for the most part, to the less attractive traits of greed, jealousy and snobbery.

She worked solidly all day, stopping only to eat an apple and a piece of cheese for her lunch, trying to weigh up her own efforts objectively. She had covered the walls and kitchen cupboards with her pinned-up sketches and the printed ads. When the doorbell rang at four she was startled; she had totally forgotten the children! She hurried to the front door and found them cluthing their weekend cases, looking a little embarrassed. Geoffrey was in his car at the kerb and as soon as she opened the door he gave a casual wave and drove away.

'How was it?' she asked.

Charlotte shrugged. 'Not too bad, but we didn't see Dad alone *once*. She hangs around all the time.'

'I did,' interrupted Jeremy. 'Dad and I went to the Planetarium. It was great. Better than watching Cape Canaveral on television because you feel you're up in space yourself.'

'How have *you* been?' Charlotte's eyes were sharp. She had worried all weekend about her vulnerable mother on her own in the house.

'Fine – I've been practising – or preparing, rather, for a job interview next week. Come into the kitchen and see what I've done,' Kate said gaily. She was dying to hear about their weekend but at the same time afraid of giving herself more pain. She knew it would be wrong to encourage any division of loyalty the children might feel, but she longed for them to say something critical about Greta Lanson.

Both children were interested in the prospective interview and Jeremy said stoutly that one of Kate's sketches was far better than the newspaper ad. She felt gratified when Charlotte whistled and exclaimed, 'Nine or ten thousand! That's huge! Do you think you'll get it?'

'No.' Kate laughed. 'But it will give me a chance to know what the set-up is like, what sort of questions they ask. It will help me when I go for other interviews. I'm going to bluff my head off.'

Charlotte was surprised at her lightheartedness and even a little jealous that her mother had seemed to manage very well without them. Jeremy hung close to her as she got them all a light supper, following her from the refrigerator to table to stove like a pet dog. 'What did you have to eat?' she asked lightly, and suffered a spasm of piercing jealousy when Jeremy said enthusiastically, 'It was smashing – a sort of fish pudding.'

'Soufflé,' interjected Charlotte.

'And a huge piece of steak with masses of chips, and a big ice-cream thing that I had to stand up to eat.'

'Knickerbocker glory,' Charlotte explained with a heavy sigh of superiority.

'But you don't like fish,' Kate said.

'I liked *this* fish. It didn't look like fish and it had Noilly Prat in it,' Jeremy pronounced the French name proudly.

'Greta Lanson must have been in the kitchen the whole time.' Kate tried to speak lightly. She wished she hadn't asked. Was she a marvellous cook as well as beautiful?

'Oh she didn't *cook* – we went to restaurants – even for breakfast,' said Jeremy carelessly. 'We went to the Dorchester and an Italian restaurant in Covent Garden and after the Italian restaurant we went round a shop that stays open until midnight.'

'Greta didn't come out to breakfast,' Charlotte interjected quickly, looking at her mother's face. 'She doesn't like to get up early. I don't think she's ever been in their kitchen – it was empty. I couldn't even find any *milk* in the fridge.'

Kate cheered up, and when Jeremy went to bed he gave her a particularly fierce bear hug. 'You're much nicer than her,' he said, muffling his head in her neck, 'though not as pretty.'

'Thanks.' Kate laughed.

Charlotte hovered after he'd gone. 'She bought me this.' She opened a Daniel Hechter bag and pulled out some cream velvet pants and a cream knitted off-the-shoulder top. 'She insisted.' Her hands stroked the fabric and her expression told Kate of her struggle between a sense of loyalty to her mother and a desire for the attractive outfit.

'Put them on. They look lovely.'

Charlotte needed no further encouragement and struggled into the tight trousers. The outfit emphasized her long-legged boyish figure and Kate realized anew how grown-up she was – and how very attractive. 'I hope they're washable,' she said quickly, to hide the rush of emotion that roughened her voice. She remembered Charlotte's self-conscious head-tossing in the pizza parlour and the preening young show-off males.

'Greta said I should have my hair short,' Charlotte pulled her hair on top of her head and peered into the kitchen mirror. 'What do you think? She has a whole make-up studio to do her hair and face. She said she could arrange for me to go in and have my face done.'

'It sounds as if you got on well after all. I don't think you need make-up yet. It's not good for your skin. Make-up is supposed to enhance your natural beauty.' She peered into Charlotte's self-absorbed little face. 'And I don't think yours needs much doing to it just yet. In any case, Daddy's programme boss of the studios; you need only ask him, you know that.'

'Well, he's so *unreliable*. But anyway, I'm going to be an actress, not a make-up artist,' Charlotte looked speculatively at her mother. 'I bet she's got a temper. You should have seen the look she shot Dad when he made a tiny criticism of the last "Lifestyles". I think if we hadn't been there she would have let fly. You could see it was an effort to hold her tongue. We don't have to go there again for a long time, do we?'

Kate kissed her good night. 'It doesn't sound as if you found it all too much of a trial,' she said good humouredly, eyeing the new clothes. 'Daddy and I will have to make some *regular* arrangements, so that we all know where we stand,' she added diplomatically.

'But I don't like her really,' Charlotte spread her hands. 'I realize she's trying to be nice, but you can tell it's an effort. She'll be glad too if we don't show up too often.'

'Bedtime,' Kate shooed her out of the room. The weekend that had seemed such a daunting hurdle on Friday hadn't been too bad after all.

Chapter Eighteen

Kate worked in every spare moment on trying to put together a portfolio for her interview. She bought a big layout pad and a set of thick felt nib pens, which she found highly satisfying to use. She sketched the children when they came home from school, asked Flip if she would mind if she sat quietly in the corner of the dining room while she coached Jeremy, and drew the two of them. She tried a cartoon technique which seemed to come off, and a romantic one which she tore up as 'soppy'. She kept reminding herself that she was selling something; it had quite a disciplining effect.

'I brought you some bedtime reading,' Flip said indicating a carrier bag. 'I'm putting myself in charge of your adult education.'

'I'm more interested in my adult career right now,' Kate answered with a distracted smile. 'I've got to see a man about a job on Thursday and he wants to see my "portfolio". Up to now it hasn't existed.'

At the end of the evening Flip looked at the sketches. 'They look bloody good to me. But I'm not so sure *you* do – can I offer you one of your own drinks? You look bushed.

'I'm not sleeping well. What do you think I should wear to an interview?' she looked anxiously at Flip. 'I don't have anything like a business suit.'

Flip roared. 'You're supposed to be an artist, aren't you? I've never met one who didn't wear old jeans and an older sweater. Still—' she narrowed her eyes at Kate, 'I wouldn't go that far. Something casual but stunning. Let's look in your cupboard.'

On hearing their voices Charlotte drifted curiously into Kate's bedroom. 'Haven't you anything sexier?' Flip asked. 'That's hardly a feminist remark,' Kate commented drily. 'I don't think so – a Fulham housewife of a certain age doesn't have much call for sexy clothes.'

'You'd be surprised,' Flip murmured, occupied in riffling through the rack. 'How about this?' she held out a narrow brown suede skirt. 'What would go with this?' 'I usually wear this beige polo.' Kate pulled a sweater from her drawer. Flip took it from her and put it back firmly. 'No – more agony aunt than advertising agency.'

'There's *my* new sweater,' Charlotte said awkwardly. Kate shook her head vigorously, but Flip ignored her. 'Let's see it.' 'I can't wear that,' Kate gasped as Charlotte went to her own room to get the sweater. 'My husband's girlfriend bought it!'

'All the better,' Flip's eyes, green tonight, glinted with amusement. 'Why shouldn't she help you get a job?' Charlotte generously urged her mother to try it on, and Flip nodded approval of the way the wide, bare neckline showed off Kate's warm skin colour, and the dolman sleeves and fitted rib emphasized her neat waist. 'That's it.' Flip nodded decisively. 'You don't mind, do you, Charley?' Charlotte shook her head, embarrassed because she guessed how her mother must feel about wearing a gift from Greta Lanson.

'I can't,' Kate shook her head.

'You can,' said Flip. 'There have been too many "can'ts" in your life. Besides, it's a lovely joke,' she started to laugh and then Charlotte joined her suddenly. The irony of wearing the sweater began to appeal to Kate.

'All right, I'll do it,' she said at last. 'She owes me something,' she said, and laughed herself. Charlotte hugged her mother in relief. 'It looks better on you than on me – you have more *shape*. Wouldn't it be hilarious if she saw you wearing it?'

The three of them went downstairs giggling to where a disgruntled Jeremy was sitting alone, having finished his maths exercise.

Kate spent every spare minute drawing and re-drawing the contents of the fridge and cupboard and took a new and avid interest in the newspaper and poster ads when she went shopping. Passing the library, she popped in and browsed through the career section. 'It won't come to anything,' she told herself, but eagerly poured over some fairly basic information about life in an advertising agency obviously intended for hopeful school leavers.

It was unfamiliar but intriguing territory. By Wednesday morning she had accumulated quite a sheaf of drawings, and she went through them, eliminating the tentative first efforts, trying to see them with an objective discriminating eye.

When the telephone rang, she answered distractedly, squinting across the room at a set of drawings she had done for an idea of her own to sell lipstick. It was Jon. 'How about coming up to have some lunch with me?' Kate felt a surge of sexual excitement at the sound of his warm, teasing voice. 'I'm rather busy,' she said reluctantly. 'I'm trying to get some work together for an appointment tomorrow.'

'Do it later. You've got to eat, haven't you?'

'Not necessarily.' But she did want to see him again.

'Even better,' his voice was caressing. 'We can carry on where we left off.' Kate leaned against the wall, feeling weak with a sudden rush of desire.

'Are you still there, Katie?'

'Yes – I was thinking.'

'Don't think, just come. Thinking's bad for you. I want to *see* you.'

'All right,' Kate couldn't conceal the hoarseness of her voice. 'Where?'

'Do you know the Neal Street restaurant in, surprisingly enough, Neal Street?'

'No, but I shall take a taxi.'

'Great. See you at 12.45 then.'

Kate arrived flustered at the cool, tiled restaurant. She felt shy and nervous, unsure of how to behave with this stranger with whom she'd made love. Jon was sitting at a round table watching the door and moved swiftly over to her once she'd struggled out of her coat. 'I like punctual women,' he said as he kissed her, and took her hand to lead her to the table. 'I'm drinking pink champagne, will that do?' He smiled into her eyes, still holding her hand. 'I'm so glad you came.'

Kate blushed and looked down at the cloth. 'I wanted to.'

'Antonio Carluccio who runs this restaurant is one of the greatest mushroom experts in the country – he's just been showing me the wild ceps flown in this morning from France. You must have some – they smell of damp woods, earth – and sex.' He kissed his fingertips, well aware of the large genial figure of Carluccio looming over their table.

They ordered immediately. 'Because you said you had work to do,' he grinned wickedly. Kate relaxed. It was high time she remembered she was verging on middle-age and not some schoolgirl on a first date.

'Well, it's true. I'm going for an interview tomorrow, in the art department of an advertising agency, and I've had to get together a portfolio of sketches.'

'I didn't know you were an artist,' he said in some surprise.

She was about to say 'I'm not' but smiled noncommittally instead.

As promised, the butter-stewed mushrooms were delicious, and so was the rest of the meal, which they washed down with a bottle of red wine. Jon sipped it appreciatively and winked approvingly at Carluccio. 'I shall go to sleep,' protested Kate.

'Not again!' Jon spoke teasingly. 'Once I can forgive, twice I might take as an insult.'

As they left the restaurant he took her hand again. She felt absurdly pleased. 'Carlos Place,' he said to the taxi driver.

'Where are we going?' Kate worried. 'I do have to get home.'

'But not yet,' he said, and this time kissed the tips of *her* fingers. 'I have other plans.'

She looked out of the window to try to control a wave of excitement again, and felt a warm wetness between her legs. People walking along Piccadilly looked so dull, wrapped against the cold, their faces blank with boredom, or with preoccupation with their work problems. Suddenly she felt carefree and glamorous. Why *shouldn't* she consider her own needs and desires for once?

At Carlos Place, Jon opened the door of a tall red brick Victorian building next to a discreet, double-fronted shop. He gave an airy wave at the shop, which bore the name Daniels in old-fashioned lettering. 'I told you I was a grocer – and like all good grocers, I live over the shop.'

Kate followed him into a dark, panelled hall; he switched on a small crystal chandelier and led the way up a curving staircase. At the top double doors opened into a vast drawing room. As he took her coat, he kissed her behind her ear. 'I've been longing for this moment all through lunch. I could hardly contain myself.' He threw her coat over the nearest sofa. 'Come, don't let's waste time,' and he pulled her through to another splendid white room, dominated by a capacious bed. As swiftly as before, with the same economical movements, he unbelted her dress, and turned her to unbutton it at the back. 'You're very practised,' she said with a breathy, nervous laugh.

'You don't want to put up with an amateur, do you?' He kicked off his shoes and slipped off his trousers. 'Especially where sex is concerned. Let me look at you.' He knelt and rolled her tights down gently, caressing her thighs as he did so, nuzzling against her pubic hair. Kate stood stiffly, looking down at his fair curly head. She wasn't sure what to do. She felt very much an amateur. Then he stood up, and threw himself on to the wide bed, pulling her down on top of him. 'Now go to sleep if you can.'

He was already erect, and supported her breasts on his hand, bringing his knees up behind her to make her lean against his body. Kate bent her head and ran her tongue experimentally over his lips and put her hands behind his head to pull him closer to kiss. She rolled her hips slightly. She was surprised at how bold and wanton she felt. Suddenly they were pulling and clawing at each other, kissing and rolling, and then he was inside her. It was over in a minute, and Kate lay breathless. Jon cuddled her close to him. 'That was altogether too quick, but I wanted you so much.' He lay with his eyes closed. Kate's heart was thumping, but she lay still in his arms, trying to calm down.

After a few moments he took her hand and put it over his penis. 'Stroke me,' he murmured, his eyes still closed. Kate touched him gently with her fingertips, light, tentative strokes. She wasn't quite sure if that was what he meant. He opened his eyes and smiled at her. 'For a married woman you're not very experienced,' he said, and took her hand to show her what he wanted.

Soon he was large again, and he began to caress Kate, murmuring to her as he took his time to bring her excitement to a peak. She hadn't realized how arousing words could be, when accompanied by insistent rhythmic stroking. He plunged deeply inside her, thrusting fiercely, watching her face with almost clinical detachment until at last Kate was gasping, 'Oh please, oh please, now, now.'

He smiled widely in triumph. 'That's better,' and let go himself. They lay against the pillows, breathing quickly. He put his arm under Kate's shoulders and pulled her close. '*Now* you can have a little sleep.' She leant on one elbow to look at him, but his eyes were shut, and his penis lay limp and powerless. She felt tender towards it and felt an urge to kiss it, but was afraid to disturb him, he looked so relaxed. She pulled the covers up gently and lay quietly, enjoying the warmth of his body beside her.

When she awoke the room was dark and the bed empty. She sat up in a panic. There was a crack of light under the door and she swung her feet to the floor to grope her way towards it, but the door opened before she got to it and Jon came in with a tray, two glasses and a bottle of champagne. 'A little pick-me-up for the snoozer.' He beamed at her.

'I thought you went to sleep too.' She no longer felt shy, just beautifully relaxed and content. 'Whatever is the time, it's dark?' He told her, handed her a glass and sipped his.

'*Five!* The children will be home and wondering where I am.'

'There's the telephone,' he soothed. 'Ring them.' Kate was trembling as she dialled. She had never before been out when they came home from school.

'Hullo?' Charlotte's voice had fear in it. '*Mummy* – where *are* you?'

'It's all right, darling – I came up to town and got delayed. I'll be home soon. Are you all right?'

'Yes of course,' Charlotte's voice was cross with relief. 'Why didn't you leave a note or something? Then we wouldn't have worried!'

'I'm sorry – I expected to be back before you. But I won't be long now.' She clutched the sheet against her as if Charlotte could see her nakedness. She put down the 'phone and looked at Jon. 'Oh dear, they were frightened.'

'Are they very young?' He sounded bored.

'No, but I'm usually there when they get home.'

'What happens when you're working?'

'I haven't had a job – so far.' She took a deep breath. To hell with her image. 'Tomorrow's the first interview I have ever had. That's why I said I couldn't come to lunch – I needed to prepare for it.'

'Are you sorry you did?'

'Of course not.' Her smile was radiant. 'I don't suppose I'll get the job anyway.'

'Which agency is it?'

'It's one of the big ones – J. Walter Thompson.'

'Why, that's just two minute's walk from here. Heavens, how convenient!' She laughed happily. That meant he wanted to see her again.

She finished her champagne. 'The bathroom, I take it, is through here?'

'Have a shower,' he called through the door.

It seemed only marginally smaller than the bedroom, with a wide bath sunk into the floor. She ran the shower, throwing back her head so as not to wet her hair, and closing her eyes as she revelled in the refreshing sting of the cool spray. Suddenly Jon was in there with her, kissing her throat, soaping her body, slipping his hands over her breasts and buttocks, soaping between her legs. She leant against the glass walls helplessly, giving way completely to the enjoyment of his rhythmic movements. It was pure pleasure. She took the soap from him and did the same to him, no longer shy of touching his penis, triumphant at producing his obvious relish. He came inside her again, the water raining over his contorted face as he thrust with increasing urgency.

When it was over he gave her a little push. 'I thought you had to get home?' He turned off the water and padded over to the towels. 'Here, dry off while I organize a taxi.' He belted himself into a towelling robe and went to the telephone.

Kate dried and dressed with panicky speed. How on earth could she face the children as if she had just been on a shopping trip to town? She felt guilty and apprehensive. Despite her efforts with the towel, her hair was still damp. It would never dry before she got home.

The doorbell rang. 'Your taxi,' said Jon. 'Luckily the Connaught is just across the road.' He seemed remote from her now, just as anxious for her to go as she was to get home. He'd pulled on some slacks and a sweater and came down to the door with her. Giving the driver her address and a tenner he said, 'The lady is in a hurry, will that cover it?' The driver looked at the note and nodded without enthusiasm. Jon shut the door on her, blew a kiss through the window, and turned to go in before the cab moved off. Kate felt a momentary pang of disappointment and then gave herself up to reliving the afternoon. She knew now what Flip meant when she had said good sex made her feel as satisfied as a fat cat. But she felt self-conscious and guilty again when she got home.

'I didn't know it was raining.' Charlotte looked open-mouthed at her wet hair. Kate pushed it aside defensively. 'It's not, but I went to the hairdressers and . . .' She paused, at a loss. 'After they shampooed me they were taking so long, and everybody looked so impossibly gilded I – I just walked out,' she finished triumphantly, so astonished at her performance that she almost expected them to applaud. Charlotte narrowed her eyes slightly, but there were none of the searching questions Kate had feared. They seemed to accept her excuse for being late at face value and were more interested in getting through supper fast so that they could watch a favourite television programme.

Chapter Nineteen

Kate had looked at her watch every five minutes. She was so nervous it seemed difficult to breathe properly. Her appointment with the agency was for noon, but since she had to be in town, anyway, she telephoned the bank manager to make an appointment. She was ready to face up to her financial situation at last. Now she thought it had been a mistake. Suppose he kept her too long and she was late? Her mind was so fixed on noon that the talk with Mr Mitchell seemed trifling, a rather tiresome routine she felt obliged to go through. It was childish to go on procrastinating, hoping that mere ignorance would save her from having to wrestle with matters she knew so little about. She'd never thought much about money. She wasn't naturally extravagant, and Geoffrey had paid into her account a sufficient amount to cover the household expenses. She assumed that her own income covered her personal spending. Usually she barely glanced at her bank statements. As long as she wasn't overdrawn, and she rarely had been, she had simply shoved them into her desk drawer.

She was irritated with the clerk's self-importance in checking that she had an appointment. 'The manager is very busy,' he said sternly, but he was subdued when Mr Mitchell bustled out, jolly and avuncular, to usher Kate into his office himself. After only a few minutes Kate noticed that the chatty deference was replaced by a slight steeliness, once she had explained her marital status. Mr Mitchell studied his bare desktop silently for a minute, and then sent for her bank statement. After a moment's examination, he looked directly at Kate. 'I suppose Mr Cosgrove has mentioned to you that he has stopped your usual allowance? I take it there will be some new arrangement put into force immediately?'

Kate had stuttered in bewilderment. 'No, er, that is, no, I mean . . . *stopped it*?' she exclaimed as the implication of what he was saying penetrated. She tried to collect her spinning thoughts. 'I'm stupid, I should have looked up my bank statements before I came. Could you tell me how much I have in my account?' She was proud that her voice had only a slight tremor.

'Yes, of course. There's under £100 – £89.60 to be exact.' His voice was non-committal but his eyes were colder. Kate's stomach churned. That wasn't enough to cope with the housekeeping for the rest of the month! Her own income was pitifully small. 'My solicitor is dealing with everything,' Kate said coolly, with some hauteur, some hidden strength making her pull the shreds of her dignity together. 'I believe there are tax arrangements to be made – as my income is unearned, it is apparently tacked on to my husband's and he is responsible for the tax. Obviously, that will be adjusted.'

'Of course, Lady Kate,' the manager said smoothly. 'But it is my duty to advise you of your true position. Even if your own income were not taxed, it wouldn't be sufficient to keep a family of four – three,' he corrected himself.

'I hope to have a job soon.'

'Splendid. That will help.' He paused, looking at her. 'And I daresay your solicitor will be sorting out with Mr Cosgrove some kind of financial support. That's a wonderful new series he's doing, by the way. My wife and I wouldn't miss "Lifestyles" for the world. Mrs Mitchell has even changed her bridge evenings in order to watch it.'

Kate got sharply to her feet at that point. 'I take it that

there won't be any problem if I need a temporary overdraft?' she said coldly. How dare he patronize her! The little blighter had had her family's accounts for years – he'd better not treat her as a poor relation now.

'I'm sure we can arrange something, Lady Kate,' he'd said over-heartily, his teeth gleaming wetly in a suspiciously even smile. Kate gave him a curt nod and left.

But outside, disoriented by the street noise and the cold autumn sunlight, her arrogant façade collapsed. For the first time since Geoffrey'd left she felt absolutely petrified. The job wasn't just desirable, it was vital. She'd have to call her solicitor at once and tell him about the money situation. She hadn't realized how much she needed to live on and how little she had, and alongside her dismay was a cold, sick contempt for Geoffrey.

Kate walked past the office building three times before she collected her wits and plucked up sufficient courage to enter it. The lobby was dauntingly large. A great many people seemed to be coming and going with an enviable nonchalance. She walked diffidently to the reception desk, where two glamorous young women were talking into telephones, exchanging repartee with visitors obviously familiar to them, and receiving a constant stream of deliveries from motorbike messengers, looking alien in leathers and helmets. She waited at their splendid desk while a blonde enamelled like a Dallas clone went to some lengths to ignore her. Eventually the blonde raised her eyebrows in silent enquiry. 'I have an appointment with Mr Grimshaw,' Kate said almost apologetically.

'Who?'

'Mr Joe Grimshaw.' Kate cleared her throat and raised her voice.

'Oh, Mr Grimshaw.' She emphasized the first syllable as

though Kate were a foreigner and had mispronounced the name.

'Take a seat, please.' She indicated two banks of deep leather chairs. Kate sat down obediently, sinking so low that her knees seemed almost on a level with her chin. She shouldn't have come – it was all too grand and high-powered. She'd made a mistake in even contemplating trying for a job here, however junior it might be. *Nobody* seemed less than superior, even the nonchalant motorbike messengers.

As she was gathering the courage to struggle to her feet and disappear through the doors into the street again, a smiling, friendly young woman came up to her.

'Kate Cosgrove? I'm Petronella, Joe's secretary. He sent me to fetch you. It's all too easy to lose people in this warren – clients have sometimes been known to go missing for days. I'm always expecting to turn over a pile of artwork and find the advertising director of one of our major clients decaying gently underneath.'

Kate found her affability warming, but not effective enough to stop her trembling, or to relax her features into more than a stiff smile as Petronella ushered her into a large, sunny, reassuringly untidy room. Joe Grimshaw came round from behind a big desk cluttered with video tapes and huge pages scrawled all over with hieroglyphics, holding out his hand.

'Hello – Joe Grimshaw. Nick Menton told me about you.' A small-boned man, casually dressed, he had bright button eyes under a fuzz of grey curly hair. He reminded Kate of Harpo Marx. He shook her chilly, trembling hand.

'What's this? Not nervous of Joe, are you? We can't have that. A cup of tea?' He looked so like a quizzical little gnome that Kate's smile lost some of its strain. 'No, thanks – I mustn't take up your time. I – er – it's good of you to see me. I hope,' she plunged on desperately, 'I hope

Nick Menton told you I hadn't worked . . .' she caught herself before she said 'before' and gabbled, 'in an agency before. I don't know whether my work is right for you.'

'Nick only said you were talented,' Joe said absently, reaching for the portfolio Kate was gripping tightly. 'Let's see.'

Kate stood beside him as he opened it. He went through it silently – and rather too quickly, she thought, to be giving her work more than the most cursory glance. It was as she thought. He was merely seeing her because Nick had asked him to as a friend. It was surely painfully obvious to anyone with half an eye that she was not a professional. Then he went through the lot again, this time slowly, and extracted one or two drawings. He took out the set she'd done for the imaginary lipstick campaign. 'Was this your idea?'

'Yes,' Kate's voice was barely a whisper. She felt mortified.

'And you haven't had any art school training?'

'No. Well, I studied with Esme Biddulph.' She dropped Esme's name carelessly, as though it was one he should know. 'She designs those marvellous greetings cards now.' Kate was stunned at her own boldness.

'I see,' Joe Grimshaw was noncommittal, looking with narrowed eyes at the drawings he'd selected. 'Did Nick tell you that the job I have is a junior one? Usually it would be filled by an eighteen to twenty-year-old more or less straight from art school. I take it you're a little older?' She nodded.

'It's a dogsbody job that's open, you know – you'd probably have to get tea, among other lowly chores.'

'I don't mind.' Kate let out her breath. He seemed kind. 'I know I haven't a lot to offer, but I think I could learn quickly. And frankly, I need the job.' She blushed. That was a mistake. 'I think I can draw,' she added hastily.

'You can.' Joe Grimshaw was unequivocal. 'There's

vitality in those drawings. I like them. You have a very clean line. But you know, this is a tough business. People think advertising is a short cut to fame and riches. It's more likely to create alcoholics or heart cases.' He smiled, his button eyes almost disappearing in a crosshatching of wrinkles. 'Generally it's sheer grind to come up with workable, professional results from what's sometimes the merest outline from the creatives. You have to stick at it, ignore the clock, put work before food, men, shopping and whatever other priority you think you have in your private life. Understand? Good.' He nodded at her murmured assents. 'In this business if you're no good, if you miss deadlines, you're out. For every new job we have on offer I guarantee we have something like five hundred or more applicants. It's rigorous and competitive. If we put in sloppy work we lose an account and if an account goes, people have to go with it. That's advertising life, my dear.'

'I understand.' Kate was sure he could hear her heart beating. She concentrated on his deft movements as he shuffled her sketches neatly back into the folder. He wasn't going to offer her a job. He would have asked more probing questions if he were. She felt a sick disappointment sweep through her. Of course. She had expected that, hadn't she? She was too old. Too inexperienced. Untalented, as Geoffrey had said. He knew more about the commercial world than Nick Menton.

'I'm afraid you'd have to come on a three months' trial basis with no guarantee that you would be kept on after that,' Joe Grimshaw said seriously.

Kate hardly heard him. She was intent on getting out of that room without any more humiliation, before this pounding in her ears got worse, before she burst into tears.

'The trouble is, I need someone immediately. We're very pushed at the moment. But I can't offer much. £9000 – is that all right? There are fringe benefits of course . . .' His voice faded in surprise as Kate said, '*What?*'

'Fringe benefits, you know the sort of thing, staff restaurant, health insurance – once you're over the trial period, of course.' He sounded a little impatient.

'No, I meant – what did you say? Did you offer me the job? I don't think I heard properly.' Her eyes had widened into a painful, fixed stare. He cleared his throat uncomfortably.

'Well it's not permanent, mind, and I can take you on only if you can start more or less immediately. I . . .'

'As soon as you like. I'm not doing anything at the moment.' Her voice sounded far away. Was she babbling? If she could get out of this room for a minute she'd be all right. She had felt so hopeless, so desperate a moment ago that she had been afraid she would fly at him wildly, shake him, tell him he *must* give her a job, he *must*. Now it seemed he had.

He looked up at her speculatively. 'Well that's all right then,' he said slowly. 'It was good of you to come. Petronella will show you out.' He must have buzzed, for Petronella's smooth, smiling face popped round the door. 'See Mrs er . . . out, will you, Pet? And take down her details, there's a good girl.' His head was down over his board again as Kate mumbled her thanks and goodbye and found herself steered outside by Petronella, whose smile seemed permanent.

'May I have your name, address and telephone number? When he wants someone it is usually in one mad rush. There's never any time to organize properly. Did he give you a date to start?'

'I thought he said immediately.' She tried to speak collectedly.

Petronella sighed distractedly. 'That means Monday – no time to write a formal letter. He's the utter limit. Personnel will go mad. Well, you'd better turn up on Monday with your P45 and insurance cards and I'll get you to sign a letter then.'

Kate's heart sank. She knew there would be a snag. What on earth was a P45? 'I don't have a, what did you say, P45?'

'Your last employer should have given you one,' Petronella was brusque, but then her smile returned, intact. She marched Kate back through the corridors to the reception desk. 'Here you are. Have the front desk ring me on Monday and I'll come and fetch you again – after that you're on your own.' She waved Kate through the swing doors into Berkeley Square.

Kate found the gate into the square and sat dazedly on one of the benches. Pigeons crowded round her feet like a flock of beggars round a tourist, cocking their heads expectantly, their bright knowing eyes sizing up the prospects of a snack. She shivered in the autumn chill. She would have to find out about that wretched form. She would have to discover just how much money she had after tax. After the shock the bank manager had given her, she wasn't going to be airily indifferent to financial reality in future. And what would happen in three months' time? It was clear she wasn't up to the professional level of a big agency. She had just been exceptionally lucky in catching Joe Grimshaw at a moment when he was clutching at straws. She would have to pull herself together and do some serious thinking.

She walked slowly to Piccadilly to get her bus. In her seat, clasping her portfolio like a badge of office in her lap, she cheered slightly as she remembered Joe Grimshaw's words. She couldn't resist peering into her folder to look at her sketches again. Vitality, he'd said. A clean line. She *would* survive the three months. She had to.

At home she poured herself a glass of wine and was looking in the telephone directory through the confusing list of government security departments, when Tom phoned. 'Katie, how are you? Can I come over? I've had to rush in to London unexpectedly for a couple of days. How about a meal?' Kate was overjoyed. 'Wonderful! Would you like the spare room? It would be so lovely to see you.' She suddenly wanted to cry. She realized how much she had missed having someone who loved her, like Tom or Esme, during these last upsetting weeks.

'I'll stay if it is not too much trouble, but I have to leave at the crack of dawn. I've got to make a presentation to the Royal Institution tomorrow; I think we've made a breakthrough on the work we've been doing. I've published a paper but now they want me to talk about it. There are some chaps in Germany who have been working in the same field and they're coming over too. I'll tell you all about it later. Will the nippers be home? I haven't seen them for yonks.'

'Yes, of course. You'll be a lovely surprise for them too. Come as soon as you like – I'll put a bottle of something festive in the fridge.'

Nick rang immediately she put down the phone. 'How did it go?' he asked without preamble.

'He's going to try me out!' She laughed excitedly. 'But I'm afraid he realized I was a total amateur.'

'Nonsense,' Nick's voice was encouraging. 'You'll pick it up soon enough. But this calls for a celebration. Let me take you out to dinner and boost your confidence.'

'That's nice of you, it certainly needs it, but I can't.' Her apprehension about work was suddenly replaced by excitement. 'Tom has just phoned to say he's in town! He's coming to stay the night. Why don't you join us for dinner, if you don't mind just family? I owe you a thank you for making that introduction.'

'Oh, forget that, but I would like to come if I won't be in the way. Are you sure you and Tom won't want to discuss private family matters?'

'I'm beginning to think of you as one of us,' Kate said

warmly. 'Besides, I think Tom is coming over early. He has a big meeting tomorrow. We'll have plenty of time to talk.'

She peered into the refrigerator. She needed to shop for some proper celebratory supplies, and *hang* the bank manager. There'd just have to be a hefty overdraft for the time being.

Chapter Twenty

Charlotte and Jeremy were gratifyingly impressed by her getting the job. And when Tom arrived, with his warmth and exuberance and the talent he had for making everything move up a gear, Kate felt a rush of love for the three of them. Flip was wrong. There was nothing to beat the warm feeling, the uncritical affection a family gave one – the knowledge that no matter what happened they'd be on your side.

When the children had been shooed off to do their homework, and Kate was preparing dinner, Tom sat companionably at the kitchen table, beating egg whites, dwarfing the small room with his huge, untidy bulk.

'I think you've grown,' Kate observed.

'I have – widthways.' Despite his happy smile he looked tired. And he *had* put on weight. 'I've been living off takeaways and sandwich lunches varied with bags of crisps. We've practically slept in the lab lately.'

'What are you up to?' Kate hoped he wouldn't tell her in too great detail – his work always sounded so dauntingly complex.

'It's all to do with cells. There've been so many developments that it is difficult to keep up, but basically, although we know the structures, we don't always know how they interact, or whether the cell walls have a more interesting function than we've previously thought. I think they have, that fluids are conducted through positive action of the membrane. There's the team I mentioned in

Germany who have come to roughly the same conclusion but by a different method. If we're both on the right track, it would affect very much the treatment of some of the genetically transmitted diseases, and the cells that suddenly go crazy, which, simplistically, is what happens in cancers. It should be possible to seal off the crazy cells in some way.'

'But isn't that tremendously important?' Kate stared at her brother.

'It could be, but there's still lots to be done. Well anyway, there's a bit of a conference on tomorrow and I've got to develop what we've done since the paper, and the German team are going to talk about the route they've taken, and there'll be a lot of chat.' He was casual but Kate sensed his excitement. He was single-minded, like their father had been. No wonder Tom had never got married – it would simply have been an interruption. She remembered how indignant she'd felt when Geoffrey had once floated the idea that Tom was homosexual. And yet, the disloyal thought crept in again. Since she'd met Flip and Jon she had thought much more about sex. Could Tom and Nick Menton be more than friends? She felt disconcerted by such thoughts and plunged into questioning about the research until Tom began laughing.

'Cut it out – you don't have to be polite! I know you know nothing about it and why the hell should you? Even I know very little and I've been studying the subject for years.'

Nick arrived, carrying two bottles of Cristal Champagne, and Kate was helpless in the face of the children's pleading and Nick and Tom's indulgence.

'Oh don't be a spoilsport Katie – this is a *celebration*,' Tom protested, handing the children their glasses. 'It's not every day my sister becomes a working woman.'

'And we must toast the future Nobel prize winner too.' Nick lifted his glass to Tom, who, to Kate's surprise, looked very embarrassed.

'You don't mean it?' she demanded.

'Course not,' Tom looked menacingly at Nick who, unperturbed, said calmly, 'He could be. I see he hasn't explained just how vital his work has been.'

Jeremy looked at his uncle with awe. 'Gosh. You'd be asked to school to talk to the chaps. We've just had Dr Aaron Klug – *he's* a Nobel prizewinner too.'

'Steady on.' Tom laughed. 'There's a long way to go yet. In any case, I thought I'd been promised a meal, and I'm famished. I'm not going to be done out of the soufflé for which I've been beating umpteen egg whites.'

Kate was surprised at how close Tom and Nick were. There was a lot of leg pulling and references to people and occasions she knew nothing about. They had the same oblique sense of humour, which in a curious way cut her out. Kate looked from the one to the other. They seemed very intimate for men who worked in different fields and different cities, surely? She was ashamed of her suspicions again.

Both Tom and Nick included the children in the conversation as a matter of course and Kate noticed the way Charlotte blossomed at their attention. Nick, particularly, seemed to have the knack of inclining his head to listen when she expressed a view, leading her on with serious questions and comments. She positively lit up when he talked about the theatre.

Kate wondered at how much more forthcoming the children were tonight than during the meals they used to have with Geoffrey, when more often than not the three of them had merely served as his audience. His evenings and weekends at home had been erratic, but he had seemed to be fond of the children, and when he had time, took a lot of trouble with Jeremy. Had she connived at putting

Geoffrey in a separate category, so that this kind of easy discussion and banter had been made impossible?

She felt rather left out now, irrationally jealous, and irritated with Nick as he joked with Charlotte. He was a bit too familiar, she thought unfairly. She struggled with her vexation, reminding herself that after all she owed the fact that she was about to become a wage-earner to him, but all the same she was relieved to see him go.

In bed later she felt compunction. Why had she become so suspicious and intolerant? Was this a by-product of divorce? Could hurt and insecurity make one jealous and cynical? She resolved to be nicer to Nick the next time. He'd looked at her with an air of puzzlement as they'd said goodbye.

Chapter Twenty-One

Kate and Charlotte spent the next evening organizing her wardrobe. 'Not too exec,' Charlotte said consideringly, 'but you need to be noticed. I think you need some things that look a bit brighter – aren't artists usually colourful creatures?'

'I wouldn't know. You mean borrowed plumage might help my confidence?'

Charlotte nodded emphatically. 'You're too self-effacing even for a mother. I think this is another situation for Beatrice to deal with. Ring her again.'

'We might see if she's free to come shopping with us on Saturday,' Kate mused. 'I mustn't spend too much money but you're right, this collection looks pretty dismal.' She eyed the clothes spread out on the bed with distaste. 'That slug of a bank manager can have a nervous breakdown over my overdraft for all I care. I can't worry about money at a time like this.' She wished she felt as nonchalant as her words. Finances were beginning to be a daily worry.

With Jeremy conveniently playing an away football match, Beatrice, Charlotte and Kate had a lovely Saturday buying an assortment of skirts and sweaters, planned, Beatrice had said with authority, to co-ordinate properly. 'Buying one top, or one skirt is a ridiculously expensive way to do things. You have to discipline yourself and your eye to make separates work properly.' Kate enjoyed being bossed by the two of them and made only a weak token protest when a deep chestnut-coloured coat was added to the pile.

'You might have to take clients out to lunch,' Beatrice warned.

'I told you I shall be washing out paintpots and making tea – I'm just the junior.'

But Beatrice was blithely indifferent. Kate rashly treated them both to a sweater and they froze in the cold autumn brightness lunching at a pavement café in South Molton Street, watching the beautiful, disdainful young women drift in and out of Brown's to a sharp running critique from Beatrice on their fashion sense.

'Never mind, Mum – *you'll* be shopping in Brown's when they see how good you are and double your salary,' Charlotte had reassured her, when Kate had said that it would be a long time before she could set foot in there again.

By Monday morning Kate was in a frenzy of apprehension and nerves. She self-consciously left the house with the children, trying to imagine her future routine. 'I don't know how soon I'll be home,' she warned. 'I suppose I'll have to stay until they haven't any more little jobs for me to do. Do you think they'll laugh at me for being so old?'

'Moth-er!' Charlotte went into her eye-rolling routine and heaved a theatrical sigh. 'For goodness sake. Didn't Mr Grimchops say you had talent? – and Nick thinks you do too.'

Jeremy laughed. 'Grimchops. I wonder what they'll call *you* behind your back? You won't be home for my tea?' The full implication of his mother's job had just struck home.

'No, you'll be a latchkey child from now on,' Charlotte said mockingly. 'We'll have social workers round in no time.'

'Jeremy, you're big enough to get your own tea.' Kate was firm. 'And I'll be back in time for supper. It's ready in the fridge – you won't starve if that's what's worrying you.'

She was much too early, but she wandered around until she found a little coffee shop in Curzon Street doing a brisk breakfast trade. She tried to read the newspaper and appear as casual as the other customers, sipping their coffee and tackling plates of bacon and eggs, oblivious to the outside world. At 9.20 she walked slowly to the Berkeley Square offices, unable to suppress a thrill of excitement as she walked through the big doors.

This time she went up to the desk with a little more confidence and said clearly to the Dallas blonde: 'Kate Cosgrove. I'm starting work here today in the art department. Would you be kind enough to let Petronella Jones know I'm here?' Two pairs of receptionists' eyes flicked professionally over Kate as Dallas said, more warmly than she'd spoken on Thursday, 'Petronella hasn't come in yet. If you sit down I'll catch her as she goes through.' Kate smiled her thanks. She actually had colleagues now; she'd be seeing these women every day – at least for the next three months, she added superstitiously.

The day wasn't the ordeal she'd feared, although it began on a shaky note. Petronella smilingly collected her, gave her one copy of a letter of appointment to keep, and asked her to sign the other one. Her eyebrows shot up when Kate explained that she hadn't got the requisite P45 or National Insurance forms. 'They're sending them on,' Kate said nervously.

'Who are?' asked Petronella. 'Your previous employer? They usually give them to you as you leave.'

'Well, you see, I haven't *got* any.' Kate twisted her hands awkwardly.

'No previous employer, no cards, or what?' Petronella rapped out, clearly irritated.

'Both.' Kate attempted a smile. 'I haven't worked before,' she said the words in a desperate rush. 'Um, I rang so many departments and kept getting transferred. In the end they said I have to go to an Employment Office with my marriage certificate and passport and they'd give me a temporary one while they check whether I have a National Insurance number . . .'

'*Everybody* has an insurance number,' Petronella interrupted witheringly.

'I'm not sure I have,' said Kate humbly. 'They have to write to Newcastle or somewhere and it takes eight weeks to find out.' She looked so confused and frightened that Petronella abandoned her bossy incredulity for a stunned, 'Well I never.'

'I can go to the nearest office at lunch time,' Kate went on, her voice so low and apologetic that Petronella had to bend her head to hear.

She'd had such a trial by telephone in order to find out about the wretched forms that in the end she had burst into tears to a kindly-sounding DHSS clerk who was telling her she wasn't in his area and that she'd have to be transferred yet again. He had relented and told her she could be issued with a temporary form until they found out if she was 'registered'.

Petronella clucked and said she didn't know *what* Personnel would say but they'd better get on. She finally showed Kate into the big art department where she'd be working. There were two or three others in the room, standing around doing nothing very much as the day lurched into gear, and Petronella introduced her briefly before smiling her way out again.

'That girl makes my face ache,' said a thin, pale man called Ian, gloomily plunging his into a mug of coffee. 'Jesus wants me for a sunbeam. Hang your coat there.' He pointed to a Victorian wooden coatstand looking incongruous in the middle of their modern office, which bristled with drawing boards, plan tables and light boxes. A plump woman, looking absentmindedly dishevelled, in a grey lacy knitted jumper and lumpy tweed skirt clumped over to Kate.

'I'm Jessica – I look after the campaigns for Chester Custard products. If Joe wants the new commercial ready for the client by Thursday I think you'll be mostly helping me, but we'll wait until Phillip comes in – he's in charge – or thinks he is,' she grunted amiably. 'Where were you before?'

Kate was unnerved by the exchange with Petronella about her insurance card, but she had steeled herself for this sort of question, and prevaricated bravely. 'I've been bringing up two children – I haven't worked for some time,' she admitted, smiling frankly at Jessica. 'I hope I haven't vegetated completely.'

'Children, ah.' Jessica looked approving. 'Important to stay with them when they're very young. I did with mine, though I did some freelancing to keep my hand in, as I expect you did too.'

More people drifted in and the day seemed to get under way in a series of fits and starts. Kate had to make copies of various visuals, thankfully discovering a young woman, not much older than Charlotte, in the duplicator room who cheerfully showed her how to work the machine. She had to get new layout pads for Phillip from a vast stationery storeroom, and was initiated into the mysteries of the work sheets which had to be attached to every job to keep tabs on the progress.

A stream of freelancers constantly came in delivering artwork, or to be given assignments by Phillip. Once three of them went down to a viewing room to look at a rough cut of a commercial that had just been shot in Barbados, and in between Kate had to work on roughing out ideas from several design briefs produced by the creative people attached to different accounts. The morning, though strange and unfamiliar, hummed along and she was startled when people started wandering off and she realized it was lunch time. 'There's a staff restaurant,' Jessica told her. 'Subsidized, so it's not expensive, but if that doesn't appeal we're knee-deep in pubs round here. I'm meeting my sister for lunch, or I'd offer to introduce you,' she added kindly. 'I'm going to the caff,' Ian interjected laconically. 'Deadlines loom. Come with me if you like.'

Ian looked underfed; his cheekbones were prominent and his clothes seemed to hang on him. Kate was astonished, therefore, to see him tuck into minestrone soup, submerged under a heap of parmesan cheese, bread rolls, roast beef and mounds of potatoes, and a steamed jam sponge pudding, followed by cheese and biscuits, all washed down with the best part of a bottle of red wine. His appetite was infectious, and she ate her pallid chicken salad with gusto. During mouthfuls he kept up a running commentary on the people in the room, what they did in the agency, offering rumours and speculation about their love life in a good-humoured, unmalicious way. Kate was grateful that she didn't need to respond or cope with questions about her past agency experience, although he did ask once what art college she had gone to.

Fortunately just then a colleague lounged over and the two men discussed the maladroit handling of an account which the agency had apparently failed to win. Ian introduced them identifying her as 'our new colleague, Kate Cosgrove – Peter Withers, Media Buyer' and Kate was aware of a physically appraising look which changed to polite indifference as he realized that she was not his normal flirtatious fare. 'Married housewife, two children, C1' she could almost hear him labelling her, still amused at the way the audience for a product was categorized on the work sheets she'd read that morning, when Phillip had initiated her into the mysteries of target groups and audience segmentation. The class division was decided by the head of the household's income, 'which puts me firmly into the C group,' Kate had decided. But it was irritating, just the same, to be dismissed so rapidly by Peter Withers.

Like the morning, the afternoon simply disappeared, and she was surprised to see that some time after six o'clock people seemed to fade away as imperceptibly as they had arrived. Phillip, his chestnut hair cut so eccentrically that he looked like a moulting pony, was concentrating deeply and merely grunted at the casual 'good nights' aimed vaguely in his direction. Jessica shuffled her work together and announced to no-one in particular that that was as far as she could usefully get tonight; she struggled into a strange, trailing arty garment made of layers of loose multi-coloured knitting, cramming a bright yellow beret over her springy grey curls. She loomed over Kate's desk. 'There's no need for you to stay late; wait until we've got a panic on and something has to be finished no matter what,' she said kindly. 'Which way do you go home?'

'I'll get a bus in Piccadilly for Fulham,' Kate said. 'It goes nearly all the way.'

'Well, I'll walk over with you – I get the tube at Green Park.'

She waited while Kate shrugged into her coat after a questioning glance at Phillip. Phillip's eyes were screwed in thought, his mouth pursed, and his arms tangled across his narrow chest as he tucked his hands into his armpits to keep them from twisting into yet another shape, so he was quite oblivious. Jessica touched her arm, inclined her head to the door, and plodded ahead to the ground floor reception area. Like the Victorian hat stand, Jessica didn't seem to belong in this smart environment, but Kate had been impressed by the sophistication in some of the visuals she'd given her to work from. She was clearly talented.

'Don't expect an office routine from Phillip. There's no

such thing in his book. Jobs come in and jobs go out and as long as we keep to the deadlines on the work sheets he doesn't fuss. But under that seemingly vague manner there's a sharp awareness, and he is amazing at knowing what's wanted, who can deliver it, and perhaps more importantly, how to brief people clearly. There's never anything ambiguous about Phillip's instructions,' she said with a chuckle.

Outside, the day still lingered in a mauve twilight, which with the office lights shining through the trees made Berkeley Square look romantically beautiful. She mentioned it, half-embarrassed; Jessica shot her a sharp, humorous glance. 'Wait until you have to trudge through rain or worse, slush, with taxis doing their best to drown you, and it'll lose some of its glamour. It's a long time since I've been starry-eyed about London. I hate it now – it's crowded, indifferent, ugly. We haven't put up one decent new building in my lifetime, in my view.'

Kate was silent, trying to think of some example to offer in defence of modern architects, but couldn't come up with one she could argue about with passion. 'I quite like the Economist building,' she said at last weakly.

'At least it's tucked away and has some pleasing form and proportion,' Jessica agreed. 'But it doesn't lift my heart very much – and that's what important buildings should do.'

'You sound knowledgeable about architecture,' Kate observed.

'I should do. My father was an architect and I married one.'

'Oh . . .' Kate laughed. 'That explains a lot. I hope he can take what you say about new buildings.'

'He's dead.' Jessica was matter-of-fact. 'He didn't do much in Britain. He found that he could work abroad without what he called bourgeois committees cramping his vision.'

'I'm sorry,' Kate was subdued.

'Oh, it was a long time ago. He was killed on a site when our little one was only four. It was harder on the children, in a way. He'd been such a good father, despite being away a lot. I was lucky to have the means of earning a living. Frank wasn't old enough to have made his fortune, and he'd just started his own practice so there wasn't a lot of cash around.' It was all said in such an even, unemotional voice that Kate found it impossible – even unnecessary – to make the usual sympathetic noises. This woman was too gruffly independent for that. And yet she sensed in her a need to talk.

'I'm just learning to be alone myself, to earn my own living,' Kate said shyly. 'My husband has left me for someone else, so I'm back to square one, in a way, except that I have two teenage children.'

'Then, my dear, don't shut yourself away from life. That's what I did, and I regret it now,' Jessica's voice was brisk. 'I was so shattered by the loss of Frank that I didn't want anyone. I think that was a mistake. It was bad for the children and bad for me. Force yourself to go out, to keep friends, and make friends even if it's an effort to begin with. Living only for yourself and your children makes you too inward-looking – you become a little eccentric, and a worry to your children. They start to feel responsible for you and worry if they go out and leave you alone.' She smiled her sweet smile at Kate. 'And one talks too much when there's a captive audience. I'm so sorry – your first day, too. Never mind. We separate here – I hope you don't have to wait too long for your bus.' She gave a large sweeping wave, tangling her knitted garment with her bag, the assortment of plastic carriers and the umbrella she was clutching, and scuttled down the entrance to the tube.

Kate jolted slowly home on the crowded bus, welcoming the way the anonymous, crowded vehicle swallowed her up, giving her a chance to sort out her impressions. It had not been as nerve-racking or as fearsome as she had imagined. In fact she was already looking forward to tomorrow.

Chapter Twenty-Two

When Kate arrived home Flip had been and given Jeremy his coaching. He was working contentedly in the dining room and Charlotte was in the kitchen, reading a book and keeping an eye on a set of saucepans bubbling gently away.

'Oh good, you've done some potatoes,' Kate said gratefully. 'And what's this? Apple crumble!'

'I thought you'd be too tired to want to bother,' Charlotte said self-consciously. 'Fresh fruit isn't the thing for such a cold day. I looked up crumble in one of your books – it's easy-peasy.' She peered into the oven. 'I think it's going to be done before the potatoes. How long are they supposed to take? I put them on ages ago.'

Kate kissed her. 'You're a thoughtful little darling – what a treat!'

Over supper, a beef casserole Kate had prepared the day before, with frozen peas, which, not to be outdone by Charlotte, Jeremy had insisted *he* cooked, Kate told them about her day at the agency.

'So they didn't throw you out,' Charlotte commented. 'I didn't think they would,' she said knowingly. 'Miss Bristow said she thought your drawings were terrific. She didn't stay long tonight. I suppose she was going on to another bash. Oh and Nick called – he wanted to know how you'd got on. I think he thought you'd be home before this. And' – she went a surprising pink – 'he asked me if I'd like to go to the theatre with him on Friday, to see Eileen Atkins in *St Joan*. He says he thinks she's one of the best actresses we have, and not used nearly enough. Can I? I won't have school the next day.'

Kate looked surprised. 'Of course. How nice of him.'

'He said that if I was really going to be an actress I should use every opportunity to see the good people live, on stage, that you learn more from theatre than watching film,' she said eagerly.

'He's probably right, but theatre tickets are expensive, and we're not going to have a lot of cash.' She felt her irritation with Nick rise again. She wanted to steer Charlotte off the theatre, not encourage her. He had no right to ask Charlotte out without checking with her first, she thought, with an exasperation she made an effort to conceal.

'Well, if Nick's taking me it won't cost anything, will it?' Charlotte pointed out.

'No, but you can't count on invitations from him very often. I'm going to have to work to a budget.' She struggled to sound mild and reasonable. 'Jeremy can help me plan it, can't you? Miss Bristow said you were doing splendidly with your maths now, and you've got that nice calculator too.' Jeremy looked pleased and owlish.

The children helped her clear up the kitchen and stack the dishwasher, something they'd never done before, and then they settled down to some television before bedtime. Apart from her spurt of annoyance over Nick, the evening had been gratifyingly peaceful and companionable.

After Charlotte and Jeremy had gone to bed Nick rang again. 'I hope it is not too late. I rang earlier – I expect Charlotte told you. But then I had to go out to dinner so this is my first chance to find out how it all went.'

Rather crisply, Kate gave him an account of the day. 'Well, I'm glad it wasn't too terrifying. By this time tomorrow you'll probably feel like an old hand. By the way, do you mind if I take Charlotte to the Old Vic on Friday? She said she hasn't seen much professional theatre, and it's one of my passions.'

'No, of course not.' It was slightly odd, surely, that he had not included her? 'But I'm not sure if she should be encouraged too much. I think she ought to go to university first. She may very well not be good enough to earn a living as an actress – there's so much competition for so little work, apparently. If she had some kind of useful degree she'd have something to fall back on.' She was surprised at her new vehemence.

'I'm sure that's sound, but letting her loose on the theatre will help her to gauge her own talents a bit. It would be cruel to thwart her and then find that she's another Vanessa Redgrave. Going to the theatre now and then won't prevent her getting a university place will it? – on the contrary.'

'I suppose not.' Kate couldn't think why she felt so nettled. 'Anyway it's very kind of you,' she added politely. 'I'm sure she'll love it.'

When he'd rung off she picked up the telephone and called Tom. She felt too wound-up for bed, and she wanted to hear how Tom had fared at his conference. He sounded so very tired that Kate said anxiously, 'Were you asleep? Have I disturbed you?'

'No, Katie, no. There's just so much to do. One of the scientists posed a new hypothesis to explain the results we were getting, and though I think we've got it right, we're having to go through all the processes again just to make sure the theory is watertight. And the bloody newspapers keep bothering me. Someone at the conference must have talked and they're badgering us for information. Publicity is the last thing we want at this stage.'

'Change your telephone number,' she suggested.

'Katie, you don't know the press. That would make it worse!'

'Can't you work from somewhere else, somewhere secret?'

'No – we have all the facilities here. No, Katie, don't worry. It's just tiresome for the moment but it will blow over. I'm glad the job went well, anyway. I thought of you. Come up here whenever you feel like a break. You don't know Edinburgh – it's splendid.'

'Hah, you just want a rest from those fattening take-aways,' Kate said jokingly. 'But I may take you up on that one weekend when the children are with Geoffrey.' She wasn't naïve enough to believe that every weekend would be as busy as the last.

Chapter Twenty-Three

At the end of the month, when Kate received her first salary cheque, she was absurdly pleased. It was the first money she had ever earned and she felt that the payslip statement, listing her National Insurance number and tax deductions, was her admission ticket to the grown-up world. Ridiculously, she felt she was at last a citizen. She telephoned Flip. 'Come and have dinner with us. I want to celebrate.'

She flashed the cheque at the children when she got home laden with plunder from a lunchtime dash to Selfridge's food hall – smoked salmon, some noisettes of lamb, a large meringue gateau, chiefly for Jeremy, fruit and cheeses. They'd been so good during these last weeks, Charlotte especially, who had invariably laid the table or started the supper. The children's relationship with her had changed. There was almost an adult companionship between the three of them, and Kate was amused and impressed at the way Charlotte had assumed supervision of Jeremy's prep.

He, too, seemed more confident, delighted that she couldn't open a wine bottle without splitting the cork, and he could, and had self-importantly taken charge when she'd wanted a glass of wine with supper. Once, he'd had to replace a fuse in the socket when the electric kettle had burned dry. When he'd come home from school and found the supply of milk running low and no fresh bread, he'd taken himself off to the little Indian supermarket on the corner and bought what he called 'the basics', clearly proud of his own resourcefulness and 'forward-planning' as he explained to Kate. Even Charlotte had forgotten to be the superior older sister and had said, 'Oh shit, I should have remembered – I saw that we were nearly out this morning.'

Kate wondered at their smooth assumption of responsibility. No-one had helped her much before. Ever since the children were born Mrs Shepherd had come in to clean, and occasionally babysit, but Kate had had to teach herself how to cook and run a household. At Cheevers, there had always been people to run the place. The only thing she *could* have learned from her mother was how to handle relics carefully. Yet here were her children capably sharing with her the chores which they seemed to know how to do by osmosis.

Geoffrey didn't ask for them every weekend, and when he didn't, they came with her on Saturday mornings to do a marathon shop. Jeremy, motivated no doubt by anxious self-interest about the supply for his appetite, usually checked the state of larder and refrigerator. Charlotte, since her first attempt at apple crumble, had watched Kate carefully as she made casseroles and piles of pancakes for the freezer, and she often came forward with 'Let me, I can do that,' and had even started to assume little cooking jobs on her own.

'Let's telephone to see if Nick is free,' Charlotte suggested when Kate said she'd invited Flip to supper. Since their theatre outing she had assumed something of a proprietorial air over Nick. He'd telephoned once or twice, and when Charlotte had answered the phone first, she had carried on a long conversation before reluctantly handing the receiver to Kate.

'Do you think he'd get on with Flip?' Kate asked dubiously.

'Flip – I mustn't get into the habit or I'll call her that at school – Flip can get on with anyone. She doesn't care if people like her or not, so she doesn't try too hard to charm them.'

Kate stared. 'Where did you learn all this psychology?'

'Moth-er!' Charlotte sighed deeply. 'I'm hardly the Lady of Shalott. I do have friends at school. It's not too hard to work out why some people are confident, or popular or whatever.'

Kate gave way. 'Well, phone him if you like, but I expect he's away or busy. It's rather short notice.'

She couldn't understand her own ambivalence towards Nick, when it was through him she'd got the job. He had phoned occasionally, not merely to ask how things were going, but also to urge her to keep up her painting. A couple of times he had asked her to lunch with him and visit his gallery, but on one occasion she had already arranged to lunch with Ian, and another she'd had some vital shopping to do. She did paint, at the weekends, solidly, determinedly, whether the children were about or not, but it was a painful process; she couldn't go into her little room without remembering Geoffrey, which refreshed her feelings of failure, and she couldn't see where she was going with the work itself. She struggled and persevered, producing quite fierce abstracts that sometimes left her feeling drained, often depressed, and dissatisfied, but it was something she didn't want to share with anyone. The painting revealed too much of her secret self, a self that she had yet to come to terms with. In any case, the children seemed to regard her painting as little more than a rather boring hobby that served to relieve them of worrying about her, but Nick, she knew, would bully her. She feared that he would probe her meanings, criticize and encourage, and she was not ready for that. It would be like undressing in public.

Charlotte returned to the kitchen to report that Nick was

not only free but would be delighted to come. Kate mentally shrugged and congratulated herself on having bought what would have been too much for four. Flip, sleek in a lime green jump suit with matching hair and eyes, arrived early, ready to help and chat. They were comfortable friends now and Kate laughed at her. 'That's a bit splendid for a family supper party, isn't it?'

'Oh I thought we'd go on to a club afterward – you said you wanted to celebrate,' drawled Flip. 'You don't have to work tomorrow – it's Saturday. I think you've been the dedicated working mother for long enough. Every time I've asked you out lately you've refused.'

'I know, but by the time I get home I'm really tired. I don't think I've got into my stride yet – I'm still terrified that they won't want me after another two months, and I guess I try too hard. At least Jessica says so.' She smiled apologetically. 'You'll have to tell me the secret of your stamina. By the time we've had our evening meal and watched the news I'm all too ready for bed.'

'I'm *always* ready for bed,' agreed Flip, 'as long as there's someone worthwhile in it. *That's* what gives me energy – sex.' She guffawed. 'Try it!'

'Try what?' Charlotte asked as she wandered in.

'A little night-life. I'm trying to get your mother to come out with me. What about you?' She peered curiously at Charlotte. 'Haven't you any boyfriends?'

Charlotte gave a self-conscious glance at Kate. 'A few – just friends.' She was saved from further questions by the doorbell.

'Don't rush her,' Kate said. 'She has plenty of time. And she's been marvellous during this past month helping me. In fact, now you mention it perhaps I've taken for granted too much that she'll always be home with Jeremy. Perhaps she's wanted to go out and hasn't liked to leave me.'

'Could be,' Flip shrugged non-committally. 'Shall I take

these plates in? Is there any lemon for the smoked salmon?' She strode familiarly into the dining-room balancing plates of smoked salmon. 'Hi,' Kate heard her greeting Nick. 'I'm Flip Bristow, friend of the family.'

When Kate went in with the lemons, Flip had moved into the sitting-room where she was perched on the arm of a chair, drink in hand, chatting unselfconsciously to Nick. Jeremy was mixing a dry Martini under Nick's apprehensive eye. 'A bit more ice, old chap, and perhaps a little more gin – I think the martini might be a touch overwhelming, but I hope your mother's going to help me out. There's enough there for ten cocktails, at a guess.'

Kate took a glass. 'Thanks, darling.' She sipped tentatively. 'Beautifully dry. You could always be a barman.'

'He's going to be an astronaut,' Flip offered, with a smile at Jeremy. 'His maths are great. What does your so-called maths master Peters say now?'

Jeremy blushed with pleasure and mimicked his teacher. 'Well, Cosgrove, a little understanding has penetrated your grey matter at last, I see. I hope we'll keep it up. Just a matter of concentration.' He did his teacher's quavery voice brilliantly.

'Just a matter of understanding, indeed!' Flip muttered indignantly. 'The fool simply can't teach.'

Nick handed Kate a bouquet of flowers with a slight, foreign bow. 'They're drooping a bit because I had to buy them from a stall holder – all the shops were shut,' he said apologetically. 'Just to say well done! You survived and, I hear,' he smiled at Charlotte, including her, 'you have a cheque to prove it.'

'My very very first one.' Kate beamed.

'It must be terrible to have to live off a husband,' Flip observed.

'Why? Do you think a man regards supporting a wife as a charity donation?' Nick's voice was neutral.

'Yep.' Flip was emphatic. 'A tax-deductible charity. He'd have to pay more for a cook/housekeeper/nanny/girlfriend, which, as we all know, are a wife's various roles. She's *his* wife, it's *his* house, they're *his* children, simply because *he* pays the bills. Talk to most of the women who have spent their lives bringing up children and running a home, letting what saleable skills and experience they once had atrophy, and see how much the fair-minded husband offers them *voluntarily* when he runs off with a young blonde and the wife's left with nothing but low-paid employment on offer – strictly what's legally enforced my friend, and not even that if he's hired a smart lawyer.'

Nick sipped his martini and looked coolly at her without speaking. 'One third of all marriages end in divorce, you know,' Flip added, glowering at him.

'That means that two-thirds don't,' he said cheerfully. 'And as I understand it, a large proportion of divorced couples remarry. Marriage must have *something* going for it.' He turned to Charlotte, changing the subject. 'How's the play going? Am I allowed to come? Kate, may I come with you? I think *Antigone* is a very brave choice.'

Kate got up. 'That's what Flip thought at first, but she knows Miss Cundell's work and thinks she'll pull it off. You think so too, don't you darling?' She turned to Charlotte. 'But let's go and eat. Lamb is so difficult to time and I'm starving.' She'd been right – Flip and Nick would not get along.

In fact the little supper celebration was a success, with Nick and Flip proving to each other how urbane and civilized they could be. At the end of the meal they all trooped into the little kitchen to stack the dishwasher and clear up among much chat and banter, and then Flip said, 'Well, are we going on somewhere?'

Kate shook her head. 'I can't. I haven't asked Mrs Shepherd to come in.'

'Mum!' Jeremy was indignant. 'We don't need Mrs Shepherd – we're old enough now to be left alone.'

'Of course,' Nick broke in. 'Aren't they on their own before you get back from work – what difference does a few hours later make?'

'You're outvoted,' Flip decided for her. 'Get your coat. Are you coming?' she turned to Nick, her eyes bright with challenge.

'Am I invited?' he returned.

'I'm not sure that the venue I have in mind is your scene.' Flip's chin lifted.

'Then there's only one way to find out,' Nick said, and grinned at her. 'Where are we going? I'll try to follow your car but I suspect you live dangerously – I'd better have the address.'

Kate couldn't believe it. Trying to imagine Nick in a jazz club or on a dance floor was beyond her. 'Are you sure?' she said uncertainly.

'No, but I'm always ready for a new experience,' he said cheerfully, shook hands with Jeremy, kissed Charlotte, and followed Flip through the front door. Kate lifted her shoulders at the children. 'I have a feeling I'm going to regret this. You won't stay up too long, will you?' She kissed them and went after the others, getting in Nick's car.

Flip wove crazily through the late evening traffic in her little black Golf. 'As I thought,' Nick muttered. 'I'm not going to keep up with that lunatic – I'm too young to die. Do you know where this place is?'

'Was it Mickey-Mike's? I didn't hear what she said.'

'No, Annabel's, in Berkeley Square. I thought that was rather smart.'

'I don't know – I've never been. But I certainly know where Berkeley Square is.'

'Well, it has four sides – which one do you suppose? Or shall we just hope to spot a flash of chartreuse between car and dungeon?'

'Yes, I think Flip will be difficult to miss if we're not too far behind.' In fact Flip was shunting angrily back and forth trying to park in an impossibly small space when Nick drove up and slid easily into a space just vacated by an enormous grey Bentley. 'Bastard,' she yelled through a fiercely wound-down window. Nick lifted an eyebrow.

'What's wrong with that?' He pointed to another space a few yards in front of Flip which she hadn't noticed. 'Bastard again.' They waited on the pavement as with protesting screeches from the engine and worrying spins from the tyres, she thrust her car into the farther space. 'I'll wipe that superior grin off your face when I get you on the floor,' Flip assured him as she joined them.

Annabel's was very different from Mickey-Mike's. There was a casual elegance about the place, and not so much noise. Flip immediately greeted a group in a small alcove and shepherded Kate and Nick in. 'Billy,' she said, greeting a small redheaded woman in a black sequinned petticoat dress, 'and Pat, Rupert, Tom, Jerry, Jane – oh you'll have to introduce yourselves . . . these are Nick and Kate.' She slumped into a chair at their table and waved familiarly to a waiter to bring more chairs. The well-dressed group smiled indulgently. 'I'm the one called Pat,' a wide-shouldered man of medium height said and smiled at Kate. 'Can I get you a drink? We're on a rather good Sancerre.'

'Lovely.' Kate smiled, her eyes raking the dance floor in case Jon was somewhere there. She had not seen or heard from him for a week or two. Jane, wearing a brown silk jersey dress, bare-topped except for a thin beaded halter collar said, 'I can tell you didn't drive here with Flip, you look far too serene.' Kate laughed. 'No, not since the last time I went out with her. I'm much wiser now.'

It was warming the way the group opened up and gathered them in, shifting into a new, amiable pattern of gossip and chat. She saw Nick talking easily on the other side of the table to the redhead, and Flip arguing fiercely with the one Kate took to be Rupert. She sipped her wine, listening to Jane and Pat discussing the film they'd seen earlier that evening.

'Let's dance.' Rupert took her hand. 'It's as good a way to get to know you as any.' The floor was tiny and crowded but Kate felt more confident than she had at the first club. She'd come a long way in a short time. Then she caught her breath, realizing with a lurch of panic that Geoffrey was a few feet away, dancing closely with Greta Lanson.

For a minute the room threatened to suffocate her, she wanted to rush out, go home, anywhere away from the stark reality of the two of them glued together, moving softly, ignoring the frenetic bopping around them. Geoffrey looked blissful; Greta, as usual, ravishing, conscious of but indifferent to the surreptitious looks they were attracting as people recognized her. Kate took a deep breath and steadied herself. 'Hello,' she said calmly to Geoffrey, and nodded coolly at Greta.

Rupert was gyrating rhythmically in front of her; she forced her body to relax and follow suit. 'Wasn't that Greta Lanson?' Rupert asked with interest. 'Do you know her?'

'Very slightly,' Kate said. 'I know her partner better. He's my husband. At the present moment, anyway.'

Rupert stared. 'That's cool. Really cool.' Aware that Geoffrey might be watching, Kate deliberately threw herself into matching Rupert's enthusiastic dancing. If Geoffrey had imagined her as a pathetic abandoned housewife he would have to revise his ideas.

* * *

The next day Kate's recollections of the evening were distinctly hazy. She remembered with amazement Nick's beautiful dancing, and the way he and Flip had had the floor almost to themselves as the band switched from rock to a fast Charleston. At the end, the people watching had burst into spontaneous applause; it had been a scene from an old-fashioned Hollywood musical, as laughing breathlessly and mopping his face, Nick had led an astounded Flip back to the table. She remembered seeing the surprised look on the face of Peter Withers, the media buyer she'd met with Ian on her first day at work, as he'd come in with a crowd, clutching an excitably giggling blonde. He had come up to her with a show of great friendliness, an evaluating eye on her party.

'I'm here with a group from the National Magazine Company,' he'd said stuffily. 'We've had a presentation from them for a new magazine. Believe it or not, I'm here purely for business.' Kate tipped her head back, looking up at him with a cool smile.

'I'm here purely for pleasure,' she'd said, and got up to dance with Pat or Tom or somebody – it hardly mattered who. And she remembered, not without a wave of shame, the warm ending in Rupert's bed in a small flat somewhere in Covent Garden. She'd made love with him hungrily, surprised that he too, like Jon, but in a different way, could produce that sensuous thrill of sexual excitement. But afterwards, stumbling into a minicab at 5 a.m., she had felt soiled, meeting the driver's over-familiar, knowing glance in the driving mirror.

She bathed and dressed – it hadn't seemed worth going to bed – and pottered uselessly in the kitchen waiting for the children to wake. They were going to Geoffrey for the weekend again. Charlotte had told her they were all going to stay in a smart hotel in Berkshire. Kate had been furious, knowing the fight her solicitor was having with Geoffrey over arranging a proper allowance for the children. He had so far refused to pay, arguing that the children's education was paid for by the trust fund and that he had 'allowed Lady Kate to keep the house.' Kate had yelped aloud in rage over that 'allowed' when James Bennett read the letter to her. Bennett had replied, with his usual imperturbability, that he thought he could get Mr Cosgrove to 'see reason', that he was legally bound to support his children and that that did not stop at school fees. Indeed, he went on, Mr Cosgrove could be made to give Kate a sizeable allowance, particularly if she didn't work, he had emphasized, bearing in mind Mr Cosgrove's own large salary. But so far the arguments had produced little more than a flurry of lawyer's letters. Mr Bennett told her not to worry about the bank. 'Arrange a personal loan, rather than a bank overdraft,' he'd advised. 'In the end, Mr Cosgrove will find *he* has to pay the interest, not you, and the longer this exchange of letters goes on without result, the higher his legal costs will be,' he'd concluded with an air of satisfaction.

Geoffrey certainly didn't seem to be short of spending money, Kate thought. James Bennett had let Geoffrey's solicitor's know that there wasn't the slightest prospect of Kate's giving up the house. 'Lord Scott was insistent that the deeds of the house were to be in Lady Kate's name, clearly wishing it to be her security for the future,' he wrote sternly. 'My client is not asking for money for herself, but the two children of the marriage must be properly provided for.'

Geoffrey had been livid and had attempted to harangue Kate on the telephone, but she'd kept her voice even and said firmly that her solicitor had told her they must not communicate directly until the legal problems had been sorted out. 'That's what we're here for,' an unsmiling James Bennett had told Kate. 'You've changed, Kate –

you've become hard and selfish,' Geoffrey had said, almost snarling. 'Probably,' Kate had agreed imperturbably and put the phone down.

Now Kate was glad the children were going away. She didn't want to meet Charlotte's questioning look or respond to her curiosity about the evening out until she'd pulled herself together. She made a pot of coffee and drank it, steaming and fragrant, as she waited for the thumps overhead and noise of rows over the bathroom to signal the children's arousal. She had no idea what had happened to Flip, or to Nick or to anyone else in the party. She remembered giving the woman Billy her telephone number, as she'd said she was giving a party and wanted Kate to come. She did remember them all swelling out on to the pavement outside Annabel's, laughing and shouting and trying to arrange who was going in whose car. She had found herself bundled into a low, rather shabby red sports car, with Rupert overflowing untidily in the driving seat. He hadn't asked her where she was going, merely driven straight off to his flat, smiling and humming under his breath. She wondered guiltily now if she was behaving like a directionless eighteen-year-old, going heedlessly wherever she was pulled or pushed.

Chapter Twenty-Four

'You're early,' Charlotte said as she entered the kitchen. She looked so scrubbed and young that Kate felt even more like second-hand goods.

'Mmmm.' She didn't want to admit that she hadn't been to bed. 'If Jeremy's nearly ready I'll make some scrambled eggs.'

'Did you have a good time? Did Nick enjoy himself?'

Nick. She'd forgotten about him. What happened to him? She hadn't seen him go, but then she hadn't really noticed much beyond the leathery interior of Rupert's TR6.

'Much to my surprise he dances very well. He and Flip gave an exhibition of the Charleston and everybody applauded.'

'I *thought* he would be a good dancer,' Charlotte said. 'He's very quick and light on his feet even though he *is* rather stocky. If he's coming to *Antigone* next week I'll have to have the money for three tickets on Monday. I suppose Jeremy will want to come, but he won't enjoy it. Nor shall I.' She fidgeted, embarrassed. 'You won't mind if I ask Dad? I suppose I ought to. There are three performances – you won't have to be at the same one.' She looked at Kate, trying to assess how upset she would be.

'As a matter of fact I saw him last night,' said Kate calmly. 'He was at Annabel's too.'

Charlotte gasped. 'What did you do? What did you say?' she asked fearfully.

'I said "Hello" and went on dancing. I didn't see them again so they must have left soon after.'

Charlotte looked admiringly at her mother. 'I hope you were dancing with some devastating man to make Dad jealous,' she burst out.

'Well, reasonably devastating,' Kate said, thinking of Rupert later, naked, his enthusiastic appetite for energetic sex leaving her limp, like an exhausted acrobat. 'But as your father was with Miss Lanson, I think most eyes were on her. She's quite stunning, and reasonably famous now.'

'Dad's a short-sighted shit,' Charlotte said hotly. 'I'll never forgive him.'

Jeremy wandered in, his hair wet, his eyes still blank from sleep.

'What are you getting worked up about now?' he asked gulping his orange juice. 'You're always making speeches.'

'Scrambled eggs?' Kate cut in. 'It's nice to have time for a proper breakfast isn't it? Sometimes I think it's my favourite meal.'

It was a relief when they both went out to the car. Geoffrey didn't come in to collect them, but merely hooted impatiently at the gate.

Kate went hesitantly into her boxroom and stared glumly at her new canvas. It was all wrong. She didn't think she could paint today. She felt distaste for herself, and the sense of drifting enveloped her again. She roamed aimlessly round the silent, empty house, peering in at the children's rooms, looking at her own smooth bed, remembering her last sight of the rumpled sheets and duvet of Rupert's bed. She went downstairs again and was glad of the diversion of the post scattered on the floor.

She seized joyfully on a letter with an American stamp. It was from Esme.

'Don't faint, but I'm coming back on Concorde,' Esme had scrawled at the foot of the third page of thin airmail paper covered in her angular writing. 'I'll be back on November 7. See you soon.'

November 7? But that was today! She jumped up. A dose of Esme's good sense and warm affection was just what she needed.

Yes, a breezy voice told her on the telephone, indeed there was a Concorde arrival on a Saturday. It would touch down at 18.10. She suddenly felt energized. She'd meet Esme at the airport and surprise her – perhaps they could have supper together.

The plane was on time. Esme, looking small but incredibly chic in an uncreased black and white dogtooth check suit and bright red shirt, was stunned to see Kate smiling at the barrier. Her eyes widened and her chin wobbled with emotion. 'Darling Kate, how lovely, I didn't expect to be met, how are you?' Laughing and hugging, they made their way to Kate's car.

'Do you feel tired? Too tired to have supper with me?' Kate demanded once they'd impatiently negotiated the exit from the car-park. 'I've missed you so *much*. Do you realize you've been away four months?' she accused.

'Is that all? It feels like four years! What a foreign country America is – I'm more at home in countries where I can't speak the language. But their weather is an improvement on this,' she commented, looking at the grey drizzle through the windscreen. 'No, of course I'm not tired – Concorde is *bliss*. But perhaps I'm a bit tight.'

They went to a cheap Italian restaurant in Putney, near Esme's flat, exchanging news over a stringy, indifferently cooked veal escalope. Kate saw that Esme was trying to conceal her grim satisfaction at the break-up of her marriage. 'Go on, enjoy having been right all along,' she teased. 'It can't upset me now.' Esme shook her head. 'It's no fun being right. I want you to be happy, you know that. I wish it had worked out.' Later, as they sipped bitter coffee that had clearly been kept simmering a long time,

Kate asked: 'Why didn't you suggest to my parents that I go to school? I have no talents, no experience, no education, and now I've got to earn my living. Goodness knows whether I'll survive my trial period.'

Esme looked at her. 'You *have* talent, you *are* educated, though not in a formal way – you have a good mind and you've always read a lot. And I *did* suggest that you be sent to school. Your father always said "Right, talk to Lady Scott," and your mother always said "Mmmmm".' They laughed, but Esme was immediately serious again. 'But you were such a fearful and nervous little thing, I did feel that to send you off like that could have been cruel. I know how pitiless school can be, remember – I did teach in a prep school. I weighed up your parents' indifference with your need for someone to give you emotional support, and I suppose you won.' She looked down at her lap. Kate put a hand over hers.

'It wasn't your fault. But I feel at such a loss now. I know nothing about the world of work and nothing, it seems, about men either.'

'Neither did I when I came to work for your parents during my summer hol – a cheap way of getting abroad I thought at the time. *I* had to earn a real living again when you married – my teaching skills had rusted and, in any case, I'd never enjoyed it much; and during the time I lived with you there was certainly no opportunity for men friends.' Kate stared at her. Wrapped in her own preoccupations, she hadn't given any thought to the fact that Esme might have had to make a fresh start. 'What did you do?' she asked curiously.

'I made a list of my assets – a very short list it turned out to be,' she said humorously. 'And I hawked them around. I was lucky in that those jokey drawings I used to do, mostly to amuse you, caught the eye of the marketing director of this card company, and that was it.'

'But what about *men*?' Kate persisted.

Esme looked uncomfortable. 'Well, it's a bit silly, really. I'm actually getting married. I mean, at my age! But he's very nice. A widower with four children and seven grandchildren and well . . .' She looked at Kate helplessly. 'It seemed like a good idea.'

Kate was shocked. 'When – and – where did you meet him?' She tried to sound normal.

'In the States. He runs a big store in Chicago.'

'Does that mean you're going to live there?' she demanded.

'Yes. Shortly.'

Kate felt a black horror envelop her. She would have no one. Losing Esme was far more of a shock than separating from Geoffrey. She realized how much she had counted on being able to lean on Esme again, having her reassurance that everything would be all right, enjoying the warm comfort of her constant, uncritical presence. She felt let down and angry. It wasn't fair. Tears made crazy patterns of the red check tablecloth and the cheap candle guttering dismally in the ubiquitous Chianti bottle.

'I'm going to sell the flat but keep the cottage,' Esme continued. A little ruefully, she added, 'Chicago isn't the prettiest place in which to end one's days.' At Kate's stricken face, she said, 'Kate, you don't need me now. Except as a friend. We are all much stronger than we realize. When you married Geoffrey I thought it was the end of my world – and it was in a way – one world anyway. But it was the beginning of another. And you'll find that it will be the same for you. Without me you've found yourself a job, you've made new friends; if I'd been here that might not have happened.'

'Come on,' she said as Kate kept her head down and didn't reply. 'We both need some sleep. What time did you get to bed last night? You look dreadful.' Kate remembered suddenly that she hadn't been to bed. She wanted to shout and scream and protest – Esme *mustn't* let her down like this. She couldn't believe that the neat, small figure leading the way so determinedly out of the restaurant, after settling the bill firmly and without fuss, was the same kind, indulgent woman who had been a surrogate mother in her bleak childhood. She seemed so inflexible now, as if she were oblivious of Kate's loneliness and need.

Driving home after dropping Esme in Putney, Kate wept. It was all so unfair; she felt abandoned. The house seemed very dark and empty. She heated some milk and sipped it in bed, feeling bereft and friendless. She didn't want to be alone. She turned like a child into her pillow to cry again. Next morning, she was quite cross when she realized she had slept soundly after all, instead of tossing distractedly throughout the night as she'd been sure she would.

Sunday was again grey with rain. Kate couldn't stay in the house, and drove to the Tate. She wanted to be with people, but she couldn't bring herself to ring anyone. She felt distinctly ashamed of her infantile behaviour now that she had had some sleep, but she wasn't quite ready to ring Esme and apologize. She felt resentful still; it was very difficult to accept that she no longer had first claim on Esme's time and affection. She shied away from the thought that it had never occurred to her to consider what Esme would do when Kate had married. Esme, except for the past four months, had always been *there*.

The Tate was a good choice. There were plenty of tourists milling about, lots of earnest students trying to impress one another, some families, and the usual sprinkling of elderly people on their own. Kate went straight to the modern section, rambling slowly through the galleries housing the Picassos, feeling peaceful again as she stood before Bonnard's 'Girl Bathing' and Vuillard's 'La Baignade'. She wished she could have known some of these painters, learned how *they* grappled with transferring the colours and visions in their mind on to their canvasses. Perhaps they too had despaired and suffered frustration over the beautifully realized pictures now hanging here. Think of how many times Cezanne had painted Mont St Victoire!

She toyed with the idea of eating out but a lonely meal seemed a bleak prospect. At least at home she could light a fire to dispel the gloom, read the Sundays over her lunch. She drove back in a much more cheerful frame of mind and fixed herself a mushroom omelette. Reading, she drank the best of a bottle of wine without noticing it until, getting up to put her plate in the sink, she staggered slightly, and realized that she was a little tight.

From habit, she went into her boxroom, unenthusiastically picked up a brush and made one or two desultory dabs at the canvas. Suddenly, she felt the whole room vibrating with colour and energy. The aloneness was positive. She felt cut free. Her mind was suddenly clear of doubts, and of the distaste she had felt for herself earlier. She seemed to be surrounded by shapes and patterns and light, and all she could think of was how to capture it in paint. She could feel a kind of throbbing fury inside her, driving her on.

She barely looked up when the children appeared, standing in the doorway in amazement. 'Didn't you hear us?' Charlotte asked.

'No. I can't stop now. I'll be with you soon.' She went on painting frantically. Charlotte looked surprised and not a little peeved, and shut the door sharply. Her mother had never shown such indifference to their presence. It was nearly seven before she realized that the astonishing charge of energy had gone, and she had begun to paint mechanically. She felt drained and tired, and threw her brush down and went out to the children.

'Hello, darlings. I'm sorry I didn't notice you come home. I was too absorbed to stop.' Jeremy was watching television and Charlotte was reading. They both turned and gazed at her in injured bafflement. 'You look different,' Jeremy said accusingly.

'How?'

'I don't know, but *different*.'

Kate gave a slight shrug. 'Do you want anything to eat?'

'We made some toast.' Charlotte's voice was chilly. 'There didn't seem to *be* anything else.'

'Well, tea and toast on a wintry Sunday afternoon is ideal.' Kate was striving to get back to normal. That strange feeling had been exhilarating and exciting, but she felt empty now. 'I'd like some myself.'

'But aren't we going to have proper supper?' Jeremy asked. 'It's after seven.'

'I haven't prepared anything,' Kate acknowledged. 'I was painting, but I'll see what there is in the freezer.'

The scratch meal was eaten unenthusiastically, and both children were unforthcoming about their weekend. Kate realized that they were offended at being ignored, regarded, virtually, as an unwelcome interruption when they'd arrived home. She disregarded their ill humour and told them about Esme, her unexpected Concorde flight and her forthcoming marriage.

Charlotte's curiosity overcame her. 'What's he like?' she asked, thawing. 'Is he rich?' and Jeremy wanted to know if Esme had said what it felt like to fly on Concorde.

It was as they were going to bed that they told her their weekend had been boring. The hotel was stuffy and old-fashioned, it had rained all the time, and *she* had said it was too depressing to go out anywhere on Saturday. Dad had said they'd go to a theme park, but she wouldn't budge out in the wet. Instead they'd sat in a gloomy residents' lounge and watched old movies on television while Dad and she had gone to their room.

'For a nap,' Charlotte said with heavy emphasis on 'nap'.

Most of Sunday they'd played ping-pong in a cold

basement games room with bald bats because Dad and she hadn't appeared until almost lunch time. Poor kids, thought Kate with amused sympathy, having a father wrapped up in a beautiful girlfriend and a mother who barely noticed they were there. No wonder they felt ill-used. 'Well, if I can get away early enough we'll go to a film tomorrow. There's *Beverly Hills Cop* with that chap you like, Jeremy, Eddie Murphy, isn't it? Or *A Passage to India* which I want to see. We'll take a vote.'

When Flip came on Tuesday for Jeremy's coaching she was enthusiastic about Nick. 'Here was I thinking you were some poor little abandoned wife who needed cheering up, and all the time you had that interesting man in tow! Where did you find him?'

'He's a friend of my brother's,' said Kate shortly. 'He certainly isn't "in tow" as you say.'

'You mean I can feel free to chase him?' demanded Flip.

'I'm sure he'd be very flattered,' Kate said calmly. 'But I thought you weren't interested in relationships?'

'Well, it could be it's time I changed my mind,' Flip said musingly. 'I'm rapidly reaching the stage where what's up here' – she tapped her head – 'is marginally more important than what's down there. Can you believe it, he came back to my flat after Annabel's and we *talked* for hours? I haven't done *that* since I was at university! He came in for a coffee and that's precisely all he had.' She gave her snorting laugh.

'Perhaps he's not interested in sex,' offered Kate.

'You're joking. He had tremendous sex appeal.'

'Well, whatever he has, it eludes me.' Kate was brisk.

'Right, then. I shall ask him to Ronnie Scott's. Does he like jazz?'

'I've no idea, but there's only one way to find out. Ask him.'

'I will,' Flip said, eyeing her speculatively. 'I will.'

Chapter Twenty-Five

With a whole month's surviving behind her, and an actual salary credited to her account, Kate felt more relaxed, although Jeremy told her with all the seriousness of an elderly bank manager that they had to be careful. 'I can't make it balance,' he'd complained, trying to work out their budget. Kate had sat with him, but she was equally surprised at how little they had to live on. What had seemed a large salary to someone who had never earned a penny before, and who had never had to manage money seriously, seemed all too little to cover their expenditure. 'How do other people manage – with *less* money?' Kate asked. They'd gazed at each other, baffled, before they'd replaced the budget in its folder.

She was surprised at how much she looked forward each day to the prospect of going into work, and never failed to feel a thrill as the revolving door ushered her into the reception hall, where she was now greeted with easy familiarity.

There was a relaxed camaraderie about the big room in which she worked, with postcards and jokey headlines and Phillip's children's drawings pinned on the walls, plants flourishing in the big wicker baskets, a jumble of video tapes and pasted-up finished work cluttering the surfaces. She no longer felt self-conscious at her lack of experience. Phillip had looked up in astonishment when she'd returned some lay-out sheets. 'Finished already? That's quick.' And he had nodded approvingly at her sketches.

She loved working with the tray of coloured 'magic markers', sketching out new ads for a client on the basis of the words and squiggles they got from the creative department.

There was a tension in the department whenever the agency was pitching for new business, when the drawings had to be much more finished. Jessica or Ian mostly did the visuals for those, and instead of the words being written with magic markers they'd go to the trouble of having them type-set. Listening to Phillip discussing it with another department who did 'the mechanicals' or talking to a printer, Kate realized that type alone was a whole new art-form. She found *all* the processes absorbing, and questioned Ian relentlessly until one day in the staff restaurant, 'The Caff' as Ian called it, he called to an attractive, well-dressed woman of about forty-five: 'Amy, do come here and get this woman off my back – I'm out of my depth.' He turned to Kate, saying, 'This is Amy, the industry's acknowledged queen of typography.'

Rather grand and aloof at first, Amy thawed when she realized that Kate's interest was genuine, and asked if she'd like to see what a difference well-chosen type could make to the look of a press ad. 'If white space and good type are used creatively, they can say as much as pictures,' she averred. 'Well, don't spread the word,' said Kate with a smile, 'lest you put me out of work.'

But she could see what Amy meant as she showed her how delicate small type enhanced a charming, tinted drawing, putting across a luxury product, and how the clear, bold, uncompromising type in a primary colour fitted a soap powder poster.

It was all very interesting to her, and she liked the feeling of being regarded as a colleague. Quite often they'd all go out to lunch together in a nearby pub, or gather in 'The Caff'. One intense, dark, very attractive young woman called Freda invariably came in late, slipping apologetically onto her stool; she asked Kate one day to help her choose some shoes in Bond Street. 'I hate shopping alone. I usually choose the wrong thing and I spend far too much.' After that, she and Freda formed the habit of mooching around the shops occasionally at lunchtime, chatting companionably.

Heading towards Selfridges one lunchtime alone, Kate felt a large arm across her shoulders. 'Katie! Where have you been?' It was Jon. Their lunch together seemed ages ago.

She went weak. 'The usual places – home or work,' she managed to say steadily. He beamed down at her, his fair curly hair beaded with the fine rain that was falling.

'Come back with me now,' he bent to murmur in her ear. She shook her head. 'I'm a working woman – I can't.'

'Tonight then? Come up for a drink on your way home – just to tell me what you've been up to. Do you like the job?'

'Love it.'

'When do you finish – six? Seven?'

'Somewhere between the two.' His smile was infectious.

'Good – I'll make sure the champagne is chilled by six. You know where it is?' he asked slyly. She felt herself blushing.

At about five she rang home to say she'd be late. 'I have some work to finish,' she lied, surprised at how easy she found it to do so. 'I expect I'll be back about eight.'

'OK,' Charlotte said cheerfully. 'I can get supper. It's that quiche and salad, isn't it? See you later, don't work too hard.'

Jessica looked up with a quizzical expression. Kate bent self-consciously over the story board for a commercial she was sketching out. 'I'd like to get this right before tomorrow,' she muttered.

She rang Jon's bell and his voice, distorted on the

intercom, told her to come up. Meeting her at the top of the curving stairs he enveloped her in a hug that left her breathless. 'Great – I've been waiting impatiently. Come and see what we have.'

In the big drawing-room a round table, laid with a pristine white cloth, sported a silver wine cooler with a bottle of champagne in it. 'And—' John pushed a bowl of crushed ice under her nose – 'caviar – the best Beluga.' He fussed with her coat, indicated a deep armchair and filled two flutes. She leaned back and sipped. 'Lovely.' He spooned great dollops of caviar on to a small piece of toast. 'Open,' he commanded, and popped it in her mouth. He sat on the floor and eased off her shoes. 'Better? Isn't that good for a poor working woman?' Gently, he chafed her cold feet.

'And what have *you* been doing?' she asked.

'Like you, working. Only my work took me to France and Germany. Have you been anywhere new, or to Mickey-Mike's again?'

'Nowhere much. I found my first two or three weeks at work quite exhausting. I just wanted to go to bed when I got home.'

'Well,' his eyes glinted in fun. 'Feel free.' She laughed. 'Another time. I have to get home.'

He topped up her glass. 'Stay a little. I have a Food Manufacturer's Federation dinner but that's not until eight. There's plenty of time.' He knelt in front of her, his elbows on the arms of her chair, imprisoning her as he brought his mouth gently down on hers. She squirmed. 'No – I must go.'

He kissed her again, skimmed his lips over her jawbone and muzzled her ear. 'Stay,' he whispered into her hair. 'Stay just a little.' She smiled at him. 'You're impossible.' She drank her wine, trying to calm her own desire.

He sat up and looked at her. 'All right – I'll be good. Have some more caviar.'

They finished the bottle and the caviar both. 'Delicious.' Kate stood up. 'I feel thoroughly spoilt.' He knelt at her feet with her shoes. 'Are you sure you won't stay a little? It seems such a waste.'

'No,' she laughed and impulsively ruffled his hair. 'Don't tempt me any further or I may change my mind, and then I'll get into a panic.'

He stood up and kissed her again, slowly and caressingly. 'I give in. I'll ring you.'

He walked down the stairs with her, his arm round her shoulders. She felt warm and cherished and, if she was honest, just faintly disappointed that he hadn't pressed her more to go to bed.

Chapter Twenty-Six

The next few months seemed to rush by in a blur of frenzied activity. Kate sometimes felt she would burst with excitement. She was invariably the first at work, feeling a proprietorial pride as she hurried along the corridors hung with the numerous awards the agency had received. She was often the last to leave.

Charlotte had been so nonchalant the first few times there'd been urgent jobs to complete, when she had phoned to say she'd be late home, that now she no longer felt the same concern about getting home for the children's sake. 'Don't worry. We've both got masses of prep. We'll get our own supper. It's easy-peasy.' They had evolved a relaxed way of having supper so that if one of them was not home by seven the other would carry on alone. Quite often Jeremy or Charlotte had school functions of one kind or another that meant they got home at odd times, and some evenings, when Kate was home, Charlotte went out with a group of school friends.

They had spent Christmas with Tom in Edinburgh, in his large, high-ceilinged flat, starkly furnished with only the basic comforts, but stacked with textbooks and scientific journals and a meticulously neat collection of notebooks.

'Do anything you like but DON'T TOUCH,' Tom had told them with comic ferocity, indicating the notebooks. Kate had looked curiously about, when he'd taken the children out, looking for signs of another occupant, but there were none. He had a fridge-freezer, and opening it, she found the freezer compartment stacked with ready-made meals labelled for two, but he spiked any suspicion of a hidden companion when he prepared them a 'home-cooked' supper, defrosting four packets in his brand new toy, a microwave oven. 'I love all these supermarket meals. My diet has improved a lot since I discovered Marks and Spencer, but they take portion control too far – a single packet would leave an anorexic hungry.'

Kate had been dreading Christmas, wondering if the children would feel especially miserable then and miss Geoffrey. He'd often had to work over Christmas, so that it had never really become the family ritual other families enjoyed, and they had few close relatives between them. So when they'd gone to a party at the home of one of Tom's colleagues, the children seemed rather wistful. Alan had six children, and he and his wife the full complement of parents. They had been so warm and hospitable that Jeremy and Charlotte had immediately become part of a large family, with presents under the tree for them, and fun games to play. They had a huge dressing-up box and played charades, to Charlotte's special pleasure. They'd loved it all. On Boxing Day the four of them had gone to a hilariously bad pantomime. It was another milestone in her independent life passed safely.

Back at the agency after the holiday, she had a sense of home-coming. She found her work absorbing and felt an increasing assurance as she realized that she was quite good at catching the spirit of a brief in a few economical strokes with the magic markers. 'Slow down,' Freda had complained once. 'You'll show us all up.' Ian kept up a continuous, good-humoured grumble about the work, sighing anew whenever another set of briefs landed on his desk. 'And what genius prompted this routine idea?' he'd ask critically, and would scowl at Kate's enthusiasm.

'You wait until you've been here as long as I have – you won't be so starry-eyed then.'

She liked being accepted as one of them, as a member of a busy, vital department. Occasionally, like Ian, she was critical of the design brief, particularly if the product was aimed at stay-at-home housewives. She felt irritated at the underestimation of their intelligence, but then told herself that both the manufacturer and the agency had done plenty of market research. All the same, in the bus going home, she would toy with her own alternative ideas about projecting the product.

She had almost forgotten she was still on trial when Joe Grimshaw called her into his office one Friday afternoon in January.

'Kate, your three months is up,' he announced looking up over two untidy heaps of video tapes on his desk, distracted, unsmiling.

'Yes?' Her voice was hushed with sudden apprehension. She had been taking too much for granted.

'Don't look so scared – this is purely routine. Phillip tells me he's very pleased with you. He had misgivings at first but lost them when he saw how quickly you grasped what was needed. He says you think filmically, which is a great advantage. And what I've seen I've liked too. I don't regret my first instinct to take you on. If you're happy to stay, I'll ask Petronella to make the necessary arrangements with Personnel.' He smiled at Kate's sudden radiance. 'Thank you – I *love* it here.' She let out her pent-up breath.

'Good.' He nodded at her, anxious to get back to his work. Kate walked back to her office on air. 'Um, it seems I've joined the permanent staff,' she announced with a broad smile to the others. 'If anyone's not rushing off tonight the drinks are on me in the Caff.'

'Great,' Ian looked up and Jessica waved her magic marker and Freda smiled.

Feeling so at home here, so much more confident, she could hardly believe it was less than four months since Geoffrey had left her. It amused her that Peter Withers now bothered to smile and chat or pull her leg if they bumped into each other. Obviously he regarded the evening when she'd appeared at Annabel's in company with a smart group of people, as one on which she'd passed some kind of invisible barrier; it was no longer necessary to patronize her.

Despite Charlotte's efforts to arrange for him to see *Antigone* on a different day from Kate, Geoffrey had been in the audience when she, Nick and Jeremy had gone to the performance. There had been a stiff exchange of courtesies. Kate had introduced Nick as 'an old friend of Tom's' when Geoffrey looked at him speculatively. The idea of platonic friendship was quite foreign to Geoffrey, and she was anxious to nip his assumptions in the bud.

In the interval Miss Cundell, Charlotte's English teacher, chattily unaware of any tension between them, had rounded them up from separate sides of the gymnasium, where tables held glasses of wine, saying, 'I'm so glad to have the chance to talk to you both about Charlotte. She is doing so well generally, but particularly in English, that she could probably get a scholarship. Unfortunately, she tells me that she doesn't *want* to go to university. I do hope you will do your best to change her mind?'

They played their part, discussing Charlotte's progress, and the play, as if they were a normal couple. Jeremy had been painfully embarrassed, not knowing which one of them to attach himself to, so he had been grateful that he could wander off and stand with Nick.

In the second half there was a tense moment when Charlotte, as Creon, had lifted her head and looked meaningfully in Geoffrey's direction as her clear young voice carried the words:

> *'And what worse sore*
> *Can plague us, than a loved one's worthlessness?'*

For the first time, Kate felt sorry for Geoffrey.

Afterwards, Charlotte was in the middle of an excited group of friends, all babbling congratulations when a large bouquet of red roses was handed to her by a grinning fourth former. 'Well done. All love, Dad.' She looked with anguish at Kate.

'Daddy told Miss Cundell he thought you were very good,' Kate had found smiling difficult. 'We both talked to her in the interval.'

Charlotte relaxed a little. It was all right, then, to show pleasure in her grown-up bouquet without upsetting her mother. She had been on tenterhooks knowing that they were both going to be there. Now Kate was struck again by the knowledge of what a burden the split loyalty was to the children. She must let them know that she didn't think that their being friends with Geoffrey was in any way being traitorous to her.

Several evenings now Kate had gone out, straight from the office. She'd been to Jon's flat several times, and they'd made love. He'd taken her to a couple of films and a play, but always it was implicit that they'd end up in bed. He would never say anything fond or endearing; he teased her, flattered her, expressed delight in her as a sex partner, but she had no idea how he *felt* about her. Strangely it was what she wanted just then – a period in an emotional limbo while she assimilated all the new experiences of working and meeting people by herself.

Independence itself was a new experience. She had

moved from the protective care of Esme, to being the subordinate half of a couple with Geoffrey. She had rarely had to take solo decisions; mostly her role had been an acquiescent, pliant one. She had felt as if part of her life had been blanked out, compared with other women's; she had had no schoolfriends, she had never shared in the fun, the swot, the worry of university students. She never had a job. Looking back, she now felt cross with herself for having been so unawake – a somnambulist. It had taken her some days to absorb the shock of Esme's marriage, to realize that she could no longer regard her as a fixture in her life. She had taken too much of Esme's time and affection for granted, and in the weeks before her departure for Chicago Kate had tried to establish a new, more grown-up relationship. Tearfully, they had said goodbye at the airport, Kate promising to visit and Esme swearing that she'd bring Martin to England to retire. But both knew that their lives were now running on separate, independent paths.

Kate was charmed whenever colleagues asked her to join them for lunch or to go out with them of an evening; sometimes Beatrice would ring her or Amy. She had been to Amy's idiosyncratic flat in Bayswater, its walls crammed with posters and framed facsimiles of illuminated manuscripts, and had sat listening to Amy's re-run of her typographical triumphs as she ground and chopped and pounded herbs and spices for the delicious Indian meal they had finally eaten at about eleven o'clock. Kate marvelled at the way Amy was able to toss off large vodkas during the process, while never once did the chopping knife falter or her concentration fail.

Unlike her hectic days of entertaining with Geoffrey, there was no ulterior motive under a social mask. She was included, in a casual friendly manner, for herself. It was a heady feeling. Freda fell into the habit of confiding her problems with her boyfriend when they wandered round the shops, and Kate stunned herself by saying to her one day: 'Why don't you give him up? He doesn't make you happy.'

'It's not so easy,' Freda had said morosely. 'I'm twenty-nine, and there aren't that many single men around. I have to hang on to Barry.'

Kate wondered if she would have said the same to Freda when she was with Geoffrey, consciously unhappy but afraid to face up to what divorce would mean. Hadn't she hung on like a ship's tender, afraid to bob around a large sea alone?

She had been surprised when Billy suddenly invited her to a party; she had spoken very little to her at that evening at Annabel's, but Billy had kept her telephone number and had phoned two days later to ask her to a supper party. Kate had had to refuse then, but this time had accepted. She had come to the tall, Victorian terrace house in West Kensington with some trepidation, and been surprised and charmed by Billy's warm friendliness.

'I don't know whether you know many people here,' she'd said, taking Kate's hand, 'but you must meet Paul Kieran; he's an artist too. Flip told me *you* were one.' Kate had gazed up into the bluest eyes she had ever seen, set in a tanned face under a thatch of straw-coloured hair. She had never seen such a beautiful man. There was no other word for it. He was talking to another man but they both broke off politely when Billy ushered Kate up.

'Paul Kieran and James Prescott, this is Kate Cosgrove. She's an artist too,' Billy said, and bustled off. Kate smiled deprecatingly. 'She means I work in the creative department of an ad agency,' she apologized. 'I only paint in my spare time.'

'Don't we all,' Paul said with an Australian drawl. 'It

takes a long time to live off fine art. What kind of work do you do? Figurative? Landscapes? Abstract?'

'Let me guess,' James broke in. 'Meticulous, botanically correct, delightful flower paintings in watercolours.'

Kate looked at him levelly. 'That's wrapped up women artists! What about Gwen John? Even her brother said she was the better painter of the two. Or Bridget Riley? Or Mary Cassatt?' She had the satisfaction of seeing that he'd never even heard of Mary Cassatt.

'That will teach you to be arrogant, James.' Paul looked down at him with a smile. James too smiled cheerfully at her. 'I deserved that. But then, I must admit, I am a dedicated male chauvinist.'

Kate stared at him. 'Would you smile as happily if you admitted you were a racist or an anti-Semite?' She'd never attempted to put anyone down before. Proximity to Flip, and some of the books she'd lent her were having an effect.

Paul roared in delight, and James looked put out. 'Women have no sense of humour,' he muttered.

'Well we have, but it becomes a little strained at that kind of remark,' Kate said steadily. 'Are *you* a painter?' She kept her voice deliberately friendly.

'No, an art critic.'

'And a very good one,' Paul put in. 'There aren't many of them about.'

'Of course.' Kate smiled frankly at James. 'I didn't connect. Your reviews always make me want to rush and see an exhibition. You did a marvellously erotic critique of the Rubens, I remember.'

James was instantly mollified. 'Do you paint seriously or are you a Sunday painter?' His tone had completely changed.

'Both,' Kate said serenely. 'I have to work for my living but when I paint, I try to paint seriously. How about you?' She turned to Paul.

'Oh I paint seriously, all right, but I don't sell much. I

shall probably be one of those artists like Van Gogh or Bomberg, posthumously famous. Mostly I teach, at the Royal College, which is dishonest of me. I should tell the brats what being a painter is really like, and urge them to be accountants or bookmakers.'

Kate had been surprised to be clapped on her shoulder by Felicity Rutherford. She hadn't seen her since that fateful birthday party. Felicity hauled Kate off to talk in a corner. 'I didn't know you knew Billy Lambton. What's been happening to you, how are you?' Her eyes raked over Kate.

'I've been working,' Kate said steadily. 'Geoffrey and I have split up.' She could say the words now without a pang. Felicity's eyes popped with curiosity.

'I didn't know. Why didn't you tell me?'

'What, send out announcements like wedding invitations?' Kate laughed. 'It's not a socially easy thing to do: an engraved card with the message: "My husband has gone off with a beautiful television presenter" perhaps? The situation is so trite. I think that disastrous so-called birthday party we inflicted on you was the turning-point. Geoffrey is going to marry Greta Lanson.' She shrugged. 'It was for the best – I'm sure we're both happier now.'

Felicity had said she must come to dinner, but Kate could tell she didn't mean it. Felicity'd had an expression of distaste in her eyes, almost as though divorce were catching. Felicity worshipped success, and successful women didn't divorce unless another, more desirable man was around and available. Kate, clearly, was alone.

Billy had piloted her around to a few more guests, but Kate had taken great satisfaction in watching Paul manoeuvre his way over to her again to say, 'Let's go and get something to eat. Billy's table is groaning with good things and I'm starving. Aren't you?' The party had ended with Paul asking her to come with him to an exhibition at Waddington's the next day. She'd felt her stock soar with the receptionists when he'd loped in to call for her.

* * *

Flip now only came once a week to coach Jeremy, but invariably Kate would go out with her afterwards – sometimes to a pub, occasionally to a disco, often to one of Flip's friends' homes. No-one seemed involved in a regular relationship, they changed partners with kaleidoscopic speed. 'I'm becoming a bohemian,' she thought with a mixture of pride and amusement, struggling sometimes to keep up. She told herself that other women would have lived like this when they were young. This was her second chance, and she was greedy for all that she'd missed. A hang-over or tiredness were small prices to pay. At other times she wondered guiltily if she were seeing the children enough, but they seemed to be sturdily independent now, sharing the shopping and cooking and leaving notes for her if they were in bed before she got home.

The morning rush never allowed time to talk. They all set off together, but parted at the tube station. Mostly their chat was about who would be in first, who would remember to get the 'basics'. Sometimes Kate would go to Selfridge's or Marks and Spencer's and lug supplies home, but mostly they relied on a big Saturday shop and on filling the freezer with prepared meals. To Kate it now felt as if they were three flatmates – the children seemed to have assumed an almost grown-up responsibility.

She was finding everything so interesting, so fresh and new that she didn't have time for much introspection. Her sense of failure over Geoffrey was still there, but she realized that the hurt was no deeper, the sense of shock and betrayal not as numbing as it had been the first time she'd realized he was unfaithful. Esme's cutting of the apron strings had been far more upsetting, and had left her feeling, unreasonably, really abandoned.

The books Flip had lent her had been something of a revelation. She could understand now why Flip had been so scornful of her attitude. She wept when she read Margaret Forster's *Significant Sisters* and understood the pain and sacrifice and sheer cussed determination a handful of women had experienced in the effort to change some of the sexual inequities of the past. Imagine how it would have been if Geoffrey, tiring of her, had simply swept off with the children, and appropriated the house together with her small income from her father? It seemed so monstrous, and yet that is just what would have happened if it hadn't been for Caroline Norton, who had managed to get the Married Women's Property Act on to the statute books after the shock of her own beastly husband's behaviour.

She felt indignant at the way Germaine Greer had been portrayed in the popular press, because once she read *The Female Eunuch* she'd realized that she too had made assumptions based on nothing more than some half-digested, hastily-regurgitated article by some jaundiced journalist. She was ashamed of her own previous apathy, her ignorance. Why hadn't she read those books for herself fifteen years ago, at the time they'd caused such a stir? Now, she gobbled up Elaine Morgan and Betty Friedan in quick succession, receiving a shock as she recognized her own mental fumblings in Gail Sheehy's *Passages*. She felt as if she'd been a female Rip Van Winkle, asleep and unconscious of everything that had gone on outside the tiny domestic circle.

'Steady on,' Flip had drawled, when Kate had tried to discuss their ideas with her. 'It's hardly news, you know. Talk like that and people will wonder where you've been hiding your brain all these years.'

'I'm wondering myself,' Kate said humbly.

'You're OK,' Flip assured her. 'Your old man hypnotized you. All you need to do is think for yourself.'

Chapter Twenty-Seven

Penelope Milsom had telephoned to find out how Kate was faring, and was delighted at the news of her job. 'Well done! And the house? You haven't let Geoffrey bully you into giving him half?'

'No. Between you and my solicitor there was no chance of that. He was very cross.'

Penelope's satisfaction was tangible. 'Would you like to come to a gala performance of *Un Ballo in Maschera*? There'll be food in the Crush Bar. It's for Save the Children – Princess Anne will be there. It should be rather grand.'

'I'd love to, as long as I can buy the tickets.'

'Two hundred pounds each? My dear, only companies and millionaires can afford that. Of course you can't pay – I have a number of tickets for my special friends. Would you like to bring anyone or shall I fix you up with one of the sponsors, a nice elderly chairman perhaps?' Kate laughed. 'If I may, I'd like to bring someone but I'm not sure if he likes opera. May I ring you back.?'

She asked Paul. 'Who's he?' Openly curious, Charlotte had listened to the telephone conversation, not missing her mother's animation as she talked, or her satisfaction when Paul had said yes. 'Oh, someone I met at a party – an artist. Penelope Milsom asked me to a gala performance of *Un Ballo in Maschera*. If he comes to pick me up, you'll meet him.'

'When is this for?' Charlotte asked.

'Next Thursday, why?' Kate was abstracted, wondering

if the bronze dress she'd bought with Beatrice would be suitable.

'I wanted to go out with some of my friends. There's a film we all want to see and perhaps we'll go to the Pizza Parlour afterwards.'

'Well it doesn't matter if we clash, does it?' asked Kate.

'I don't like leaving Jeremy alone.' Charlotte's voice was flat.

'You sound like a hen with one chick. Weren't you both telling me not so long ago that you were too old to have anyone look after you?'

'Well, we are. But you're always out now and I can never make firm arrangements with my friends. Jeremy finds the house spooky on his own when it's late. I had to go out one evening when you were late home – I didn't know you were going to be out too. When I got back he was as white as a sheet. He watches too many horror films on television and frightens himself to death.'

'You haven't said anything before.'

'Well no – you're always so busy.'

'I'll say "no" to the opera if you're really worried.' She looked sharply at Charlotte.

'Oh, that's OK. We'd talked about Wednesday. Do you think you could be home early then? I won't have time to get supper. The film starts at 6.30.'

Kate was nettled. Charlotte talked as if, if it weren't for her, the whole place would collapse. 'Of course I will if you're going out. I know I've been late a lot recently but at this time of the year the agency has to clear all its spring campaigns and my department has a lot of work. But I can work through my lunch hour.' She was cross with herself for feeling guilty.

Charlotte, expressionless, had turned away with a flat 'OK.'

Kate had been surprised when she got home at six to find

Jeremy slouched over his prep in the dining-room and Charlotte laughing and giggling in the kitchen as she cut a sandwich for herself and a thin dark boy she introduced as Nathan. He had a sharp, clever face and it was obvious he already shaved. Kate had assumed Charlotte had meant her school girlfriends. She frowned as she saw Charlotte had poured them each a glass of wine. How often did this happen?

When the doorbell rang she was relieved to see four other noisy teenagers crowding into the small kitchen, demanding that Charlotte and Nathan hurry if they weren't to miss the vital opening. They flowed out again like the bathwater disappearing noisily down the waste-pipe.

'Finished your prep?' She poked her head round the door. Jeremy looked up startled. 'Nearly. Are you home tonight? Where's Charlotte?'

'She's gone to a film. Didn't she tell you? How about you and me having supper by the fire and then a game of Scrabble?'

'All right,' he said unenthusiastically. After two highly unsatisfactory games, when he'd been silly and giggly and made up so many ridiculous words that Kate had become thoroughly cross and irritated, he said abruptly, 'I think I'll go to bed – I'm tired.'

Kate was relieved, but it was unusual for him to take himself off without any urging. His eyes looked glittery and his cheeks were red. She hoped he wasn't sickening for anything. She felt his forehead. It was clammy, but Jeremy twitched away.

'There's nothing wrong. I'm just a bit tired.'

'OK then. Go to bed. Good night.' She kissed him. He seemed to lapse into sulkiness. Perhaps they'd lost a football match. She should have asked.

She was startled when Charlotte came in later, looking

very pink and pretty, to find that she'd dozed off. 'What a middle-aged thing to do,' she said to Charlotte.

'Too many late nights.' Charlotte said it lightly, but there was an unmistakable edge to her voice.

'How was the film? What was it?'

'I *told* you: *The Lacemaker*. It was a revival with Isabelle Huppert. She's a beautiful new French star.'

'Yes – I'd forgotten. And Nathan? Have you told me about him too?'

Charlotte looked self-conscious. 'He's no-one special. I met him when I went for a coffee after school. There's a café near the tube station that my form all go to. He's at Barnaby's. Miss Griegson is organizing our debating society to have joint debates with them. I may join,' she added carelessly. 'Miss Griegson says debating makes you marshal your thoughts, helps you to be less self-conscious in public.'

'Good idea,' Kate said, and stood up, yawning. 'Let's push off to bed? I expect we're *both* tired. By the way,' she plumped up the cushion on her armchair, 'how often do you have a glass of wine by yourself?'

'Mum, I *am* sixteen! You've let me have drinks before.'

'Occasionally. Very specially. It's not a good idea at your age to have one as a matter of course. Leave some things until you're properly grown up. Don't get there too fast.' She kissed her good night, giving a playful pat to her bottom, but Charlotte merely looked annoyed.

Next day was a frantic one. Freda was away ill and a client had increased his budget. The original campaign had to be re-thought to bring in a regional television area to test-market a new product. But this had to be slotted into the campaign without jeopardizing the existing press and national television spend, which was already running, because if the new product was a failure and had to be withdrawn, the whole meticulously synchronized plan would be ruined and many thousands of pounds lost. It was complicated, and for once Kate found herself echoing Ian's predictable scorn at the puerility of the thinking. 'There won't be another award to frame for this one,' she muttered to Ian. 'Is this the result of the client's interference or our own idea?'

'Dunno. I'm paid to draw out the bilge, not think it up, but I bet my kid could do better on this one.'

Kate thought she'd like to have a go at some ideas herself and let Phillip see them, but just getting through without Freda was an ordeal. She concentrated on drawing as fast and effectively as possible, and felt a glow of satisfaction when she was finished by 6.15 and could go. Hurrying to the door, she was lucky to catch a taxi dropping his fare, and she took it on gratefully, telling herself it was a necessary extravagance.

When Paul arrived, she wasn't quite ready. She called down to Charlotte to show him in and give him a drink. When she hurried down the stairs minutes later, she found Charlotte unusually silent. She was clearly stunned at the sight of Paul in evening dress. He looked like something straight out of Hollywood, and when he smiled, flashing very white teeth at her, she could hardly speak. She signalled a 'now I understand what all the fuss was about' glance at her mother, but there was no conspiratorial smile, as Kate expected. She seemed apprehensive. Jeremy mooched in as Paul was finishing his drink, but merely said 'Hello' and stood with his hands in his pockets, eyeing Kate's dress, looking glum. There wasn't the same fun and collusion that there had been when she had worn it the first time, when she had been *urged* to go out with Flip. But she was looking forward to the opera so much that she ignored the air of resentment and disquiet the children were projecting.

Kate had forgotten how enthralling the opera house

itself could be. She hadn't been since the early days, when Geoffrey was cultivating the Milsoms, and had urged her to accept Penelope's invitations. Tonight, perhaps partly because it was so long since she'd been, everyone seemed glamorous and there was an almost tangible anticipation in the air. She saw Penelope busy darting about smiling and talking to people. 'She never misses a trick,' she mused, admiring the way Penelope managed to leave a trail of animation as she hovered briefly here and there, going from one group or couple to another like a couture-clad butterfly sipping nectar.

In the interval, still bemused by the music, she and Paul made their way to the Crush Bar. Here Penelope seized her, whispering, 'Darling, *devastating,* absolutely devastating,' and hauled up the nearest people to introduce before bustling off. Kate laughed up at Paul. 'She's always like that. Incredible,' and turning to look over her shoulder at the departing Penelope, found herself staring straight into Nick's eyes.

'What a surprise!' she exclaimed. 'I'd forgotten you knew Penelope too. Paul, this is an old family friend, Nick Menton – Paul Kieran.' Paul engulfed Nick's hand. 'Nick Menton of Menton Galleries?' Nick nodded.

'I've been longing to meet you, but you have a dragon of a secretary – I've tried for months to get past her.'

Nick was unsmiling. 'Indeed. It's her job I'm afraid, but perhaps she's sometimes a bit too protective. Why don't you call me on this number?' He gave Paul his card, nodded briefly to Kate and walked over to join a very pretty dark girl.

'Frosty,' Paul commented, and looked at Kate who was gazing after Nick in some surprise. 'He made me feel like an encyclopedia salesman. Let's have another drink, little one – it's free.'

His last words grated a little; she hoped he wasn't a

sponger. But he was certainly very agreeable. Although clearly not an opera buff, he professed himself entranced by the music. He put himself out to be charming to the few people she knew, and made a point of telling Penelope before they went back to their seats that he deeply appreciated being there.

After the opera Paul drove her home to Fulham. 'Now for the best part.' He turned to her, and putting his finger under her chin, tipped up her mouth to his. 'Let me come in,' he breathed into her hair.

'No, it's late, and I have to make an early start.'

'I'll wake you up in time.' He pulled her towards him, kissing her eyes and mouth. 'Making love in cars is only for teenagers.'

'No, I can't, really. The children are home.'

'They won't see me. Please. I'll wait until you all go off and then creep out as discreetly as a house detective.' His hands were stroking her back bared by the bronze dress.

'No, Paul, *please*. Let me go. I *must* go.'

'All right,' he sighed and sat up suddenly. 'But come away for the weekend with me, will you? I sometimes borrow a friend's cottage and paint there. You could bring *your* paints too. What could be more blissful? Making love, painting, making love – we might even have time to eat.' He smiled. 'Say yes, now while I have you captive.'

Kate laughed at his boyishness. Why not? He was very attractive. She'd already made love with two men she barely knew, so it was a bit late to start having moral misgivings now. Geoffrey was having the children this weekend. It would be a change to go away. 'All right – yes. Now let me go in.'

'Where did you meet him?' Charlotte asked breathlessly as they practically jogged to the station the next morning. Kate had slept through the alarm and had to be roused by Charlotte, and they were all late.

'At a party. He's a friend of Felicity Rutherford's – at least I met him at a party where she was. He wants me to go painting with him this weekend. He's an artist. You're going to Daddy's, aren't you?'

'But you hardly *know* him.' Charlotte's voice rose indignantly.

'Well, a weekend is a chance to do just that, get properly acquainted. We'll be painting – I am rather elderly to have maidenly scruples about being compromised, if that's what's worrying you.' She attempted a laugh but Charlotte only frowned. 'I'm beginning to hate the weekends,' she muttered. 'And what about the shopping? We're out of so many things. We used the last of the cornflakes this morning, there's no more butter and just about a crust of bread left,' Charlotte grumbled on.

'Don't worry – I'll go out at lunch time. 'Bye now.' Kate made a final sprint as Charlotte turned for the opposite platform. But she didn't have a chance to shop in the middle of the day because a client had turned down the last campaign and a new one was being prepared against the clock. They all worked solidly, and practically in silence, until the revised storyboards for the commercials and the back-up press campaign were finished by the 4 o'clock deadline. Kate stretched. Her back ached and her hand felt stiff. She yawned as a call came for her.

'Kate? You haven't changed your mind about the weekend? I've got the cottage.' Paul's voice was low and warm. 'It's a lovely quiet spot in Suffolk, but we need to get there early to warm it up and make up the bed. Particularly the bed. How soon can you get away?'

Kate glanced round the room. Now the panic was over everyone was relaxed and sitting back. 'I might be able to leave earlyish; we've had a rush on but it seems to have subsided now. If I can't I'll ring you.'

'Good. Try, there's a good girl. And can we go in your

car? Mine seems to be in trouble. Perhaps you could pick me up?'

Kate put the phone down feeling extraordinarily nervous. Some of Charlotte's disquiet seemed to have rubbed off. Going away with someone was a bit more serious than tumbling casually into bed for what Flip called frustration's safety valve. She felt a twinge of doubt and guilt, quickly stifled when she thought of how nice it would be to get away from London for a change. And she would take her paints.

When she got home the children's bags were packed and ready in the hall, and the two of them were sitting in the kitchen, reading over the remains of tea.

'You're early!' Jeremy looked up in surprise. Charlotte gazed irritably at her. 'Where's the shopping?' she demanded. 'You said you'd get it at lunch time.'

'I know, but I didn't *have* a lunch hour – we all worked through. I'll get something. But I've got to rush now. Paul's car has broken down and we're taking mine, and have to get there early enough to switch on the heating and stuff.'

'You are going, then? I thought it wasn't definite. Who else is going? Just the two of you?' Her tone was hostile.

'I suppose so.' She wasn't going to let Charlotte bully her. 'When is Daddy collecting you?'

'About six, he said. But I expect it'll be nearer seven,' Charlotte turned her back pointedly.

'Then if I push off as soon as I'm ready, you won't have long to wait, will you? I won't need much for the country.'

She bundled sweaters and trousers into an overnight bag, but her paints and brushes were more of a problem. She packed board and turps and oil in an old rucksack and hoped they wouldn't leak on the way. Charlotte seemed more satisfied when she saw the painting gear go into the boot. 'She thinks it will keep me out of mischief,' Kate thought, amused at the way she hovered. ''Bye kids.' She kissed them warmly. 'Have a good time. See you Sunday evening!'

Two glum faces watched her drive away; she felt a pang. They did look a couple of sad orphans. It couldn't be much fun being shunted between parents, feeling unwanted by their father's girlfriend, and watching their mother blithely drive off for a weekend with a strange man. For a minute she had an impulse to turn back and call the whole thing off. Would it be better for them if they felt she, at least, was stable, and always there at home? She herself didn't know what it felt like to have a domesticated mother constantly around. Perhaps it was just as stifling, in its way, as a remote mother was chilling.

They drove slowly out of London, going through the congested East End before they hit the fast motorway. On the way they turned off the M11 to stop for food at a pub Paul knew. 'Specializes in meals suitable for Australian outback appetites,' he said as Kate gazed in astonishment at her piled-up plate. 'Make the most of it – there won't be much in the cottage. We'll have to shop in the village early tomorrow or starve. Damn, I've left my wallet in my grip. Let me have the car key.'

'I'll pay,' Kate said scrabbling in her bag. 'We must get on – how much further is it?' He sat back without demur as she settled the bill.

The cottage wasn't very pretty, and it was furnished in a very cheap way, as if for letting to transient visitors who wouldn't care for it, hardly the romantic white-washed thatched place she'd envisaged. It felt damp, too, but Paul lit a huge fire, and there was, she was thankful to see, an electric heater in the bedroom. They'd made the bed together, and Paul fell on to it pulling her on top of him. 'Now the weekend can start.' He kissed her and fumbled at her jeans. 'I'm having a hot bath first,' she protested. 'You promised there was hot water.'

She felt better after her bath, and once in the clean white sheets on the high, old, surprisingly comfortable, iron bed, she lost the faint feeling that coming away like this was a bit sordid. To her surprise Paul, already hunched under the bedclothes, simply gave her a sleepy kiss and was soon gently snoozing. Relieved, she snuggled gratefully against his warm back and fell asleep quickly herself.

Just before six she woke to the dawn chorus and the first faint morning light. She slid quietly out of bed and went to the window. The view was marvellous and made up for the cottage's lack of appeal. She tiptoed into the bathroom where she'd left her clothes, and slipped outside. Despite the birdsong the atmosphere was full of gentle peace. The rough grass surrounding the cottage was wet, but over a low nearby hill the sun was already streaking the sky with the colour of a freshly-squeezed orange. She caught her breath, entranced, and went to the car boot for her paints. She felt an intrinsic part of the landscape, not an observer, but part of the waking day as though she too was a light spreading over the grass and trees. There was that same intense feeling of energy and colour she'd felt on that lonely Sunday afternoon, an insistent internal rhythm that threatened to overwhelm her if she didn't release it. She propped up her board against the car and spread her painting paraphernalia on the ground. The light was getting stronger all the time.

Painting fiercely, oblivious to everything but the stimulating struggle to make her hand and eye work together to force the blank canvas to yield, she was startled by Paul's voice calling from the window, 'Hey, you cheat! What are you doing down there?'

She felt cold and stiff and her back ached from discomfort and the tension of the past two hours. 'Lazybones,' she called. 'You're missing the best part of the day.' She propped her board against a decrepit apple tree, shoved the paints and rucksack next to them, and went in. Paul had come down to the kitchen and was looking bad-tempered. 'It's not my idea of a great weekend to wake up to an empty bed,' he said.

'I woke early, and it looked so lovely outside I couldn't resist it. We have two whole days. Want some coffee?'

'There isn't any – we have to go into the village for provisions – I told you that last night.' He turned abruptly to the kitchen door. 'Well, we might as well go now. It's just after eight – by the time we get there at least the baker's will be open and we can get eggs and coffee in the paper shop.' He was forced to grin as she laughed at the incongruity, and he seemed to recover his good humour.

With the sun quite strong behind them, they drove into the village. The baker's was not only open but busy, and Kate sniffed the air with sensuous pleasure. 'I don't think I've smelt freshly baked bread for years.' On the way in, they'd noticed a farm offering free-range eggs and vegetables and the paper shop had apparently become a small supermarket, surprisingly well-stocked.

'Hey, we're here for a weekend, not a month,' Paul said eyeing her basket.

'I know, but I'm shopping for home as well – Charlotte reminded me in no uncertain terms that the cupboard was bare.'

'Oh well, then you can pay. A teacher's pay doesn't stretch to family groceries.' Again she felt the flicker of suspicion; was he mean, or really hard up?

They stopped at the farm for eggs and vegetables that a shy teenager obligingly harvested from the kitchen garden behind the cowsheds as they waited. 'Organic?' Paul said, cocking an eyebrow and sniffing the pungent air. 'I'm ravenous.'

The early spring sunshine was thin, but it lit the hills still hung about with veils of mist, with a sharp, happy yellow as the rays spread over a sloping field. She turned enthusiastically to Paul. 'Let's be quick with breakfast and make the most of the light.' He smiled, caught by her excitement, with no trace of his earlier irritability.

With the sun unseaonably warm, it was lovely to be out of doors, and they both painted contentedly for most of the day, breaking off for a picnic lunch of bread and pâté and fruit.

When Kate saw Paul's work she was deeply disappointed. It was competent but facile, a faithful copy of the scene, but wooden. She tried to cover her surprise with polite, vague remarks. It made her feel worse that he was enthusiastic about her painting, criticizing it with genuine perception. She could see that he could be a good, encouraging teacher, but wondered if he really believed he could paint well enough to expect Nick to consider his work for his gallery. Perhaps he's more at home with portraits, she thought.

'You're right – you're a *serious* Sunday painter,' he said later. He had watched her intense absorption, the total loss of consciousness of anything about her except the scene she was trying to capture. She looked up in surprise, her eyes blank from some inner vision. 'You've got something,' he said. 'I didn't think you'd be so good – much better than me. You've got the spirit of the landscape, whereas I've made little more than a map.' Kate felt pity as he gestured deprecatingly at his own effort, but relief too that he understood his inadequacy. 'There's real feeling there,' he went on, 'a touch of the Ivon Hitchens. It's formless, in a way, yet I can see the hills exactly, and you've caught that yew; I didn't see its menace until I looked at your painting. Now it gives me the shivers. Come on, let's go inside before I decide to cut my throat.'

Supper was delicious, Kate coaxing the ancient stove to produce a good casserole; the beef stewed gently in the fresh vegetables and a mixture of herbs she'd found in the overgrown garden, and Paul produced two bottles of wine from his bag. At the end of the meal, Kate felt somnolent from the day in the fresh air, the emotional activity that painting entailed, and the wine.

Paul had irritated her by constantly pinching her arm, or her bottom as she cooked, sometimes quite painfully. 'Stop it, that hurt,' she complained once, rubbing her forearm. 'Did it?' he looked into her eyes and she felt a twinge of nervousness as she saw how light and cold his were now.

She was realizing how inviting bed seemed, after her long day, when Paul, sitting in front of the fire on a sagging old sofa, caught her as she attempted to pass into the kitchen, and pulled her on to his lap, gripping her firmly. 'Now we have to punish you for being a bad girl this morning and leaving my bed, don't we?' Kate attempted a laugh and pulled away but he tightened his arm. 'Don't we?' and he slapped her hip with his free hand. She was nonplussed, unsure how to react. It seemed so odd. She attempted a laugh, to show she realized he was joking, when he suddenly yanked at the arm held behind her back, so that her body spun and she was lying across his lap, with his right elbow planted between her shoulder blades, and his right hand keeping a firm grip on her arm.

'I said, "Don't we?"' and he hit her buttocks with his left hand.

'Paul, don't be silly – let me up,' she gasped.

'Silly, am I? Then you must be punished again.' He leaned his chest over her back, sandwiching her between his torso and his lap and started to pull her jeans. 'That's for calling me silly.' He hit her again and ripped off her briefs, exposing her bottom, 'And that's for painting better than me.' This time the flat of his hand came down painfully hard.

'Paul, stop – you're *hurting* me. This has gone far enough,' Kate was now both angry and frightened.

'I'm not finished yet,' he grunted, and hit her again. She could feel his penis hard against her chest, despite its being restricted by his tight jeans. Holding her in the same iron grip, he used his free hand to unzip his jeans and wriggle out of them. She felt a wave of revulsion as she felt his penis hot and hard against her thin sweater. He shifted his elbow from her shoulder blades to the back of her head and pressed her face down on his penis. 'Eat it,' he commanded. She gagged and he hit her again. 'Do as I say or it will be the worse for you.'

She tried to turn her head, moaning as he thrust his hips up. 'Take it, go on, in your mouth.'

She clenched her teeth and pressed her lips together as she felt another stinging pain on her buttocks. She could hardly breathe as he wriggled and manoeuvred his hips to force his penis into her mouth. Her mind was rushing wildly as she tried to think how to get out of this nightmare. Her eyes watered with pain as he grabbed her hair and pulled her head up and grabbed her nose. 'Do as you're told,' he said through gritted teeth, his face red and contorted. As she was forced to open her mouth he pushed her down again on his penis. She felt as if she would choke. Then the warm sticky emission filled her mouth. She gagged again and found he'd released her. She spat out the semen, took one look as he leaned back limp and exhausted against the back of the sofa, grabbed her jeans and fled to the bathroom, locking the door before being violently sick. She bathed her face and stared at the horrified face in the spotted mirror. Her ears were ringing and she didn't know what to do next. How was she to get out? The man was a lunatic! God knows what might happen next. She could not stay here now. She listened intently but she could hear no movement downstairs.

She picked up a metal tube, covered in hideous flaking

pink paint, slotted through the top with a narrow bar holding a half-empty toilet roll. Some piece of redundant armoury from the First World War by the look of it, but she could wield it if necessary. Cautiously, she opened the door and crept into the bedroom next door. With her free hand she grabbed her bag. She had to get out. She looked out of the window. If need be, she could try that way. It wasn't far to the ground and there was a kind of ramshackle porch she could drop on to. She dropped her bag out of the window just before Paul came into the room. She clutched the toilet roll object close to her side as he said pleasantly, 'I didn't mean to frighten you, Kate. I'm sorry.' His face was still flushed and he was breathing heavily, but his eyes had lost the empty look. 'I thought you were a little more sophisticated.' She stared at him warily. 'I mean it – I'm sorry. Come down with me to the fire and let's play some music. There's still some wine. Don't let's spoil our time here. Put that object down.' He pointed to her potential weapon.

'You have already spoiled it,' she said coldly, but took some steps towards him and the door. She didn't want to show alarm, and it was important to get downstairs. She could tackle the window if need be, but she would risk spraining an ankle or breaking a leg that way.

He spread his hands and lifted his shoulders. 'Every man has some little aberration. Surely you've come across that? After all, you came away readily enough with me – you must have done this sort of thing before. I expect there are quite a few variations *you* could teach *me*,' he said, with a leer.

She felt sick and ashamed of herself. It was perfectly true. She hadn't needed much persuading. 'I admit that it was my fault for coming away with someone I hardly knew.' She paused. She didn't want to antagonize him into violence again. 'But no, I haven't ever been forced into that kind of – of sadistic rape.' Despite her efforts, her voice held contempt. His face hardened. 'Rape? You don't know the meaning of the word,' he sneered. He moved over quickly and hooked her arms over the rail of the bedstead. 'I could tie you up here and rape you. Then you'd know what it was like. I'd enjoy it.' His eyes were looking strange again.

Her mind was still racing. 'Perhaps I'd enjoy it,' she surprised herself by how calmly she spoke. She mustn't provoke him any more. She smiled up at him. 'I think we both need a drink first. Where is that wine you offered just now? You're right, it's silly to spoil the weekend. It has been lovely up until now.'

He smiled, and she was amazed at how quickly the astonishingly handsome, charming persona slipped back into place. 'OK,' he said, and lifted his hand in agreement. 'You're intrigued, aren't you? You think you might like a bit of the rough stuff?'

She made herself stroll slowly and casually to the door, now he'd released her again. 'You put on some music and replenish the logs whilst I just wash up, then we'll relax.'

He grinned wolfishly and turned to the fire. Kate slipped into the kitchen. Her bag was somewhere in the dark, to the left of the porch she reckoned, and the car was parked about ten feet from there. Her handbag with the car keys was still on the kitchen table where she had dumped it when they came back from shopping. She turned on the kitchen tap, as if she was indeed starting to wash up, snatched her handbag, and flew out of the back door. The light from the curtainless sitting-room window and the open kitchen door was just enough for her to spot the dark bulk of her overnight bag. Scooping it up, she hurtled into her car, grateful that he'd asked her to bring it, and reversed out of the gate. She bumped over the rutted farm lane to the narrow metalled road they'd taken to the village that morning, and turned blindly right, pressing on the accelerator. She looked fearfully in the mirror, somehow sure he'd find some way of coming after her, but there was just the anonymous black of the night.

She drove on. She had no idea where she was going but she'd just drive until a signpost gave her a clue. Now that she was safely away she started to shake. She felt overcome with shame and humiliation and anger with herself, and waves of revulsion swept over her as she relived the nightmare scene. She didn't care how he would get back to London; that was his problem, she thought viciously, but at the same time she admitted her own stupid connivance in coming away so blithely with someone who was, after all, a perfect stranger.

Chapter Twenty-Eight

When at last she let herself into the little Fulham house, she could have wept with relief. It was nearly 2 a.m. and she was dropping with fatigue. She leaned heavily against the front door, groping blindly for the light switch, not sure if her shaking legs would support her to the stairs, when the light flooded on. She blinked in sudden fear and couldn't believe her eyes as an equally blinking shirt-sleeved Nick stood outside the sitting room door with his hand still on the switch. They looked at each other in astonishment.

'I thought you were away for the weekend.'

'Whatever are you doing here?'

They both spoke at once. Nick came up and took her bag, and led her into the sitting room. 'I was dossing down there,' he indicated the sofa.

Kate gazed fearfully at him. 'What happened? The children . . . ?'

'It's all right.' His voice was hushed and soothing. 'They're upstairs, asleep.' He poked the fire and threw on some coal and went over to the drinks. He raised his eyebrows questioningly as he held up a bottle of whisky. Kate nodded speechlessly. He poured each of them a whisky.

'Geoffrey's secretary rang, soon after you left apparently, and cancelled the arrangement to have Charlotte and Jeremy this weekend. They were in a bit of a state because they couldn't talk to him direct for some reason, and they didn't know how to reach you. And—' he paused to sip his whisky – 'they didn't have much money. Luckily, I telephoned to see if you were free to come to the cinema with me.' He smiled crookedly. 'And so the story poured out. So I took *them* to the cinema instead. We all enjoyed it. We went to some Pizza Parlour that Charlotte knew so everything was all right, but I thought I'd better stay, so I've been sleeping here.' He patted the sofa. 'Very comfortable it is too. Of course I didn't know you were coming back tonight, I thought the children said Sunday afternoon. Anyway we did a bit of shopping – I must say Charlotte's very practical; we had to follow her list exactly, she wouldn't allow me to buy what she called extravagances.'

Kate shook her head miserably. 'I don't know what to say.'

'Well, between us we cooked a jolly good lunch, and then we drove out to Richmond and walked right across the park. I must say I couldn't face cooking or the Pizza Parlour – dreadful name – again so I took them to a little restaurant near my place in Notting Hill, as I needed to collect a shirt and a couple of other things – this morning I went out unshaven to the shops and bought some of those disposable razors – I felt like a shady character in a detective movie. Then we went to the cinema *again*. And now you're up to date.' He smiled genially at her. 'Drink up – you look as if you need it.'

Kate bent her head over her drink. Hot tears spilled on to her hands. She couldn't speak.

Nick got up and strolled uncomfortably about the room. 'I'm sorry if you think I've made myself too much at home. I didn't know what else to do. My flat isn't big enough to have them there. I suppose they are old enough to be left on their own but somehow I didn't like to do that.'

He gulped his drink, obviously distressed by her silent weeping. 'Look, don't worry. I'll go home now,' he went on as Kate still didn't speak.

'Please don't go.' Her voice was muffled. 'I don't know how to thank you. I think I'm in a state of shock. I never dreamt anything like this would happen. Geoffrey should not have got his secretary to cancel, he should have spoken to me. It's *outrageous*,' she said furiously. Then she subsided again, to blame herself. 'But I'm *just* as much to blame. I shouldn't have gone off before I saw them handed over. But we had to get to darkest Suffolk – it was a long way and very remote.' She gulped at the whisky, glad that it made her choke and splutter so that it looked as if her still-brimming eyes were due to the drink. 'I'm sorry you've had all this trouble. I hope it didn't upset your arrangements too much. You've been very kind – I can't thank you enough.'

'Then don't.' His voice was gentle. 'Why don't you get to bed? You look all in. I'll stay here.'

'There *is* a spare room.' Kate was still smarting with humiliation.

'Charlotte offered it, but it meant making up a bed and frankly, we couldn't face it when we came back late from the cinema. Much easier here with a blanket. I was very comfortable.' Kate looked at him. She hadn't noticed before how very kind and understanding his eyes were. She raised her hands and dropped them again, helplessly. 'Good night.' Anything more was beyond her then.

Despite two consecutive nights short of sleep Kate woke early on the Sunday morning. She grimaced in the mirror as she brushed her hair, thinking of Paul. She went cold with horror at the thought of what might have happened in that remote cottage, that didn't even have a telephone.

Downstairs she put the kettle on and made some tea. Taking a cup, she knocked gently on the sitting-room door. There was no reply. Opening the door quietly, she peered round and saw Nick still asleep, his face more rumpled than ever, his dark hair ruffled. He looked younger. Catching him asleep was curiously intimate. Awake, he always had an alert, slightly amused watchfulness. She started to close the door when he grunted slightly and opened his eyes.

'Good morning.' He was instantly conscious. 'Tea? How lovely. No-one brings me tea in bed except when I stay in a hotel.' Kate's smile was strained. She felt embarrassed at what he must think of her behaviour. 'I hope you slept reasonably well,' she said formally.

'Perfectly. And you?'

She nodded. 'I'm all right. I'm going up to see the children. Have first call on the bathroom – there's a little shower tucked into a cupboard upstairs but I can never get it to work properly. It either scalds you or gives you frostbite.'

Charlotte looked at her disbelievingly. 'I thought you were away.'

'I was. I came back last night. I heard about the fiasco with Daddy.'

Charlotte shrugged. 'He's always been unreliable. But Nick was wonderful.' She looked accusingly at Kate. 'We didn't have any money, and you hadn't done the shopping as you promised. If Nick hadn't called we would have starved!' she added melodramatically.

'I doubt it,' Kate said crisply. 'There's food in the freezer and tins in the larder, and you could always have gone round to Mrs Shepherd's, but still, I'm glad Nick came to the rescue. It was very good of him.'

'He's *fun*,' said Charlotte. 'We had a much better time with him than if we'd gone to Daddy's with Greta Glamour draping herself over him all the time.'

Jeremy stumbled in, yawning and rubbing his eyes. 'I didn't think you were coming back until after lunch.'

'I changed my mind,' Kate said evenly, conscious of Charlotte's sharp, wondering look. 'I brought the shopping back from the country – lovely farm eggs and home-cured bacon.' She suddenly reached out and hugged them both tightly. 'Thank goodness nothing happened to you. I'd never have forgiven myself!'

'We were all right,' Jeremy stiffened resistingly. 'We saw two good films.'

Kate got off Charlotte's bed. 'It sounds as if you've been thoroughly spoilt. Let Nick have the bathroom first, he's the guest, and then hurry downstairs.'

'He's hardly a guest any more,' Charlotte pronounced with assurance, and swung her feet to the floor. 'More like one of the family after this. You owe him a *lot* of money,' she said. 'He paid for all the shopping, and the films and restaurants.'

Over breakfast Charlotte openly questioned Kate about her return. 'What happened?'

'The cottage was damp and comfortless.' Kate headed her off. 'But the country was lovely, and I did some painting. I got up very early and started right away.'

'Hitler was a painter. Maybe you'll be a dictator and start another world war, like him.' Jeremy giggled helplessly at his own wit. Charlotte gave him a withering look and picked up the *Sunday Times* magazine, flopping on to the sofa.

'You *are* still painting then?' Nick's calm voice broke in. 'I'm so pleased. May I have another look later?'

Kate wished she'd kept quiet. She didn't want Nick to look at her paintings. She couldn't understand her own reluctance – unless it was because she felt he was much too penetrating; he'd see too much, more than she wanted anyone to see. She sipped her coffee.

'Please,' he urged. She coloured. She was being ungracious again in the face of his kindness.

'If you like,' she shrugged. *Damn.*

'I suppose we won't be going on the river now?' Jeremy looked at Nick, who looked apologetically at Kate. 'I promised we'd rent a boat and potter up the river,' he said. 'It looked so attractive in the sun yesterday when we went to Richmond Park. Would you like to go?'

'That sounds fun.' She didn't want to go; Nick made her feel uncomfortable. She always seemed to be in his debt. But the children had obviously been looking forward to it, so after breakfast she prepared lunch while Nick and Charlotte read the Sunday papers and Jeremy disappeared to his room, presumably to do some prep.

Nick wandered out around noon with a sherry for her. 'Are you going to let me see those paintings or are you hoping I'll forget all about it?' She was right, he was much too observant, but his voice was teasing and he was smiling.

'OK. Yesterday's effort is still in the car. I expect it's smudged now. It's not dry of course.'

She fetched it from the boot, thankful that she'd stowed the paints straight in there after they'd finished painting. There was Paul's stiff little scene. She'd have to get it to him somehow. She'd get one of the motorbike messengers to take it to the college.

Nick followed her into the boxroom; he stopped abruptly when he saw her Sunday painting on the easel. 'When did you do this?' he asked sharply. Kate shrugged. 'A few Sundays ago. It's not finished. I ran out of time.' He took the still tacky landscape carefully from her and propped it on a table against the wall. 'And this yesterday?' She nodded.

He walked back from the easel, and again closer to it. 'Have you done anything else I haven't seen?' he demanded.

'A few things. Mostly unfinished.' She indicated a few boards and canvases against the wall. He picked them up, scrutinizing them carefully, turning them and propping them in a row along the wall. He walked round and round, occasionally picking one up and turning it to the light. He stopped in front of the easel again for a long silent moment and then spun round suddenly to face Kate.

'You've developed enormously,' he waved at the easel. 'That is tremendous – and *that.*' He pointed to the landscape. 'There's real feeling, a natural sympathy there, and yet you've put a strange spirit in it; you've somehow indicated that Nature isn't altogether kindly, there's a feeling of struggle for survival.' He indicated some vigorous, curling greens. 'Look at those forms, vying for their share of the sun and the rain, toughened in the fight against predators.'

He shook his head and turned back to her again. 'Kate,' he said quietly, 'I was right the first time. You are a real artist. Your work has a rare quality of emotion and vision, and your technique is amazing, especially considering that you've had no proper training. In the short time I've known you it has grown sure, confident. You have an extraordinary colour sense. I—' he broke off and shook his head in wonder. 'How have you managed to keep all this stoppered up for so long?'

'It's just that I've been able to practise since Geoffrey left.' She looked at the work on the easel. When she had painted that she had been aware of that amazing vibrancy and moving colour all around her for the first time. It was strange but now she realized that she was always conscious of it, as of a tune running through her head. The act of taking up her brush and squeezing paint seemed to have given it form, like switching on an electric light and seeing objects in a room illuminated and clarified. Her cheeks were hot. She breathed quickly. 'Are you sure? Are you really any judge?'

'Yes.' He nodded decisively. 'I am. I'll prove it. If you can work on a few more, say at least another five, I'll give you an exhibition, and I guarantee you will sell them all.' He looked serious. 'Can you do it? Do you really want to?'

'I can't think. I have to work to earn a living. There isn't always enough time.'

'You'll have to make time. This has to be your priority. You can't ignore a talent like this.'

She felt as if she were sweeping along on a fast-moving river. She could see where she was going. The rush of the currents didn't seem worrying. She didn't feel afraid, only excited.

'All right. I'll try,' she said abruptly.

Chapter Twenty-Nine

Just before lunch on Tuesday, the telephone rang. Freda turned round in astonishment. 'Someone's asking for Lady Kate Cosgrove. Does he mean you?'

'I expect so,' Kate pulled a face of dismay. It must be her solicitor, which was a relief in one way, because she didn't want to speak to Paul or Jon or Rupert just then, but maddening, in that she had kept her title a secret at work; it could be an embarrassment there. Her thoughts were in turmoil.

But it was Jeremy's headmaster. 'Lady Kate, I wonder if you could spare me a few minutes? I would like to talk to you about your son.'

'He's not ill?' she gasped.

'No – not exactly. But it would be a good idea to have a word with you. Could you possibly manage this afternoon? I understand that you work – your son told me where you were. But this is rather important.'

Kate's head spun. 'Yes, I'll come of course. When?'

'Will two o'clock suit you?'

'Yes, yes – you're sure he's not ill?'

'Quite sure. Two o'clock then. Goodbye.' The line clicked but Kate kept hold of the receiver, her face white. The others looked at her questioningly.

'Something up?' asked Ian.

'That was my son's headmaster. He wants me to go and see him today. He made it seem urgent.'

'Then you must go,' Jessica said in her comfortable voice. 'They never believe anyone has anything to do but suit their convenience – I bet it's nothing more serious than Jeremy's slipping in chemistry, or there's a foreign trip the school wants to organize. But we can manage, can't we, Phillip? There's no panic on?' Phillip lifted his head, blinking absently, ready to nod in agreement so that he could get back to his briefing of an illustrator.

'Did he really say *Lady* Kate Cosgrove?' asked Freda curiously.

'Excuse me,' Kate gasped, and bolted to the cloakroom where she threw up.

Pale, trembling, her head aching, she went back to the office. 'I'm sorry, I'm not feeling myself,' she said in excuse. She bent over a blur of work on her drawing board. What *could* be the matter with Jeremy? She'd already diagnosed her own trouble.

Later, facing James Roberts, the headmaster, she felt that she would either be sick again or faint. He'd told her in a clipped, disapproving voice, his face creased with distaste and concern, that Jeremy had been found smoking cannabis. When he'd been questioned, Jeremy had admitted that it was not the first time, but refused to say where he'd obtained it. He'd had no option but to suspend him. Jeremy was at that moment in the sick bay.

Kate had a feeling of unreality. He *couldn't* be talking about her son, Jeremy, who'd always seemed so young for his age, to her so little changed from the small boy he had been, ready for a cuddle and a bedtime story. The headache that had suddenly descended at the office throbbed ceaselessly.

'I can't believe it. Are you sure?' she whispered, her lips so stiff she could hardly move them to form the words.

'Quite sure.' The head nodded decisively. 'I have no need to tell you, I'm sure, that we consider this very serious. I'm not sure that we can keep Jeremy here.'

Kate stared at him. 'You mean you'd expel him?' She

gazed at him in horror. 'That would be terrible. I'm sure there is some awful mistake or misunderstanding. Could I talk to him?'

'Of course. Indeed, I was going to ask you to take him home for the rest of this week while we consider what is to be done. As far as I know this is the first time he has behaved badly. Until very recently his school work was improving, particularly in maths, and then, according to his form master, he became rude and quarrelsome, making what he thought were immensely amusing jokes out loud in class, giggling uncontrollably at his own inanities, and generally being thoroughly disruptive. It would seem that such behaviour started about the time he first got hold of this drug.'

'I can't believe it,' Kate said again, and stood up. She felt sudden fury towards this smooth, cold man. What a contrast to the cordial character, so anxious to impress them favourably, who had shown Geoffrey and her round the school when they'd first considered sending Jeremy there. 'May I ask you not to take any decision about his future here until I've tried to get to the bottom of it?' she asked, with icy dignity. 'After all, he is coming up to O-levels. As he hasn't been in any trouble before, I think that asking me to take him away at the first hint of misbehaviour could be considered harsh and not a little unreasonable. Besides . . .' her voice broke, 'he's had quite an upset at home which may have gone deeper than I realized. His father has left, and we're in the process of getting a divorce. It has meant my having to take a job and Jeremy has tried to shoulder some of the domestic responsibilities. Indeed, he and his sister have been towers of strength.'

Dr Roberts' expression softened slightly. 'I'm sorry – I didn't know. If only parents would take us more into their confidence our job would be so much easier.' He sighed uneasily. 'Very well. I can see there are extenuating circumstances. But you must remember that drug-taking is illegal. The School cannot condone law-breaking.' His lips primmed and he sighed again. 'I'll not take any decision for a day or two until you've had a chance to talk to him. Perhaps you would telephone to make an appointment so that we can have another discussion? Now I'll take you to the sick bay to meet the young delinquent.' He suddenly smiled and put his arm comfortingly across her shoulders to shepherd her out of the room.

'I'm very sorry to have given you this shock. This isn't the first time such a thing has happened, nor I fear, will it be the last, but some parents don't seem to care, or even realize the danger of drugs. Indeed, I am even assured by some of our more er . . . trendy masters, that cannabis is less dangerous and addictive than alcohol or tobacco. I can't believe that is so, but in any case, while it remains an illegal substance we have to take a strong line with offenders.'

Jeremy was sitting on a hard bunk in the small, cheerless sick bay looking white and frightened. Crossing swiftly to him, Kate put her arms round him. 'Poor darling, whatever has been the matter?' she murmured into his hair as she hugged him to her bosom. The door clicked softly shut behind Dr Roberts. 'I was only trying it out.' His voice was muffled against her shirt, but he was snuffling.

'Darling, don't worry – we'll sort it all out. You're coming home with me now, where we can talk. Get your things.' Jeremy lifted his head in shock.

'You mean I'm expelled? Are they going to get the police? Robbie said it was a police matter.'

'No, no, don't be so dramatic, you'll make Charlotte jealous.' She smiled, trying to cheer him. 'Dr Roberts and I are going to have another talk shortly. Let's get home now and have some tea. It's ages since we've had tea together after school, isn't it?' She talked in a soothing, everyday voice to try and inject some sense of normality into the situation.

In the taxi home, both were silent. Kate held his hand and made the odd remark about the scenes they were passing but there was little response from Jeremy, who sat with his chin sunk on his chest, seemingly riveted by the state of his shoes.

Kate made them some tea and toast and lit an unnecessary fire in the sitting room. They sat by it quietly, until Jeremy said haltingly, 'Some of the older boys went on a school trip to Holland with the art master; they're doing a project or something on Dutch painting for their As, and they got it there. They were passing it round. Everybody in our form had some. And I liked it, it made me feel good so I got some more. Everybody kept laughing at my jokes. Usually no-one takes much notice of me.'

'Who gave it to you?' Kate demanded. 'Did he just *give* it to you? I thought drugs were supposed to cost a lot of money.'

Jeremy looked mulish. 'I can't tell you his name. I swopped it for the Cup Final tickets Dad gave me – I was going to ask Josh to come with me. I was sorry afterwards because I really wanted to go to that match. I think Dad had quite a bit of trouble getting them, too. He'll be angry about it. But at the time it seemed like a terrific dare.'

'Oh darling.' Kate looked at him sorrowfully. 'You were silly. But what about now? Do you have any more?'

He shook his head emphatically. 'No – the last time I had some I felt awful. I didn't want to do it again.'

'You *are* telling the truth? I can't help you if I can't believe in you.'

He looked directly into her eyes, his own still bright with unshed tears, his chin not totally under control. 'I'm telling the truth. I don't tell lies,' he said earnestly, hurt that she should even consider the possibility. She touched his hand gently. 'Good. I'm sure you don't. Let's forget it now. I'll talk to Dr Roberts tomorrow. He'll want to know the name of the boy you got it from, you know.'

'I'm not sneaking!' Jeremy said defiantly.

'Come and help me in the kitchen. I thought you were going to the Astronomy Club, but I don't suppose that's on now.' A bit of punishment wouldn't hurt, she thought, and he would miss the Cup Final. Her mind buzzed, trying to think of how best to deal with the problem. She didn't want to press him on the name of the boy from whom he got the drugs; he might reveal it inadvertently sooner or later. She had very little knowledge of drugs; of course she'd read stories of pop stars and drug addiction. She could understand the need for people caught up in the competitive adulatory hothouse of the pop music world, but how could an unfamiliar drug attract one small immature schoolboy?

'Don't tell Charlotte, will you?' Jeremy looked up at her anxiously. 'She'll never let me forget it.'

'No, of course not. Stop worrying. Scrub those potatoes – they're nice new ones. And see if there's any mint showing in the garden. It spread into that cold frame, so there may be a bit. I brought these English lamb chops back from Suffolk, they look delicious.' She strove for normality.

A shattering bang of the front door announced Charlotte's surprisingly early return from school. Kate went into the hall to greet her and was met by a blazing-eyed daughter, red spots burning her cheeks. 'It's your fault!' she yelled, throwing her bag of books on the hall floor. She stormed up the stairs, stamping on every tread and crying noisily. Kate was appalled.

Running up after her, she just managed to hold on to the door Charlotte attempted to slam in her face.

'Whatever is the matter?' Kate cried as her daughter flung herself on her bed, sobbing bitterly.

'I didn't get the part! I didn't get the part!' she yelled, turning a contorted face to her mother. 'Cundy said I hadn't prepared properly, I read like a wooden top.'

'What part?' Kate was perplexed.

'There, you see? You don't even know what's going on. You're not interested in anything or anyone but yourself.' She turned into the pillow with a fresh storm of weeping.

'You mean the Birthday Celebration play? But that's not until next term – you told me it was the first week of the new term, the centenary of the school!'

'But we have to rehearse it – it's an *important* one. Both schools are going to make sets and design and make the costumes and *everything*. Cundy began casting it today and I'd set my heart on being Raina – it's the best part. Now Serena Somers has it, and she's vile. She's never forgiven me for being Creon when she was just a senator. Both heads want the schools to be closer because of all this fuss about co-education, so there are only three parts for us.'

'How is it my fault?' Kate tried to sound amused but she felt as if this whole day was beoming a kind of nightmare.

'Well, you're never home. And you forget things. And I'm worried sick about money. It never balances. We spend too much and you don't even know or care – you leave it to a thirteen-year-old to do the family budget! It's been getting Jeremy down. I have to do *everything* – I didn't have time to prepare properly. You have to psych yourself up into a part! There's always too much to *do* now! I have my prep, and I have to look after Jeremy, get the shopping, cook our supper . . . and look at how we nearly went without food at the weekend because there was no money and you'd gone off with some man!'

'That's not fair,' Kate cut in sharply. 'Stop that noise. How can we talk when you sound like a banshee?' Charlotte stopped in sheer surprise at her mother's tone and looked round.

'And why are *you* home so early?' she demanded. 'What else has gone wrong?'

'Never mind that now. It's true, you've been very good and helped me enormously while I was trying to learn my job; I've been very touched, and very proud of you both. But I've *had* to work late – it's part of the deal. I can't be the only one dashing home early when there are deadlines to meet. Jessica has *three* children and *she* stays when there's a panic on. If you have clients spending millions of pounds they want to see their campaigns when it suits them, and if they want to have changes made, we have to revise all our roughs and storyboards. And I thought Jeremy would *like* to feel the man of the house, particularly as he's had problems with maths. I thought balancing the books would encourage him, show him I believed he could do it.' Her voice shook.

'Yes but you go out a lot too,' Charlotte said accusingly. 'And you're always tired. I'm terrified in the mornings in case we all oversleep and you'll lose your job. I don't think you know how big your bank loan is now. *I've* kept a check and it gets bigger every month. You're not paying *anything* back. And you say you'll bring something in and then you forget.' She started to sob again as she catalogued her mother's crimes.

Kate tried to speak evenly. 'Very occasionally, I do forget the shopping, that's true. And I have been out a few times – you urged me to go with Flip. I thought you were glad I wasn't a burden for you, that you would not like to think of me as a pathetic rejected wife sitting alone at home feeling sorry for herself. And,' she added with a continued attempt to defuse the situation, 'to be frank, it was very pleasant to meet new people, even to having one or two men flirt with me. It was something novel for me.' Her cheeks flared in embarrassment as she admitted to herself that it had been more than flirtation. We can't be having this conversation, Kate thought. I can't believe that in one day both my children should become strangers. She felt the already-familiar black taste in her mouth and rushed to the bathroom. She walked slowly back to Charlotte's bedroom. Charlotte gave a frightened glance at her pale face, and looked down at her hands uncomfortably.

'I'm sorry,' Kate said quietly. 'You see, I'm afraid I might be pregnant.'

Charlotte jerked up her head, her eyes wide with horror. 'That's disgusting!' She was so outraged that she stopped crying.

'I am sorry.' Kate felt deeply ashamed.

'Was it that phony film star you went away with?' Charlotte's eyes were hot with indignation.

'Absolutely not.' She marvelled that Charlotte had spotted Paul's turpitude when she had not.

'Trust me to have an unmarried mother for a mother!' Charlotte exclaimed. They looked at each other in shocked silence, and then, simultaneously, started to laugh, giggling helplessly at Charlotte's words. They put their arms round each other, rocking backwards and forwards on the bed, crying and laughing shakily, relieved at the breaking of the tension.

Kate straightened up first and said firmly: 'This is no way for me to behave. I'm sorry, you're quite right, darling. I don't think I've handled my so-called independence at all well. I think I've been too bowled over, trying to learn all at once things I should have known since my teens. A mother in her mid-thirties is supposed to know it all. I suppose that I've confused independence and irresponsibility. You've both been such bricks I'd forgotten how young you still are, and how much schoolwork you have.' She gave a gesture of helplessness. 'You're so right,' she conceded again. 'I've made a thorough mess of things. But I'll work something out,' she said decisively. 'You're not to worry any more.'

Charlotte shook her head in miserable apology. *'I'm*

sorry – I didn't understand. I was furious with Daddy and wanted you to get back at him, but somehow I didn't like you going out with other men. I haven't minded helping, really, but it has all got on top of me lately, and Jeremy has been so difficult he's driven me round the bend. I don't know what's got into him but he's been behaving strangely –idiotic and noisy and threatening to do stupid things. He stood on his bedroom window-sill and said he could float down into the garden. I had a terrible job to make him get down.'

She leaned her head into Kate's shoulder. Kate put an arm round her, and stared at her reflection in Charlotte's dressing table mirror. Why hadn't she noticed? She had become self-centred and neglectful. She drew a deep breath. 'First of all, we'll have to look at that play. Cundy won't overlook you altogether – you're far too talented – *Antigone* proved that. It's not always the star role that has the most depth either. I bet she didn't want you to get too complacent. We'll go through it together and see what else you can try for – it's not all cast, is it?' Charlotte shook her head.

'But what about you?' she whispered. 'Are you really pregnant?'

'I think so. Stupid, isn't it, at my age? But that's *my* problem. And you must stop worrying about the budget. I know it doesn't balance properly yet but Mr Bennett will sort things out – apparently I may have a tax rebate on my allowance from Grandpa's estate. I arranged with the beastly bank manager to run up a loan for the time being. Look,' she added and got up, 'don't let's leave Jeremy alone. Don't tell him about me, that's *our* secret for the moment. Let's have supper and discuss how I'm going to arrange things better at home. Go and splash your face. I'm sure if Greta Glamour saw you now she'd send you straight to make-up.' They both smiled wet-eyed at the shared joke, and Kate went downstairs.

Chapter Thirty

When the doorbell rang they started in surprise. 'Nick!' said Charlotte first. 'You were going to the theatre with him, remember?' Kate had totally forgotten that on Sunday, after the trip on the river, she had promised to go to the theatre with Nick on Tuesday. When she had said decisively she didn't want to go out and upset the children again he had said good-humouredly: 'Well, I can fill you in on their plans. Jeremy is going to the Astronomy Society because they have the Astronomer Royal, no less, coming to talk to them, and Charlotte says it's the first joint debate with the boys' school at which they're discussing the fiendishly original motion "This house believes a sportsman's life is nasty, brutish and short".' They'd both laughed and she'd agreed to go.

Jeremy went to let Nick in, but Kate shook her head in dismay. 'I *can't*.'

Nick came in. Looking at their faces, he asked, 'Something up?'

Kate shook her head. 'Jeremy's Astronomy Club is off, and *I've* simply got too much to do. Nick, I'm sorry, I *can't* come. Is there someone else you can phone at this hour?'

He looked at them shrewdly again. 'Well, what a relief. I read the reviews this morning and it sounds awful. I was wondering if you'd ever forgive me for inflicting such a dire evening on you, and this solves the problem.' He took the tickets out of his pocket and calmly tore them up. Charlotte gasped. 'That's sacrilege!'

'Probably,' he agreed. 'I thought you were going to a debate?'

Charlotte glanced quickly at Kate. 'I was. But it doesn't matter.'

'Oh, Charlotte,' Kate said contritely. '*Please* go. I was getting carried away.'

'No, I think I'd rather stay with you.' But she was half-hearted. Kate realized that Nathan was probably one of the team.

'I'll run you there,' Nick cut in smoothly. 'It won't take ten minutes and then,' he turned to Kate, 'as you've stood me up I shall expect you to give me a drink if not an omelette to go with it.'

Kate lifted her shoulders in agreement and Nick ushered Charlotte out.

'What shall we have for pud?' Kate turned to Jeremy. 'Can you make a fruit salad with one elderly banana, a rather spongy imported apple, and some of the remaining blackcurrants in the freezer? Or shall I whizz it all up with some cream and hope for the best? Gracious living's in short supply at the moment, I'm afraid.' Jeremy grinned and produced some chèvre they'd bought on Saturday. 'Nick won't mind what we have. He just hates eating alone, he told us.'

Nick was back inside of twenty minutes with a bottle of wine under his arm. 'A crowd of young men were waiting around the gates looking doleful until Charlotte turned up. I think she's having a Zuleika Dobson effect on Barnabas. If she hadn't gone a great many would-be orators might have slit their throats,' he reported. He handed the bottle to Jeremy. 'Here, you're much more efficient with a corkscrew than I am.'

When Jeremy had gone rather early to bed after a supper time that seemed extraordinarily normal and cheerful, Nick leaned back in an armchair and said, 'What's up? You don't need to tell me if I'm intruding. But if I can help, let me.'

'It's not what you can do, it's what I must do. I feel as if a ton of bricks has fallen on me today. Charlotte's failed to get the lead in the school play on which she has set her heart. She regards it as largely my fault because I've let her assume too much responsibility for running the house and looking after Jeremy, who has been getting beyond her, and I quite see why. Apparently, he has been smoking pot, which has made him behave in this strange way. He has been caught in the act at school, and is now suspended pending "sentence".' She paused, and gave a trembling sigh. 'It's my fault. I was so excited by having a job for the very first time that I got too wrapped up in it. In effect, I suppose they feel they've lost *both* parents. They have behaved in a very grown-up way over Geoffrey's leaving. And of course, they've been more upset by that than they realize. He wasn't ever at home much, but he is their father and I know he's fond of them, particularly Jeremy.' She looked up at him. 'It's at times like these that I wish I smoked – I can see how it would be a comfort in moments of stress.'

He wrinkled his nose in distaste, got up and moved about the room, his hands thrust into his pockets. 'Pot-smoking isn't serious. I'll bet most kids have a go at it. Curiosity is healthy, after all.'

'That's not the view the head takes.'

'Oh, that's just to frighten you. He'd be laughed out of the Headmasters' Association or whatever it is if he made an example of an obviously innocent young kid like Jeremy. It probably hasn't been going on very long. He has to appear to take a strong line, because it *is* illegal to smoke the stuff, but I wager he'll find some excuse for getting off his high horse. Have you told Geoffrey?'

'No, of course not.' Kate looked at him in surprise.

'I think you should – it's his problem as well as yours, and, as you say, Jeremy is very fond of him.'

'I hadn't thought of it,' Kate said slowly. 'Of course I

should. I've tended to wipe him out of our lives, but that's unfair. I'll ring him tomorrow. Dr Roberts asked me to telephone him tomorrow but I'll speak to Geoffrey first.'

'I don't think Charlotte is a problem.' Nick was still strolling thoughtfully about. 'She's very adult; she'll get over it once the sharpness of the disappointment wears off. In any case, it is very good for her to learn that star roles don't always go to the most talented or deserving. It's a useful early lesson if she's serious about the stage.'

'Nick, you are a great support.' Kate leaned back in her chair and gazed up at him gratefully. He did have a solid maturity and shrewd commonsense about him that was immensely comforting. He irritated her from time to time, but there was no doubt that he'd helped her with the job, although he had never once alluded to the fact that he'd arranged her meeting with Joe Grimshaw. Without that she would never have got inside JWT. He had fortuitously turned up when the children were feeling abandoned and frightened, and had taken charge, staying with them and giving them such a good time that what could have been a nasty incident was merely another source of their annoyance with her; and now his reassuring presence seemed to shrink her problems to a manageable size.

He looked uncomfortable. 'Isn't that what "old family friends" are for? Isn't that how you think of me?'

'Yes, of course. I'm immensely grateful. Your mere presence is soothing, even without your good advice,' she smiled. But there was more behind his remark, an unusual emphasis on 'old family friend'.

'Not a very glamorous role, is it?' He made a grimace and stopped his pacing to stand directly before her. 'An "old family friend" doesn't cut a very romantic figure. I suppose it hasn't occurred to you that I might be in love with you?'

He bent down and put his hands on the arms of her

chair and brought his face close to hers. 'I don't want to be an old family friend, especially not yours.'

Kate pressed back into the chair, gazing in shocked surprise at his kindly face, now darkened by an expression of mixed intensity and embarrassment. 'I'm sorry. I had no idea, truly. It never occurred to me.' Of course, she should have realized. Why would he have taken so much trouble with them if he hadn't another motive? Here was someone else she had taken too much for granted. She felt very tired.

'But you have been out with other men; they don't apparently have the same difficulty getting you to go out with them as I have. I always have to find an excuse to see you.'

'Is that why you're encouraging me to paint? So that you can pretend to criticize my work and come round to see it?' Kate demanded, bridling. She felt a sense of betrayal, because she had begun to feel so much more assured about her work.

'No,' he said, and straightened up crossly. 'Don't be so – so feminine. I don't confuse my work with my affections. You have tremendous talent and I'd like to see you go on to what I believe will be really great work. I'd encourage you in that direction in any case – even if I disliked you. At least give me a little credit.' He turned away, trying to hide his hurt.

'I'm sorry,' Kate said again. She felt helpless and totally drained, as if she were seeping silently away through the armchair. This at the end of a distressing day was too much. 'I'm very sorry.' She pressed herself into an even smaller, more miserable heap. How could she explain that she didn't find him attractive? She had been carried away on the heady tide of freedom once Geoffrey had left, intoxicated with Flip's freewheeling behaviour and the men she'd met through her, so different from the others she had known. She'd been shocked out of that temporary aberration by the ugliness of Paul's conduct, and the children's problems, but the last thing she now wanted was for Nick to be in love with her.

He bent down and tilted her chin up. 'Don't worry, little one. It's not your fault. I shouldn't have let myself love you – I could see it coming when I first met you and you looked so forlorn and vulnerable.' He brushed her lips lightly with his. 'Good night. I'll take myself off. Tell Charlotte not to worry about the loss of her part. There will be scores she'll be able to choose from in the years ahead. Like you she has a real talent.'

He virtually melted through the sitting-room door. She heard his car start up and drive away. She remembered the time, long ago, when she had been swimming in the sea, believing herself to be within her depth, with Esme comfortingly behind. When she became tired and tried to stand up, the sandy seabed was no longer there under her nor was Esme near. There'd been only water – cold, deep water.

Chapter Thirty-One

Kate was surprised at how coolly and efficiently her mind functioned the next day. She'd lain awake thinking about how to cope better with all the problems. Jeremy was in trouble; Charlotte was upset; they weren't making ends meet – and she was pregnant. Not an auspicious start to her independent life. She tried to avoid thinking about Nick. But she was not going to fail. She *could* do better – mentally she pulled a face as she recognized the echo of a recurring remark on Jeremy's school reports.

She telephoned Joe Grimshaw and Phillip at home to ask if they'd mind if Jeremy came with her to the office, while she sorted out a minor family crisis. Having had their unenthusiastic agreement, she telephoned Geoffrey and said it was vital for them to meet that very morning to discuss Jeremy.

His voice, like hers, sharpened with anxiety as he immediately asked, 'Is he ill?' and, only partially reassured, he agreed to meet her at a café just off Berkeley Square.

Jeremy was quiet and shy as he came with her through the foyer of JWT. He looked about him, curious and impressed. She was glad they were the first in the office. She found Jeremy a seat and showed him, briefly, some of the campaigns they were preparing. 'I'll show you how to work the duplicator machine later; you could save us a lot of time if you can manage that.' As the others came in, she introduced them, and was glad that Jeremy's presence prevented Freda from probing about her title. Jeremy had brought some books and seemed quite content when she slipped out to meet Geoffrey.

He looked very strained. 'First Greta, now this,' he groaned, when she filled him in.

'Greta?'

'Yes – that's why I had to cancel the children's visit. She's been offered an enormous salary increase to go to work for Neptune, and I spent the weekend trying to talk her out of it. I thought a trip to Paris might bribe her. She's very popular; we can't afford to lose her.'

'Did you manage it?'

'I don't think so. I don't know. She's only twenty-six and it's a big compliment to be wooed by one of the established, heavyweight stations.' His eyes looked bleak. 'But I'm shocked about Jeremy. How did you let him get hold of the stuff?' His old belligerence returned. He immediately assumed that it somehow was her fault, and – she acknowledged – perhaps it was. But she held her tongue.

'I didn't know anything about it. He hasn't seemed quite himself lately but I thought he was sickening for flu or worrying about his schoolwork. Unlike Charlotte he finds a lot of his subjects uphill work. As I haven't met anyone who takes drugs I didn't recognize the signs, but apparently he'd merely tried them out of curiosity. Dr Roberts is being sticky, though. I have to ring him to discuss it further but meanwhile I'm to keep Jeremy at home.'

'I'll come with you to see Roberts,' Geoffrey said indignantly. 'I won't have him bullying me. It's *his* responsibility to keep drugs out of his school. Poor kid.' His voice softened. 'I expect he took my leaving much harder than I realized. I'll have to spend more time with him.'

Her lips twitched at Geoffrey's assumption that, as

usual, he was the centre of interest. She wished she had a little of his arrogance. But he was right. Jeremy was very fond of his father. She thought of how sick he'd been when Charlotte had threatened never to see him again.

She told Geoffrey it would be a comfort to have him there when she saw Dr Roberts again; he was rather intimidating, and she promised to let him know as soon as she'd made an appointment. Back at the agency, she rang the school and was relieved when the head suggested 5 p.m. that day. The sooner the agony and suspense were over the better. When she got through to him again, Geoffrey sighed heavily, like a man carrying all the troubles of the world single-handedly, but agreed that though he was extremely busy, he could manage to make time for something as important as his son, and arranged to call for her.

She then asked to see Joe Grimshaw, and put her cards on the table. After telling him the whole story she added, 'You see, what with the break-up of the marriage and my taking a job I think the children have found adjusting more difficult than I realized. They've helped me cope with things at home, and *appeared* to be taking things in their stride, but it's obvious now that they were knocked off balance, at a time of heavy school pressure as well. I think the strain has been a bit too much for them lately.'

Joe folded his arms on a pile of videos and rested his chin on them. 'Difficult. I've a son taking a couple of A levels for the second time. It's agony for him – and us.' He grimaced. 'Don't worry about the pot-smoking. I bet half the people we know run on the stuff – I'm in favour of it being legalized. I don't think it's any worse than alcohol – probably a lot less dangerous, and they'll prove it sooner or later. How can I help?' he asked kindly. He gave no sense of hurry or pressure though Kate knew how busy he must be.

She smiled gratefully. 'I was just wondering if it would

be possible for me to work part time here and take work home each day? Then I could be on the spot when they come in from school. Phillip says I'm quick. I could bring in the afternoon work first thing in the morning and if there were a crisis, well, I could stay, on occasion, or use one of the motorbike messengers. Naturally I'd pay, in that case.' Joe's eyes disappeared into their thicket of wrinkles as he rubbed his grizzled hair into a mad halo. 'Possible. Possible. But I have another idea,' he said, looking directly at her and stretching his eyes to their widest extent. 'I was thinking about broaching it to you shortly anyway. I think your touch is much too good for roughs. Phillip was talking about it when we lunched recently. We wondered if you might try to have a shot at the finished work, some of the illustration?'

'Oh, I'd love it,' she gasped. 'But I'm not sure I can vary my style enough to suit different products.'

'You wouldn't have to. Develop your own – a strong, individual style is much the best. As long as you can draw – and you can. That was clear to me from the first. If that idea appeals, you'd only have to come in for briefing from time to time. I think Phillip likes to have you here because you work fast, and he'll be a bit reluctant to let you out of the office, but I think we might be making better use of your talents.'

Kate's mind raced. Her confidence had increased so much as she'd learned more about advertising, that she knew she could do the work. Without the strict daily schedule, she'd be able to arrange her own – and even, if she managed well, get on with her painting. She wanted desperately to complete the pictures for Nick.

She looked frankly at Joe. 'It sounds lovely, but I have to be practical now. I *have* to earn a living. I can't afford to earn less. If I don't get enough commissions from you for the finished art work, could I top up with the roughs?'

'Silly muggins – you'll earn *more!* Our problem, I

foresee, will be keeping you exclusively to us. Agency personnel constantly change, as you may have noticed.' He pulled a face. 'When someone goes to another agency the first thing they do is try to poach the best staff and contributors from the old one.'

'What a lovely position to be in!' Kate cried. 'I do hope someone tries to tempt me. If you mean it, then of course I accept. It would solve a lot of my problems.' Impulsively, she leaned across and planted a kiss on his forehead. 'You've been very understanding, I do appreciate it.' He looked embarrassed and his eyes disappeared again. 'Ask Phillip to come in and I'll tell him what we've discussed. If I'm as clever as I think I am, he'll think it was his idea.'

When it was time for Geoffrey to show up, Kate had collected a pile of unfinished work and, promising she'd be back with it all done in the morning, ushered Jeremy out to the waiting car. He looked with apprehensive eyes at his father and smiled feebly when Geoffrey patted his knee and said 'You silly bugger,' in a genial tone. 'I thought you'd given up playing with fire when you set the bedroom curtains alight that time. Now I've got to lick Roberts' boots and try to get you off the hook.'

'Sorry,' Jeremy mumbled, hanging his head. Kate turned to look out of the window. Had Geoffrey *always* been so egotistical? Had she really never noticed the excessive use of 'I?' The driver cut through the traffic and Kate pondered the difference between the cosseting Geoffrey received from his secretary and chauffeur and her own daily sprints for bus or tube train, often with bags of shopping.

But she had to admit Geoffrey was impressive in Dr Roberts' study. Adopting a mixture of urbane worldliness, understanding of the other's 'difficult' position, and subtle flattery, nodding agreement and interjections of 'Quite right' and 'I do understand' and 'How do you manage to put up with the little horrors day after day?', he won Roberts round to a jovial man-to-man rapport. Turning on all his earnest, little-boy charm, he promised, 'I'll keep a firmer eye on the young idiot myself in future.' Kate kept her indignation under control but she seethed with the injustice of it. The situation had somehow been turned into a case of an incompetent mother giving a son too much loose rein.

Geoffrey ended by inviting Dr Roberts and his wife to the studio to participate in the audience discussion with distinguished panellists in one of their 'Citizen Speaks' programmes.

Outside the now-affable headmaster's study, Geoffrey rubbed his hands with satisfaction and turned to Kate. 'I don't think you'll be hearing any more about expulsion. It was just as well I was able to come with you. I'll talk to Jeremy. He'd better not muff it again.'

Kate pressed her lips together on a rising retort. She forgot it on seeing Jeremy's scared face, watching for them through the car window, break into a huge relieved smile when Geoffrey gave him a triumphant thumbs up sign. 'Thanks, Dad,' he said warmly when they got into the car, and heard that Dr Roberts had said he could return to school tomorrow, and that the incident was closed.

'Now, where would you like to be dropped?' Geoffrey's air of high-pressured executive returned.

'Fulham,' said Kate, looking straight ahead.

'I have to get back to the studio,' Geoffrey protested.

'There's an empty taxi,' she pointed at a couple cruising round Westminster Square. 'It won't take you long by cab whereas I think Jeremy and I ought to get home as soon as possible. We've had a lot of strain.' Geoffrey stared at her for a moment, and then got out of the car. 'Take Lady Kate home to Fulham, Fitzer,' he said to the driver. He put his head through the window again. ''Bye old chap. Hope to see you Friday. Goodbye Kate. You *have* changed.' He shook his head sadly.

As they drove off Kate burst into giggles and, after squirming uncomfortably, Jeremy uncertainly joined in.

The two of them had a comfortable hour or two before Charlotte's return. Kate organized part of the supper, while Jeremy laid the table and prepared the vegetables. They chatted companionably, without the underlying tension of the last few days.

'Mum,' Jeremy said, standing awkwardly in the centre of the kitchen holding a handful of knives and forks. 'I'm really not a drug addict. I did try it out but you have to believe me – I won't take it again.' She touched his cheek, a lump in her throat. 'I know. We all make mistakes. You grow out of some and make others. Who was it said something like "a wise man profits by other's mistakes, a fool learns by his own"? I'm still, at my advanced age, being very much of a fool, so you're entitled to a few mistakes here and there. Not for a long time, mind you.' She grinned broadly. 'You've had your quota for the time being.'

When Charlotte came home Kate was reading *Arms and the Man*. 'I suppose you wanted to be Raina?' she asked. Charlotte nodded, her eyes searching her mother's face.

'Louka is so much stronger. She knows where she's going, she won't be manipulated or put-down, she's a realist. She could steal the play . . . if she wanted to. What's more, she has a sense of irony which is lacking in Raina – *she's* just a pretty face. Though I'll bet the Boy's School chose this play? Shaw rarely wrote a decent part for a woman – I'd have thought they'd have chosen something with more characters.'

'I think it's cost – more characters, more costumes. Anyway, it's supposed to be quality, not width. Cundy has something up her sleeve. I think she wants to have a real theatre funded for the schools and this is her launch pad.'

'Who's being Bluntschli?' Kate asked.

'Nathan.'

'Ah.'

Charlotte blushed.

After supper they read the play together, dissecting and arguing, with Jeremy reading some of the parts.

'You're right, Mum. I can put more into Louka. I'll make sure that cat Cundy has no option but to give it to me on Thursday.' She lifted a determined chin. 'And I'll be so good that Serena will be sick as a parrot.' She kissed Kate exuberantly. 'How are you feeling?' she asked with a meaningful change of tone.

'Fine,' Kate said hastily. 'Fine. But I have some work to do for the office before the morning, so I'll work in the dining-room. You two go to bed. Jeremy, set my alarm please, dear. I don't feel I can rely on it if I do it.' The last thing she wanted then was for Charlotte to question her about her pregnancy. It was so bizarre that it still seemed unreal. Yet she had delayed action on too many things in her life. This was one she couldn't duck much longer.

Nick phoned a bit later, to say that he was off to the States, where he was setting up a New York office. He'd been thinking about it for some time and casting around for a suitable opening, because New York was where all the art money was today. His agent had telephoned about a small but reputable dealer who had an eye on retirement, but in the meantime was interested in some form of partnership. It was too good an opportunity to miss, so he'd be flying off tomorrow, and if all went well, would be away for some time. It was time he had a look round again there anyway.

She was relieved that they wouldn't have to meet very soon in the embarrassed aftermath of his declaration of love, and grateful for his tact. She had recovered her equilibrium and was able to say 'I'll miss you,' meaning it.

'So will the children,' she added quickly, to avert a too-personal interpretation. She told him about Geoffrey and their visit to Dr Roberts, and that Charlotte had calmed down.

'Good. I was sure it would all turn out all right. But you – you *will* go on painting? I don't wish to keep on repeating myself to the point of tedium, but after your unfair assumption last night, I'm terrified that you'll let mundane everyday details get in the way.'

'I won't,' she promised. 'I'm sorry if I was mean – it had been a rough day. I've now made an arrangement with Joe for me to work from home; I'm just finishing off a pile of roughs now, which I'll take in tomorrow. That gives them a breathing space, and then I am going to work on a freelance basis, which means I'll be able to spend much more time on doing some work for you to see when you get back.'

'Good.' There was a long, slightly uncomfortable pause.

'You *will* write to me or telephone from time to time, Nick?'

He gave a short laugh. 'I'm sure your life is much too busy and crowded for you to want to hear from me. And I'll have masses to do – all the legal arrangements will be very involved.'

'*Please.*'

'All right.' His voice lightened a little. 'Take care of yourself. Goodbye.'

Kate put the phone down sadly. Nick was hurt and she was unable to assuage his feelings. She *would* miss him. Recently he seemed to have materialized whenever she needed advice or support. But she could not think of him as any more than a friend of Tom's. She understood how he must be feeling. Rejection was bitter, as she knew only too well. It took a bit of concentration to clear the reminiscent blur from her eyes, that made the roughs in front of her seem so out of focus.

Chapter Thirty-Two

Joe was right, Phillip did act as if it was all his idea. When she gave him the work she'd slaved over until the early hours, he behaved like a kindly old master to a bright pupil who had begun at last to fulfil her potential.

Kate was worried about the reaction of her colleagues. Would they resent her now? She couldn't bear to lose the easy, casual relationship she'd achieved with the three of them. Freelance artists were accorded a grudging respect, as befits people hired solely on their creative ability, but they weren't one of them. They didn't share the daily crises and triumphs, the in-jokes and the domestic gossip.

Tentatively she suggested treating them all to lunch. 'It's not a farewell lunch,' she said nervously. 'I hope I'm going to come in lots.'

'I thought you'd ask us to dine in the baronial hall,' Freda said waspishly. But Ian swept a low bow. 'Charmed, my lady. This peasant's paycheck was exhausted days ago.'

Kate blushed. 'Oh please, don't,' she begged. 'That's all such nonsense.'

'Well, *are* you a Lady or not?' Freda's tone was still a little acid.

'Let's go and eat and you can hear the whole riveting story.'

Kate was being exaggeratedly bright in her efforts to make everything seem normal. Jessica smiled, a little distantly, thought Kate ruefully as she got her hat and coat. She was grateful to Ian for making them all laugh with an exaggerated pantomime of obsequiousness, opening doors for her with a flourish, pulling out her chair in the restaurant with swaggering display, tugging his forelock and calling her 'My lady' at every opportunity, making a farce of it.

'I've never seen anyone climb the ladder so fast,' Freda said into her drink. '*I've* been here longer than you and no-one's asked *me* to do the freelance sketching. I've always *heard* that a title isn't exactly a drawback.'

'Oh, do be fair,' Jessica cut in with an admonitory look at Freda. 'We said ourselves that Kate was too good for the work she was doing. I'm glad for you,' she said generously to Kate. 'But are you really a Lady?'

'I'm afraid so. It's ridiculous I know, but there's not much I can do about it.' She didn't know how to play it. She wanted desperately to keep their friendship. They were her first colleagues, people who had made her first tentative weeks at work supportable. They had welcomed her as one of them though they must have spotted how raw she was, surely. She decided to plunge.

'My father was a rather impecunious earl who spent what little money he had financing his fairly fruitless archaeological expeditions. The only time he discovered anything of importance, an amphitheatre, was at the moment when I made my arrival into the world. My mother never forgave me. She was stuck in some nursing home while he had the glory. It cast a blight over my entire childhood.' She laughed and suddenly realized it was the first time she'd been able to tell the story without feeling bitter and swamped with resentment. It made her feel tremendously light-hearted, as if she had suddenly let slip a burdening rucksack.

'I'd rather like to be Lady Mitchell,' Jessica said unexpectedly. 'I can see all sorts of advantages, mostly unfair ones, but whoever said life was fair?' She knocked back her wine. 'I'm going to make a mad, extravagant dash to Daniel's; I have a friend coming to dinner and there's nothing in the house.' She brushed Kate's cheek and scuttled off.

The others looked knowing. 'We think Jessica has an admirer,' said Ian, tapping his nose like a Victorian actor. 'She's had her hair done, and,' he looked from side to side elaborately as if to make sure no-one was listening, 'she was seen in Miss Selfridge's trying on a boater.' Kate threw back her head and laughed. 'You're a clown. What a lovely idea! What a lucky man it will be to get Jessica.'

'I need some new shoes,' Freda said suddenly. 'Have you time to come and help me choose them? You know what I'm like.' It was her way of indicating that everything was all right again. Kate felt immensely relieved.

The first weeks of being an accredited freelance were disorientating. Kate felt jealous as Charlotte and Jeremy rushed off to the station without her. The house seemed much too quiet, and she pottered about restlessly, tidying a cupboard, making shopping lists, drifting in the garden, amazed that she'd never noticed before not only how empty the house was during the day, but how the very street seemed lifeless. At first she worried herself sick too about whether Joe and Phillip would actually give her any work. Maybe it was a heaven-sent opportunity for them to get rid of her in favour of someone more experienced? When Phillip finally telephoned, asking her to come up the following Wednesday to talk over some work for a client's autumn campaign, she fairly babbled with relief. 'Oh, I do miss you all,' Kate said, sitting on the briefing stool beside Phillip. 'The house is so quiet I find it hard to settle down to work. I'd never noticed it before.'

'It's quiet in the office too,' said Ian, teasing her. 'I never realized what a chatterbox you were.'

Going home late she hoped she wouldn't bump into Jon. He hadn't telephoned lately, so she assumed he had another inmate for the big white bed. Her own eagerness to make sexual progress, to attain that 'good in bed' label, had abruptly subsided after the frightful experience with Paul. She was ashamed of her rash, promiscuous behaviour now. The previous evening, glancing at one of the many feminist books Flip had lent her, she had opened at random Germaine Greer's to read: 'Sex for many has become a sorry business, a mechanical release involving neither discovery nor triumph, stressing human isolation more dishearteningly than ever before.' It had struck forcibly home. Why couldn't she have worked out for herself that sex had to be a physical expression of love, not merely a physical exploration?

She smiled to herself, thinking over the morning's meeting at the studio. They were a warm, friendly bunch. She'd make sure she asked them home to a meal; in fact, she'd make sure she asked anyone else she liked to a meal. She didn't have to moulder away in solitary state simply because she was separated, nor did she want to go on another feverish search for a lost youth in a round of parties and discos. Flip was a stimulant and interesting. She had been very good for her, but now she wanted to stand unequivocally on her own feet. She felt rueful as she realized she had never taken any initiatives; she hadn't decided to end a thoroughly unsatisfactory marriage, it was Geoffrey who had left *her*. It was Esme who had adamantly moved on, refusing to let Kate lean on her again; Flip who'd made her go out and meet people; Nick who'd engineered an introduction so that she could get a job. She mentally squared her shoulders as she thought that she was now really on her own, and whatever future direction her life would take, it would be her hand on the tiller.

It wasn't long before she settled into a sort of routine. Work from JWT came erratically; either a great deal at once or none for days, one interval stretching into three weeks, so that she agonized about whether they'd dropped her for good and whether she'd be able to cope with the bills. When she had no agency work to do she painted, but she found it hard going. She persuaded both children to let her paint them. 'I hate the smell of turps and linseed oil,' grumbled Charlotte. 'You have no soul,' Kate said imperturbably. 'Wait until you've smelt greasepaint and ancient dust from bare floorboards – you'll find it the most evocative scent in the world because it'll be *your* milieu; you'll love it as much as I love this. You can read or do your prep in here. I need a bit of inspiration after I've been alone all day.'

Quite often the sitting would end with all three of them crowded into the room, talking over mugs of tea. Kate was bemused at how they discussed their father and Greta Glamour with her as though Geoffrey were someone Kate had only known slightly in some distant past.

She kept putting off doing anything about the pregnancy. She knew she was being foolish, but somehow it still had no reality. When she managed to pull herself together about it she had to admit she was deeply squeamish about the idea of arranging an abortion. She had been careless and irresponsible and another child was unthinkable, yet she couldn't stop herself imagining how awful it would have been if the circumstances had been the same seventeen years ago, and she had aborted Charlotte or Jeremy. She was, what's more, abashed when she allowed herself to reflect that she wasn't even sure whose baby it was – Jon's or Rupert's. She would go and see her doctor soon. After all, he didn't know that she and Geoffrey had split up. It would be perfectly reasonable to say that at her age she thought she was too old to have another baby. Each night in bed she resolved to ring him first thing in the morning, but each morning she got on with other things. It seemed as if she were deliberately letting the days drift by.

When Geoffrey called for the children one Friday he was unusually early and actually rang the bell. Kate, covered in a paint-smothered overall, opened the door to him in surprise.

'Aren't you going to ask me in for a drink?' he asked genially. She opened it wider. 'Of course. You're usually in such a rush.'

'Well, I was very peeved to begin with. I thought you were very stubborn over this house.' He had the grace to look away. 'And your chap was making excessive demands for an allowance. I didn't think women wanted support these days – "equality" has got a bit one-sided, it seems to me. But of course I don't want you all to go short because I've taken myself off.'

Kate bit back a retort. It wouldn't do any good, and there would be less strain on the children if they seemed relaxed and amiable together. It felt strange, though, to see him plop himself familiarly in what had been his usual armchair. Charlotte wasn't quite ready, but Jeremy fidgeted uncomfortably, eyeing Kate to gauge her re-action.

'You're painting again, I see,' he said, gazing at her smock with distaste.

'Yes, I very much enjoy it,' she said looking at him levelly. He met her eyes blandly.

'What do you do at J. Walter Thompson?' he asked chattily. 'They're one of our best clients. Perhaps I could put in a word or two on your behalf.'

Kate's mouth twitched. 'That's very nice of you, but I am managing. The people you know would be too grand to worry about art departments.'

Charlotte came in, and gazed in such amazement at her father that Geoffrey got hastily to his feet, knocked back the rest of his wine, and said, 'Ready at last? Right, off we go. Goodbye, Kate, thanks for the drink.'

When she told Flip about the little scene over supper later that evening, she said grimly, 'I'd have slipped in some cyanide. What a pompous prick. Now perhaps you'll see why marriage is not for me. Incidentally, what have you done to Nick? Why has he gone to America in such a hurry?'

'A business opportunity cropped up suddenly and he had to act fast,' Kate spoke lightly. 'I didn't know you were still in touch?'

'If you can call it that.' Flip grimaced. 'I asked him round to my place a couple of times and he took me to supper, but I regret to say that most of the conversation always managed to veer round to you, despite all my efforts to show him my grasp of current affairs, Dixieland jazz and the German versus the Japanese business mentality.' She grinned and shrugged. 'He was one of the ones that got away.'

Sitting at her drawing board one morning a few days later, Kate felt irritation and deep dissatisfaction with the brief she'd been given. It seemed trite and boring. But it had come from the Creatives and had been approved by the client in rough form, and she had to do it to order. A poster to go in bus shelters, advertising a paint brand to catch the spring-cleaning DIY market, it showed bunches of flowers arranged in the paint tins, to indicate the colour range. She carried out her instructions obediently, but two days later, when she had finished the illustration, she put it crossly to one side and started to work out an idea of her own that had come to her as she worked.

Another two days and she sat back smiling. She'd done one finished poster and sketches for three others, showing endearingly comic lambs, rabbits, a Jersey cow and a flight of birds busily painting their respective burrows, nests or barn. She wanted to convey a young, fresh, new spring feeling in clear, flat colours almost like those in a child's colouring book, but with a cartoonist's sense of the ridiculous. She hoped people bored in bus queues would find them entertaining.

'Dear Phil,' she scribbled on a note. 'I've done an alternative for the paint job. It's a gift, so don't be cross, but I was bored stiff with the flowers.' She sent the lot up by motorbike messenger and went into the garden to get some fresh air. He'd think she had cheek; if so he need only throw her ideas away.

Chapter Thirty-Three

The weather became almost summer-like, and Kate set up her easel in the small back garden. She painted compulsively every day when she didn't have any agency deadlines to meet, not only because of Nick and his promised exhibition, but because an inner hunger now drove her on. Something had been released in her, a consuming passion that sometimes frightened her by its intensity. She would feel cross and resentful when she had to stop to do an illustration, or cook or shop, though she tried to stifle such feelings. It didn't seem to matter whether her work would be considered any good or not, she simply knew that at the times when she worked at the easel she experienced an excitement and frenzy that totally dispelled her old feelings of inadequacy, of being unwanted and unloved. Before her easel she felt herself grow physically bigger and stronger, and the euphoria was tempered only by the impotence she felt when she had not captured her vision on the canvas, and by an increasing frustration at the restriction of working in her small boxroom.

She felt better out of doors. The leaves were still soft and tender, like a baby's skin, and the sun sifting through the black tracery of a beech tree, diffused by the trembling leaves, created incredibly beautiful shifting patterns. Kate painted the row of houses that backed on to the small walled gardens, flanked by the clear yellow and vivid forms of the tree, and was astonished, when she stepped back to look at the canvas some time later, that she had somehow woven through, on the patchy black and ochre-coloured weathered brick-work an imaginative creation of the people who lived there and the lives they led. It was an allegory, and she had not been the slightest bit aware of doing it. It was positively scary that her hand and inner eye had so taken over from her conscious self.

Penelope rang. 'Are you all right?' she demanded. 'You sound odd.'

'I *am* odd, I think.' Kate strove to speak lightly, to recover from the curious sensation her painting had generated. 'Just short of a dose of your crisp common sense. How about you and Michael coming to dinner, as soon as ever? It's time I began to organize my own social life.'

Much to her surprise, Penelope promptly accepted. Kate had always imagined that she had a string of engagements stretching from one year's end to another, but now she said it looked as though the following Monday was free.

Good, thought Kate when she'd put the phone down. Now instead of talking vaguely about having people to dinner, I can start being positive. She thought she'd ask Phillip and his unknown wife; she'd like to know him a little better, and he had been so kind to her.

She dialled his direct line. 'Kate, oh good – I've been trying to find a moment to ring you all morning and haven't managed it. This place is more of a madhouse every day. Look, those alternative drawings you sent in . . .'

'Oh don't worry about them,' Kate broke in hastily. 'I was just toying with another thought. I told you to chuck them out . . .'

'Don't interrupt. Creatives *love* them, they rushed them round to the client and guess what? They've scrapped that poster campaign.'

Kate felt sick with disappointment. 'I'm sorry. I should have stuck to the brief but it seemed so trite. I *am* sorry.'

'No, wait. They want to turn them into animations, not posters . . . they've scrapped that campaign and are substituting yours as a series on *national* TV!' His voice dropped to emphasize the importance of what he was saying.

'But I – I know nothing about animation or film or . . .'

'You don't have to.' Phillip was patient. 'They have specialists to do all that; it's the idea, and the witty characters, they liked. It means they've practically tripled their adspend. You'll get a very fat fee for this, Kate.'

'That's wonderful! I'm overwhelmed. It was all so easy. I – I was just doodling really.'

'Well, doodle some more,' Phillip advised. 'It paid off.'

Kate laughed and explained that she'd really telephoned to invite him and his wife to dinner. 'Why, that's lovely – it will give me a chance to have dinner with Julia for once.' Phillip's laugh was rueful. 'I've hardly been home before nine or ten for the past three weeks. She'll soon divorce me for neglect.'

Flip was free on Monday too, and Kate thought for a moment and decided that Jon would be a good sixth. He was easy, charming company and wouldn't be so insensitive as to assume that, with the children around, an invitation to dinner included bed and breakfast.

He was cheerful but cagey. 'It's all right,' Kate teased. 'You're not being wheeled out for approval by friends, there's nothing more ominous about the invitation than that I want you as a civilized sixth to complete my dinner party.'

'You mean I know which knife and fork to use?'

'Exactly. I haven't done any entertaining since – since I became a career woman,' she said quickly. Jon, reassured, gave a laconic yes. Kate felt a thrill of pleasure at the prospect of the party; and pleased with herself for being able to talk to Jon without embarrassment or that disconcerting hot rush of physical excitement. The thought of sex with Jon reminded her that she had still not done anything about the pregnancy. 'Be positive a little longer,' she lectured herself, and at once rang her doctor and made an appointment for the Tuesday, after the dinner party.

Charlotte offered to help with the preparations for the dinner party when she got back from the weekend with Geoffrey, but added offhandedly, 'I won't be able to be there – Nathan's taking me to the theatre.' She blushed.

'Lovely,' Kate said warmly. 'Will you and he have time to have a drink with us all before you go?'

'I'm not sure.' Charlotte was endearingly shy. 'We're going to the Lyric in Hammersmith, so it's not far. I'll ask him.' She gave Kate an impulsive kiss. 'I think I'm in love,' she announced, looking challengingly at her mother. 'And don't say I'm too young – Juliet was only fourteen.'

Kate laughed. 'I wouldn't dream of it. I think of the two of us you're easily the more mature. Just don't follow Juliet's example too far. Her behaviour was a bit extreme, don't you think?'

When Geoffrey called to collect the children, he again implied that he expected to come in. He seemed to think Kate would be grateful for his occasional presence. She poured him a whisky and soda without comment. Sorting out Jeremy's little trouble, as he put it, seemed to have assuaged some of his guilt at leaving them all. His manner was casual, as if he were quite at home, apparently seeing nothing extraordinary in his behaviour. Kate wondered if his feelings ever went deep, but then remembered the look of happiness on his face when he'd told her he wanted to marry Greta.

Tonight, though, he was sunk in gloom, and hunched dejectedly in 'his' armchair. 'Greta has gone over to Neptune,' he told Kate bleakly. 'She's a terrible loss to the station. I can't think of any other woman presenter to replace her who has a tenth of her looks and audience appeal. Even Charles Wootton is involved in the search for a replacement. We were actually talking about letting "Lifestyles" drop, but it has been so popular. We're trying out a temporary guest presenter, an actress, but she can't hold a candle to Greta, and anyway she has a new play booked in a couple of weeks.'

'Why don't you get a male presenter?' Kate said lightly. 'Then there need be no odious comparisons.'

Geoffrey's head shot up. 'My God, what a brilliant idea! Why didn't I think of that?' He got to his feet, his old animation returning. 'I didn't know you had it in you, Kate.'

Kate pressed her lips together in amusement at the back-handed compliment. 'It's hardly like discovering the specific gravity of gold – rather obvious, I'd have thought.'

He looked at her sharply, but he was clearly anxious to get to a telephone at once. 'Ready?' he demanded impatiently of the children.

'We're waiting for you,' Charlotte pointed out coolly. ''Bye Mummy.' She kissed Kate and led the way to the front door with reproving dignity. 'See you Sunday.'

Kate got up early on Saturday. It was another fine day, and she drove to Soho to shop for the party. She was entranced by the new season's fruit and vegetables cramming the stalls in the Berwick Street market – some she'd never heard of, let alone seen. She bought extravagantly, deciding that she'd buy anything that caught her eye and plan the menu round the ingredients. By eleven she was on her way home again, eager to get at her easel.

She set up again outdoors, aware that the little gardens had more life in them than earlier in the week, as people went about their weekend pottering. She waved cheerily to her next-door neighbour, who was peering down curiously from an upstairs window. She remembered a large, flat chestnut-coloured basket she had displayed on the top of a kitchen cupboard, one she'd brought back from Biot, in France, after one of their first holidays abroad. She got it out and piled the exotic fruit and vegetables from the market on this, marvelling at the way a snowy white cauliflower, looking so round and agreeable, took on a cosmopolitan flavour tucked in among the shiny peppers and aubergines, the kumquats and spiky artichokes. Greater artists than she had made do with a lemon or two, she thought to herself, but she was so tired of the boxroom, and she needed a spill of colour to stimulate her.

At first her strokes were routine, as she began the ritual of painting in a thin background colour, but her absorption increased as that new but now-familiar feeling of energy and colour vibrating around her increased her speed to keep up with the tumbling visions in her head. The still life formed and reformed in colour and texture as she tried, with a mounting tension of excitement, to capture it in paint.

Just before five she stopped. The sun had given up for the day, and it was now grey and cheerless. She shivered, feeling drained, tired, and ravenously hungry. The Biot basket held a slightly jaded vision of the morning's arrangement; but her canvas glowed. She packed up and went inside. The house seemed so unappealingly cold, quiet, lonely. She made a clumsy sandwich with some of the Continental sausage she'd bought that morning and poured herself a glass of red wine. She felt suddenly low and dispirited, bitterly aware of her shortcomings as an artist. She wished Nick Menton had left her alone. When she'd regarded her painting as mere dabbling she hadn't suffered this disquieting drive.

By Sunday lunchtime, however, she had recovered her spirits and was able to look at her new work dispassionately. The still life, though unfinished, was very promising – much better than she'd thought yesterday. She also liked the portrait of the children, sprawled in a gangling arrangement of arms and legs over an armchair and the floor, the light stroking the planes of their faces, absorbed over books. Then there was the one with the houses . . . Nick wouldn't be able to accuse her of not trying, she thought. She wished he'd telephoned, but there had only been a scrappy letter or two, telling her of the protracted negotiations of the new partnership deal, and mentioning with some excitement some new American work he'd seen.

She wished he would come back. Not only did she miss him, she realized, but she felt in need of his judgement. She didn't know anyone else she could entrust with the emotion revealed in her work who would also understand the painful exploitation of technique involved in putting it all on to canvas. What if she were drifting too much? Nick would be able to spot where she was going wrong and get her back on the track. She shut the door on the little room firmly. She was getting too self-absorbed and introspective. It would be much better to give the whole thing a rest and concentrate on preparing for the dinner party.

Chapter Thirty-Four

Penelope and Michael were the first to arrive on Monday, Penelope's pixie face wrinkling even more as she stepped into the hall and sniffed. 'Not a dish I recognize. Are we having some nouvelle *nouvelle cuisine*?' she demanded. 'A carefully-composed salad dressed with low-calorie turpentine instead of vinaigrette?' Michael looked apprehensive.

'Beyond my creative skill,' Kate assured them. 'That delicious aroma comes from my newly active boxroom, not the kitchen.' She led them into the sitting-room, where Jeremy was hovering proprietorially by the drinks cupboard. He poured Penelope a huge gin and tonic which made her cross herself behind his back as he turned to Michael.

'Can you mix a dry martini, old chap?' Michael asked. 'It's my best drink,' Jeremy told him proudly. He tonged ice into a jug, added hefty measures of gin and tiny ones of vermouth, gave it a noisy shake, and twisted a piece of lemon peel over the contents with a flourish. Michael smiled. 'By jove – wonderful! You've been taking lessons from James Bond. Tell me, have you seen pictures of your grandfather when he was at school? No? Then let me tell you, Jeremy, you are the image of your illustrious grandfather. Did you know we were at school together?'

He and Jeremy were soon chatting about school and Kate told Penelope about the rest of the guests. 'Flip is a rather colourful member of the teaching staff at Charlotte's school, but she's become quite a friend since she came to coach Jeremy in maths. She seems to change the colour of her hair with some magic concoction almost as often as her clothes. It says a lot for the headmistress that she can accommodate someone so outrageous, but she's apparently an excellent teacher and very popular with the girls. Phillip is my immediate boss at J. Walter Thompson, but I haven't met his wife Julia yet, and Jon runs Daniel's.'

'And is he a special friend?' Penelope was uncharacteristically arch. She had been disappointed when Kate had told her in answer to her questioning that the 'devastating' Paul was no longer on her horizon.

'Of course not,' Kate said hastily. 'Please don't embarrass him or me by implying that there's anything between us,' she implored, wondering if the probable father of her child could be described as no-one special.

The other four arrived simultaneously on the doorstep, having introduced themselves, colliding with a breathless Charlotte who was rushing a reluctant Nathan off to the theatre. 'I thought you said your mother invited me for drinks,' he was heard protesting as she dragged him down the path.

Kate was disappointed that Flip's hair was an unremarkable black, and that she was wearing a decorous black, long-sleeved, high-necked dress and her wide red lips and matching earrings giving the only touch of colour. Yet she still managed to convey an errant, sexy chic. Julia, surprisingly for the wife of the rumpled, sweater-wearing, eternally preoccupied Phillip, had the silvery blonde beauty of a Swedish model, and Kate saw Jon give her a swift appraising look before he moved over to her chair. 'Oh, oh, *trub*-hole,' Flip murmured to Kate as she helped to pass drinks. 'I hope her husband isn't a Black Belt – or, on second thoughts, maybe it would be more amusing if he were.' It was a good mix; Phillip had left his harrassed air at the office and became an amusing raconteur, telling them some no-doubt apocryphal stories about clients and campaigns that had gone wrong. Penelope and Flip seemed to speak the same witty, irreverent language, and both Michael and Jon expanded under the cooing admiration of Julia. 'He must be mad if he works late and leaves her too much on her ownio,' Flip commented as she helped Kate bring in the last course. 'I bet Jon gets her phone number before the evening's out.'

'I hope not,' Kate looked troubled. 'Phillip is so sweet and he has been very kind to me.

'Don't worry. Jon's passions never last long or come to anything. Oops, sorry – I'd forgotten he made a play for you.'

'You get more ridiculous the longer I know you.' Kate poked her in the ribs. 'Stop speculating and bring in those plates.'

They all lingered round the table with their coffee, too comfortable and content to move to the sitting room. Kate was happy. The food had been praised, and Michael, something of a wine buff, had asked to see the label on the bottles, and had nodded approvingly at Kate. 'You have your father's eye for a good bottle, I see,' he remarked. Kate had smiled. 'No credit due, Michael. I let the man in the shop choose it.'

She didn't want the evening to end, but Phillip got to his feet reluctantly and caught Julia's hand. 'We must go. I've just had the awful thought that tomorrow is yet another working day,' he groaned and clutched his head theatrically. 'When will it end I ask myself.' They all got up then, and there was a flurry of goodbyes and expressions of pleasure in the hall. Phillip had parked his car on the other side of the road and Kate stepped off the pavement so that she could wave them off without being obstructed by the cars parked all along the road.

'Don't forget to doodle,' Phillip called through the open window as he pulled away.

'What?' Kate tried to hear his remark over the revving up of the engines. There was a sudden thump and she looked down in utter shock as the backboard of Jon's Porsche cut unbelievably into her body. She opened her mouth just as a stab of excruciating pain robbed her of breath, and another thump, this time from behind, knocked her forward across the top of the backboard. She heard a scream and saw Charlotte's agonized face racing towards her as she slumped into unconsciousness.

When she opened her eyes she was lying on the road, covered in a blanket; Penelope was holding her hand and muttering over and over again, 'Don't worry, darling, you'll be all right, just lie still, an ambulance is on its way.' Jon's white face was bending over her, and Flip had her arm round a frightened, weeping Charlotte. 'Where's that fucking ambulance?' Jon yelled, as on cue Kate heard its siren. 'Is that really for me?' she murmured and passed out once more.

When she came to again she was in a hard narrow bed, with a small, mousy nurse sitting beside her, knitting. Her every bone seemed to ache, and her head was throbbing. She tried to move, but thought better of it at once. The nurse looked up. 'Hello, dear. Feeling better? Don't move – you have a drip in your arm.'

Kate's eyes swivelled to the two bottles suspended above her bed. Her lips felt dry and crusty. 'Where am I?' she licked her lips, trying to manage the thick tongue that blurred her words.

The nurse bathed her lips with a swab. 'Don't talk, dear. You're still under the anaesthetic. You're in St Stephen's hospital. You had a little accident, but you'll be all right.' Kate closed her eyes again and slept.

When she awoke the second time it was to see two frightened children and Flip at her bedside.

'Some party,' she croaked.

Charlotte burst into tears. 'Oh, Mummy!' she buried her head in Kate's neck. 'I thought you were *dead*!' she wailed. Jeremy clutched her hand convulsively, eyeing the drip apprehensively.

'Nothing serious,' Flip said gently, her eyes kind and concerned; her usual glinting ironic look was gone. 'You've got a bilateral fracture of the tibula – or is it fibia? Anyway one of dem bones, and a bit of severe bruising round your middle. It seems Jon and Michael treated you a bit like a sandwich filling, trying to spread you thinly between two thick slices of car. Jon had left his car in gear for some extraordinary reason and it leapt back when he started the engine, just as Michael tried to reverse out of the tight space in front. Neither of them realized you were standing there waving like a maniac to Phillip. They're both sick as parrots and, if anything, look worse than you do. I reckon you can sue them both.'

Kate smiled weakly. She thought Flip must be underplaying it. The way she felt, every single bone was broken and there was a tight pain in her abdomen. 'Charlotte—' She tried to turn her head to kiss the little face wetting the nape of her neck with tears. 'How was the play?'

This simply produced a fresh storm of weeping. Jeremy looked agitated. 'Charlotte was coming back just as you got hurt,' he explained. 'She saw it all. She's been very upset.' His own chin began its babyish dimple and wobble. Kate tried to smile, but it felt more like a grimace. 'Drama seems to run in this family. I'm all right. Please don't worry. I'm just dying for a drink. All the nurse would give me was a damp swab. I need one of your martinis, Jeremy.'

Charlotte sat up and tried to mop her face. 'If Greta Glamour sees you like that she'll give you the address of a good plastic surgeon, not just send you to make-up.' Kate wished they would go and leave her to endure her aches and pains without the strain of trying to appear brave.

Flip gave her a small sip of water from a feeding cup. 'Just a little or I'll be doing something wrong. Half the labels on the doors along this corridor say "nothing by mouth". I thought I'd pinch one for that lousy restaurant near me. Come on, kids, we'll come back later.' She stood up. 'You probably haven't noticed but this room has more blooms than the Chelsea Flower Show – conscience money from Jon. I'm staying in your house so don't worry – a week or two away from discos will be good for me.' She gave Kate's hand a good squeeze of encouragement and turned away as both children kissed Kate, a fresh set of tears brimming over in Charlotte's eyes.

Kate drifted on the edge of sleep or unconsciousness with no sense of time. Nurses bustled in and out, changing her bottles and taking her pulse and temperature and doing inexplicably intimate and uncomfortable things to her. There was a contraption over her legs to keep the bedclothes off and she could feel the heavy weight of plaster on her right leg. Once when she awoke another nurse was sitting beside her bed. 'Good. Dr Edwards wanted me to let him know when you woke up. He wants to see you.'

Dr Edwards looked tired and frail and not much older than Jeremy. 'How are you feeling, dear?' he asked, sounding so incongruously avuncular that Kate wanted to laugh. 'Not my usual bouncing self, I'm afraid.'

'Well, you were very lucky. You could have had some serious compound fractures from the impact of those two heavy cars, but we could only see a bilateral fracture of the femur, and severe bruising. There are some lacerations across your pelvis and abdomen, but you didn't lose a lot of blood from them.' But he looked nervous.

'Then why am I still having a transfusion?' demanded Kate, sure he was keeping something from her. 'The nurse changed the bottle a short while ago and said I'd lost a lot of blood.'

He cleared his throat. 'You did. I'm afraid you lost your baby. You haemorrhaged quite a bit, so we're having to top you up and give you a saline. But we'll be able to take the plasma off tonight, all being well.'

Kate felt tears come. It was stupid. She hadn't wanted the baby, it should be an enormous relief, but somehow it seemed just terribly sad. Dr Edwards patted her arm awkwardly. 'I'm sorry, my dear. There was nothing we could do. You'll be able to have another child later.' Kate began to sob and he left the room. He was quickly replaced by a bosomy sister who had kind eyes but who said briskly to Kate, 'Now, now, no more of that. It doesn't help matters. What's done is done, you just have to get on with life you know.' Any minute now she's going to say it's no use crying over spilt milk, Kate thought, but the bracing voice did make her pull herself together and she felt a bit calmer. 'That's right. Now how about some tea? You'll have to have the feeding cup for the moment but we'll have you sitting up soon enough.'

In fact within two days Kate felt surprisingly better. Her head still ached a bit, and she felt stiff and uncomfortable, but the drips were removed and she was able to read and enjoy visits, including one from Jon, who looked anxious and upset, and Penelope, who said that Michael was suffering so much from shock and remorse that she was seriously thinking of sending *him* into hospital, just to stop him getting on her nerves. Kate wrote him a note to say how stupid she had been to see him into his car and then stand right behind it. 'It must have been that wine you admired so much,' she wrote. 'Next time you'll have supermarket plonk. It doesn't seem to addle my brain as much.'

Each day she had to do battle with a muscular physiotherapist who seemed to believe she was ready for a Jane Fonda workout, but within a short time she had Kate hobbling round the corridors on crutches. Her femur had been pinned, she told her. She was ready to give Kate a detailed explanation of every operation on the corridor.

Her lacerations were left to heal. 'New technique,' said Sally, one of the cheerful Australian nurses. 'No more plasters and strapping. Wounds heal more cleanly left to themselves, providing you practise normal hygiene.'

Kate was shocked the first time she saw her body. Great bruises in ominous colours covered her abdomen and ribcage. 'And that's just the outside,' Sally said matter-of-factly. 'You have internal bruising as well. No, Lady Kate, you're not a pretty sight at the moment.'

'Thanks. You're a great morale-booster.'

'Well you could make up your face to match and become a punk, and charge tourists to photograph you.' She looked judiciously at Kate's light curly hair. 'You'd need to do something about that, though.'

'It was once aubergine,' Kate boasted. 'I'm not entirely out of touch, you know.'

A mere two weeks later Kate was allowed home. Penelope came to fetch her in the Mercedes, and Kate looked at its rear end with interest. 'No sign of any dents,' she commented. 'But I can quite see why it got the best of the argument. A case of irresistible force with me as the stupidly immoveable object. I hope Michael has stopped agonizing.'

The children had filled the house with flowers, and Flip had arranged for a bed to be made up downstairs. 'Your Mrs Shepherd has a sister-in-law who's a retired nurse, and she's coming to look in every day.' Her eyes gleamed. 'Jon is footing the bill. Shut up,' she ordered, as Kate started to protest. 'He knows very well that if you wanted to, you could sue him. What are car rear mirrors for? And he can well afford it.'

Flip had been a brick, staying in the spare room and cheering the children. 'Your brother telephoned every evening,' she reported. 'He said he'd be coming down as soon as you're out. We got quite pally. Pity he's stuck up in Edinburgh,' she said with a wicked moue.

Kate leaned back on the sofa. 'You must meet him, but I warn you, he's very dedicated. I haven't known him to have a girlfriend, even at Oxford. He's obsessive about his work.'

'Sounds the kind of challenge I like. But I've got to go now. I've had enough of being saintly, looking after your kids, nice as they are. I'm going to beat up the town tonight, so I've got to get my warpaint on. They ain't seen nothin' yet.' She gave Kate a kiss and a cheerful wave and left.

Chapter Thirty-Five

Jon telephoned every day, sent her flowers and every known edible delicacy, delivered by a brown-liveried chauffeur who much impressed Hiney, Mrs Shepherd's sister. He visited her several times but it was obvious that illness or pain made him uncomfortable. His usual light, teasing conversation was replaced by carefully brought-out stilted news items, and he was clearly relieved when he could decently flee. Penelope too telephoned every day and kept the house full of flowers and new books and magazines.

Kate had persuaded Phillip that she could go on with doing illustrations for him, as long as his briefs were carefully written so that she didn't have to come up to the office. Hiney and Mrs Shepherd fixed up a work table in the sitting-room, which she had turned into a virtual bedsit. Painting was difficult. She tried it sitting down but the results were wooden; she needed more freedom of arm movement. She doodled instead with her magic markers when she hadn't any work and didn't want to read.

She'd told Charlotte about the baby. Her face had gone white.

'Did it hurt, Mum?'

'No, not so I noticed – it was all part of the general pain. I didn't even know anything about it until afterwards. It was much better than a deliberate abortion. I'd have hated that.'

They seemed to have a much closer, more grown-up relationship now. Charlotte told her lots more about school; not about the work, which she did with an uninvolved competence, but the people and personalities. Nathan figured a lot in her accounts, but other boys were also mentioned. Kate thought that her being in love might have lost some of its intensity and novelty. She suggested that Charlotte ask some of her friends home to a meal. 'I'd like to meet them, and Hiney and I can manage a meal between us. A buffet party perhaps?' Charlotte considered. 'I think the Pizza Parlour's safer. I don't want to play Louka in plaster. Besides, my friends seem unable to digest food unless it's washed down with loud music.'

Charlotte refused to leave Kate at weekends to stay with Geoffrey. 'Mum *needs* me,' Kate heard her saying firmly on the telephone. Jeremy too stayed with her the first two or three weeks she was at home, but then Geoffrey insisted on his visit, bribing him with sports outings. Jeremy reported that Greta Glamour wasn't there much at weekends. Her new channel had meant a total rearrangement of her work schedule, and Geoffrey was fed up.

'He'd be lonely without me,' said Jeremy. 'He's very depressed because now he can't tell Greta about the idea for a new series he had had in mind for her. He's trying out new people for it but he says he can't find anyone as pretty or with as much personality as Greta.'

Kate watched 'Lifestyles' and saw that Geoffrey had got hold of a likeable young feature writer from the *Sunday Times* to replace Greta. He was a very good interviewer, and seemed sympathetic, so that people opened up for him, but Jeremy reported that the ratings had dropped. 'That's why Dad must have a new series for the autumn,' he added. 'They need to bump up the advertising revenue.'

When Penelope called one afternoon she said in her direct way, 'When will you really be able to move about again?'

'I think in about three or four weeks,' Kate replied. 'They are taking more x-rays on Monday. Apparently my bones are sticking together again quite well. Why?'

'Because I think you should have a little holiday and I've the perfect idea. One of my friends, an opera singer, has offered me his villa in Tuscany for a month. It's quite charming and comfortable, with lovely views. If you can get about a bit by then there are Siena and Florence nearby but really there's little incentive to move much, which is why I think it would be ideal.'

'But what about *you*?'

'Michael and I are going to Australia. He has some companies and a plant there that he has to look at, and I can poke my nose into Sydney Opera House. And after all, it *was* Michael's car that reversed into you. We both feel guilty, and this will be a little way of making up.'

'Nonsense, it was nobody's fault but mine. What a fool, to stand waving right between two cars about to move off!'

'Well, I do think you ought to go. We'd stand you the fare,' she said, 'and there's even a maid Carlo would be anxious for you to have around, because he has to pay her anyway if he's to prevent her running off to holiday-makers – there's a lot of letting in that area.'

'I wouldn't dream of letting you pay my fare,' Kate protested, 'but it does sound tempting. I was thinking before my accident how much I'd like to get away to somewhere fresh – it's difficult to keep painting in my little boxroom.'

'Well, there you are. What could be more inspiring than the Tuscan countryside? All that rich coloured soil and the misty blue hills; no painter worth her salt would turn down such a chance.' Her small pixie face stretched in a triumphant smile.

'You're a total manipulator,' Kate laughed. 'All right, I'll accept! I'm *very* grateful. What a convenient coincidence that the school holidays are about to start.'

'Very coincidental,' Penelope said this so matter-of-factly that Kate shot her a suspicious glance. She wouldn't put it past her to have checked out such things in advance.

'That's settled, then.' Penelope got up to go. 'I'll get Michael's secretary to fix all the travel – she's so used to it. Just find out exactly when the children can get away from school. It will be a good break for them too if they've had exams.'

Kate pulled her down as Penelope bent to kiss her and gave her a hug. 'Don't think I can't see through you, you old fraud. It's a good job you're not a politician or you'd have Mrs Thatcher trembling in her shoes.'

'Who *says* I'm not a politician? They're not always in the House, you know.' Penelope blew a kiss, and went out to have a gossipy chat and say 'goodbye' to Hiney.

It all seemed so simple in the end. Charlotte's exams ended exactly the same time as Jeremy's term did, and Flip was sure there'd be no problem with the head if she nipped the last week off the term. 'They do nothing much then but get in everybody's hair.' Phillip had obligingly given Kate a pile of work, which meant that she had earned a fat cheque and could afford to take the time off, and she was touched when Tom came down the week before they went and said he'd come along to help them settle into the villa. 'You're still a bit unsteady on your pins. You might fall and end up back in St Stephen's.'

His work on cells had been published and was now undergoing carefully controlled tests in several hospitals in different parts of the world. He seemed confident and relaxed, and had lost the look of strain he'd had last year.

When she invited Flip to dinner to meet him, Kate was astonished at how quiet she was, how attentively she listened when Tom answered her and Kate's questions about his work and its implications. They seemed to have an easy, teasing camaraderie, forged during his nightly telephone calls when Kate was in hospital, but Flip was like a different person with him. She seemed to forget her challenging sharp retorts and biting sarcasm.

At the end of the meal Tom said he was going out for a stroll, and Flip offered to go with him. 'It's not far to Putney Common or Richmond Park by car,' she said, 'and there's more chance of fresh air.' The evenings were light now, but Tom didn't return until after Kate had gone to bed. The next evening she heard Tom telephone Flip to ask her to go to the cinema. 'You don't mind, Katie? I want to see that film and Flip seems to be something of an expert on Bertolucci – we were talking about him last night.'

On the third day he said diffidently that he thought he'd ask Flip out to dinner. 'She was so kind when you were in hospital. She seemed really concerned about you and very responsible about the children.'

'Darling, you don't need to jusify taking Flip out! I'm very fond of her – I'm *glad* you like her. Don't worry about me – I still seem to get very tired by the end of the day and I'm quite glad to go to bed early. Besides, you've been shut up here most of the day, and we're off to Florence at the weekend. Just beware of Flip on the dance floor. She's lethal.'

'I don't dance, unfortunately.'

'If you see much of Flip, Tom darling, you will, you will.'

Chapter Thirty-Six

Although the flight to Florence and the car journey to the villa that Michael's secretary had organized weren't onerous, Kate was tired out when they finally reached the villa, and very glad of Tom's presence. He acted like a good-tempered shepherd, equipping them for their stay with paperbacks and insect repellent, buying Charlotte and Kate some scent at the duty-free, and Jeremy a little automatic camera.

Perched right on top of a high, snub-topped hill, overlooking farmland and a small forest, the villa, when they finally came to it in the late afternoon, looked as if it had grown there. Geraniums and rosemary and a mass of wild flowers tumbled over rocks and forced through cracks in the wide stone terrace. Inside, shuttered against the sun, it was dark and cool, with gleaming bare wooden floors. The children ran all over excitedly, opening shutters and claiming bedrooms. Virtually the whole of the ground floor was taken over by the large L-shaped sitting-room, with one end used as a farmhouse kitchen and the other dominated by a large piano and old, comfortable sofas. The refrigerator was stocked with milk, butter and eggs, tomatoes, cheese and a selection of sausages. 'Everything for a feast,' Tom commented, opening a cupboard containing crusty bread and some anonymous bottles of wine.

'The maid comes in the mornings,' Kate said. 'Penelope says we should let her do the shopping because she'll know where to go. And not to question the bill too much – it's one of her perks.' She sat down suddenly. 'I think I'm going to have a snack and go to bed. I feel energy draining out of me.'

'OK. I think you should have this room next to the kitchen, because it's on the ground floor and the doors open straight on to the terrace, and I imagine it gets the morning sun. Let the kids sort out their own rooms, and I'll take what's over. I have only a couple of days, so it doesn't matter to me where I sleep. I'll take the kids for a look round outside and then we'll get our supper. You go to bed.' He poured her a stiff whisky from a bottle of duty-free. 'Here, gulp this down and you'll feel better.'

He cut a wedge off the bread, topped it clumsily with some salami and passed her the plate. 'This do for a snack?' Charlotte came in, took a swift look at Kate's wan face, and said, 'I'll unpack for you.' In no time, head buzzing gently from the whisky and general tiredness, Kate found herself ushered into the cool, dark bedroom, and she slid gratefully between thick stiff cotton sheets. It was still early, and the light struggled through cracks in the shutters, but she turned with a contented sigh into the pillows and slept.

Next morning, Charlotte came in, wearing brief shorts and a thin strappy t-shirt, bearing coffee and rolls and some black cherry jam on a tray. 'The maid's here already. She's called Carla, she brought the rolls. She doesn't speak any English but we're getting on fine. It's a wonderful day, and the countryside is bliss. There are a few other villas around – one just behind the forest with a *swimming pool*, and there are about three close together with several cars outside. A lot of people were eating on a terrace, like ours, only on posts, over some kind of barn. They waved at us, and there's a table tennis table in a kind of big shed at one side. We played last night, but the bats aren't much good.

Uncle Tom said we could buy some new ones when we go into the village if we can find a shop.' She stopped for breath.

'*You* haven't wasted much time!' Kate sipped the fragrant coffee. 'Did you find out anything practical, like is there any hot water? I'd love a bath.'

She felt so much better, and well-rested, and when she opened her shutters and saw the fresh morning and the hills rolling away into infinity, with the sky a clear, light, happy blue, she felt energy seeping back. The others had breakfasted outdoors, and Carla was already sweeping the spotless living room. She smiled hugely at Kate, flashing a generous supply of gold fillings, and greeted her with an enthusiastic '*Buongiorno*'. Kate's Italian was fairly primitive but equal to '*Buongiorno*'. Carla indicated a pile of shopping on the table, '*Signora, zucchero, fragole, pomodore, pane . . . altro*?' Kate laughed, shaking her head, saying, '*Io non parle Italiano bene*', which caused Carla's teeth to flash again. Carla picked up a notepad, pointed to Kate, the pad and herself and indicated that she was to write down anything she wanted her to bring the next day. She nodded her understanding, and looked in the refrigerator and cupboard. There seemed enough food for lunch, and they could go to a restaurant tonight. She let Carla get on with what was obviously a familiar routine and went outside. Jeremy came running up the bare, rocky hill. 'I've seen seven lizards and there are millions of grasshoppers, or crickets Uncle Tom says they are. He and Charlotte have gone to see if that little village we passed as we came in has a restaurant. Can we explore?'

'Well, let's wait until the others come back, then we can go in the car to get an idea of the place. It looks lovely. I feel even my bones warming up, and the scent is wonderful! I wish I'd bought a book about wild flowers, there are so many here I don't recognize.'

When Tom and Charlotte came back they reported that

they'd met the people from one of the villas in the little shop where they were buying ice-cream, and they were all to go there for a drink. 'They rent their villa every year – they've been coming here forever,' Charlotte said. 'And they speak Italian, although Uncle Tom is quite good too,' she said generously. 'They had a boy just a bit younger than Jeremy with them. We said "yes" – is that all right?'

'Well, you *have* settled in quickly. Jeremy and I thought we'd like a drive round to get our bearings. Carla wants us to write down on the notepad anything we want – have you unpacked the Italian dictionary? We're going to need it. Blast Esme – I do wish she'd taught me languages.'

'Italian's a bit like French,' Charlotte said airily. 'We'll soon pick it up. We have a whole month – yippee!' She stretched up her arms and ran across the warm curve of the hillside in sheer high spirits. Tom and Kate's eyes met. 'She's still a kid in spite of having all the Italian male talent in the village eyeing her,' Tom said. 'I think they thought she was my girlfriend and my stock went up enormously. She'd better watch those shorts if she goes out alone though – she won't be safe.'

The self-drive car they'd picked up at the airport was like an oven when they got into it. 'Ouch!' Jeremy cried. 'The leather's too hot to sit on.'

'It will be OK when we start moving,' Tom said, starting up. 'Don't complain about sunshine – remember how little we get of it in England.'

Kate was entranced by the countryside. She felt her spirit expanding as the road wound secretly up a hill, dropped into a valley and climbed up another. There seemed an endless supply of hills, each steeper than the last, some covered in mysterious forests, others carefully cultivated in a series of terraces. There were sheets of sunflowers, turning their dark sun-burnt faces fringed with blonde petals perpetually to the sun, and poppies, their days numbered, bobbing in a non-stop dance. Tiny little villages clinging to sheer cliffs, dominated by cool yew-shadowed churches, would suddenly appear round a sharp bend. Old men and wrinkled women in long black dresses sat contentedly on stone benches under trees in the narrow streets, gazing at them as they drove through, curious but detached. Sometimes they responded with toothless smiles when Kate called '*Buongiorno*' at them as they stopped to wander round the narrow streets. 'In Britain they'd be tidied away into an old people's home,' Tom said soberly. Jeremy too was soon greeting everyone with a confident '*Buongiorno*', and was thrilled when a shopkeeper, leaning against his bead-curtained doorway, smiled at him and gave him an apple. '*La mele*,' he said. Jeremy repeated it carefully, casting a blue-eyed smile at the shopkeeper, '*Grazie*,' he added. 'Now I'll have to buy something,' Kate said. 'Oh dear, what's Italian for peaches? I'd better have a pound – no, a kilo, I guess – of those. We'll eat them in the car and have some for later on.' Kate struggled with the unfamiliar money, managed to buy her peaches amidst much hilarity in the shop. 'Chinky chento,' Jeremy chanted. 'Chinky chento quattro . . . no wonder Italians sing.'

They drove back to the villa, Tom teaching them to count in Italian, and Jeremy carolling the numbers that strung together so happily. They walked over to the neighbouring villa, Kate, finding the hill a bit of a strain, glad of Tom's arm. It was one of the three close-clustered ones on another gentler hill a little below theirs. A very sun-tanned blonde woman, bare-footed, wearing white shorts and a black and white halter top was lying on a wicker chair reading. '*Buongiorno* . . . is it still *giorno*? You lose track of time out here.' She got up languidly and held out her hand. 'Ros Jones. Are you settled in? You're in the Gentili villa I gather. Better views than ours, but a longer trek up if you walk to the village.' She was a little older than Kate, friendly and attractive. Kate grimaced. 'I won't be doing much walking, alas. I'm still getting over a fractured leg.'

A big, burly, grey-haired man wearing red and white striped shorts came out through the French doors of the villa, carrying a tray of drinks and a jug clinking refreshingly with ice. 'I saw you coming up the track. So you found us without difficulty. Mind you, there are so few houses around it *would* be difficult to make a mistake. Bob Jones,' he said turning to Kate, and offering his hand. 'Been exploring?'

'Not much yet – just a little drive this morning, but it all looks so enticing.'

'The kids and I chuntered around a bit last evening,' said Tom. 'It's so lovely I can't bear to leave at the weekend. My sister is convalescing from a nasty accident so she has to take it easy. You've met Charlotte, and this is Jeremy who's already getting to grips with Italian.'

'*Buongiorno*,' Jeremy said shyly.

'Marty,' Bob boomed. 'Greg, Angie, come here.'

'They won't hear you.' Ros settled back in her chair and waved at the others to sit down. 'They're at the pool. We share a pool with the two other villas here, and the children seem to spend all day there. You're welcome to come up for a swim any time – it's not as big as the Fontana's behind the woods, but you can splash around.'

'Come with me, I'll show you,' Bob said kindly to Charlotte and Jeremy. 'It's round the back.'

Charlotte and Jeremy followed him with alacrity, exchanging looks of anticipation, while Kate and Tom sipped their drinks. 'Charlotte said you've been coming here every year for ages,' Kate remarked. 'You'll have to tell me about a few restaurants. Carla, the maid, has stocked the fridge and larder with so much food that she must think I'll be spending all my time in the kitchen.'

'Oh, Carla.' Ros Jones laughed. 'She's the sister of the

local farmer, the sister-in-law of the village shopkeeper, and is married to the chap who runs the bar. She keeps them *all* going by supplying the holiday villas with stores. A nice little business. But she doesn't rob you *too* much, and it's so convenient to arrive and find all the necessaries on hand. But I don't think you'll find the wine very drinkable.'

Bob came back and started giving them a run-down of places they should see and the restaurants to eat in. 'Come with us – we're going to our favourite in Colle Val d'Elsa tonight.' Kate saw a resigned look pass over Ros's face. Bob was clearly the gregarious type. 'Oh really, you're much too kind. We can't muscle in on your holiday – I expect it's one of your few chances to have time together as a family.'

Ros turned to look at Kate. 'That's probably the last thing Bob wants. He gets claustrophobic if we're the only ones around – it's all that conviviality in the wine trade. They're not happy unless there's a perpetual party going on.' She didn't sound resentful, but Kate sensed that it had been a source of irritation in the past.

'Another time,' she said. 'My big brother goes back to Scotland on Saturday and since we live in London, I never see enough of him. We've promised ourselves a quiet family dinner tonight. I have to make the most of his company – besides, I want him to sit beside me while I tackle driving on the right. I am highly nervous of Italian roads, and terribly out of practice.'

Bob was clearly disappointed, but Ros looked at her with eyes full of understanding as they stood up to go. 'Come over again – get your leg functioning again by walking here. At least it's downhill one way.'

Jeremy was full of talk about the pool and the three children. 'Marty has a snorkel, and Greg can do three lengths underwater. They say it's more fun in the sea, but it takes ages to get there so they don't go very often, but they're smashing at diving for pennies on the bottom. Angie just floated about on a rubber dinghy with her legs in the water, but she's ever so brown. They said I can have a swim after lunch – can I, Mum? And there are two kids of eleven and thirteen in one of the other villas next to them, but they'd gone off somewhere for the day so we didn't meet them, and Greg has a bike he said I can borrow.'

'Well, fine, but don't be a nuisance. They seem very friendly but I expect they want to be on their own too. I was thinking we'd go into the little town this afternoon and look round – don't you want to come?'

'*I* do,' Charlotte said unexpectedly. 'Angie says there are some great little shops. I'm going to buy a bikini. I only have my school swimsuit because I didn't think we'd do much swimming, but Angie had about half a dozen bikinis drying by the pool. And she said you can get some marvellous sandals. I wish I'd telephoned Beatrice before we came away, I have nothing to wear!' Tom and Kate exchanged a grin. 'Charlotte's found a soul mate,' Kate said. 'They'll spend hours trying on each other's wardrobes. I'm starving, aren't you? I think we'll be clearing out Carla's supplies in one fell swoop.'

Chapter Thirty-Seven

While Tom was with her Kate didn't do any painting but she felt a mounting hunger as each day seemed more beautiful than the last and she itched to try to capture the hills with their changing shadows as the sun moved round the serene and settled villa, the way the clouds wreathed the lower hills in the distance towards Siena as the sun rose in the morning, the fields of sunflowers. It was easy to get up early and when it was just getting light Kate sat out on the terrace outside her bedroom watching the sun rise, revelling in the soft, wreathing beauty of the clouds before they were dispersed by the sun's warmth, the peace and isolation of their hill.

She didn't like driving into Val d'Elsa. Her leg ached, and she didn't feel in control. 'I'd give it a miss,' Tom advised. 'It's early days. I bet Carla can fix you up with someone to drive you if you want to get about a bit.'

'To be truthful, I don't, much' said Kate. 'I want to paint and it seems so lovely just being here, but I expect the children will find it a bit dull in a day or two. They ought to see Siena and Florence, and Pisa and that lovely little town full of towers, what is it called, San Gimigniano?'

'They'll be happy enough with the Joneses. They've hit it off with their kids and apparently, another family the Joneses know is taking over that rather luxurious villa behind the woods that Charlotte and I noticed on the first night. I think the young ones will make their own fun.'

But before he went he asked Carla if she knew of a driver for Kate. '*Si, si, certo.*' Carla's head nodded in time with the words. Very soon a handsome young man in his early twenties came up the hill, introducing himself as Carla's nephew Guido, and at their disposal as a driver. He had some halting English. 'You want I come,' he picked up the notepad and waved it. He pantomimed a note on the pad. '*Carla me*', he nodded emphatically and pointed to himself. Kate too smiled and nodded vigorously to show that she understood.

When Tom had gone, Kate moved her painting gear out on to the terrace and worked contentedly all day. The children disappeared to the Joneses after breakfast and returned briefly for lunch, but otherwise she was left in peace. The colony of children had swelled to eleven, counting the four new neighbours. They now went to their larger pool where the swimming was more ambitious. Jeremy boasted daily of his under-water prowess, and his ever-more-complicated and daring dives. The boys had built a camp in the damp forest of oak and chestnut where they had their lunch and pretended to hunt. Painting in that climate and among that scenery became an obsession. Kate realized guiltily that she had allowed the other families to more or less adopt her children. 'Ask every-body to come to supper tomorrow,' she told the children. 'I'm being very neglectful.' Carla beamed at the size of the shopping list, and prepared potatoes and washed lettuce, and picked a bunch of wild rosemary for the chickens. Kate made a huge fruit salad which, with the ice-cream Guido brought up with the wine, would take care of the pudding, and there was plenty of cheese. She laid the table on the terrace, and switched on Otto Gentili's tape deck, which included some of Otto's solos. His singing could hardly be compared with Pavarotti's but it was a thrill to listen to his disembodied ringing voice in his own villa. She pictured him singing his heart out on some crowded stage for a cosmopolitan audience somewhere, while she, a perfect stranger, talked tranquilly and happily in his very agreeable villa.

The three families knew each other so well that there was an easy, relaxed rapport between them as they puffed up the last steep bit of Kate's hill. The children took themselves off to table tennis and various secret occupations of their own, Charlotte and Angie disappearing to Charlotte's bedroom no doubt to compare wardrobes. The Andrews' oldest daughter, a fat and rather spotty fifteen-year-old, was left to herself, and Kate saw her on the periphery of the adult group, sitting on the warm stone of the terrace, gloomingly scuffing her sandal in the dust. 'Caroline – come and help me, will you? I've never cooked on a barbecue before. I bet *you* know how to do it.' She kept the lonely, unattractive teenager by her side while the others were drinking, with Bob as the self-appointed barman, and felt cheered when she saw the girl's scowl lift. She felt again the pain of being unwanted, an outsider, and she was cross with Charlotte for conspiring to exclude Caroline. 'Would you let me paint you?' she asked her at one point. The child looked up, so astonished that Kate had meant her, that Kate felt a lump in her throat. 'You have such lovely colouring – it goes so well with the countryside,' she said, smiling.

It was a boisterous, jolly evening of eating in the flickering candlelight, and though a breeze had sprung up and they needed sweaters, it was still warm. After the meal, while they were sitting in that replete content that comes from good food and wine at the end of a sun-drenched day, Graham Andrews disappeared, and then suddenly they all became silent as the music of Chopin, played with real feeling, drifted out to them. Kate stared out over the valley, a sad yearning stirred up in her by the music. For the first time since she and Geoffrey had separated she felt a chill loneliness, a need for someone to share this beauty, to hold her close. She shivered.

'That's what I felt,' Ros Jones said softly at her elbow. 'Someone walking over my grave. I love this music, but on a night like this it's almost unbearably sad. It makes me think of all the might-have-beens and if-onlys.' She glanced at her husband and gave a tiny shrug. 'Bob,' she called. 'It's getting cold. I think I'll stroll back.'

'Not just yet, Ros, I was just going to propose a game of bridge. Do you play?' He cocked his head at Kate, as, oblivious of his protests, Ros walked off down the hill. 'No, I'm afraid not,' she said, sorry to disappoint him.

'Oh well, I'll go and stir up Graham and see if he can play something more cheerful at least.' He went inside and the music stopped abruptly.

Janey Andrews looked at Kate. 'Not a music-lover, our Bob, but he's very kind. Ros tells me you paint? What kind of thing?'

'I'm not sure,' Kate said slowly. 'I suppose you could say it's abstract – everything seems to break up into patterns and shapes, but I have tried to paint the children. They're not very willing sitters, I'm afraid. But Caroline has kindly said she'd let me paint her.' She smiled at the girl sitting beside to her. 'I suppose since I've really only been painting seriously for the last few months I haven't anything that can be dignified by the term style.'

'I'll sit for you,' Janey said unexpectedly. 'I used to be an art student myself but got disillusioned, and then once I had four children I didn't have enough left-over energy to go on trying. But I wouldn't mind coming up here and reading while you paint.'

'That's awfully good of you – I'd be very grateful. I am painting the countryside but it would be lovely to have a figure in it or see how I'd get on with an actual portrait.'

'Righto, I'll come up when we're not going anywhere. It's heaven to get away from this mob from time to time.'

She made a wry face as the children came rushing up. 'Mum, Harry has trod on something sharp and it's hurting.' She looked at the child's upturned sole as he whimpered and squeezed his face into expressions of excruciating pain. 'So I see,' she said calmly, pulling out a long, sharp thorn. 'Ouch, Mum, that *hurt*!' Harry was indignant.

'I'm sorry, but you shouldn't run about without shoes. Especially at night – all sorts of things could bite you. Come on, it's time anyway we all cleared off. You're all too hot and excited. Good night Kate – thanks for a lovely meal.'

Bob Jones looked disappointed at what he considered an early end to the evening, but collected his three and resignedly followed the Andrewses and the Scott-Felloweses back down the stony rutted track. 'Good nights' and 'Thank yous' drifted up as they disappeared into the gloom of the trees below.

'You were terribly mean to Caroline,' Kate said in reproach to Charlotte as she put what was left of the food away. 'I've never seen anyone so left out and miserable.'

Charlotte shrugged. 'Oh, she's such a pain. Angie says she's fatter than ever this year.'

'She probably eats to comfort herself,' Kate said tersely. 'I didn't expect you to be unkind and thoughtless.' She was pleased to see Charlotte look a little ashamed. She didn't often criticize her and her rebuke had gone home.

'I'm for bed,' she said. 'Carla can clean up tomorrow.' She gave her daughter the briefest good night kiss, to underline her disapproval.

Chapter Thirty-Eight

The days quickly fell into a happy, comfortable pattern. The various children would spend the day together, and quite often the families would join up in the evening at some restaurant. Kate painted with a burning dedication, irritated when she had to force herself to stop to go with the children for ice-cream or to one of the medieval hilltop villages and stroll round the cool, narrow streets.

Guido drove them. He was very good-natured. Kate's bad temper evaporated as they all dissolved into laughter as they tried to exchange language instruction. Charlotte somehow managed to sit in front with him most of the time, tossing back her hair and glancing up at him sideways, under her lashes, as they talked. 'She seems to have been born knowing how to flirt,' Kate thought, amused and a little alarmed at her coquettish mannerisms, which seemed, however, to disappear naturally as soon as they returned home and Guido drove off.

Caroline came first to sit for her, and then Janey Andrews. Kate did a quick photographic study of Caroline, slimming down her fat cheeks, arranging her body so that her bulging puppy fat didn't show. She felt guilty at employing such flattery, but consoled herself with the thought that most fashionable portrait painters did the same. She was rewarded by the touching delight of the child when she gave her the picture.

'Is that really me? Do I look like that?' Caroline asked, unable to take her eyes off the portrait. 'In a year or two when you look in the mirror you'll see that doesn't do you justice,' Kate assured her.

'That was a master stroke,' Janey commented a few days later, as Kate arranged her in a rustic wooden seat against the table tennis barn. 'Caroline has been a different child since you gave her that painting. Even that detestable Angie has been a little gracious to her, and she's bloomed.'

'It just shows what a little confidence can do for you,' Kate said, thinking of her own painful childhood. 'She sees that not everyone thinks her fat and spotty. I was like her once.'

'Then you've got over it remarkably well,' Janey commented, yawning in the sun. She kept professionally still as she read or talked desultorily. Kate wouldn't let her see her work.

'Later, later,' she said hastily, turning her canvas to the wall. 'I can't bear anyone to look, particularly when it's not finished. It feels too, too *intimate*. It's like people being able to read your thoughts. You feel naked and vulnerable.'

'You're painting me, not going for deep analysis, I hope,' Janey said mildly. 'I don't want any sexual repression coming out in my picture!' They talked in a disconnected, amiable way. Janey was patient and friendly.

'Where's Mr Cosgrove?' she asked suddenly.

Kate looked uncomfortable. 'I'm afraid he's not around any longer.' She concentrated hard on the paintings.

'You mustn't mind me – I'm like Mrs Noah. I want everyone neatly paired up. I was just wondering who we had among our lot out here to provide a holiday romance.' She chuckled at Kate's embarrassment. 'You can't shut yourself off painting day after day.'

'It's what I want to do, what I'm here for. I've never had the time or encouragement before and I'm trying to be serious.'

Janey stopped teasing. 'But do let me see it.'

'Yes, yes I will. But later. It's not ready.'

'You said yesterday it was nearly finished.'

'I know.' Kate was agitated. 'But it still isn't.'

'Fiddling can go on forever,' Janey said knowingly. 'It then becomes fussy and self-conscious.'

When Janey had gone Kate felt repentant. 'You may not be an artist, but you're acquiring an "artistic temperament",' she scolded herself sardonically as she looked at the three canvases she'd done since they'd come. She hoped Nick would think she had improved when he finally arrived back in London. She felt tremulously excited about Janey's portrait. She had painted her against the bleached wooden side of the table-tennis barn, the soft hills curving at the side, flowing into the curves and rhythms of Janey's rounded, mature body, her long brown hair merging with the grain of the wood, her lap filled with the wild flowers that grew in such profusion over the hill. She could feel Janey's warmth and maternal comfort coming out of the picture, the tranquil oneness with the countryside, together with her own delight in the unspoiled beauty of the place in the clear, soft colours, of the flowers, the distant hills and the trees. And yet the picture couldn't be called figurative, there was still that unconscious breaking down into pattern. But here it was softer, less energetic than in some of the feverish work she had done in London.

She was painting alone again a couple of days later. Bob Jones had suggested they all trekked to the beach at Punta Ala, and Guido had offered to drive the children, since there wasn't really room in the other cars for what would mean a couple of hours' journey. He'd asked, since they were going to swim, if his friend Cesare could come. Kate had agreed. She didn't really want to go. The days left to them were all too few, and she couldn't stop work now – there was still too much she wanted to do. She was appalled to think they had less than a week to go.

Working concentratedly, she was startled by the sound of feet on the loose scree of the hill. She looked up to see Janey and Graham smiling at her.

'Sorry, we didn't mean to startle you,' Graham apologized. 'We were walking over this way and I though I'd ask if I could play the piano for a bit. And perhaps even beg a cup of tea. It's hot work walking up your hill.'

'Of course.' Kate put her brush down. 'I thought you'd all gone to the beach. I brought some Lapsang Souchong with me – I wasn't sure I could buy it here, but it seems they have everything in the *supermercato*.' She went through into the cool kitchen and put the kettle on and got out some cups. She put milk and lemon on the tray and took it out to the terrace and then stopped aghast as she saw Graham and Janey looking at her paintings. 'Oh no,' she wailed.

'I'm sorry,' Graham said, without sounding in the least apologetic. 'Aren't we supposed to look?'

'She's neurotic about her work,' Janey said easily. 'But you promised I could see them later. Isn't this later?'

Kate shrugged in resignation but made a face. 'I suppose I *am* being soppy,' she agreed. 'Oh, let's get it over with. Have a look if you like, it can't matter now. I've got to go back on Friday.' She poured the tea. 'The others are inside the barn behind an old horsehair sofa – watch out, one or two may still be tacky.'

She drank her tea, pretending to be casual. Was this how tense she would be at an exhibition? If so, she didn't think she could go through with it.

Graham came up and took a cup and went back to contemplating her paintings and then came back and sat on the terrace wall. 'Well, speaking strictly as an amateur collector, I think those three are quite superb. I'd like to buy that one of Janey, of course, to begin with. As it happens, a friend is coming to stay tomorrow for a day or two – an international art dealer. He often pops over when we're here when he wants to nose around Florence. I bet he'll agree with me. If you like, he can fix the price of Janey, if you'll sell it to me.' Kate felt overwhelmed. 'I – I don't know what to say,' she said slowly. It would be a good idea she thought, if another dealer saw her pictures – then she'd know for sure Nick wasn't just trying to be kind.

Janey took a quick sip of her tea. 'Graham does know something about art,' she said. 'I think those three are beautiful. I didn't dream you were painting me like that. And that little one of the view out there, the wooded hills and sharp splashes of colour from the fields of sunflowers, well . . .' she waved. 'You've got it.'

'Thanks.' Kate smiled. 'Bring your friend if you like but I have promised a dealer in London to let him see any pictures I've done out here. He was at school with my brother Tom so I've never been sure whether he was simply being kind when he urged me to go on.'

'In my humble view, he wasn't,' said Graham and moved towards the piano. Janey and Kate leaned back in their chairs, eyes shut, listening to the piano part of Mozart's E Flat concerto. When Kate opened her eyes silent tears were pouring down Janey's freckled cheeks.

'Whatever is the matter?'

Janey opened her eyes. 'I can't help it. I saw your painting and wished it had been me,' she said ungrammatically. 'And then listening to Graham. You don't know, but he should have been a professional pianist. Listen to that – he might have been another Brendel! And instead I've ended up Mother Earth and he's a – a *stockbroker*! It's all so unfair,' she said with a grimace of pain.

'I'm sorry.' Kate tried to control her impulse to laugh, but failed. 'That does sound so funny,' she said in embarrassment. 'There you are, in the lap of luxury, with four smashing children, and you're complaining.'

Janey stopped weeping abruptly and started to laugh

herself. 'It's middle age. I'm beginning to think of all the things I've never done, of all our unfulfilled hopes and ambitions. Yet I was never any good, except I suppose I had a kind of facility with a pen which earned me a crust as a fashion illustrator before I was married – and I despised that. But Graham, as you can hear, is *good*. Whenever he plays like that I feel my soul break up into thousands of regretful pieces.'

The conversation ended abruptly as the car drove up with Guido and Charlotte in the front seat and Cesare and Angie in the back. Both girls looked rumpled and flushed and the men seemed anxious to get away. Kate saw Janey's eyes narrow. 'It's a good job you're going back on Friday, I would think,' she breathed. 'Guido is married, with three children under five, and Cesare is the local up-to-no-good Romeo.'

'Oh no.' Kate looked sharply at Charlotte. 'Where's Jeremy?'

'He wanted to come back with Marty and the others in the other car,' she said airily, avoiding Kate's eye. Janey and Graham melted away with a wave.

'What have you been up to?' Kate demanded. 'You look as guilty as hell.'

Charlotte attempted to stare guilelessly into Kate's eyes but failed. 'What do you mean?' she said feebly.

'You know quite well what I mean,' Kate said grimly. 'Have you been to the beach with the others – *all* day?'

Charlotte looked away. 'Well, no. The beach was so crowded and noisy it was no fun. Guido wanted to show us a special place.'

'I bet he did,' Kate felt a black anger. 'Did he have sex with you?' she gripped Charlotte by the shoulders to make her look at her.

'What's the matter with you?' Charlotte twisted and moaned. 'It was nothing. Guido has fallen in love with me. He wants to come to England.'

Kate felt ferocious. 'Bringing his wife and three children, I suppose?'

Charlotte gasped. 'That's not *true*!' She looked shocked.

Kate let go her shoulders. 'It *is* true.'

Charlotte burst out crying. 'You're just saying that. It can't be true.'

Kate's anger left her suddenly. She put her arm round Charlotte. 'Darling, it is true. You're not the first pretty young tourist to make an unsophisticated villager feel he has a chance with her. Tell me truthfully, did he make love to you?'

'Not quite,' Charlotte's voice was low. 'It was too difficult. I couldn't quite . . . well, anyway, it was so uncomfortable. There were horrible hopping sandflies.' She began to cry again. 'And he smelt of garlic and sweat.' Kate tightened her embracing arms. 'All right, all right,' she said in deep relief. 'No harm done. You were both very silly. What about Angie?'

'I don't know.'

Jeremy's arrival, stumping up the track, stopped further questioning.

'What happened to you?' he said to Charlotte. 'We waited ages for you to turn up and then came back on our own. It was smashing.' He turned enthusiastically to Kate. 'Marty and I went right out in a pedalo, and then we took it in turns to dive off. Marty said there were sharks out there. It was scary but exciting. Ever so deep. I tried to dive to the bottom but I never reached it because my lungs nearly burst. I'm going to get an aqualung next time. Then I could get right down to the sea bed.'

His chatter relieved the tension. They had a quiet supper on the terrace, no-one but Jeremy talking much, but then even he began to yawn.

'Bed,' said Kate. 'We've all had quite a day.'

Chapter Thirty-Nine

Next morning Charlotte was very quiet. She moped about on the terrace, refusing to eat any breakfast, hiding behind sunglasses and pretending to read a book. Jeremy as usual raced through his breakfast and disappeared to one of the other villas.

'Cheer up.' Kate's heart went out to her daughter, as she saw her mouth drooping and her hands picking at the wicker of the chair. 'We go home on Friday and you can put all this behind you. We all behave stupidly at times, even middle-aged mothers, as you well know, and there's something about a hot sun and a holiday that makes you forget that you have to face up to an everyday life sometime. Let's go into Val d'Elsa and buy presents for the people at home.'

'How are we going to get there?' Charlotte's voice was low. 'I'm not going in that car with Guido again.'

'Well, I'm sure I can drive now. We can go very slowly. I have to find out where the nearest Hertz is so that I can leave the car, and we'll have to enquire about how to get to the airport, though I don't think I can drive as far as the airport. There's probably a train – or perhaps a taxi won't be too expensive. Guido has at least helped us learn a little Italian. I don't feel quite so at sea now, do you?'

Charlotte got up and came over to Kate.

'Mum, I do love you. I bet Angie's mother won't be as nice to her if she finds out about Cesare.' She threw her arms about Kate. 'I didn't like it. I don't think I'll ever want sex with *anyone* ever.'

'Oh come – I want to be a grandmother some day. Not just yet,' she added hastily, pulling a comic face. 'I haven't quite got over being a teenager myself yet. Here. Let's have some coffee and tackle that little trip to town.'

But as they were finishing their coffee Janey crunched up to the terrace. 'Good. You're home.' She looked searchingly at Charlotte's drooped head, the sunglasses quickly back in place. Kate gave a warning shake of her head. Janey nodded in understanding.

'When we got back last night our friend had already arrived,' she said. 'He's recovering from the journey with a swim, but we wondered if we could bring him up to lunch? He has to go to Florence this very afternoon, and he says he wants to cram in a trip to Rome and Paris before going back to New York. He won't be staying as long as we hoped. We're very disappointed.'

'Of course you're welcome to lunch, but if he's so busy, you oughtn't to drag him here on a fruitless errand. It will be so embarrassing – Graham was probably just carried away yesterday. In any case, as I explained, I promised the pictures to a friend in London. He has a small gallery, but it's quite prestigious.'

'I don't think Graham's ever wrong about pictures. Even when he was at Cambridge he bought a Kitaj and a Bacon – well before they were famous,' Janey said with some pride.

Kate shrugged. 'On your head be it, then. Lunch is the inevitable salad with cold cuts and cheese and Carla's anonymous wine, but I could rise to some avgolemono to make it seem a little grander, if you like.'

Janey waved over her shoulder as she turned to slither down the track again. 'He's not at all grand or fussy. I think you'll like him. We were art students together long ago.'

'Sorry, pet.' Kate made a face at Charlotte. 'I got caught up in that yesterday. But we can go to the shops after the siesta – they're open late. Will you help me get lunch?' She very much wanted Charlotte to stop brooding.

'I think I'd better go and see how Angie is,' Charlotte got hastily to her feet.

'All right. If you want to bring her with you this afternoon, feel free.' She turned into the open kitchen and started to wash lettuce. Then she got out the lemons. She was glad she had made some chicken stock from the carcasses after the supper party. Would it seem to Nick like disloyalty if she let another dealer see her work? Whatever they were really like, she had worked seriously, had tried hard to conquer the medium and solve the composition problems.

She suddenly felt a strong wish to see Nick again. She missed him, and was surprised at how much she had thought about him. No telephone calls and a couple of scrappy letters showed he was putting a distance of some sort between them – or perhaps a protective screen. Perhaps, now, he would make his base permanently in New York. It was not a comforting thought.

Kate was deeply engrossed in a book when the Andrewses came up the path again. She had propped her paintings on a crude platform of logs she'd stacked against the north side of the barn. She jumped at their voices and her stomach churned with tension. When she got to her feet to greet them she stood rooted to the spot, her jaw dropping open. With them was none other than Nick.

'I don't believe it,' she cried, staring at him. 'Nick!' She rushed across to him, a huge smile lighting her face, and hugged him.

He looked shaken. 'You!' He'd gone white, and turned helplessly to his friends. 'You didn't mention your undiscovered artist by name. Kate is an old family friend. In fact I was at school with her brother.' There was a distinct tremor in his voice. He's still upset, thought Kate, dismayed at the slight emphasis on 'old family friend'.

'What an extraordinary coincidence,' she babbled. 'Nick is the London dealer I was telling you about.' She turned back to him and took his hand impulsively. 'How *are* you? You promised to telephone and you didn't. I've missed you,' she said shyly. 'It's lovely to see you again.' She felt his hand trembling.

'Well, then, my opinion is confirmed if Nick has already seen your work.' Graham was gratified. 'Do let him see the one of Janey.'

'Have a drink first.' Kate dashed into the house; she needed to pull herself together. She had rushed at Nick like a gauche schoolgirl, while he had been cool and restrained. She returned, bearing the tray before her like a shield. She had an attack of compulsive nervous prattling. What marvellous country. How the children loved it. Everyone had been so kind and generously shared their swimming pools. The children were in their element with so many others of their own age around. The big regret was that they hadn't been to Florence. Everyone said it was spoilt by tourism at this time of the year and the queues for the Uffizi were impossible, and her leg, though practically healed, wasn't up to driving far. But at least the children had seen Siena when some of the others had kindly included them in an outing.

Janey began to shoot her looks of puzzlement. Nick barely grunted, or responded with an occasional slight nod. Graham stirred impatiently. 'Where have you hidden those paintings?'

Kate felt sick. The climate between her and Nick was so cool that now she didn't want him to see them, didn't want to endure his polite, frigid remarks.

She gestured helplessly at the barn when the silence lengthened embarrassingly and Janey was openly staring at her. 'They're there. I'm going to get lunch,' she said abruptly. She wished it were Friday already.

'What on earth's the matter with you?' Janey asked, charging in behind. 'You sounded like some hysterical escapee from the cocktail circuit.' Kate smiled weakly. 'Shock, I suppose.'

They were gone a long time and she poured herself nearly all the remains of the whisky. Carla's wine was not strong enough. When they came back Graham was talking volubly and Nick had his head down and his hands clasped behind his back. He looked thinner, older, Kate thought. A wave of pity swept her.

He lifted his head and looked straight at her. 'I'm glad Graham agrees with me. He's always had a discerning eye. You have done an extraordinary painting of Janey. It has a disturbing, physical intensity that I find quite amazing. All three confirm that you have an original internal vision, a grasp of composition, and a sympathetic colour sense, as I knew before, but you have also managed to paint this clear light remarkably well. Light is so difficult to handle.' His expression was sombre, his tone professional.

She stood looking at him, absurdly disappointed, despite his praise. What did she expect? She wanted his old warmth and friendliness back, the personal interest he'd once shown in her. 'I'm glad,' was all she said, and swallowed.

'Have you any more in London?' Nick still had his professional voice, but she sensed he'd relaxed a little, and was recovering from the ordeal of meeting her again so unexpectedly. 'Yes. I've been very obedient. There are at least four or five others in London – I've been churning them out in every spare moment like a factory.' She managed a smile. 'But it sounds as if you're not coming back?'

'I wasn't intending to,' he said noncommittally. 'There didn't seem to be any reason to. My gallery runs just as well without me. It's a sobering thought, to learn you're so dispensable.'

She had an irrational wish to exclaim, 'You're not, you're not! *I* need you', but Graham was going on about his new various acquisitions, boasting, praising, querying, criticizing, dropping names like Gilbert and George, Craigie Aitchison, Elizabeth Frink. Janey joined in; together they blurred the fact that neither Kate nor Nick was talking or eating much.

Charlotte and Jeremy came back. 'Nick!' Charlotte practically screamed in delight and rushed over to him, and Nick's face broke into his first real smile of the visit, as he put one arm round her waist and grasped Jeremy's shoulder with the other. 'Golly, you look like a couple of gypsies – so brown and so well.'

'Have you eaten, Mum?' Jeremy looked anxiously at the depleted dishes on the table. 'We haven't had any lunch.'

'There's plenty – go and get yourselves plates.' She smiled at Nick. 'I never know whether they'll be back to lunch – sometimes they're out all day. The neighbours have put up with a lot.'

'Nonsense,' said Janey. 'I have a theory that the more children there are, the less trouble they are – big families amuse themselves.'

The children's arrival broke the tension. Charlotte sat close to Nick, and Jeremy gave him a blow-by-blow account of his diving prowess and the sharks bobbing around their pedalo.

'It's news to me that there are sharks in the Mediterranean,' Charlotte said crushingly.

'*Marty* said there were.' Jeremy regarded his authority as final.

'You can come into Val d'Elsa with us this afternoon,' Charlotte informed Nick happily. 'We're going to look for presents, but Mum's not really ready to drive yet.'

'Oh, I see. I'm needed as a chauffeur,' Nick said, teasing her.

'Charlotte! Nick has to go to Florence,' Kate broke in, embarrassed. It just showed how much they'd all taken Nick for granted in London

'Oh Nick, please stay, *please*,' Charlotte pleaded. 'We haven't seen you for yonks.'

'Yes, stay,' Jeremy added. 'And then you can watch my diving.' He clearly thought this prospect sufficient bribe for anyone.

Nick looked sheepishly at Janey. 'Is there still a phone in the bar down the road? I could do some rearranging if that's all right with you. It does seem a shame to rush through when it's all so beautiful.'

Janey was enjoying the drama. Her eyes kept switching from Kate to Nick and back again. 'You know we'd love you to stay. We're here for another fortnight. There's plenty of room as always for you.'

'You can stay here,' said Jeremy with his mouth full. 'There's the room Uncle Tom had.'

Kate looked at him, smiling. 'You see, you're not at all dispensable.' His eyes held hers, slightly questioning.

'Let's get to the telephone.' Charlotte was anxious for it to be settled. 'I'll come with you—' She stopped, blushing scarlet as she realized that she might bump into Guido in his uncle's bar where the telephone was, and looked uncertainly at Kate.

'Yes, go with Nick,' Kate said reassuring her. 'It's a good idea. And bring back some ice-cream.'

'Well.' Janey leaned back in her chair as Charlotte and Jeremy bundled Nick into the car, and Graham was again drawn irresistibly inside to the piano. 'I think that was his shortest visit to us on record: arrived last night, moved on midday.'

'I don't think he can stay here,' Kate said hastily.

'Perhaps not,' Janey touched her hand. 'I didn't know it was like that between you two.'

'I don't know that it is "like that". I hurt and offended

him terribly the last time we met. I was thoughtless and unfeeling. I didn't think he meant any more to me than as a friend of my brother's. I'm not sure he's forgiven me.'

'And does he mean more now?'

Kate was silent. Her thoughts were in turmoil. Nick seemed so dear, so right to be there with them. 'I don't know,' she said at last.

'Well, don't hurt him any further.' Janey was brisk, a little cool as she stood up to brush crumbs from her skirt. 'Nick is absurdly sensitive. His parents were divorced and each married several times over. He was constantly shunted around to various "steps" all over Europe. But he's pure gold. I'd hate anyone to take advantage of him.' Her eyes measured Kate judiciously.

'Don't worry – I do appreciate him. He's been extremely kind to us all,' she said formally, annoyed by Janey's assumptions.

Chapter Forty

When the children returned with a cheerful Nick, Kate was sitting quietly on the terrace, her eyes fixed unseeingly on the distant view. She felt shy and diffident again.

'I hope you haven't let my children hustle you into doing something you don't want to do.'

'I think being here is what I want to do,' he said, his face serious. 'A man can change his mind just as easily as a woman. The children made me feel so welcome. They're going for another swim, they tell me. I suspect they'll turn into fish any minute, but meanwhile I'd like to sit here with you until the shops open. Then if you still want to, I'll drive you into Val d'Elsa to shop and perhaps have dinner there?' He looked at her quizzically.

'I'd like that very much.'

They sat silently together, gazing over the hills. Kate turned her head against the back of the chair and looked at him, profiled against the light, his eyes apparently focused on the tiny patch of a distant poppy field. She felt such a warm rush of affection that it was as much as she could do not to seize his hand and press it to her lips.

'I think this is the first time I've just sat quietly and looked since I went to New York. No-one ever strolls or meanders there – every trip has to have a purpose. Time management is big business. It's so lovely to sit and just *spend* it. I don't even feel guilty. Would you like to come with me to Florence tomorrow? I have to see some people there. It is crowded, but they live a little outside the city. I think they could even arrange for you to look round the

Uffizi when it's closed to the public. Would you like that?'

'I'd simply love it, but are you sure? Nick, I was very insensitive when last we met in London, I . . .'

'Sshhh, don't talk about it. I was presumptuous, and the timing was way off too. Damn, I forgot I promised to go down for a diving display. There, you see, it's quite hard work trying to do nothing after all. Are you going to come? You're not still working, are you?'

She matched his tone. 'No, not really, but time is so *short*. No, I won't come. I've seen the aquatic displays, and very damp they are if you stand too close. I'll see you all again later.'

She was aware again of that insistent internal buzz, like an engine sparking into life, the urge to capture again the shapes forming and reforming kaleidoscopically in her head. She felt excited, could hardly wait to pick up a brush. He nodded in understanding and trudged down the path to the swimming pool.

She found a small canvas – there wouldn't be time to finish a bigger one. She painted intensively, quickly, trying to release the feeling inside her. At the end of the afternoon she'd achieved a bright, explosive little painting in golds and yellows and white, with the sharp scarlet of the ephemeral poppies and the clearest, brightest blue she could mix. When it was done to a certain point she hid it carefully. She would finish it if necessary in London, but this was strictly for private viewing.

Chapter Forty-One

The three of them came back to collect her, hair plastered damply to scalps, Jeremy's eyes pink from too much underwater swimming.

'He's like a seal,' laughed Nick. 'You'll be able to hire him out to a circus.'

Jeremy looked highly gratified. 'Nick can dive too,' he announced, as if it were a big surprise. 'And he's done snorkelling.'

'I asked the Andrewses to join us for dinner,' Nick said, to Kate's disappointment. 'Unfortunately—' he paused, his expression giving nothing away, 'they've been rounded up by Bill and Ros Jones to try out some new farmhouse restaurant in the hills Ros has heard about. Graham is fed up; he's been caught by Ros's enthusiasms for gastronomic discoveries before. "It'll be watery minestrone and the ubiquitous veal", he's forecast. I think we'll do better than that. Have you tried that old abbey restaurant in Colle d'Elsa? I think you'll like it.'

They trailed round the little town gathering up gifts which looked charming in the tiny shop windows but which Kate knew would seem dreadfully tatty and trite back home. She was cheerfully unconcerned; it was all part of the holiday entertainment.

Later they strolled up to the Colle d'Elsa, an older, cooler village, unspoilt by tourist shops, where they were to have dinner. Kate was baffled by the change in Nick. Now almost noisily extrovert, amusing, teasing, he had the children in giggles and her fascinated by his stories of the Colle's history. He also described the Palio in Siena, the festival culminating in the race by horsemen in medieval costume, tearing dangerously round the beautiful shell-shaped central piazza.

'You must know this district well,' she said a little enviously.

'Yes, I've often spent holidays here, in the villa Graham rents. It belongs to friends of mine, as a matter of fact. But I also lived in Florence for a time.'

'Then you must speak Italian well,' Charlotte said. 'Maybe you can teach us!'

'I can count in Italian,' boasted Jeremy.

'OK, then you can pay the *conto*.' Nick tossed a vast number of notes on the table and they all laughed as Jeremy struggled with the bill, with a bit of discreet help from their friendly waiter.

Mid-morning next day Nick came to pick up Kate for the drive to Florence. He asked if the children wanted to come, and roared at the sight of Jeremy's shocked face at the suggestion that he should go and look at great paintings rather than go swimming as usual.

'Marty and me are arranging a treasure hunt, and everyone can join in,' Jeremy said persuasively. 'We've already thought up some very difficult clues.' Charlotte struggled between disdain at joining in anything as childish as a treasure hunt and a similar unwillingness to waste time in an art gallery, though the Florentine shops were tempting. 'I think I'll stay here,' she decided finally. 'I half-promised to wash and style Caroline's hair for her.' She gave Kate a virtuous glance.

Anna and Roberto, who acted as scouts for Nick in Florence, welcomed him with obvious affection and enthusiasm. It was clear that they were old friends. They turned eyes bright with curiosity on Kate, but looked slightly disappointed when he described her as 'one of my new finds, Kate Cosgrove, who is going to have an exhibition in the gallery in September, and is worth coming over to see.'

Nick was to look at some of the pictures they had ready for him in a long white room at the back of their villa, and as they walked through Kate exclaimed in delight at a large ceramic bowl on a low table. 'How lovely!'

Nick smiled approvingly. 'You've said the right thing – that's one of Anna's. I forgot to tell you, Anna is a wonderful potter.'

'Would you like to see?' Anna asked, and at Kate's nod she took her to a wooden studio below the terrace. Kate was entranced. Her work was quite beautiful, with an attractive eggshell glaze that was so appealingly tactile she couldn't resist touching and stroking it. All the colours were pastel, but used with such sophistication, that they were not at all sugary.

'Can I buy something?' Kate asked diffidently. She was afraid that Anna might try to make her a gift, but she was too businesslike. 'How nice of you. Thank you.' Her English was perfect, Kate remarked. 'That's because, sadly, Florence is now a tourist town,' she answered with a grimace. 'It is necessary.' She made up an invoice, wrapped the parcel, consulted the current exchange rate and dealt with Kate's traveller's cheques with efficiency and despatch.

'I wish *I* were a business woman,' Kate said admiringly. 'I work as an illustrator now for an advertising agency, and I was immensely grateful that they employed me at all, but I have no idea of the going rate.'

Anna shrugged. 'It will come. My family have been traders for generations – it is one of the first things I learned, how to write an invoice and how to fix a price level. Let's go and have lunch – Roberto at least will be starving.'

Afterwards Nick took her strolling through the town, criss-crossing the river Arno by the crowded Ponte Vecchio with its expensive little shops. 'Would you take it amiss if I bought you something – purely as a souvenir?' he added hastily.

'No.' Kate smiled ruefully at his anxiety to keep their relationship on this new level of unemotional friendship. 'As long as you let me buy *you* something too.'

'Agreed.' He chose for her a smooth silver necklet with a deep turquoise set in the centre. Kate settled for an exquisite little silver pill box. 'Ah – you think I'm a hypochondriac. For my vitamin pills?'

'Or stamps. Or just to look at on a desk. I think it's pretty.'

'So do I.' He bent and gave her a chaste kiss on the cheek. 'Thank you. Now let's have a cool drink in the piazza and go to the Uffizi. Roberto is going to meet us at the private door and take us in.' The galleries were emptying as the remaining public dutifully padded out, some with the eager step of those ticking off another chore completed, looking forward to a drink as reward, others reluctantly, casting irritated and puzzled glances at the trio, wondering what *they'd* done to be so singled out for special entry. Kate walked a little ahead, greedily trying to absorb as much as possible. 'Do you think it's possible that Leonardo looked at this, thought "It doesn't work", and abandoned it?' she asked, peering at the unfinished 'Adoration of the Magi', trying to unlock for herself the secret of that sure hand. 'Possibly. No true artist ever sits back satisfied – or not for long. Or else—' Roberto mimed slitting his throat – 'they are dead. I sometimes wonder how pictures are ever wrested from some artists – they go on repainting, improving, never happy. There's one I know who gets so gloomy at the end of a picture he wants to rip it up in self-disgust. Someone has to stand by and rescue his work.'

Kate knew how he felt. Subjecting one's work to another's scrutiny was like a medical examination – you were naked and shivering and convinced you had some repulsive disease.

Afterwards they met Anna for dinner in an elegant little restaurant on the fringe of the tourist centre. 'You must have a Florentine beef steak,' urged Anna. 'They are the best in Italy.'

'Careful,' Nick said, laughing 'She's quite small. I doubt whether she'll cope.'

'*Si, si,* she must.' Roberto nodded vigorously. 'Here they are the best of the best.' A rapid Italian exchange with the smiling, totally round proprietor followed.

'Well, *he's* a good advertisement,' Kate said. 'I hope I'm not going to end up like that.'

'If you have too many of his steaks, you will,' Nick assured her.

They had a tomato salad to start with, fragrant with basil, dressed simply with oil and salt and pepper. When the vast rib of beef arrived Kate was glad she'd refused the more substantial antipasto misto. She gasped, as she looked at the charcoal-grilled steak, virtually covering the plate, with what seemed to be half a pound of melting butter on top. 'It's enough to feed all of us,' she exclaimed. But it was so delicious that she kept cutting off a little more, even after she had laid down her knife and fork, sure that she couldn't eat another morsel.

When they drove back through the warm night to the villa, Kate leaned back against the seat and sighed with satisfaction. 'I don't know, art dealers seem to have a lovely life. Travel, private visits to great galleries, friends *everywhere* – you can never be lonely.'

She felt Nick turn to her in the dark. 'That's where you're wrong. I've been lonelier than you'll ever know, particularly in New York.' She heard the slight catch in his voice. Did he mean his last stay in New York, after he'd said he loved her? But his voice was back to normal a second later when he said 'Marriage is lonely too, if it's to the wrong person.' Did he mean her marriage to Geoffrey? Or was he speaking from personal experience? Again she wasn't sure, but she wasn't going to ask. It would trespass across the invisible boundaries he'd erected. Their present relationship was too fragile to risk.

Chapter Forty-Two

Early Friday morning Angie and Charlotte clutched each other in tearful farewell, promising to write; and, to Kate's satisfaction, Charlotte also kissed Caroline, and gave her one of the presents they'd bought in Val d'Elsa. The boys swore they'd meet in London and join a swimming club for instruction in deep sea diving. Kate thanked their parents for their kindness and generosity, as they all nodded emphatically, yes, certainly, they'd meet up here again next year.

Nick drove them to Florence for their flight to London, before going on to Rome and Paris as he'd planned. Their parting was friendly, and he said he'd be back in London shortly to arrange Kate's exhibition. There was something curiously unsatisfying about this new, careful friendship. Kate felt nervous, as if she were obliged to walk on eggs with Nick. That irritated her, and she was cross with herself; she knew such irritation was irrational.

London was its usual cool, grey self. There was a grumpy note on the doormat from Geoffrey, saying he hoped the children would be back in time for him to have them on the weekend, at which Charlotte groaned, 'Must we?'; and three large padded envelopes from Phillip marked 'Urgent', 'Extremely Urgent' and 'Yesterday'.

Kate was surprised when Geoffrey telephoned shortly after they'd arrived. He said he just wanted to find out if they were back, and ask if they'd had a good time.

'Lovely.'

'I suppose you didn't see *Campaign* in Tuscany?'

'I don't even know what *Campaign* is.'

'My dear girl, you work for J. Walter Thompson and have never heard of the trade paper for the industry? How typical! Well whether you've heard of it or not, they've heard of you. You've won one of their creative awards for a television commercial.'

'But I haven't done one.'

'Well, it says here you have. It's for a paint – Majestic.'

'Oh!' Light dawned. 'Oh, I only did the idea and some sketches. I knew they were going to turn it into a commercial but I hadn't anything to do with that.'

'Well it seems to have been credited to you. There's a big story about it. I suggest you subscribe to *Campaign*, you might be better informed.'

'Thank you, Geoffrey. You are always so encouraging, so good for my self-confidence.'

'Well anyway,' he growled, 'I'll pick up the children about eight. I suppose they'll recognize me after four weeks?'

'I'm sure they're looking forward to seeing you.' Kate thought of Charlotte's pout. 'I doubt whether they'll have any clean clothes, because we didn't get back until an hour ago, but judging by the weather here they can go back into winter woollies.'

She called Phillip. 'Kate! Congratulations – that Majestic paint job has won top creative prize in the *Campaign* awards! The chairman's delighted, and the client thrilled to bits – not because they care tuppence about creativity but because it means free publicity for them. You'll have to put on your best bib and tucker for the presentation thrash. All the agencies go. It's a monumental PU as a rule. And it's jolted Joe into drawing up that contract we talked about vaguely. He doesn't want anyone else to steal you.'

'Hold on – what's a PU, and surely offering one idea isn't like inventing a better mousetrap?'

'Piss-Up, dimmo! And one doesn't have to eat a whole meal in order to see that the cook knows what he's about. Anyway, there were enough good notions in that last batch of graphics to please everybody. Creatives are using some of them. Joe wants you to have lunch in the executive dining room with him and some of the Creatives and me, I hope, and sign the contract then. Very hallowed hall that, Kate. There's a real live butler and waitresses. They've never done it for me,' he said cheerfully. 'It's what I always say – you have to leave or be fired to be appreciated. Oh, how's the leg?' he asked as an afterthought.

'Ready to kick over the traces,' she said gaily, feeling elated and triumphant.

When Geoffrey called later, he looked at Kate in amazement. 'You look wonderful.' He stared, trying to figure out what the difference was. 'Have you changed your hair?'

'No.'

'New make-up?'

'I'm not wearing any!' He shook his head in disbelief, his eyes running speculatively over her.

'The children are repacking, having just unpacked. They won't be a moment. Would you like a drink? I should warn you, Jeremy is now mad on diving. You probably won't hear about anything else.' She handed him his whisky and soda and noticed how quickly he downed it. 'How's Crystal Television?'

'We have our problems,' he said heavily. 'One of our senior newscasters has followed Greta to Neptune. Charles Wootton is not at all pleased. "Lifestyles" ratings have steadied, but they're down on last year. We paid a small fortune for an American drama series which has gone down like a lead balloon, but still . . .' he held out his glass for a refill '. . . my new series launches next week.

It'll pick up the autumn schedules. It's all about the environment – it's the latest fad.' When Kate ignored his empty glass, he stood up to help himself and leered at her slightly. 'I can't get over how well you look, Kate. And now you're in the big time in the advertising business. Who would have thought it?'

'Geoffrey, are you driving? Remember you have the children with you.' He took a deep swig from his glass.

'Isn't it amazing how even attractive women feel the need to nag. You sound just like Greta. Nag, nag, nag. She's hardly ever home now with all the fuss they make of her at Neptune. No wonder I drink. I have to have something to do.' He reverted to his glum mood.

'Hurry, you two,' Kate called up the stairs. 'Daddy's here.' Geoffrey frowned as an audible 'Shit' in Charlotte's voice floated down.

'I don't suppose she can find anything to wear,' Kate said diplomatically. 'That's been the cry the whole holiday.'

When the children came back early on Sunday afternoon they had long faces. 'Daddy's drinking too much and Greta Glamour's bitchier than ever,' Charlotte announced. 'She said my skin looked *sallow* and asked if I'd like to use her blusher. When Dad suggested an Italian restaurant she said, "Look at what pasta has done for Charlotte, she must be a whole size bigger".' Charlotte looked murderous until Kate laughed, when they all joined in.

'She wouldn't talk all afternoon.' Jeremy put in his bit. 'She said she had to read a filmscript a producer sent. She said she didn't see what Daddy was so fussed about – film acting was no different from television and if she liked the part she'd take it.'

Jeremy was staring at the ceiling with his hands behind his head when Kate popped in that evening to say good night. 'Mum,' he said seriously, 'I think Dad's ill. His hands shook a lot this morning, and I heard him coughing in the bathroom. His face keeps going a bright red and he took a lot of Paracetamol. He said he had a headache.'

'I expect he's under a lot of strain,' Kate said to soothe him. 'The station is facing stiff competition and he's working on a new series, he told me. I expect he'll be more relaxed when that starts next week.'

Charlotte spent hours on the telephone catching up with her friends. They were all getting worked up about the school play and had been rehearsing in the holidays. 'I'll be the worst one,' Charlotte wailed when she reported this development. She plunged into reading Shaw, and couldn't wait to get to the empty school where the cast and an assortment of stagehands were working. The A-level art students of both schools had designed the costumes and sets, and Charlotte felt left out. She cheered up considerably when Nathan started to pick her up for rehearsals in his mother's car. He'd passed his driving test while they were away. There seemed precious little languishing after Guido.

Kate helped Jeremy to find a swimming club where aqua-lung training was a feature, and he trotted off there nearly every day. The new term would start shortly, so they'd soon be back to their old routine.

She went to lunch with Joe and some of the Creatives, and was glad Phillip came along too. It was delightful to be made such a fuss of. She felt her spirit stretching and blooming in the warm praise and approval, and found herself joining in the discussion of new campaigns, listening to the strategies being outlined to win a larger share of the 'market cake' as they called it. She'd never dreamed that a job could be so fascinating and enjoyable. When she made a point, or, as she became a little bolder, offered the odd suggestion, she was thrilled that they stopped and listened. She could finally understand Geoffrey's total absorption in Crystal Television. It was like being stage-struck.

'Why don't you come to our planning meetings?' Greg, a smooth-faced, bespectacled Creative suggested. 'You have a good grasp of what it's all about and it would save time if you have some input before the roughs reach you.'

Kate looked shyly at Joe.

'Marvellous idea! Of course you should, Kate. We could make you a consultant on a selection of accounts.'

'You mean to give the housewife's view?' she teased.

But he meant it. When they went back to his office to look at the contract he said seriously, 'If you have time to come to those meetings, it would be worthwhile. Your ideas are so uncluttered by preconceptions, so simple and direct.'

She made an effort to appear impassive when she looked at the contract, remembering Anna's cool businesslike approach, but the fee seemed so astronomical that she thought there must be some mistake.

Joe was watching her. 'You're worth it,' he assured her, his eyes doing their disappearing trick. 'And there'll be a consultant's fee on top if you think you can organize your schedule at home so that you can come into the office from time to time.'

As she jolted home on the bus, she thought back to the first time she'd left Joe's office, less than a year ago, clutching a portfolio of hastily-assembled roughs. She had been totally inexperienced then, terrified of not surviving the three-months' trial. How thrilled she'd been when she'd got her first pay cheque! And here she was being made a fuss of in the executive dining-room and cajoled into signing a contract. She wondered, with a stab of deep regret, if her mother would have been proud of her if she were alive now, if she'd have liked her better?

The telephone was shrilling when she got in and she rushed to it hoping it was Nick. It was Tom.

'Katie! How are you? Is the leg quite better?' he sounded as ebullient as she'd felt on the bus.

'Very much better. How are *you*? Any more news about the tests?'

'Oh, it's early days. The medical profession is ultra-cautious you know – we measure in years, not weeks. But an eminent American physiologist has done some correlating work and he's convinced this is the right track to pursue. Have you seen Flip since you've been back?' He switched the subject suddenly.

'No – I've been quite busy. I must call her.'

'Do. I think she has some news for you.'

'For me? What news?' Her imagination failed her.

'Flip and I are going to be married. I went back to London instead of Edinburgh after I left you. I suddenly changed my ticket at the airport, and it was the best impulse I've ever had. Imagine an old bachelor like me getting married, Kate. I never dreamed I would.'

Kate sat down. 'I can't believe it! That's wonderful news! She's very, very lucky,' she said warmly. 'And so are you, dear Tom. When is the happy day?'

'Oh, when we can all fit it in. It'll be just a registry office occasion – no splendid do. Flip feels desperately embarrassed about behaving so conventionally, and I'm too old for that kind of fuss.'

They talked excitedly a little more, and Kate promised to ring Flip right away. When she answered, Flip's voice was apprehensive.

'You don't mind?'

'Mind? It's the best news I've had!'

'Well, but you know what a bad character I am, and Tom's so wonderful. He makes me feel humble. When he talked about his work I realized how important it was, and how dedicated and selfless he is. I can't go on racketing around as I have done. I went on a week's disco-bender after Tom went back to Edinburgh, hoping he'd prove to have been a mere novelty, a change from most of the men I seem to know, but instead I suddenly realized I was bored – *bored stiff* with those unrewarding characters. Looking after him seems so necessary, so much more vital than teaching maths to unwilling kids.' There was a slight pause, a sound between a sigh and a slight sob. 'Do you think I've gone soft in the head?'

'No, but I think I heard the sound of a few feminist principles crashing?'

'Yep. Well.' Flip's familiar low, rasping laugh came down the line. 'In fact Tom is more of a feminist than I am. That's another nice thing about him – he's so *fair*. In any case I don't suppose my high-minded self-sacrifice will last long,' she said. 'I shan't turn into a simpering handmaiden overnight.'

'Just don't hurt him.' Kate suddenly remembered Flip's two brief marriages. 'He's vulnerable, and as far as I know, hasn't had a serious relationship before.' She and Tom were only too alike in that.

'I know.' Flip was serious. 'And I know what you're thinking, but this time *I* care. For the first time in my far-from-blameless life it seems more important to me for Tom to be happy, and that's the difference. And Kate,' she added strangely shy, 'I haven't been with any other man since I met Tom; I haven't wanted to.'

'Then I'm glad, and I hope you'll both be very happy.' Kate's voice broke. Flip and Tom sounded so sure, so *joyful*. She envied them. 'We must celebrate. Come and have some champagne and a meal.'

'I will,' Flip promised. 'But later – I'm going to Edinburgh again tonight.'

When Kate gave the news to the children they were astounded.

'Do you mean Flip will be my *aunt*?' Charlotte asked incredulously. 'It will be impossible at school. I won't know how to treat her.'

'She'll be in Edinburgh,' Kate reassured her. 'You'd probably have been the envy of the Upper 5th.'

'I don't suppose Uncle Tom will get the Nobel prize now,' Jeremy said despondently. 'It doesn't seem to go with being *married*.'

'I think one or two *have* been married,' Kate said, and switched on the television set. There had been a lot of newspaper comment about Geoffrey's new series on the environment, and the first instalment was being shown tonight. The three of them watched it through in silence.

'Well, he's not going to push up the viewing figures with that kind of crap,' Charlotte said, and changed channels.

'It's early days,' Kate said. 'New series don't always get off to a good start.' But she was surprised at the banality of the programme. Geoffrey had always had a sure, popular touch. This material was self-conscious and preachy, with a whey-faced self-confessed vegetarian as a presenter who talked like a born-again Christian about the 'end of the world as we know it' unless we all changed our wicked profligate ways. Jeremy remained silent but he looked troubled. He knew his father had been counting on this.

Chapter Forty-Three

Kate was glad the agency was piling work on her; she felt too restless to paint. She'd stacked all her canvases against the wall except for her last small one, which she'd tried to finish but couldn't. The inner song that had impelled her to do it was missing. In fact it now depressed her. She put it out of the way in a cupboard.

Both children were absorbed in their own affairs. Kate did want to become more involved with the agency, but she didn't want the children to feel neglected again. She knew she would have to be more organized. She talked to Mrs Shepherd about coming in daily, now that she could count on a regular income from her work.

Mrs Shepherd listened carefully. 'You mean, you'd make out shopping lists for me, leave out the laundry and cleaning, you'd want me to do a bit of ironing, peel the potatoes, that sort of thing?' She pursed her mouth in consideration. 'That's right, Mrs Shepherd, be a sort of daily housekeeper.'

'Well, of course it would be nice to have something regular, I must say; I have to have so many little jobs to make my money up, like, and my ladies are always chopping and changing. But I'd have to have some security, like. I mean, if I was to stop my other ladies and then you didn't want me any more, well, I'd be in a right old, know what I mean? Alf's asthma is that bad sometimes he can't work regular. We have to rely on my money, see?'

Kate nodded. She was impressed that this little woman

was businesslike too. 'You go to an agency and find out what I ought to be paying you, and we'll have a proper employment contract if you like, with a month's notice on either side.'

She herself understood now the security one's own money gave. Mrs Shepherd beamed. 'Don't you worry. I'll take care of things. I used to be in service before I married my Alf, I know how things should be done,' she said, with self-assurance.

Kate then felt free to take up Joe's offer. It wouldn't affect her painting; she could still do that. She hadn't found any conflict so far – in fact, one kind of work seemed to stimulate the other at times. Besides, she wanted to bathe some more in that professional approbation, after years of being considered of no importance, of having nothing to contribute beyond purely domestic skills. She knew how much she had to learn, but the prospect seemed thrilling, not frightening. If she'd had a normal education, if she had not married Geoffrey so early, would she have discovered any potential in herself? She thought about the rows of books on careers she'd seen in the library when she'd gone to look up the activities of advertising agencies. Probably teachers at school would have urged or encouraged her in one direction or another, as they were trying to do with Charlotte. Esme could not be blamed. Her parents had loaded too much responsibility on to her shoulders and abandoned their own.

Having been given fresh impetus, she rang Beatrice. 'Let's have lunch. I need the services of my wardrobe adviser once again. I've a new contract, so I'm going to splash out on some glamour,' she told her. 'I think I might even treat myself to an executive suit in case I have to hold forth to a client. You never know.'

'There, I *said* you'd be taking clients to lunch before long.' Beatrice sounded gratified at her own wisdom. 'You should have bought one before – clothes send messages about how you would like to be perceived. If you look like a nonentity, that's how you are treated.'

'Yes, well, don't overdo it,' Kate said hastily. 'I'm not quite ready for psychological analysis. I'm simply going to join in agency discussions a bit more. I've decided I'm going to have a career.' She had to laugh – it sounded so incongruous.

Kate took Beatrice to Cecconi's, where JWT's account executives spent thousands, according to Phillip. 'You've changed,' Beatrice said admiringly, as Kate ordered. 'You seem so positive now, so assured.'

'Well, as long as I seem it, that's all that matters. How about a really chic black suit?'

Beatrice shook her head decisively. 'No – too sharp, too hard for you. Cream perhaps, or olive, with a beautiful silk shirt.' Lunch was spent happily planning. 'And perhaps something for a rather special private view,' Kate added diffidently, as she paid the enormous bill. 'Oh – whose?' Beatrice asked carelessly. 'Probably mine.' Kate blushed as Beatrice squealed.

'Hurry up and get to thirty-five, Beatrice. It seems that's when everything starts to happen. It's as if my life has been videoed and the fast-forward button has jammed. It's unbelievable. When you bullied me into buying that bronze dress about a year ago everything looked so terribly bleak and difficult. I felt, I *was*, incredibly naïve.'

'It was the dress, of course,' Beatrice asserted. 'It bears out everything I feel about clothes. Well, I knew you painted a bit, but I thought it was a *hobby*, not a profession. Cor!'

Chapter Forty-Four

Charlotte refused to go to Geoffrey's for the weekend, pleading dress rehearsal at school.

'I'll go alone then,' said Jeremy firmly. 'Dad looks *forward* to our visits.'

'I can't stand their constant bickering if you must know,' muttered Charlotte.

'Well, you make it worse.' Jeremy rounded on Charlotte. 'You deliberately wind her up. You're always forcing Dad to take sides.'

Kate looked at Jeremy with interest. He was growing up. He had never shown that kind of perception before.

She drove him to the Regent's Park flat because Geoffrey's car and driver were taking Greta to the airport. 'There's some shindig going on in Montreux,' he said, once Kate had been persuaded to come up. 'She's getting an award as Television Personality of the Year or some such kudos.' He handed Kate a brimming glass. 'You women seem to be taking over the world.' He sank most of the contents of his glass at one go.

'Never forget who it was who made you,' he said, staring belligerently at Kate. 'You – you were a dull little thing with no brains and no dress sense when I first met you. Look at you now, you're chic and attractive, and an award winner working for J. Walter Thompson, one of the world's biggest agencies.' His bloodshot eyes attempted the flirtatious glance he seemed to think mandatory in the presence of personable women, and then returned to his tirade. 'And Greta – she had done *nothing*, been *nowhere* when I, *I*, mark you, made her a star.' He downed the rest of his drink and poured another. 'But there's no gratitude.' A drop of spittle made a slow motion descent and sank into his tie. Kate looked away.

'Still, my son's all right.' He brightened as Jeremy returned from dumping his grip. 'You love your ol' Dad, don't you son?'

Jeremy looked embarrassed at the maudlin mumble. 'Are we going to eat out again?' he asked impassively.

'Whatever you like, my boy.' He turned to Kate. 'Or perhaps your mother will cook us something. Like old times, eh, Kate?'

'Hardly,' said Kate coldly. He was drunk. She didn't like leaving Jeremy with him.

'Please, Mum, stay,' Jeremy was agitated. 'He's been like this before but GG was here then. I don't think we should go out,' he muttered, turning his back to Geoffrey. 'He'll drink more in the restaurant and I won't be able to get him back again. He's heavy. Won't you stay here with us?' He'd obviously experienced Geoffrey's heavy imbibing before.

'But I *can't* – it's not my home.' Kate was frightened. Geoffrey had dozed off, and was snoring, the remains of his drink slopping out of his glass as it slipped in his unconscious hand. She removed the glass. Geoffrey couldn't be left alone like this. Equally, she didn't like leaving Jeremy alone with him.

'Where's the kitchen?' She sighed. 'Perhaps he'll be better if he has something to eat.'

Jeremy tugged her gratefully into the tiny kitchen. It had the dead look of something discarded before it was ever used. There was nothing but some soda and tonic water in the fridge, nothing but a musty smell in the cupboards.

'I'll have to shop,' she said somewhat dismayed. 'I'll

have to go to Baker Street. Will you be all right? It's not far.'

Jeremy nodded, secure now she was taking charge. 'I'll just let him sleep.'

Kate raced round a supermarket, picking up ready-made quiches, pâtés, tinned soup, cooked chicken, eggs, bread and butter, cereal, milk, spaghetti, fruit and vegetables. Jeremy would be able to cope for the rest of the weekend from that lot. Were there any saucepans? She hadn't noticed. How did they live like that?

Back in the flat Jeremy's disembodied voice sounded relieved over the security intercom when he realized it was Kate. 'He's still asleep,' he whispered. Kate found a saucepan in a lower cupboard and heated soup, made a salad, put out a selection of cold meats, and washed a grimy plastic bowl to hold the fruit.

Geoffrey woke with a loud snort when she came into the room again. 'Greta? Oh – Kate.' He fell back in disappointment and groped for his drink.

'Supper's ready, Geoffrey,' Kate said crisply. 'I don't think you want another drink just now.'

Jeremy looked apprehensively at his father but Geoffrey simply muttered, 'Nag, nag, nag, that's all women do, nag, nag, nag,' as he shuffled to the table. He wolfed down the food, nevertheless. 'Delicious, Kate, I always said you were a good cook.'

'I didn't cook it, Geoffrey. It's an assembly job. You just pick it all up in a supermarket.'

'Really?' he seemed astonished. His eyes were bloodshot and bleary and he seemed far away. He went back to his armchair and switched on the television set. Greta, looking fresh and quite lovely, was smiling out of the screen, introducing a well-known author, on one of the recorded chat shows she did so well. 'Give me a drink, old chap,' he said to Jeremy without turning his head. Kate poured a very weak whisky and soda.

'Geoffrey, I think you ought to go to bed,' she said when the programme was over and Geoffrey remained slumped in front of the blank screen, 'You've had a hard day.'

'I always have a hard day.' He fixed his eyes unseeingly on Kate's face. 'But you never appreciate that, do you? You only think of your own career.'

Kate realized that he thought she was Greta. 'Come Geoffrey, bed,' she said firmly, as if to a small boy, heaving on his arm. Jeremy took his other arm and they supported him along the corridor.

'In here, Mum.' Between them they took off his shoes, jacket and slid off his trousers. Kate covered him with the duvet. 'He'll sleep until morning now,' she said comfortingly to Jeremy. 'He'll be better then. He's just had too much to drink and not enough to eat. There's plenty of food in the fridge. You can fix breakfast. Make sure he eats.'

'You're not going, Mum?' Jeremy's eyes widened.

'I must – I can't stay here. Besides, Charlotte's alone.'

'*She* won't mind. You can ring her. I'm frightened! Suppose Dad's sick and chokes on his vomit – a pop star died that way the other day,' he said, his eyes showing panic. 'I read about it.'

'You're being melodramatic, darling. Leave that to Charlotte.' But she was anxious too. 'All right, I'll stay if you're really worried. But you'll have to protect me if Greta Glamour suddenly turns up.'

Jeremy sighed in relief. 'There's a room Charlotte uses at the end of the corridor.'

'I'll doze here,' she indicated a sofa. 'I won't feel so much like a trespasser, then. Go to bed, dear. I think *you're* over-tired too.'

Chapter Forty-Five

It must have been about four in the morning when Jeremy shook her awake. For a minute she couldn't take in the surroundings, the opulent flat, her stiff limbs, the cold, but Jeremy's agitated expression pulled her together.

'Come quickly – Daddy's ill! I heard him groaning and choking and I went in but he can't speak or move. His eyes are rolling about. Please *come*.' His voice was a hoarse, scared whisper. She leapt to her feet, stumbling as pins and needles in her hurt leg let her down.

Geoffrey's head was twisted, his tongue lolling, and his body was shaking. He wasn't asleep, he was unconscious. She lifted an eyelid and saw his eye roll up. She picked up an arm and it was lifeless. He had a pulse, but a faint one. She turned him on his side.

'Get a handkerchief, quick, roll it up like a gag to stop his tongue choking him. Don't be frightened, Jeremy, he'll be all right.' She was petrified herself. She had no idea if what she was doing was right. Just a blur of information from reading medical dictionaries when Charlotte and Jeremy were small and suffering from childish complaints, and a mix of television programmes on health.

She looked wildly round for the telephone and dialled 999 for an ambulance, and went back to the bedroom. Geoffrey had turned a strange colour, and there was a strong smell of urine.

Jeremy was crouched in fear in a bedside chair. 'Is anyone coming? Will they be quick?' he implored. Kate put her arms round his shivering body. 'They'll be here in a minute. Don't worry. They'll take care of him.'

Ten minutes later the intercom buzzed and Jeremy darted to release the security door. The ambulance men were bluff and genial. They took one look at Geoffrey and ushered Jeremy out of the room.

'Are you the wife?' they asked.

'No. Yes.' Kate was surprised to find she still was.

'There's no point in your coming to the hospital with us now, madam, but perhaps you could give us full details. Name, age, religion, when did this happen . . .'

After they'd gone she made some tea, and sugared Jeremy's heavily. 'Drink this, darling. It will make you feel better. I think we'll go home now. Do you know where Greta is staying? We ought to ring her.'

Jeremy shook his head.

'Oh, well, it doesn't matter now. The studio will know. I'll get them to telephone her tomorrow.' She turned back the bed and opened the window. In his unconscious state Geoffrey had wet the bed, but she had no intention of doing anything about that. Greta would have to cope with the laundry.

Neither she nor Jeremy, she suspected, slept much, but she was dozing when Charlotte came in with a cup of tea.

'What happened? Is Dad going to be OK?' she asked, her eyes frightened.

'I think so. He's been working and worrying too much and it brought on a stroke. At least that's what one of the ambulance men suggested it was. As he's comparatively young I'm sure he'll be all right.'

'He's been worrying about that bitch, if you ask me,' Charlotte burst out.

'Jeremy was marvellous,' Kate said, to divert her. 'Have you been into his room?'

'He's up. He's mooching around the kitchen. He doesn't want any breakfast.'

'Poor love,' Kate said, throwing back the bedclothes. 'What's the time? Nearly ten! Heavens, you shouldn't have let me doze like that. Were you all right on your own?'

'Of course.'

Kate spent the morning on the telephone. The hospital offered the usual message – Mr Cosgrove was 'as well as could be expected.' He was conscious, there was quite a bit of paralysis and his speech was impaired. This was normal after a stroke but provided that there wasn't a relapse during the next twenty-four hours, they were hopeful. His blood pressure was very high and they were working to bring that down.

Kate called Charles Wootton and gave him the news. 'I'm not surprised, Kate,' he said gloomily. 'Something like this was bound to happen, the way he was going on. Greta Lanson may be beautiful but I bet she's hell on earth to live with and Geoffrey's used to his creature comforts. I'm sorry, Kate.' He broke off, embarrassed. 'That's all right Charles,' she said calmly. 'But do you know where we can locate Greta? She ought to be told. She'll want to be with Geoffrey.'

'You think so?' Charles gave a short laugh. 'You haven't lost your faith in human nature, have you, Kate? Have you telephoned her new station?'

'No. Please, Charles, you can help. *You* do it. You can get through to the right people so much more quickly than I. I only know that she was going to Montreaux to pick up some television award.'

'Right, OK,' he said reluctantly. 'Bang goes my golf. I'll call Rodney and find out where she's staying.'

A couple of hours later he reported back that he had eventually telephoned her hotel, but the porter had said she was out shopping. 'Kate, you'll have to ring again yourself. I have to drive to Hereford now and I'll be on the road for about three hours and then involved in some local event where *I'm* presenting the prizes. Rather more than a million miles from Montreux, but I know where I'd rather be.' Kate realized he was opting out of further involvement. She felt indignant. Geoffrey was one of the senior directors and had been largely responsible for setting up and getting the station going. They'd once been so close, but it was obvious that Charles and he were no longer on very good terms.

At her third attempt she managed to get hold of Greta. 'Geoffrey ill?' she said in a voice that seemed far-away. 'Speak up, I can't hear you. Who is this?'

'Kate Cosgrove,' she enunciated clearly. 'Geoffrey was taken ill last night and is now in the Royal Free Hospital. He seems to have had a mild stroke, and I think you had better come home.'

'I can't.' Greta's voice was frosty. 'This is a very big occasion – I can't walk out now. I'm receiving one of the awards, and all sorts of important people from the film industry and television are here.'

'I thought Geoffrey was "important people" too,' Kate said. 'It will be upsetting for him to come round and not find you there.'

'But what can I do? He's in good hands. I'll be back next Tuesday. I promised to see someone in Rome on Monday. I *can't* come now.' Her voice was far from having the low, seductive tones she used so effectively, so caressingly, on television.

'Greta, I don't think you realize that Geoffrey is *seriously* ill. I'm sure – I *hope* he'll get better, but I think you ought to be with him now,' Kate persisted.

'Well, I *can't*,' Greta snapped. 'You can give him my love and say I'll see him Tuesday, no, Wednesday, by the time I unpack and have a bath. Tell him I'll see him

Wednesday. I'll send him some flowers meanwhile. Royal Free, did you say?' The phone went dead. 'Bitch,' thought Kate.

She phoned the hospital again. Yes, as next of kin she could visit, but she mustn't stay long.

Kate drove off, watched by two anxious children. They were suddenly being made aware of mortality and it was clear they didn't like it.

Geoffrey was conscious but unable to speak properly. His words were very slurred, and one side of his face dropped, dragging the lower eyelid down so that a red-rimmed white eyeball rolled disconcertingly. His right arm lay useless on the hospital counterpane. He stared helplessly at Kate, who talked to him determindedly.

'Greta will be here soon,' she lied. 'And Charlotte and Jeremy will come when you're a little stronger. I've talked to Charles Wootton and he says you're not to worry about a thing.'

He gave what she interpreted as a nod and muttered something. His left hand clenched slightly and he muttered again. A blue-eyed sister bustled in brightly with a thermometer. 'Don't you worry, Mrs Cosgrove,' she said. 'We'll soon have him better.'

Geoffrey muttered more urgently and the sister listened intently.

'Aunt Ellie, he wants Aunt Ellie,' she translated helpfully. Kate looked puzzled. She stared at Geoffrey. Aunt Nellie! The penny dropped. He meant the tiny, nervous woman who had been at their wedding. She was dumbfounded. She hadn't seen or heard of her in the eighteen years since that fateful day.

'Do you want to see Aunt Nellie, Geoffrey?' she asked clearly.

There was a grunt and a half-nod.

'I don't know where she is. Can he write?' she asked the sister.

'Try him. He can't use his right hand at present but he can probably scribble with his left.'

Kate gave Geoffrey a pen and her notebook. Nellie Brown, he wrote in shaky handwriting, Belitha Villas, Balham. The effort was painful but his expression seemed triumphant.

'Very well.' Kate nodded like a mandarin. 'I'll try to ring her.' His eyes closed and she tiptoed out, leaving the sister writing on his chart at the foot of his bed.

Chapter Forty-Six

Kate looked up Aunt Nellie in the directory when she got home and rang the Balham number. 'Aunt Nellie? Kate Cosgrove. Do you remember me?'

There was a silence, and a whispery voice said, 'Does Geoffrey know you're phoning me?'

'Yes, of course. Geoffrey *asked* me to. He's not well at the moment – he's had a slight stroke and he's in hospital.'

There was a deep, anguished moan.

'Don't worry, Aunt Nellie. He's going to be better, but he'd like to see you.' A thought struck her. 'Have you a car?'

'No.' There was a little bark at the idea.

'Would you like me to pick you up and take you to see him? It's quite a way from Balham to Hampstead.'

There was another long silence. Then: 'If you don't mind, if Geoffrey won't mind. But I thought . . . I'm sorry, dear.' She sounded embarrassed. 'Geoffrey told me you were getting a divorce.'

'That's right,' Kate said over-heartily. 'But we're still friends.'

She made arrangements to pick up Aunt Nellie the next day, Monday, and went to see Geoffrey again. Greta had not telephoned but there was a vase with some vividly coloured flowers from her. 'Why do florists think mixed colours are so desirable?' Kate thought, looking in disgust at the telegraphed bouquet, with a stiff branch of unrelated greenery stuffed in with them, and the cheap card written in an illiterate hand with Geoffrey's name spelled wrong. Greta hadn't exactly taken a lot of trouble to comfort her beloved.

Aunt Nellie lived in a terrace house, immaculate among its down-at-heel neighbours. The red-tiled porch was smoothly polished and a sparkling, empty milk bottle was set neatly on a little mat. The yellow privet hedge was clipped with such precision that it might have been measured with a slide rule. As she drew up, the lace curtain behind the glazed door twitched, and the door opened before she had time to ring.

'Ready dear, didn't want to keep you waiting.'

Kate realized that Aunt Nellie had been waiting for some time, hatted and coated, with her little bulging PVC carrier bag.

Words poured from her once Kate had reassured her that Geoffrey wasn't at death's door. 'Geoff' as Aunt Nellie called him, was her sister's boy. She'd died when he was two. She hadn't been married. Geoff's father had come home on embarkation leave for Singapore and that was the last Jean had seen of him. She knew his parents kept a pub, near Clapham Common it was, but when Jeanie had gone to see them they didn't want to know. 'Thought they were a cut above her, they did. Oh, she was so angry. A real temper, Jeannie had, no wonder Geoff's got one. She stormed out and wouldn't tell them she was pregnant. 'Course when she died I sort of thought I ought to let them know they had a grandson, but when I went there, they'd gone. Taken a boarding house in Devon the people thought, but didn't know any more than that. Well, I thought, it must be meant, sort of. So I kept him meself.' She clasped her hands over the frame of her old-fashioned bag with satisfaction. 'Such a bright little boy he was, and ever so good.'

'How did you manage, Aunt Nellie?' Kate kept her eyes on the traffic. 'Did you have a husband?'

'Husband? Not me,' she snorted. 'Never had any time for men, loud untidy creatures, always up the pub. I'd had enough of men when I saw how my father treated my poor mother. I managed, dear. You do, don't you? And Mr and Mrs Goodman were ever so good. They let me bring him to the shop, haberdasher's it was, you don't see many of them now, do you dear? He stayed out the back in a playpen. He knew he hadn't to make a noise when customers came in. I think that's why he was so good at his schoolwork – I used to give him books to keep him quiet. Little rag books at first and then big pictures books. He could read when he was four,' she said proudly. ''Course when his headmaster said he ought to go to college I was so proud. He won a scholarship, you know, and that helped, and then I took on a little extra job or two, and he worked in the holidays. I could never call him lazy. He's really done well now hasn't he, dear? I'm so sorry about you and him . . .' she shot an embarrassed glance at Kate.

'Why haven't you been to see us?' Kate asked.

'Well, it wasn't fitting, was it? Your family is so posh. But Geoff comes to see me. He bought me a new three-piece suite at Christmas. And he helped me buy me house. I was only renting it, lived there over forty years I have, but then the landlord wanted to sell and Geoff said it was a good idea because I was a sitting tenant and he wouldn't be able to charge much. Geoff paid the deposit. He's ever so good.'

Good my foot, Kate was seething. The poor little woman had struggled to help Geoffrey put up a show at Oxford. Then he'd kept her out of sight in case she spoilt his image. 'Well, when he's better he must take you to meet Charlotte and Jeremy,' she said. 'They'd love to meet you.'

'Oh I'd like that. I have lots of snaps of them in my front room.'

Geoffrey was sitting in a chair in the ward when they

arrived. Kate tactfully went out as Aunt Nellie proceeded to pile an amazing number of things on his locker.

Kate sought the sister, who said there was continued slight improvement. The physiotherapist was seeing him again tomorrow. She pursed her mouth. 'And we mustn't let Mr Cosgrove drink so much again, must we? That was partly his trouble. That and stress.' She shook her head at Kate whose reflex to apologize was so strong that she had to kick herself mentally.

When she finally got back after returning Aunt Nellie to her little villa, listening again to an endless tale of Geoff's brilliant childhood, she was worn out. The traffic had been thick and she had lost her way. She ended up going round the Imperial War Museum about three times, shunted and hooted at by huge lorries as she hesitated at baffling road signs. She hated the noisy, unfamiliar congested South London streets. Greta could chauffeur Aunt Nellie after this – she had a studio car and driver at her disposal. Kate wondered how Greta would react to the sight of the sick man propped up so strangely in a chair, with one eye pulled down and a crooked, dribbling mouth.

There was a note from Charlotte. 'Nick phoned. He went on to New York after Paris, and is just back. I've asked him to my play. I've gone out for a drive with Nathan. Jeremy's gone to play tennis. Nick says please ring him.'

Kate was about to pour herself a drink when Flip phoned. 'Come out and have supper. I want to bore someone about Tom's virtues, and I don't think any of my other friends would stand for it.'

'I'm so tired, Flip, I don't think I can bring myself to go out again. I'll listen when I'm stronger, I've spent most of the day hearing about Geoffrey's virtues, I don't think I can stand Tom's as well.'

'What's up?'

She told her about Geoffrey and the past four days.

'I'll come round, then, make you an omelette or something. I promise not to say one word about your wonderful, clever, considerate, handsome brother. Put your feet up now.'

She dialled Nick while she was at the telephone. 'How are you? Charlotte tells me Geoffrey is very ill. How lucky that you were with him when he was taken ill.'

'He's on the mend. The sister told me this afternoon that he will have some physiotherapy tomorrow.'

'That's good.' His voice was cool, detached. 'I wanted to make an appointment to see the rest of your pictures, to agree on a date with you for the exhibition, and to discuss framing. There's quite a lot of detail we must talk over.'

'To make an *appointment*? Goodness, how formal!'

'I'm sorry, yes, that did sound a little too businesslike for an old family friend.' He gave a slight laugh. 'Well, shall I come round now? Perhaps you'd have supper with me?'

'I can't tonight, I'm sorry.' Kate cursed Flip.

'Of course,' he said hastily. 'You're much too much in demand. Well I'll ring tomorrow and we'll fix things.' He rang off.

Kate kicked the telephone table. She was getting thoroughly tired of cracks about old family friends. They had become friends again in Italy. What had made him revert to this frosty politeness?

'God, you look terrible,' Flip greeted her when she opened the door. 'A fat lot of good the holiday did you.'

'I'm fine, really. It was just pretty grim on Friday and Saturday with Geoffrey. And Greta refused to come back. And today I've been lost in beastly traffic, and because of all this to-ing and fro-ing from the hospital, I'm getting behind with my work for the agency. Anyway, let's have some champagne, our first celebration since your big news.'

Flip's face was radiant. 'Isn't it amazing? I of all people acting like a lovesick schoolgirl! I suppose when it hits you late it hits you harder, like measles or is it chicken pox that's so much worse in adults? The real shock, which nearly made me scuttle to hell out of here, was learning that your brother was an hereditary peer. I didn't think I could take that, and the whole thing was nearly off before it was on. I had to tell him I couldn't live up to being Lady Scott of Trenthulme, but he said I was being a snob.' She laughed in delight. 'I must say the two of you kept it a dark secret. Anyway, I promised I wouldn't talk about it. I've brought pounds of smoked salmon for supper, and a roast chicken – you needn't worry, I didn't cook it – and some Marks and Spencer salad. So we'll just sit comfortably and eat off our laps. Where are the kids? I suppose they'll need feeding too? There's enough, I think.'

It was so good to feel the warmth of Flip's easy friendliness. Kate felt herself relaxing and the strain going.

'Oh, Charlotte's out with her boyfriend, I expect Jeremy will be back later but he can help himself. The fridge and freezer are stuffed. I've got Mrs Shepherd coming in every day now, as I'm newly affluent. The agency has given me a contract and lots more money. I'm going to be a career woman at last.'

'That's *marvellous*. We're *both* late developers. It looks as if I shall turn into a cosy little wife while you're going to be like one of those sharp New York women in trousers and a business suit.'

'I've just bought a business suit, as a matter of fact,' Kate admitted. She told Flip about her lunch with Beatrice. 'And Nick Menton, he's offered to show my pictures in his gallery. Well, give me a tiny exhibition really, so I had to buy something nice for that.' Her voice was so carefully casual that Flip's eyes narrowed.

'How *is* Nick? I haven't seen him since he went chasing

off to New York. It was so sudden I thought you'd had some row. I realized he was interested in you when he wouldn't talk about anything else when we went out. Is he back?' She watched Kate's face.

'Apparently. He rang just before you came to make an appointment.' She swallowed. She was still smarting. 'By sheer coincidence he came out to Tuscany to visit friends of his who were renting a nearby villa and so we met again. He seemed to like the paintings I'd done out there.'

'Well, a *lot* seems to have happened in the last month. My cataclysmic love affair. Geoffrey's stroke. A dizzying take-off of your career – let's get stuck into the champagne!'

Flip talked about the school play to change the subject. Cundy had roped her in as make-up artist. 'The school's getting hysterical about it all. You'd think Peter Hall and Trevor Nunn were coming. The head's invited some "distinguished guests" as she put it – I think she and Morgan, the Boys' School head, are trying to outdo each other on that score. It is the Founder's Centenary Celebration, so I suppose it's one of the few occasions when they can push the boat out without the Governors making a fuss. The head's going to use the opportunity to launch an appeal for a proper theatre, an idea cleverly suggested by one Cundell, English teacher extraordinary. Cundy's like a demented slave-driver. I'm glad I'm not in the cast. All her frustrations over not being a theatre director are surfacing.'

'Charlotte's been wringing her hands because the rest of the cast have been rehearsing behind her back – while she was on holiday, in other words.'

'She'll be fine. She's a natural. I'll just be glad when it's all over and we can get the new term under way. I've given my notice, so this will be my last term. I can't *wait* to get to Tom and Edinburgh.'

As she left, Kate kissed her. 'I shall like having you as a

sister-in-law but I'll miss you. I seem to lose everybody.'

'Idiot. Your life is just opening out.' She loped down the path to her car. As she shut the door Kate realized that Flip's hair was the same colour as when they'd gone away. Now she knew she was serious.

Chapter Forty-Seven

Nick rang to see if it was convenient to call about eleven the next day. 'I'm sorry to hustle you, particularly when you are worried about Geoffrey, but framing takes time and I need to make a selection of just what we're going to show.'

'Of course.' Kate was equally brisk.

When he arrived, her heart sank. He had that same distant, professional air he'd shown when Graham and Janey had ushered him up her mountain that morning in Tuscany. Gone were the smile and the banter of the evening they'd had dinner in Colle d'Elsa with the children, the warmth and closeness that had developed in Florence.

'I have two possible dates. The first, which I prefer, is a bit precipitate, perhaps – it's the week after next, and it means we'll have to lean heavily on the framers. We rarely do an exhibition at such short notice but I have already arranged to show two young artists then, though it would have made a pretty thin exhibition. If you wouldn't mind sharing the event with them, we can swing it.

'The other possible date is a month off, but it clashes with several other important events in the art calendar. The first has the advantage of the early season; the critics will be hungry for something to write about so they won't be quite as cynical as usual about the emergence of a new artist.' He paused and looked at her questioningly.

'Whatever you say,' she shrugged, trying to match his coolness with offhandedness. 'It's better to get it over with quickly, I think. I won't have so much time to get nervous, and I anticipate being busy for JWT later on.' She told him about her new contract in a flat voice.

'I'm so glad,' he said formally, as she led the way to the boxroom. All the pictures were propped in readiness against the wall. 'You see, I did as instructed. I kept at it; you have quite a few to choose from.' She waved a hand. 'Don't worry about my feelings if you want to reject any. I'm beginning to develop quite a thick skin. It seems a vital ingredient.'

He glanced at her quickly but she left the room saying over her shoulder, 'I'll make some coffee.'

Kate was fiddling unnecessarily in the kitchen when Nick eventually joined her. He took a cup from her and half-sat on the edge of the kitchen table.

'Kate, whatever happens, however your personal life is going to turn out, however much you are in demand to work for advertising agencies or any other commercial concern, I want you to promise you won't let anything interfere with your painting. It would be *criminal*. I don't expect to be around to prod you like this,' his eyes were fixed intently on hers, his face was sombre, 'but you must put your painting first. I shall exhibit *all* those paintings, if you let me – perhaps not that very first one I saw; you've developed so enormously since then it would be a distraction to the critics. When I do, you will see that both Graham and I are right about your talent.'

She gave a half-laugh. 'You're making it sound as if you are disappearing from our lives.'

'Perhaps I am.' He turned to the kitchen window with his coffee cup. 'I feel like the wandering Jew or the rolling stone – anyway someone who has no place.' He turned back, shrugged and smiled. 'Let's load the car. I can't wait to get started on the arrangements. I'm so excited about your work. Thanks for the coffee.'

There was a superficial bustle and artificial cheerfulness as they loaded the back of his car with the paintings. 'Let my secretary, Peta, have a list of whom you want to invite to the private view – just leave me room for the critics and some of the paying customers – and she'll send out the invitations. Oh, by the way, Charlotte asked me to her play. Is that all right with you? If you'd rather not, I'll make some excuse.'

She stared at him. 'Nick, I don't understand. *Why* should I mind? Charlotte would love you to come, she would be very disappointed if you didn't.'

'Oh well, in that case—' he broke off, embarrassed. He started to get into the car.

'Oh, I forgot!' She clapped her hand to her head. 'You haven't heard the real news.' She laughed, glad to switch to another subject, away from the growing tension and mystifying undercurrents between them. 'Tom is getting married.'

'Good Lord. Who's the lucky woman?'

'Flip!'

His face went from blank incredulity to a broad beam. 'How absolutely right. I'd never have matched them in a million years. Nor can I imagine either of them succumbing to matrimony without a struggle, but now that you mention it, it seems so obvious. Good old Tom, I'll give him a ring. Perhaps I can be best man.' His mood had changed and he was smiling naturally. She bent as he got behind the wheel chuckling, and impulsively kissed him through the open window. 'I don't pretend to understand you but *Ciao*.'

He looked at her, his smile wiped off by surprise, seemed about to say something, changed his mind, gave a little wave, and drove off.

She turned back into the house, confused and depressed. His behavioural about-turn was totally baffling. She paused at the telephone, tempted for one minute to ring Jon, to suggest meeting. It would be a relief to be with someone so straightforward and uncomplicated, whose only demand was unemotional lust. Instead, she opened the portfolio of work for Phillip and immersed herself in that. At least it was profitable.

Charlotte came home later, heavy with despair. 'Everything is going wrong. I forgot my lines twice, my costume doesn't fit. There's a gink who can't remember his bloody cues and is always staring with a dumb expression on his face as though he's in the audience, and has nothing to do with the cast. It's all going to be a disaster.' She threw herself into a chair. 'I don't think I want to be an actress after all. I'm going to tell Miss Martin I'll *take* her bally chemistry A-level, or politics or economics – *anything* but acting.' She put her arm across her forehead and heaved a tremendous sigh.

'Yes, dear, that's just how Maggie Smith would have done it. Now do you think you could leave the rehearsals behind at St Anselm's and lay the table?'

'Ohhhhh.' Charlotte got to her feet. 'You don't understand what it will be like. There will be real people in the audience, not just parents. There are all the governors of both schools, and the head's in a twist because she and Mr Morgan are joint hosts at a big dinner afterwards for important guests. Serena thinks the arts minister is coming, and Cundy is ab-so-lutely like a whirling dervish. I just know it will be so embarrassingly *amateur*.' It was the most devastating word she could use. She pulled open the cutlery drawer with such ferocity that it came right out and sent knives and forks in all directions.

Kate laughed. 'I bet you couldn't do that on the night if you tried. A fine dramatic flourish!'

Charlotte picked up the scattered cutlery, unwillingly laughing herself. 'It's less than a week away and all the others have had so much more rehearsal time. I'll let them all down,' she went on muttering. 'You sound like Dorothy Parker,' Kate observed.

Charlotte looked up questioningly. 'A girl's best friend is her mutter. For goodness sake get on with it.'

Jeremy came in from cricket practice. 'I'm starving. Have you phoned up about Dad? Can we go to see him?'

'Yes, I rang this morning. "Continued slight improvement" was the bulletin. I think that's very encouraging – hospitals are ultra-cautious. Greta Lanson is coming back today. She can take over from now on. He'll be out so soon I think you'd better wait now until he's settled into the flat. Sister thought he could even go home tomorrow. It depends on Greta.'

She told them about her exhibition. 'Crumbs,' said Jeremy. 'What with Charlotte and now you, I think I'll ask for the bed next to Dad's. Hospital seems the only place I'll get any peace. I suppose no-one wants to hear how many runs I scored?'

She didn't see Nick again before Charlotte's play, although he telephoned several times to discuss details, and to warn her that one of the *Sunday Times* magazine feature writers might want to interview her. 'My secretary does a little PR for the gallery and I think she's "sold" you personally as a story. Do you mind?'

'I think I do,' Kate said slowly. 'I'd rather only my work is mentioned, if it rates it – I can't think of a story angle about me – what is it? "Mother of two paints"?'

'Ouch. Well, if you feel like that we'll put them off. It will only make them more persistent I suspect, but publicity is not a bad thing at the beginning of an artist's career. Think of all those who desperately needed it.'

'I hear what you're saying. I should be grateful,' she said. 'Peta was doing her best.'

She felt ashamed. His attitude was bringing out the worst in her. She drew a breath and tried to get on a better footing. 'Tom is coming down, ostensibly for Charlotte's play, but of course to see Flip. We're going to dinner afterwards, would you like to come?'

'That's very sweet of you—' He paused. 'Won't Geoffrey be there?'

'Geoffrey?' She was puzzled at his question. 'I don't think he'll be well enough for one minute.'

'I just thought – well, thanks, I'd love to. It will be good to see old Tom too.'

Arms and the Man was a big success. As soon as the curtain went up on an excellent set Kate knew that this was going to be no ordinary production. All the long rehearsals and work during the school holidays had paid off. The set revolved from the interior of Raina's bedroom to the exterior of the house and garden and back to a drawing room. Only a few spotlight beams unkindly picked up the strings that turned the slightly unbalanced, circular platform.

Charlotte was superb. Kate was prepared to be proud of her after her performance in *Antigone* but this time she excelled herself. Kate had a lump in her throat as she watched her young daughter's polished performance, the effective little mannerisms, the well-timed pauses, the scornful sniff, the disbelieving toss of the head, the busy little scuttle across the stage before stopping to deliver, more potently, the next line of her speech. She had got under the skin of the scheming, intelligent, likeable Louka, acting Raina right off the stage. Kate felt a little story for Serena.

Nick looked at her in the interval. 'How can you prevent her from becoming an actress now? She *is* one.'

Tom smiled sympathetically at Kate. 'Poor little mum, watching her cygnet turn into a swan before her eyes.' He bent and kissed Kate. 'I bet GBS himself would be tickled pink. She's going to be great. I don't think you have a hope in hell of persuading her to go to a university now.'

Kate's eyes brimmed.

'Oh Mum!' Jeremy was embarrassed. 'It's only a school play. It's not the National. No need to get so worked up.' He looked so anxious that she was going to be emotional that he made her laugh.

Afterwards, the applause was wholehearted and enthusiastic. The head made a graceful little speech about all the hard work both in front and behind the scenes and brought the bashful stage managers and scene-shifters on to take a bow. Bouquets were handed up just like a real first night. Then Mr Morgan, the Boys' School head, had the spotlight shine on the arts minister in the front row, who stood up, bowed to the audience, and then went up to the platform and launched the appeal for a proper theatre.

There was more applause and the audience broke up into chattering groups. Kate and Tom fought to kiss and congratulate Charlotte, standing with Nathan's arm proprietorially round her shoulders, in the midst of an excited crowd of cast and friends. Flip joined them, running her fingers through hair already standing in exasperated spikes. 'Phew, there's enough emotion back there to fuel an Oscar ceremony. I don't think I shall survive two more performances – I had to slap three coats of base on Nathan, he was sweating so much, and that silly twit Serena Mayhew fluttered her eyelids so much the eyelashes I'd stuck on with such care came off twice. In the end, I wouldn't let her wear them. She'd cause too much of a draught I told her. She was furious. Hullo,' she slipped her hand inside Tom's and gazed up at him. They beamed foolishly at each other.

'Let's go,' Kate said quickly. 'I've booked a table. Charlotte is going on to a party for the cast at Serena's. There's just us, and, like Jeremy, I suspect, I'm starving.'

It was one of the unpretentious local restaurants, and what it lacked in polish it made up for in value. The waiter ushered them into their seats without ceremony so that Tom, Flip and Nick were sitting opposite her and Jeremy. Nick at the end of the three seemed very far away, which in their present climate she thought was just as well. 'I think your colleague Miss Cundell did a brilliant job,' Tom said, turning to Flip. 'I don't think I've ever seen such a polished school play. They must have put in *hours*.'

'And *hours*,' Flip said feelingly. 'It all started last term and seems to have gone on intermittently the whole holidays. I don't think Cundy has been away at all. I suppose we can forget about coaching Charlie for her A-levels?' she asked looking across at Kate. 'She could get them all right but I bet she won't try – not unless Sir Peter himself told her it was the best thing she could do.'

'Well, *I* think she *should*,' Kate said firmly. 'She doesn't want to end up like her mother, ignorant and without a skill to her name, suddenly having to earn her living at thirty-five.'

Flip pretended to scrape soulfully on a violin. 'My heart bleeds. I think that with a fat lucrative contract under her belt and an exhibition coming up, her mother's example might simply reinforce her arguments for not going.'

They all laughed, and Tom asked her about the contract, while Flip talked to Nick. As far as Kate was concerned, it wasn't a very satisfactory party except for the sight of Flip and Tom together, so obviously right, and clearly besotted.

Afterwards, Kate dolefully drove a sleepy Jeremy home. Charlotte was still out. It may have been the contrast with Flip and Tom's closeness, but she felt unutterably lonely.

Chapter Forty-Eight

When Kate telephoned the hospital the next day it was to be told that Mr Cosgrove had gone home. 'Greta Lanson, the television star, came to collect him,' Sister said, clearly impressed. 'I'm, er, sorry, Lady Kate, I didn't realize you were separated. Miss Lanson explained; I'm sorry I addressed you as *Mrs* Cosgrove. You didn't make it clear.'

'I'm sorry, Sister. Miss Lanson was abroad when my husband was taken ill, and it seemed simpler. Legally, I am still his next of kin.'

'Well, all these details are relevant – we have to fill in our record cards correctly.' Sister was determined to scold. 'Anyway Mr Cosgrove will be fine as long as he keeps up the physiotherapy and watches his blood pressure. The doctor's put him on aspirin and forbidden him alcohol. I hope we won't see him here again. Miss Lanson said she'd look after him. I must say she looks even prettier in real life than on the screen.'

'I quite agree, Sister. I'm afraid I must go.' Kate put the phone down, cutting short Sister's desire to talk about Greta. She hoped Aunt Nellie had been told that Geoffrey had gone home. She had visions of her determinedly struggling through London Transport's mystifying route maps, plotting her bus journey from Balham to Hampstead.

On Saturday, when a yawning Charlotte finally put in a late appearance in the kitchen, she told Kate that Geoffrey had come with Aunt Nellie for her last performance.

'He was suddenly in the audience. I was so stunned when I spotted him I almost forgot my lines. He looked better than before he went to hospital. He came up to me afterwards and introduced Aunt Nellie. He mumbles a bit, and his arm hangs down, but he was walking. His driver was waiting and Aunt Nellie tucked him into his car as if he were a baby in a pram. She was so sweet.'

Jeremy looked open-mouthed. 'Where was GG?'

'I've no idea. You don't think I'd ask, do you?' Her lip curled.

'Well,' Kate said. 'Makes the midnight drama seem a touch overplayed, as he's recovering so quickly. He might have lingered at death's door a day or two longer.' She laughed quickly to show she was joking. 'Anyway, that's a relief. I don't suppose Daddy will want you to spend the weekend, but you might telephone and suggest you just visit.'

Charlotte pulled a face. She was feeling restless, now that the rehearsals and the play and subsequent fuss were over. It all seemed so flat. She sipped a coffee, trying to think up a convincing reason for not going to see Geoffrey just yet, when the doorbell rang. Jeremy went to answer it and returned wide-eyed with a huge basket of flowers. 'For you,' he said handing them with a flourish and a bow to Charlotte. 'They're addressed to "The Star In The Making".'

Charlotte squealed and seized the large white envelope. 'I expect they're from Daddy,' Kate said. 'Now you really must go . . .' She broke off as Charlotte suddenly sat down, looking faint. 'It's from the director of Bristol Old Vic Theatre School!' Her voice was breathy. 'He says he was in the audience last night and thought I was excellent, that any time I want to go and see him and discuss my future I have only to ring this number. Mum-*my* . . .' she suddenly shrieked, and threw her arms round Kate and whirled her round the floor. 'I can't believe it, I can't *believe* it, please read it.' She was crying and laughing as Kate took the card and read it out loud again.

'That's what it says. We all said you were good – now perhaps you'll believe us. Well done!'

'I'll ring him now,' Charlotte went rushing to the telephone, her dressing-gown sleeve catching on the door-handle. 'Oh shit,' she said, struggling to disentangle herself.

'Calm *down*.' Kate grabbed her arm. 'Sit down and *think* a minute. This isn't something you do in a rush – what are you going to *say*?'

'Oh Mum, I can't delay. He may forget about me. Perhaps he has an opening, oh *please*.'

'All right, all right, but he's hardly going to forget over a weekend. What about your A-levels, and university? The theatre is such a competitive life, you should have some qualifications – you can still be an actress after you get a degree.' Her voice sounded like a recording.

'Oh Mum, we've been through all this!' Charlotte was impatient, passionate. 'I don't *want* to go to university. I want only to act. You know I do, I've told you often enough. This may be my chance to get started . . .'

'I don't see why she can't do what she wants to do,' Jeremy broke in, in such a firm voice that both Kate and Charlotte looked at him in open-mouthed surprise. 'She's *good*. People should always do what they're good at it – Dad did, and now you have. I will, if only I can find something I'm good at,' he ended lamely.

'OK, I give in – as far as telephoning to make an appointment to see this chap goes. He might not be suggesting anything more than a talk to give you good advice. He might be a white slave trafficker,' she said with a mock-leer at Charlotte, who was re-reading the note. 'Telephone if you like, but most would-be actresses would play it cool. If you ring now you'll sound breathless with excitement. Go and have a bath and get dressed. It's not far off lunch time.'

* * *

In the afternoon Charlotte went off to see some of her cronies and discuss her news, her feet barely touching the ground, and Jeremy took off for some distant tennis game. Kate was pottering in the small garden. It was looking particularly pretty, despite having been neglected a lot during this last eventful year. She wanted to divide some of the perennials and make more room for the spring bulbs. An extra long peal of the front door bell made her start; she realized that someone must have been ringing for some time and she hadn't heard. She hurried to the front door and was stunned to see Geoffrey leaning against the wall of the small porch, his little-boy smile in place, only slightly distorted, an extravagant bouquet in his hand.

'Hello, Kate, I thought you'd never answer. May I come in?' His car and driver were at the kerb.

'Of course. What about Fitzer?'

'He'll wait. I'm not up to driving yet.' His words were very slow, his movements clumsy, but his colour was better and he'd lost a little weight in hospital, which was all to the good.

'You look very well, Geoffrey,' Kate said. 'You've made a quick recovery.'

He made a deprecating gesture. 'It was only a mild stroke, brought on by stress,' he said. 'They have these physios who have no mercy. They work you over as if you were a rag doll and hadn't a bone or a muscle in your body. Mine put me through hell, but it seems to have done the trick. You see,' he gave another lop-sided grin, 'I'm as good as new again. I wanted to thank you for looking after me.' He thrust the flowers at her. 'If you hadn't got me into hospital that quickly, I might have been very much worse. It was very good of you, Kate. And Aunt Nellie told me you'd fetched her,' he looked intently at the carpet. It cost him something to mention Aunt Nellie.

'I think it's a shame you never invited her here,' Kate began severely. 'She told me she'd brought you up. You never mentioned her – I've only ever seen her at our wedding.'

'I know, I know,' Geoffrey held up his good hand. 'I've made a lot of mistakes. The biggest one was leaving you and the children. They say you only appreciate things when you've lost them. Kate, I have had time to do a lot of thinking. Really what I've come for is to say I think we should call off the divorce proceedings and start again.' He smiled at her. 'It has been an unhappy year for both of us. But it's not too late to clear up the mess. I'll just move back and we will be as we were.'

It took Kate some seconds to take in what he was saying. She stared at him in amazement.

'Just like that? What about Greta?'

His expression changed immediately. 'It doesn't work for us any more. She has tried, poor girl. And so have I. Since she went to Neptune our schedules have been out of sync. But she's not really interested in a home life. Her career is all-important to her and I – well I can't go on living in restaurants and whizzing round clubs all the time. I suppose it's middle age.' He gave a self-deprecating cough, pausing for her to contradict him. 'I've missed you, Kate.' His words were halting and the slurring made some of them indistinct.

'It sounds as if you just need a good housekeeper, Geoffrey,' Kate said crisply. 'I myself have had so much work that I've had to get Mrs Shepherd to help out more. You are both so busy, it must be difficult to organize a home life. It takes some doing,' she grimaced. 'You could find someone like her, I'm sure. Would you like a cup of tea?'

She'd had a job to speak so reasonably. She needed to calm down or she'd explode. 'I'd rather have a whisky but I promised the quack, yes please, Kate darling.'

He smiled fondly at her. He clearly thought she would be delighted that he wanted to return. Kate's feelings were divided between fury and pity. Geoffrey had such a narrow focus. He couldn't see beyond his own needs. He'd never change.

When she came back with the tea tray he said: 'Kate, I haven't put it very well. I suppose I sound as self-centred as I used to be. I promise you I'm not.' He had an earnest expression on his face, willing her to understand. 'I'm not an invalid. Another couple of weeks and I shall be as right as rain. I don't want you to think that I've come to talk over beginning again because I need a good nurse.' He attempted a laugh. 'I realize now how much you and the children mean to me. I don't want you to go on struggling to earn your living when I can help. And it will be good for Charlotte and Jeremy to have us back together again.'

'Have you told Greta all this?'

'Well, I didn't have to. We hadn't been getting on too well before I was ill. And we had dinner last night and she put into words what I'd been thinking – that I missed you and the children more than I had realized.'

He was sincere, she felt sure. There was a diffidence about him that had not been there before. He wasn't taking her response for granted, as she had first thought. She was touched, aware how he must be sinking his pride to talk this way.

'I'm sorry, Geoffrey.' Her voice was gentle. 'I can't.' It wasn't Geoffrey's fault. He had been brought up by Aunt Nellie with a strong sense of his own cleverness and importance, just as she'd had her ego shrivelled into an apologetic, self-effacing spirit. 'It won't work. It hadn't for years, only I was too cowardly to admit it because it meant taking some action, and I shrank from doing anything positive. But since we've separated I've had to get a job and I find that not only do I enjoy it – very, very much – but I'm quite good at it. I understand now, more than I used to, I confess, how you came to be so absorbed in television.

'The children have missed you, but they've got adjusted now, and in any case they will soon be moving on. Charlotte is passionate about the theatre as you know, and it looks as if she might manage to get taken on by the Bristol Old Vic School. We don't know yet, but there's a chance. Jeremy – well, Jeremy is doing better at school. I know he is very fond of you, but he'll be fourteen soon – it won't be long, really, before he moves on to university or somewhere.'

Geoffrey dropped his head and stared at the carpet. 'I was afraid I was too late. You have seemed so happy lately, and you look so marvellous. I suppose you have a whole raft of men after you.' He looked despondent. '*Is* there someone else?'

But he didn't wait for an answer. 'I thought you were upset at my going, if you want me to grovel a bit more I will, I . . .' A sudden thought struck him. 'Is it that chap you were dancing with at Annabel's?'

She laughed. 'No, Geoffrey. Look, I think you should go back home and rest, and get thoroughly better – have a holiday. You and Greta have had a worrying time; she with a new job and you with various problems at the station. You do love her – I saw the way you looked when you first talked about her. You can work out your difficulties if you give yourselves time. In any case, there is no future for you and me. It wasn't a good idea before, it would be an even worse one now.'

'This is my home,' he mumbled. He was staring at her as though he were seeing her for the first time. He started to struggle to his feet and she held out a hand to help him but he brushed it aside.

'Geoffrey – why don't you let Aunt Nellie look after you and Greta? She'd love it. And then you'd have your home comforts *and* Greta.' She held out her hand. 'I hope we can go on being friends.'

He looked at her, and gave her a clumsy kiss.

'Goodbye,' he said dolefully and fumbled to open the door.

Fitzer had obviously been watching the door. He got out of the driver's seat quickly and took charge, touching his cap embarrassedly to Kate.

'Goodbye, Geoffrey,' she called as he was tucked into his seat. 'Take care of yourself.' He didn't look up as the car drove away.

Chapter Forty-Nine

Kate was planning to go to Berkeley Square to deliver her latest lot of drawings to Phillip personally, and to have a gossip with her old colleagues. It was the day before her exhibition and she was feeling nervous and apprehensive; she wanted a bit of banter and leg-pulling to dispel the butterflies. The children were back at school. Mrs Shepherd was defrosting the freezer and humming in a maddening off-key that seemed to penetrate the house. She was glad when the telephone rang to create a diversion.

It was Nick, and her heart sank as she steeled herself for another icy exchange of instructions about tomorrow. But his voice was lighter, more friendly. 'Kate, how are you feeling? Nervous? Would you like to come and have some lunch and look at the gallery while there's still time for any last minute changes? I think you'll be pleased.'

'I was coming up to town anyway to deliver some stuff to JWT – that *would* be nice. Are you sure you're not too frantic?'

'Of course not. Come to the gallery as soon as you've finished and we'll go on from here. I look forward to it,' he said, and rang off.

Kate shook her head. What a moody person!

She decided she'd wear her new suit. So far she hadn't had to attend any meetings at the agency, and the suit was hanging unworn but tempting in her cupboard. Beatrice had chosen something from someone called Arabella Pollen. It wasn't so ferociously smart that she felt it would be wearing her, and the sludgy green colour was prettier on her than the black she'd secretly coveted. It had a very shapely matching silk print top. Kate felt she needed the boost of wearing something new and attractive.

She went by bus. She loved the slow lurch through New King's Road and Chelsea, the chance to look at people in their unguarded moments. She'd like to paint the King's Road, its vulgarity and cheerfulness, the sudden glimpse of a beautiful square full of plane trees and the narrow side roads of carefully preserved houses. Toulouse-Lautrec painted the Moulin Rouge, Edward Burra low pub life, perhaps it would be a woman artist who could capture the spirit of a shopping street.

She dropped her folder of sketches on Phillip's desk and waved to her former colleagues. 'I can't stop now, but I'll see you all tomorrow, I hope. I shall need a friendly face or two.'

'You bet,' Ian said. 'We'd come to the opening of an envelope if there was a free drink going.' He grinned as she waved and hurried off, skittering across Berkeley Square as she wondered what sort of mood Nick would be in by now. If only he would drop the barrier he had erected since Tuscany. She was glad to see that he was wearing his relaxed smile when he met her at the door of the elegant little gallery; he took her arm and tucked it under his. 'Come and look,' he said happily.

She gasped. Her paintings, beautifully framed and lit, were hung at eye level right at the entrance of the gallery. They didn't look like hers. They seemed so professional. Nick toured her round them slowly and then took her back into the street. 'Look there,' he said. In the window was one single picture, the portrait of Janey, with a card announcing the exhibition. There was a red dot in the corner of Janey's picture. 'Graham has bought it.' He smiled at her questioning glance. 'You'd better look at the other work – the artists are young, with talent and a certain promise, but they are not in your league, Kate.'

She toured round silently again, unable to credit that she was looking at her own work. She felt her heart lift. She glanced up at Nick. 'Does it sound conceited if I say they look wonderful? I mean the way you've hung them. I can't believe I did them, now, they look like real paintings,' she said, shaking her head unbelievingly.

'Come and have some lunch. There's a place near here with a tiny courtyard at the back of the restaurant. I think it's sunny enough to eat outdoors, don't you?'

They walked to the restaurant, Nick telling her about the daily threats they had had to make to get the framers to finish the work in time, the problems with the critics, one of whom was determined to come this afternoon and steal a march. 'I've said no, but he's a powerful villain. I had to give in. The others have solo appointments tomorrow morning, so I hope each will believe he has an exclusive,' he grimaced. There had been a printing error in the catalogue and they'd only got the corrected ones back about five minutes before she arrived. 'Peta likes everything orderly, all these panics make her bad-tempered. I don't think we've ever put on an exhibition in such a short time. She's threatened to resign every day. I've given her the afternoon off to get her hair done and calm down.'

It was a very narrow restaurant; they headed for the far end, where a couple of tables basked in the sunlight of the open courtyard. A spindly silver birch trembled in a tub in the middle of the floor, giving each table a shifting pattern of leaves on the tablecloth.

'How pretty,' said Kate.

'It's Italian,' Nick said looking at her. 'The proprietor comes from Tuscany, from Val d'Elsa in fact.'

'I don't believe it,' Kate looked back at him. 'You're making it up.'

'Lorenzo,' Nick called to a tall, dark man standing nearby. 'Tell Lady Kate where you lived in Italy.'

'Ah, Signorina,' Lorenzo bowed smilingly. 'The only place, Tuscany, of course, Val d'Elsa.'

'I have just come back from there,' Kate exclaimed. 'It's lovely country. I had a blissful working holiday.' She wrinkled her nose at Nick to show he was responsible for the 'working'.

'You see, you're too suspicious. You can even have a Florentine steak here, but perhaps that is too much?'

Kate hastily agreed. She told him about Charlotte's flowers and the Bristol Old Vic Theatre School. 'She's still in the clouds. I think she's floated six inches above the ground ever since. She's going to see the chap next week. Once she does, if he does offer a place, or some real encouragement, I'm afraid I shall have to give in gracefully. She's quite determined she won't go to university. She regards it as a sheer waste of time.' She gave a little shrug of defeat as she sipped her chilled wine, a Vernaccia di San Gimigniano that Nick had chosen, relishing the cool, clean taste.

'Perhaps for her, it is,' Nick said. 'It must be lovely to be not only talented, as she most certainly is, but single-minded. She'll make out.'

Their food was brought, with Lorenzo watching his waiter carefully to see that he served them impeccably, as befitted anyone who had visited his home town.

'I had dinner with Flip last night,' Nick said casually. Kate looked up in surprise. 'Flip?'

'Yes, she asked me to go to her flat and share a Marks and Spencer take-away, as she called it. Very good it was too. I suspect Tom will be well-fed even if it won't be with home cooking.'

Kate smiled, but she was puzzled, and waited for enlightenment.

'She told me you weren't back with Geoffrey?'

Kate put her knife and fork down. 'Is that a statement or a question?'

'Well, I suppose hoping for confirmation,' he said lamely.

'No I'm not back with Geoffrey – whatever gave you that idea?' Her brain raced. No-one but Geoffrey knew of his visit.

'Charlotte,' he said shame-faced; he started drawing patterns on the cloth with a fork. 'When I rang on my return from New York, she said you were staying with Geoffrey, the night he was taken ill, and so I assumed, I suppose, that you had been reconciled.'

Kate looked at his bent head. She suddenly understood his frostiness and distant behaviour. She felt a slow surge of joy seeping through her. She tried to keep her expression still. 'I *was* there. Greta had gone to Montreux and when I dropped Jeremy, it was clear that Geoffrey was too drunk for me to leave Jeremy alone with him. Jeremy didn't want to leave him in that state because he'd read some newspaper story about a pop star choking on his vomit – sorry to mention this in the middle of a delicious lunch. And there was absolutely no food in the house. I shopped for a meal, Jeremy and I got Geoffrey to bed somehow, and I dozed on the sofa until I was awakened by the drama of his stroke. *Nothing* would make me go back to Geoffrey. That marriage was over a long, long time before he left me,' she said, reaching across to take his hand. 'But why, Nick? Why should it worry you if I *had* gone back?' She held her breath.

He looked up suddenly. 'It just would,' was all he'd say.

She picked up her fork again. It wasn't quite what she had hoped to hear but it was better than his earlier coldness. Suddenly he was gay and exuberant, as in Colle d'Elsa. He chattered on about the show, who was coming, whom she had to beware of. Then he looked at his watch.

'It's maddening, but now that I've given Peta the

afternoon off I have to go. It's crazy, but there's still quite a lot to do and there's that arrogant critic coming. I want everything to be perfect. But, could we have dinner somewhere quiet, tomorrow, just the two of us?' He was still smiling, but he looked anxious, his eyes too bright, his hand twisting and tipping the wine glass.

'I'd feel very upset if we didn't. If Charlotte can have a first night party I don't see why I shouldn't have a celebratory dinner – after all, one picture has already been sold. We can eat on the proceeds.'

Nick paid the bill to the accompaniment of much chat and fuss from Lorenzo. Outside, he called a cab for her, and as he put her in he kissed her – on the mouth. 'I had to do that,' he said breathlessly. She turned to look at him standing staring after the cab. She felt as if the string pegging her spirit down had been cut and it was soaring up, way beyond the solid slabs of office blocks and hunks of hideous hotels fracturing the skyline as the cab passed. She lay back against the seat and laughed out loud. Dear Nick. Darling Nick. Deliciously diffident Nick. She wanted to tell the taxi driver all about him, but instead told him she was in a terrific hurry, could he take the fastest way home. 'Fly, if possible.' He was a young driver. He gave her a conspiratorial look over his shoulder and scorched home to Fulham.

The inner song had started up again. The wild music had begun when Nick had kissed her, those insistent rhythms that could be assuaged only with brush and pigment. Once inside she flung off her new suit and headed for the boxroom. Fishing out the little canvas she'd started after Nick had arrived in Tuscany, she began at once to paint. She didn't need Italy's light and colour any more; it was in her head. She painted steadily, confidently, gratified as what she had tried to capture on the villa terrace emerged. Then she locked the door, and dialled Flip.

* * *

Jeremy came home, helped himself to milk and biscuits, and disappeared to his room saying he was going to finish his prep early so that he could watch a film on the box. Charlotte sat at the kitchen table and repeated virtually word for word a long talk she'd had with Miss Cundell about Bristol.

'She said it has a very good reputation, that all sorts of well-known actors have come out of that particular stable – like Greta Scacchi,' she added significantly. 'Oh I do hope he'll take me, I'd do anything, *anything*, sweep the floors, mend the costumes . . .'

'Sleep with the director, I suppose,' Kate teased. 'Don't try to get on that way – you'll never live it down. Promise?'

'Oh Moth-er,' Charlotte rolled her eyes in disgust. 'Oh I wish next week would come quickly. Shit – Mum, I'm sorry, I forgot it was your debut tomorrow. Are you feeling all right?'

Kate threw her arm across her forehead. 'No, my dress doesn't fit, I shall forget to be nice to the critics, the pictures will be awful, it will all be so, so *amateur*.'

Charlotte grinned. 'Well, Maggie Smith did it better but I get the point.'

At five o'clock next day Kate stood beside Nick in the gallery, wearing her new silk dress, as friends and strangers crowded into the gallery. She was so happy that she'd lost her nervousness. The exhibition seemed of only secondary importance, but she did her best to talk to some of the critics, who had already had a preview and were seeking her out. She tried not to sound too naïve.

'So you are a serious painter after all?' It was James Prescott, the critic she'd met with Paul at Billie's fateful party. She looked swiftly round in case Paul had arrived with him.

'I found them quite a surprise. To look at you, one

wouldn't dream you were capable of such strong, confident colour, or that raw emotion.' He was so solemn that Kate had a wild impulse to giggle.

Penelope and Michael Milsom came up, Michael still muttering in embarrassment about her accident.

'Michael, it was the best thing that could have happened to me – do stop worrying. It got me to Tuscany and there . . .' She wanted to say, 'There I fell in love with Nick', but instead waved her hand vaguely and said, 'I was able to paint. It was bliss.' She beamed at them. What dears they had been.

'What are you up to?' Penelope asked curiously. 'You look as if you'll go off pop any minute. Are you hiding something?'

'If I am, you'll be the first to know,' Kate assured her. Jeremy kept rushing up to her with reports of sales: 'Another one's gone – and it was £2,000! That makes five!'

Kate was shocked. 'Oh no!' She turned to Nick.

'Underpriced,' he said unrepentantly. 'Wait until next year.'

Beatrice came in with an exquisite young man in tow whom she introduced as designer Anton Cecil. 'Another new account, Kate, my very own, be nice to him. He's not as awful as he looks,' she whispered, and flickered her finger at Kate's dress. 'You have great taste,' she winked wickedly. Janey and Graham arrived, Graham telling a critic he was introduced to almost immediately how quickly he'd spotted Kate's potential.

After a couple of hours Nick came up and said, 'We can leave Peta to cope with the stragglers. They'll stay forever if we let them. She has a technique that would do credit to a sheepdog. Where are Charlotte and Jeremy?'

'They've gone off with Tom and Flip,' Kate said airily. 'We can have that dinner on our own. I've already booked a table. It's my treat.' She gave the taxi driver the address of a hotel in an exquisite square in Knightsbridge. It had once been a private home, and the young French couple who owned it had tried to retain that atmosphere. The husband cooked and had quickly won a reputation among gourmets for the tiny restaurant, where his wife presided like a gracious hostess in the dining-room.

At their table, there were fresh white flowers, and champagne already in a bucket. 'It seems we're expected,' Nick breathed. 'You're quite a schemer.' The bottle was opened for them by a smiling Madame Flore.

'I hope you don't mind,' Kate looked at him over her glass, 'I've ordered the meal – it seemed less disruptive. The menu is always small anyway.'

He raised his glass. 'To a great new artist,' and sipped.

'Nick, you told me once that paintings reveal the painter's thoughts and feelings. Do you still believe that?'

'Yes. If the artist is any good, and if one has any sensibility to understand. After all, it's another form of communication.'

'Then what do you think this says? It's for you.' She gave him the small canvas, now inside a beautiful box to protect the still-tacky paint.

He opened it and gazed at the little picture, at the confident, happy strokes, the clear, singing colours, the intimate scene.

'Is it really meant for me?'

'Just you. You're never ever to exhibit it. I started it the afternoon you climbed up to my Tuscan hilltop, but afterwards, when we came back, you were so remote and hostile, I couldn't finish it. Yesterday afternoon I could.'

He looked from her fond, smiling face to the picture and back again as if he couldn't believe his eyes.

'I don't dare to say what I hope it means – it would be unbearable if I were wrong.' He held the picture with one hand and clutched hers with his other.

'It's meant to say "I love you",' she said softly. 'If it doesn't, then I'm not the painter you think I am.' He looked at the picture again, drinking in the warmth and sensuality, the secrecy of that particular Tuscan view, the unmistakable love spilling out. 'It's called "Private View".' Her voice was low. 'Private private view.'

Madame Flore tactfully motioned the tray away as her young waiter came out of the kitchen door with their food, and smilingly withdrew.

THE END